Praise for *Never A Bride*

"Lively pace, appealing protagonists, and sexual chemistry that almost visibly shimmers between them in a charming, lighthearted, and well-done Regency."

—*Library Journal*

"Witty dialogue and clever schemes… Both of Grey's vivid characters will charm readers."

—*Booklist*

"I absolutely adored this story. The characters are beautifully developed, their chemistry is unmatched, and the story is written so superbly that you fly through the pages and are swept away."

—*The Long and the Short of It Reviews*

"Captivating… a delightful tale full of mystery and intrigue."

—*Fresh Fiction*

"A delightful Regency romp. You'll have lots of fun with this one!"

—Kat Martin, author of *The Handmaiden's Necklace*

"Charming and delightful—a must-read! Fresh and original and destined to be a keeper."

—Joan Johnston, *New York Times* bestselling author of *Rebels*

Also by Amelia Grey

A GENTLEMAN NEVER TELLS

AMELIA GREY

sourcebooks
casablanca

Published by Sourcebooks Casablanca, an imprint of Sourcebooks, Inc.
P.O. Box 4410, Naperville, Illinois 60567–4410
(630) 961–3900
FAX: (630) 961–2168
www.sourcebooks.com

Printed and bound in the United States of America
QW 10 9 8 7 6 5 4 3 2 1

One

All the perfumes of Arabia will not sweeten this little hand.
—Shakespeare, *Macbeth*, (5.1)

WHORLS OF LIGHT GRAY MIST HUNG IN THE DAMP AIR. His long strides scattered patches of dense fog that hovered above the ground. Hyde Park wasn't a place anyone should be before dawn, and was the last place he wanted to be on an early Sunday morn with a stubborn female at his side.

As they entered through the west side, he shook his head over the fact that the wet chill of autumn hadn't kept her in bed no matter how many times he'd tried to get her to stay a little longer. Viscount Brentwood chuckled ruefully at how temperamental she was when she wanted her way and couldn't get it, and she wasn't shy about letting him know when she was unhappy. They'd always had a love-hate relationship, and that hadn't changed since their arrival in London a few days ago.

In the distance, he heard the rattle of what sounded like a cart or wagon approaching, so he moved to the side of the well-worn path. In this area of the wooded park, it was damn near impossible to see anyone or anything until they were almost upon you, unless it was a clear night with a bright hunter's moon, and there were far too few of them at this time of year. He picked up his pace, wanting to get this shackling ritual behind him and get out of the park before full daybreak.

"Hurry up, now, Pris."

All he got in answer was a disdainful sniff.

A minute or two later, a rumbling cart emerged out of the mist. It was being pulled by a strapping lad with a felt hat tugged low on his brow. Two young women wearing tattered wool coats and white mobcaps on their heads walked beside it. Over the clanging of milk cans and rattle of squeaking cart wheels, Brent heard feminine giggles as they passed him. They looked at him and laughed again behind their gloved hands. Even the youngster with them glanced back at him and grinned from ear to ear.

Not that he could blame them. It must be quite comical to see a man as tall and broad-shouldered as he walking a dog that wasn't much bigger than some of the rats seen down at the wharf. Though the deeper into the park he walked, the fog swirled so heavily on the ground he was surprised they could even see the small dog at all. Her head was barely visible above the hovering mist.

"They're laughing at us, Pris," Brent murmured softly, his warm breath stirring the moist air.

Judson Allan Brentwood, seventh Viscount Brentwood, took off his hat, smiled good-naturedly, and bowed to the milkmaids who'd turned to watch him and snicker some more. He slurred his words as if a drunkard and said, "What's da matter there, gels, haven't ye ever seen a proper gentleman walk his dog in da park before? Come closer, I'll let you have a pat or two."

Brent bowed when the girls gasped and quickly turned away from him. Within moments, the trio and cart disappeared into the heavy mist. While holding the leash with one hand, he reached up and settled his hat back on his head. He then lifted the collar of his greatcoat against the chilling air seeping down his neck. He didn't really mind the milkmaids and lad having a good laugh off his walking his mother's cherished pet, but he wasn't so sure he wanted anyone he knew seeing him walk the dog.

If it hadn't been for his promise to his mother on her deathbed, he would have left the aggravating little mongrel at his estate in Brentwood. He had started to do just that, but at the last minute, his conscience had gotten the better of him, and he'd grabbed up the dog and put her in the carriage. But if she kept yelping before daybreak, the Mayfair town house might not be big enough for the both of them. If that wasn't bad enough, whenever he was at home, she seemed to always find a way to be underfoot, or scratching on his door, whimpering to get inside and sleep on his bed.

His mother had always treated the dog as if she'd come from a Pomeranian lineage right out of the King's kennel. Brent harrumphed at that thought. In truth, his mother had no idea of the dog's ancestry, though it was mixed to be sure.

Oddly though, he was growing a tad fond of the little devil, though he had no idea why. He'd made a vow to his mother that he would take good care of her dog, going so far as to promise her to take the dog for an early morning walk a couple of times a week. That hadn't been a problem at his estate in Brentwood, but now that he was in London, he could see how the oath to his dearly departed mother would be harder to keep.

Brent allowed the dog to take the lead and adjusted his pace to her stop-sniff-scratch-and-go routine. The horizon lightened from black to light purple and gray as daybreak fanned across the bottom of the sky. The trees and bushes thinned, and some of the fog dissipated the farther into the park they walked, gradually making it easier for him to see.

In the quietness of the morning, Brent couldn't help but think fondly of his mother. She was a firm believer in being well read, and she saw to it her three sons were, too. She was always quoting someone. She didn't care if it was Keats, Shakespeare, Byron, or the Bible. She had even been known to use a line or two from a dreadful horrid novel. If she took a fancy to a quote she had read, she'd find a way to use it before the day was over.

But with all her loving sternness, she carried a dark secret. A secret Brent had kept for ten years and would have kept the rest of his life if he could have. But fate stole into their lives with its own plans. He had tried to spare his brothers the nasty gossip about their parentage that was now being whispered behind fans at parties and churned around the gentlemen's clubs in London like a deadly whirlpool. Though, most of the time, it seemed the ribald rumors and high-stake wagers bothered him more than his brothers. He was thankful his mother hadn't lived to see the day when her younger twin sons arrived in London.

When it was clear he couldn't stop Matson and Iverson from making the move from the Americas back to the home of their birth, he'd felt duty bound to join them. Besides, at the age of thirty, it was past time he should be looking for a wife. Over the years, none of the few young ladies who lived in the villages around his Brentwood Estate had caught his fancy, not enough to propose matrimony, anyway. He decided since he had to winter in London, he would make friends among the ton so he would be ready to peruse the marriage mart come spring when the Season started.

Suddenly the mongrel stopped and started barking viciously.

"Quiet, Pris," Brent said. "You'll wake the hounds of hell with all that noise. Come on, let's get this walk finished and get back to Mayfair. I promised to take you for a stroll; I didn't promise I'd do it for any set length of time. I have better things to do today than mollycoddle you."

They walked a few more feet, and the dog stopped again and started snarling. Her body stiffened, and she lunged forward. Her eyes fixed on a stand of trees not far away. The hairs on the back of Brent's neck bristled, and a prickle of something he couldn't put his finger on moved up his back. He knew Prissy detected something more than just a rabbit or squirrel rustling the bushes.

She sensed danger.

Brent's hand tightened on the leash. A chill skittered

up his spine, and apprehension caught between his shoulders. He strained his senses to see, hear, or feel whatever was alarming Prissy. And then, through the light mist he saw a figure shrouded in a black hooded cloak walking toward him.

The dog continued with a deep, warning growl. Brent's gaze never wavered from the person. He paid careful attention to every detail and almost immediately recognized from the slight build, moderate stride, and gentle sway of shoulders it was a woman who approached him. But before he could relax, surprise rode through him when she drew closer with the biggest damn dog he had ever seen, walking calmly, unfettered beside her.

After Prissy's own start of surprise, his mother's dog went fiercely crazy, barking fast and loud. She half choked herself with the leash, trying to get to the huge mastiff coming toward them.

"Stop barking, and be still, you silly little devil," Brent mumbled, holding the dog back.

The young lady stopped a respectful distance from him and regarded him warily. He could barely make out her features, but there was no mistaking her deep blue eyes, full, tempting lips, and alabaster skin so smooth it looked ethereal in the slowly brightening sky.

She took a confident step toward him, a hint of a smile pulling at her mouth. "For such a big man, I would think you'd be confident enough to know how to handle such a darling little dog."

Brent raised a brow. "If by darling dog you mean this spawn from the gates of hell, then pray tell me, how do you suggest I get her to be quiet?"

The corners of her beautiful lips lifted even more. "You quiet animals the same way you calm people, by speaking softly to them."

He realized he had somehow managed to amuse her. That didn't sit well with Brent.

"Not this one," he said, moving the leash from one hand to the other while he continued to assess the lady.

Her smile widened, and his irritation grew.

His voice was a little more than testy when he said, "Don't try to tell me her shrill barking isn't piercing to your ears, too?"

She seemed to consider what he'd said before walking even closer. He watched her with deep interest. She was tall; the top of her head reached his chin. Her frame was hidden beneath her heavy cloak, but he had no doubt she was slender and not boyish in her figure. Her gaze stayed boldly on his face, and for some reason, that show of confidence sent heat pulsing through his body.

"Can't you see your dog isn't disturbing me or Brutus?"

Brutus?

Her dog was named Brutus?

Oh, hell.

Brent glanced over at her dog. The mastiff looked to be about the size of a small bear and stood completely still and obedient by the woman's side, acting as if he couldn't be less interested in the little terror screeching like a banshee at an exorcism. To make matters worse, here he was, well over six feet, holding a small, fancy dog on a leash, while one of the loveliest ladies he'd seen since coming to London was with a dog who looked capable of ending a man's life with one bite.

Prissy, who obviously had more courage than brains, was still frantically straining to get at the larger dog. Brutus, who could easily swallow Prissy whole, remained calm and undisturbed as a windless night by his mistress's side. It was no wonder Brent had made her smile.

The young lady removed her hood, exposing long golden blonde hair. Brent swallowed slowly. He had an immediate urge to reach over and gently glide his hand down the silken length of her tumbled locks. He watched in awe as she lifted her hair from beneath her cape, spreading it gloriously over her shoulders.

She had to know how alluring that was. And especially so to a man who hadn't been with a woman in far too long.

A delicious quiver started in his loins.

There was just enough of a breeze to flutter a stray tendril across her lovely cheek. She quickly brushed it behind her ear.

His breath quickened as she knelt in front of him. She pulled off one short black glove and let Prissy sniff her hand while she spoke softly to her. The dog stopped barking instantly and allowed the lady to pet her head and gently stroke her back as if they were long-lost friends reunited.

Oh, yes. Brent would be silenced and soothed, too, if she were stroking his head and talking so lovingly to him.

"See, a whisper is always better than a shout."

"I didn't shout at her," he felt compelled to argue in self-defense, but wished he hadn't the moment the words left his mouth.

"No, you didn't. But you were speaking gruffly, and that is just as upsetting to an animal."

Upsetting? This time Brent held his tongue and remained silent.

"Male or female?" she asked without looking up at Brent.

"Female," he responded, his throat suddenly dry.

"What's her name?"

He didn't want to tell her, but as his mother was so fond of saying, in for a penny, in for a pound.

"Prissy," he said with as much masculine bravado as he could muster, and then couldn't keep himself from adding, "She's my mother's dog."

The woman looked up at him and smiled so sweetly he almost felt hypnotized by her.

"Prissy," she repeated. "That's a lovely name for such a brave dog. I don't think I've ever seen a Pomeranian this small."

Brent started to tell her that was because the father was of questionable breeding but silently cleared his throat instead, and then said, "And I've seen some big mastiffs before but, without question, Brutus wins the ribbon."

She stared up at him again and laughed softly. The sound wrapped around him like a promise on a spring morning, while her captivating charm sent heat rushing through his body with the warmth of a blazing fire on a bitter cold night. The way she was looking at him played havoc with his lower body. He couldn't help but wonder what this alluring woman was doing in the park so early and so obviously alone.

"My precious Brut simply didn't know when to

stop growing." She reached behind her and patted her dog's big head. Brutus gave her a woof of approval. "But he's as harmless as a kitten, most of the time."

Her speech and the expensive fabric and tailoring of her cape spoke of wealth, but no lady of quality would be in the park at any time without a chaperone or companion. She looked a little young to be a well-set courtesan, but then he supposed they were all young once. And she certainly seemed too confident for an innocent maiden. Could it be she was some lucky gentleman's well-paid mistress? She wore no crested rings on her fingers that he could see, so he doubted she was married, but whatever her case may be, ferocious dog or no, she was living much too dangerously for a lady.

"Pardon my question, miss or madame, but is there anything wrong?"

She rose, straightened her shoulders, and looked directly at him once again. Her expression remained confident as she pulled on her glove.

He sensed a measure of hesitancy in her voice when she calmly said, "I'm not sure I know what you mean."

He didn't believe for a moment she didn't know what he was referring to, but he decided not to call her on it. He simply raised a questioning eyebrow again and said, "Perhaps something unusual has happened this morning, and that is why you are in the park without benefit of a proper chaperone or guardian."

Brent was certain she blushed, and then she intrigued him even more by lowering her lashes for a moment, as if she wanted to shield something from him.

But what?

The first shards of daylight spread across the horizon, making it easier for Brent to see just how lovely she was. He hadn't seen the sky on a cloudless summer's day that could hold a candle to the blue of her eyes. Every movement she made seemed graceful and natural for her, but to him they were inviting and seductive.

"No," she said, not meeting his gaze. "I just had to clear my, I mean, I just wanted to get away and be alone for a little while before the day began."

He doubted whatever had brought her to the park was as simple as that. "Surely I don't have to tell you it is not in your best interest to be in the park by yourself at this time of morning, or at any time for that matter."

She lifted her chin as if to challenge his concern. "I am not worried about unsavory people out to make mischief, sir. As you can see, I have Brutus here to protect me."

Brent knew it to be true the breed of mastiff was a good guard dog, but now that it was brighter, he could see Brutus more clearly. The dog looked to be quite old. A closer look at the black soulful eyes, gray muzzle, and droopy face, not to mention a total lack of interest in sniffing Prissy, confirmed Brent's assessment that the mastiff's best days were behind him.

"No doubt Brutus has a heart as big as the ships that sail the Thames, and in his younger years, it's not hard to imagine he would have been a fierce protector. His size alone might still send some ruffians running; but whether he can protect you from danger now or not, he cannot protect you from scandal, and that might be your greatest concern."

She shrugged her shoulders, and even that common, unobtrusive gesture aroused him.

Her gaze stayed locked on his. "Perhaps you are right about that, sir, but I have no fear from someone who is considerate enough to walk his mother's dog."

"It's true you have nothing to fear from me, but alas, I cannot be your chaperone."

She stepped closer, though for half a second he had the distinct feeling this confident young lady was suddenly uncertain. But the thought vanished when she surprised him by reaching up to touch the side of his face. Even though she wore a cotton glove, he felt heat and gentleness in her hand, and he caught the intoxicating scent of rosewater on her skin.

"You seem a kind and decent man." She hesitated, and then drew a deep breath. "Forgive me," she whispered.

She rose on her toes and placed her lips on his. Brent was stunned by her action, but as her body leaned into his and her lips pressed against his, surprise was replaced by an intense and immediate feral desire to possess her, which he struggled to control.

Her lips were soft and warm despite the chill of the morn, and he was lost to her tender kiss. It took a moment before it filtered into his brain that she wasn't really very good at kissing, though she was trying hard to play the seductress. That simple fact made her all the more intriguing and desirable.

When her arms wound around his neck and her lips parted, Brent dropped Prissy's leash and drew her gently into his embrace. Though he had no idea why, this woman was obviously serious with her intentions, and his body could no longer resist her attempt at seduction.

Brent coaxed her lips farther apart and tasted the warmth of her mouth, teasing her with his tongue. He slid his hands inside her cape and around her waist to the small of her back and felt her feminine softness. She gasped into his mouth when he brought her tightly against him. She was slender, yet very womanly melting into his arms. Beneath her wrap, his hand roved up and down the sensuous curve of her small waist and gentle flare of her shapely hips.

He couldn't believe how wonderful and sweet her pliant lips felt beneath his. A rampant hunger sprang up inside him, and he deepened the kiss, letting his mouth cover hers more fully, frantically seeking her inner depths. She matched his hunger as if she had been yearning just for his touch. His hand moved up her rib cage to settle over the soft, tempting swell of her breast, and his insides quivered at how delicious she felt. Beneath his hand, her chest heaved with each determined breath, each skillful caress. A soft, involuntary whimper passed her lips, and her arms tightened around him. Her fingers dug into the thick fabric of his greatcoat.

Somewhere, at the back of his mind, he heard Prissy barking again, but the sound barely registered. The little creature was always barking at something. Brutus woofed a couple of times, but there was no way he was leaving the golden-haired beauty with the enchanting blue eyes who had walked freely out of the mist and so amazingly into his arms.

Brent reached up and pushed her cloak away from her shoulders, letting it fall to her back, giving him more freedom to touch her supple body as he desired. His lips left hers, and he kissed his way down the slender column of her neck, past the tied, corded sash that held her cape on, to where a bit of lace at the neckline of her dress teased and tickled his cheek and chin.

"Gabrielle!" a man shouted.

"Unhand her, you scoundrel!" another man bellowed.

Startled, Brent released her. A button on the sleeve of his coat caught on the lace at the neckline of her dress and ripped it as he stepped away.

In the blink of an eye, Brent saw four men charging toward him. Two of the men were well-dressed gentlemen, and the other two were wearing servants' garb. He glanced over to his seducer. Her eyes held firmly on his. He expected to see fear or maybe regret in their depths, but what he saw was guilt.

Guilt?

Surely not, but the expression on her face told the tale. She wasn't frightened of him or the men barreling down on them.

Had she planned this?

Was it possible that barely a fortnight in London and he'd already been caught in a parson's mousetrap by the conniving, sweet-smelling hand of an angel?

While it was true he had planned to look for a comely, well-suited wife while in London, he had no intentions of being leg-shackled by anyone he didn't choose.

"Sirs, I'm Viscount Brentwood," he said as the men skittered to a halt in front of him. "I assure you this is not what it looks like. I was not attacking this young lady."

"Lord Brentwood," the taller of the two gentlemen said, "I am the Duke of Windergreen, and I assure you, I saw you kissing my daughter!"

A duke's daughter! Blasted hell!

He didn't know what kind of wretched plan was in that lovely head of hers, but he knew how powerful dukes were. This little scheme of hers could easily land him in Newgate if he wasn't careful.

Brent turned to face the bewitching young lady, who still stood close to him, and whispered, "You did this deliberately, didn't you?"

Her blue eyes rounded in horror. "No, of course not. How could you think that?"

"Right now I'm finding it very easy to think that."

"Explain yourself, Brentwood," the duke demanded.

Damnation!

He turned back toward her father. What could he say to the duke? That his daughter was the one who had kissed him? Would the duke believe him or even care that this lovely young angel he called Gabrielle was the one who initiated the kiss?

Somehow, Brent thought not.

In the dark recesses of his mind, Brent realized he heard Prissy barking again. It wasn't her yappy, irritating bark or her snarling growl at blowing leaves. It was a painful whine.

Brent tensed again. Something had happened to his mother's dog.

He glanced down. It wasn't the mastiff giving her trouble. Brutus stood quite innocently beside his mistress.

Prissy cried again, a piercing screech of alarm as if something had hold of her. Brent's mind went blank, and without thinking about consequences, he bolted toward the sound.

"Catch him!" Brent heard the duke shout behind him, but he kept running toward the dog.

But not much more than a few steps farther, he was slammed to the ground from behind, a heavy body landing on top of him.

Brent grunted and winced. He struggled to throw the man off his back as a beefy hand shoved the side of his face into the hard, wet ground.

"Stop!" he yelled. "I'm not running away. I hear my dog. I need to go to her. She's hurt."

"Sure she is, my lord," the servant muttered above him as he pushed Brent's face harder into the cold, rocky earth. "And I have a manor house in Kent, too."

What a hell of a mess he was in. Something was wrong with his mother's dog, and he'd been caught in the park at daybreak kissing a duke's daughter.

"Damnation," he rasped into the hard ground.

No wonder his mother had always said it would be a cold day in hell before she went back to London.

Two

GABRIELLE'S HEART JUMPED TO HER THROAT. PANIC threatened to overwhelm her.

She watched in horror as her father and her fiancé's father yelled at their footmen to catch the retreating viscount. Heavens above, she didn't blame him for running away. If she were him, she'd be trying to get away too!

He thought she had deliberately tried to leg shackle him, but that couldn't be further from the truth.

She only wanted to kiss him.

Gabrielle knew her father and Lord Austerhill occasionally enjoyed a smoke, a talk, and a long early morning walk in the park. But she had been too consumed with her own troubles to even consider that they might be in Hyde Park this chilly morn.

Heavens above, what had she done? But, of course, she knew the answer to that.

With a brief squeeze of her eyes, she tried to blot

out the image of seeing her fiancé and her sister wrapped together in a passionate embrace in a dimly lit corridor where the Autumn Ball was being held. She feared that scene would be forever etched in her mind. How had she missed their love for each other? She had always considered herself so discerning, so intuitive, but obviously not when dealing with matters of the heart.

With what she witnessed, a different young lady might have thrown herself out a window or across her bed and cried like a fool, but Gabrielle had never been a fool... other than being foolish enough not to notice her fiancé and sister were in love. This, in turn, had made Gabrielle wish for a window. Instead, she had grabbed her cape and her faithful dog Brutus and had gone to the park and thrown herself at a gentleman!

What in heaven's name had she done?

Watching the servants chasing after Lord Brentwood, she had to wonder if the window might have done less damage.

She didn't know what madness had come over her, but when she'd seen the tall, handsome man standing in the swirling mist, for a moment she couldn't breathe. He was beautiful, regal, nearly otherworldly, which could be the only reason she had forgotten all about this world and approached him. When his gaze had drifted down her face, she'd felt a quickening of something wonderful skimming along her breasts and then sailing inexplicably to the lowest recesses of her abdomen. Just remembering how she had felt when he looked at her brought the elusive sensations tingling back into her body, feelings she'd never experienced when her fiancé had looked at her.

In the distance, the sound of a body being slammed to the ground, followed by a loud grunt, cut off everything but her own distressed gasp. With a wince, she turned to see her father's footman sprawled on top of the viscount, and Lord Austerhill's servant pressing the innocent man's face into the ground. Queasiness filled her stomach, and Gabrielle thought she might be sick. She swallowed past a thick throat and steeled herself for the backlash she knew wasn't far away.

Brutus sensed her distress and nudged against her hip with his body, growling low in his throat. Out of habit, she reached down, and with a pat on his big head, assured the dog she was fine. He reached up and sniffed her hand.

"What in the name of Hades are you doing out here with that man?" her father demanded. Grabbing her upper arm, he turned her around to face him. Brutus growled again, but her father paid the dog no mind.

Feeling as if her breath was trapped in her chest, and unable to move, Gabrielle stood in mortified silence, staring at the two enraged men glaring at her. The raw fury in their faces spoke of dire consequences and suddenly rendered her speechless.

"Gabrielle!" her father said more sharply, squeezing her arm.

Her father had always been a short-tempered man, but he had never touched her—in kindness or in anger. She hated disappointing him, but there was no changing what had happened. She calmly took hold of her father's wrist and removed his clenched hand from her arm before Brutus decided to attack. That would prove a bigger disaster than she was facing right now.

"It's clear we'll get nothing out of her," Lord Austerhill spat, not bothering to hide the contempt he felt for her. "As I suspected, she is too filled with guilt to speak."

"No, Lord Austerhill," Gabrielle said, struggling to pull herself together. "I am not afraid to speak. There is simply nothing I have to say about my presence in the park."

Her father shook with uncontrolled rage. "You better have something to say, young lady, and you can start by telling me what you are doing out here alone with that man."

"I believe we saw what she was doing here, Duke," Lord Austerhill argued. "What I want to know is why, when she is to marry my son a week from today."

How could she tell her father she had enticed the viscount because something about him drew her, and she wanted to be kissed the way she saw her fiancé kiss her sister last night? How could she admit to Lord Austerhill she wanted to experience the unbridled passion she saw on her sister's face when his son had kissed her? Though one look at her father's thin lips, not to mention Lord Austerhill's bulging eyes, let her know she didn't want to tell either man the truth. Besides, how could she explain to them what happened when she was as astounded at what she'd done as they were? No, it was best to remain silent and let them think what they wished.

Gabrielle had never been a witless ninny who was led by fanciful dreams of romance and feminine emotions.

She was calm, sensible, and never flustered—until today. The truth was, she had never done an impetuous thing in her life. She was her father's oldest child. She was dependable, rational, and obedient. That was why she had accepted the practical, unemotional marriage her father had arranged for her in the first place. That was what those of her kind did.

Or so she had always believed. Now she wasn't so sure. After what she experienced with this viscount, this stranger, Gabrielle had to wonder if she had only buried feelings of passion and desire in order to please her father.

But, what in heaven's name had come over her this morning to make her throw all of her upbringing away and want to be kissed and held in the arms of a handsome stranger? What was there about Lord Brentwood that had awakened the wanton desire she'd felt when she looked at him?

"Speak, girl, speak," her father demanded again.

"Have you absolutely nothing to say in your defense?" Lord Austerhill snapped.

Gabrielle was forced to ignore her father and the nobleman. She had no answer. She felt as if her whole life had suddenly shifted, and she didn't know herself.

She glanced back at the man on the ground. She watched in horror as the two footmen struggled with Lord Brentwood. No matter what her father or the earl thought about what they witnessed, she was the reason the viscount was being manhandled like a common footpad, and it was her responsibility to help him.

Suddenly, Gabrielle was not concerned about her father's ire, herself, her sister, or Lord Austerhill's son. She was appalled to watch the handsome viscount dragged unceremoniously to his feet, his hands held firmly behind his back by the servants.

She turned to her father. "Papa, tell Muggs not to hurt Lord Brentwood. What happened was not his fault; it was mine."

Her father's jaw was set with rage. He was a rigid man, straight as the blade of a soldier's sword and just as hard. In his younger days, a mere glance from him could send a shudder through the household staff, and her younger brother and sister racing to hide beneath their beds.

"I'm not the least concerned whether Muggs hurts the man. He can kill the scoundrel for all I care. And for your information, young lady, when a man puts his hands on an untouched maid of quality, it is never her fault as far as I'm concerned. The blame is always with the man, though the girl is always the one punished."

"Notice whom her concern is for, Duke," Lord Austerhill remarked scathingly. "Did you hear her say one word about how this shameful act of betrayal she's committed is going to destroy my son?"

Gabrielle smothered an angry retort about his son by pressing her lips tightly together. Her ill-advised words of concern for Lord Brentwood didn't sit well with the earl or her father and wasn't going to help the struggling viscount.

"Clearly, your daughter has been carrying on an affair with this man behind my son's back with secret assignations."

Gabrielle gasped. "That is not true, my lord. I haven't," she said earnestly, and immediately wondered if letting them know this was the first time she had ever met the man made her seem more a wanton doxy than if she and Lord Brentwood had been long-standing lovers.

Apparently her fierce denial did nothing to salve the earl's rancor. His bushy gray eyebrows rose with skepticism, and a nervous tic worked each side of his wide, sneering mouth.

Indignation dripped from his words as he said, "That is not what it looked like to me. You two seemed to know each other very well indeed, consid-ering the way you were wrapped in each other's arms, with your lips locked together as if you were trying to swallow each other. Your torn gown and gaping cape were falling off your shoulders."

No longer able to hide the turmoil churning inside her, a shiver of outrage shook her. Gabrielle gasped so loudly Brutus growled a warning.

Gabrielle's chin lifted defiantly. "Lord Austerhill, you owe me an apology. My gown was never off my shoulders." She looked down at the bodice of her dress and winced inside when she saw the delicate lace that had edged the neckline of her dress was torn free. Hastily she added, "A bit of lace was ripped away from the fabric when it caught on the button on Lord Brentwood's sleeve. That is all."

"Ha!" Lord Austerhill shouted loudly. "As if any of that matters anyway. Tell the story any way you like. It won't change what was going on here or the outcome it has now created."

Resentment and anger at the man's pompous attitude festered inside Gabrielle. She was the one who had been wronged by his son carrying on a tryst with her sister. Gabrielle opened her mouth to protest and tell the man the ugly truth she had discovered just hours ago at the ball at the Great Hall, but caught herself. Accusing his son would mean telling on her sister, as well, and while Gabrielle wanted to strangle the impetuous Rosabelle for her deception and betrayal, she couldn't risk ruining her by telling Lord Austerhill and her father what had been going on between Rosabelle and Staunton.

"Now see here, Austerhill," her father stated firmly. "That is enough of that kind of talk. There has to be a reasonable explanation for what we witnessed."

Austerhill took the bowl of his pipe and knocked it quite firmly against his palm, sending ashes fluttering to the ground. Somehow, Gabrielle knew the man was telling her that, to him, her worth was no more than ashes to be trampled beneath his feet.

The earl looked up at her father with steely eyes and a grim expression. "Maybe you need clarification to satisfy your questions concerning your daughter's actions, Duke, but I do not. My son is not going to marry a woman who was caught alone with a man for any reason. All I can add is I thank the saints in heaven I found out what kind of person *she* is before *she* married my son and became his wife."

"Austerhill. There is no call to get—"

"I'm done here," the earl said, sticking the pipe in the pocket of his greatcoat. "If my son's wife is ever with child, I damn well want to be sure he is the father."

Gabrielle gasped, and anger surged inside her. "You go too far, my lord."

Lord Austerhill twisted his lips into a sneer at Gabrielle, turned, and stomped away.

"Wait," her father called furiously to the earl's retreating back. "You can't leave. Where are you going?"

"To tell my son his wedding is off because his betrothed is…"

Gabrielle didn't hear Lord Austerhill's last words and was glad she didn't. By the revulsion in his parting glance and the loud gasp from her father, she could imagine what he'd said.

"Damn you, man," her father yelled and started after him. "This was not her fault, I tell you. Get back here!"

Lord Austerhill called to his servant, and the man immediately dropped his hold on the viscount and followed the earl until they disappeared into the mist.

Gabrielle's father turned on her with rage. "By all the angels in heaven, what made you pull such a foolhardy stunt as this? I could imagine something like this from your sister, or even from your brother, but not you! You have always been my sensible daughter. Now look what you have done!"

Once again she retreated into silence. She had no answer for him.

"What in God's name was going on between you two?" her father barked. "You have ruined everything! Do you know what you've done, the money this is going to cost me, girl?"

Gabrielle blinked at her father's harsh tone. She had

always known the wedding was for her father's financial benefit and not her own happiness, but hearing him actually say the words pained her and, once again, her stomach quaked.

"Yes, Papa, I know," she said softly, keeping her gaze locked on the viscount.

"Then explain yourself, Daughter. Have you no shame? By all that's sacred, tell me why you agreed to meet him." Her father threw a finger toward the viscount.

"It wasn't planned. It just happened," she said, knowing it was the truth but also knowing it didn't explain anything. There was no logical answer for what she had done.

"Really?" her father asked in an incredulous voice as he threw a glance in Lord Brentwood's direction. "Do you expect me to believe you woke before daybreak and decided you were going to take Brutus for a walk in the park and, by chance, you happened to meet a stranger, embrace him, and end up kissing him by accident?"

Yes, that is exactly what happened.

"After more than nineteen years of living with me, just how big a simpleton do you take me for?"

What she had done to her father was horrible for a well-behaved daughter; what she had done to the viscount was unforgivable. She feared there was no way she could make it right for any of them.

For the present, Gabrielle saw no way out other than capitulation. She lifted her shoulders and chin, and said what she knew her father wanted to hear. "I'm sorry for the distress I've caused you, Papa.

Though I never intended for this to happen, I'm without excuse."

"Yes, you are!" he said, anger rising in his tone again. "And now I'm left with the task of sorting all this out! If there is any chance of salvaging this engagement, the only way will be if I give more lands than were exchanged in the betrothal agreement, not to mention everything else we had worked out. With the wedding date just days away, funds, lands, and business ventures have already been mingled. It will take our solicitors weeks to sort it all out."

Gabrielle stiffened. Salvage the engagement? Marry the earl's youngest son, knowing he and her sister were in love? She couldn't.

"No, Papa. I will not marry Staunton."

"Nonsense," he said gruffly. "You will, if I can talk him and his father into forgiving you."

All thoughts of capitulation vanished. "It's not nonsense. I've never wanted to marry him. You and his father arranged this marriage for financial profit, not for any love between Staunton and me."

"Love?" His lips thinned in exasperation. "What is that, Gabrielle? Of course the marriage was for money. There's no such thing as love. I should have known it was a foolish notion that brought you out to the park this morning to meet that man. It's just as well you learn here and now that whatever it is you think you feel for him it isn't love, and it has nothing to do with what makes a good marriage."

No such thing as love? Did she believe that?

Maybe, yesterday. Maybe, before she saw the passion between Rosabelle and Staunton. Maybe, before she kissed Lord Brentwood and felt those wonderful stirrings of desire down in her soul.

Gabrielle looked toward Viscount Brentwood again. He was tall and lithe for such a wide-shouldered man, walking with far more ease than she would have anticipated considering what had happened to him. She expected him to be seething with uncontrolled anger like her father and Lord Austerhill, but when his gaze locked onto hers, all she sensed from him was a deep burning to know why.

A shiver of awareness slithered through her. He seemed to consume her with his dark eyes as he drew nearer. The way he looked at her played havoc with her breathing. She felt flushed and out of breath, as if she'd been the one running and in a struggle. A seeping warmth settled low in her stomach, an unwelcome warmth. That feeling had caused enough trouble already, and she wouldn't give in to its comfort again.

The closer he came to them, the faster her heart beat, and not from fear of reprisal, but from very raw, very real attraction. There was a jagged red scratch on his cheek where his face had been shoved against the ground. His black greatcoat fell open and hung off one shoulder. His top hat was missing, and his thick, light brown hair was mussed and fell carelessly across his forehead. Despite all the recriminations she'd heard from her father and Lord Austerhill, she wanted once again to wrap her arms around Lord Brentwood's strong, broad chest and feel his full, sensual lips on hers.

She couldn't comprehend the reason she was so affected by him.

Lord Brentwood and the servant stopped in front

of Gabrielle and her father. She was supposed to be making final preparations for her wedding next week and, instead, she was staring into the intense dark brown eyes of a stranger that were asking questions she knew she couldn't answer.

That old eagerness to please stirred inside her. She wanted to take a step toward him, plead with him to forgive her, but something in the quiet way he looked at her made her remain where she was.

In a voice much less emotional than she was feeling, she said, "My lord, I assured my father this was not your fault."

A brief moment of surprise flashed in his eyes before they turned dark and stormy again. She could see that he wrestled with something deep inside. Was it loathing for her, or for her father and the footmen who tackled him?

"I don't need you taking up for me, Lady Gabrielle."

She threw a cautious glance toward her father, surprised he was letting her talk to the viscount. "But I must," she protested. "I never meant for any of this to happen."

His gaze stayed on her face, as if he was taking careful note of her every feature. "Really?" he asked quietly. "None of it?"

Stunned by what he asked, Gabrielle sucked in a hasty breath. He was reminding her of their passion. Her cheeks heated. He was seducing her right in front of her father, and she was powerless to stop him.

"Please don't," she managed to whisper softly so only he could hear, before saying in a stronger voice, "You must know I didn't want this to happen."

His eyes turned quizzical. "I don't know that."

"How could you not?"

"Because I don't know what games you are playing, Lady Gabrielle, and I don't know why you chose to involve me in them."

"There is no game. You are just an innocent victim."

The viscount drew back suddenly as if she had struck him below the belt. "I am no one's victim, my lady."

"No, of course, you're right. I only meant I'm sorry you were treated like a common criminal just now."

"Nevertheless, I willingly made the bed, and I will lie in it."

Her stomach clenched at the implication of his words. "I'm not sure what you mean by that," she said, though she feared she did.

"I will do whatever I must to make this right for you."

She blinked rapidly. Merciful heavens! He was too blasted calm about all this. He was making her crazy. "What is right for me? You are the one who was wronged."

"That is not up to us to decide," he said, glancing toward her father.

"Indeed it is not," her father chimed in as if on cue. "And I'm glad to hear you are going to be sensible about this debacle. But, of course, the first thing I intend to do is see what can be done to save her engagement to the earl's son."

Lord Brentwood jerked toward her, the fierce glare from his eyes cutting her as if it was a sharp knife. "You're betrothed?"

"Don't tell me you didn't know of this?" her father barked.

"I didn't," Brent said tightly, keeping his hot gaze on her face. "I'm new to London and hadn't heard."

"I've heard of you," her father said. "Your brothers are the talk of the clubs and scandal sheets."

The viscount grimaced but said nothing.

Gabrielle swallowed past a thick throat. She, along with everyone else in town, knew about his twin brothers' resemblance to the well-known and well-liked Sir Randolph Gibson. The scandal sheets mentioned them every day.

"I'm sorry," she said. "Of course, I should have told you I was to marry the Earl of Austerhill's youngest son next week," she admitted, knowing how terribly awful that made her sound after the way she had thrown herself at him.

Anger seeped into the viscount's face, and from between tightly clenched teeth, he said, "Next week? And you didn't see the need to let me in on that important detail about your life a little earlier?"

Her emotions were frayed. No answer she could give would satisfy him, so she simply said, "It didn't seem relevant at the time."

Lord Brentwood's mood changed quickly, and he took a menacing step toward her. Brutus growled a warning. The servant's hands clamped tighter around his arms and held him back as he said, "With you betrothed, tell me, what the devil were you doing kissing me?"

"That's what I have been trying to find out for the past ten minutes," her father added brusquely. "And it's past time for one of you to tell me!"

Gabrielle's gaze shifted from Lord Brentwood to

her father and back to the viscount again. They both demanded and deserved answers.

Heavens above!

Surely there was something she could do other than tattle on her sister? But what?

Three

*Courage is doing what you're afraid to do. There can be no courage
unless you are scared.*

—Eddie Rickenbacker

GABRIELLE PACED IN FRONT OF THE WINDOW IN THE
drawing room of their Mayfair home. Her faithful
companion, Brutus, slept peacefully on his giant pillow
in his favorite spot near the softly burning fire.

She kept reminding herself she was a calm, rational,
and sensible person, even though her actions earlier
that morning disproved that fact. Most of the shock
of everything that had happened had worn off, and
Gabrielle was feeling stronger and more capable of
dealing with the crisis she'd created with her unchar-
acteristically impulsive and scandalous behavior in
Hyde Park.

Staring at her father and the viscount, she became
so emotional that, for a moment, she was on the verge
of spilling all and telling them about Staunton and
Rosabelle's romance and deception when, thankfully,
they'd heard someone approaching them in the park.

Her father told Lord Brentwood they would talk later. He had then grabbed her arm, quickly whisked her to his waiting carriage and back home where she had been ever since.

After telling her he'd deal with her when he returned, he had left immediately to see Lord Austerhill. Her father desperately wanted to undo the damage she'd done by being caught in a compromising embrace with Lord Brentwood. In the hours since he'd been gone, Gabrielle didn't care what kind of agreement her father might reach with Lord Austerhill, she would never marry the earl's son.

She was over the shock of Rosabelle and Staunton's love for each other and was thinking more rationally about that, as well. If the two of them truly loved each other, wasn't it her duty to try to make it possible for them to be together? Just because Gabrielle had been willing to settle for a loveless marriage in order to be the obedient daughter didn't mean Rosabelle must, too.

She was glad she hadn't had to face her sister since she returned home. It wasn't yet past noontime. Rosabelle was a late riser and always took an enormous amount of time with her toilette in the mornings.

With little more than a year's difference in their ages, Rosabelle had always been very competitive with Gabrielle, but she never minded and often would let her sister win if they were playing cards or other games. To please her sister, Gabrielle had even postponed her debut at court a year so she and Rosabelle could debut together. They had always been close, sometimes talking until the wee hours of the morning about friends, books, beaus, and clothing. That is, until recently. Gabrielle had noticed her sister had been avoiding her. She had thought it was because Rosabelle was upset to see her leaving to have a home and family of her own. Now Gabrielle knew the real reason.

A shiver shook her. Gabrielle couldn't even think about how dreadfully awful it would have been if she had married Staunton and then learned of her sister's love for him.

Gabrielle heard the rear door open and stopped in front of the window. That must be her father. She squeezed her eyes shut and clenched her hands into fists. She willed herself to be courageous and strong. She had learned long ago how to reason with her temperamental father, and she had to do that now. It was best to be patient with him, let him have his say, and then calmly make her point. Slowly, her hands relaxed. Her eyes opened. She took a long, steadying breath.

In the past, it had always helped her to think of the worst that could happen and then come up with a solution. What exactly could her father do to her for her indiscretion? She supposed the worst thing he could do would be to try to force her to marry Staunton. She had already decided she'd never do that. So the next worst thing would be if she were forced to marry the viscount. That was almost as objectionable as marrying the earl's son.

Almost, but not quite.

If she acquiesced to that, she would not only be agreeing to another loveless marriage, but she would be ruining Lord Brentwood's life, too. She couldn't do that to him.

She had to give her father another option. She would ask that he send her away to one of his many estates. She knew from gossip that each Season more than one young lady was sent to the country to live for a time. Some returned to London and Society, and others preferred to stay in the country.

Gabrielle had always loved the hustle and bustle of living in London. She loved riding in the parks, walking the streets, and looking in shops. She loved going to Vauxhall Gardens, the opera, and on the few occasions her father had allowed, to the theatre. She would probably be lonely in the country for a time, but with enough books to read, needlework to stitch, and her painting, she would find a way to cope and fill her days.

Her father's voice drifted down the corridor. He was talking to Mrs. Lathbury, a short, rotund woman with a soft voice, who was frightened of her own shadow. She was the latest in a long string of house-keepers who had managed the duke's Mayfair home over the years. Her father had never been an easy man to work for, and turnover in their staff occurred frequently, certainly more often than Gabrielle would have liked. She was only six when her mother died giving birth to her only son, Ellis, who was currently finishing his studies at Oxford. Gabrielle had often wondered if her father would have been a kinder, softer man had her mother lived longer.

A few moments later, she heard the duke stomping down the corridor. Listening to his heavy footfalls, Gabrielle knew he was heading straight to his book room, which was opposite the music room.

Gabrielle wished she didn't have to have this discussion with her father, but there was no way around it. And she wasn't going to stand around worrying, fearful, waiting for her father to come to her. She was going to him to determine her fate.

She waited a reasonable amount of time and then squared her shoulders and headed that way. She stopped at the doorway to the drawing room when she heard Brutus moving behind her.

Looking back at the dog, she saw him half standing, struggling to lift his back legs and get them moving. "Stay," she said and held out her hand. "You've done enough walking for today."

Brutus made a low growling sound in his throat, as if to argue with her his right to go, as he continued struggling to stand.

"Stay, Brutus," she said more firmly. "Down."

Brutus stopped but continued looking at her with big, soulful eyes, panting heavily, as if hoping she would change her mind.

"I'm only going to the book room to see Papa," she said gently, not wanting him to think she was scolding him. "There's no reason for you to disturb yourself. Now be a good boy and lie back down on your soft pillow."

Seeing he wasn't going to win this battle, Brutus eased back down onto his bed with a groan, laid his head on his front paws, and stared at her with a sorrowful expression.

Gabrielle felt as if a cold hand gripped her heart. She knew the cold of their morning jaunt had seeped into his old bones and sapped a lot of his strength.

It was heartbreaking to know her big brute of a dog and faithful companion could no longer climb the two steps by himself to get into her father's coach. Muggs had struggled to help lift his hind legs and get him into the carriage. Brutus's age was showing more and more as each day, week, and month passed.

She smiled lovingly at Brutus. "That's my good boy. I'll be back soon."

Halfway to the book room, fluttering butterflies attacked her stomach, and that angered her. She wasn't a simpering fool. Whatever weakness had come over her in Hyde Park that had caused her to deny her good common sense and kiss a stranger was gone.

Forever, she vowed.

She was back to being Miss Practical. But as she neared the end of the corridor, she couldn't help but ask herself if she really wanted to return to life as it was before her few enchanting moments in Lord Brentwood's arms.

Gabrielle stopped at the open doorway of the book room and, pulling from an inner strength that had served her well in the past, knocked on the casing. Her father looked up from pouring himself a drink but didn't speak to her.

"Papa," she said and stepped inside.

"You are either very brave or very foolish, Gabrielle, to seek me out knowing how upset I am with you at this very moment. You would do well to give me time to have a drink, perhaps several, before you approach me."

Gabrielle wasn't afraid of her father, and until today, she had always obeyed him.

"What's done is done, Papa," she said, grateful her voice sounded stronger than she felt.

"Yes, yes, I know, and can't be undone. Believe me, I've tried. Unfortunately, by the time I arrived at Austerhill's house, he had already awakened his son and told him about your brazen indiscretion. Of course, Staunton made a good show of wanting to immediately call out the viscount, but thankfully, his father and I talked him out of that foolhardy idea. Neither of us wanted scandal heaped upon scandal."

"Oh, thank goodness, Papa! That would have been madness."

"So was my time there. From the moment I arrived, the entire household treated me as though I had brought the black plague to their doorstep. I hope you are happy now that your wedding and my financial plans are officially canceled."

As a matter of fact, she was happy and relieved her wedding was canceled, but no matter how difficult a man he was, she couldn't find delight in her father's misery. He may not have been a doting father through the years, but he'd certainly never done her harm. Gabrielle wished she could tell him that she took it all back, but that wasn't true. She knew she wouldn't want to have missed those few incredible minutes she'd spent in the viscount's strong arms for anything in the world.

"But surely, Papa, you will regain the properties you promised to the earl as my dowry when the betrothal was arranged; so all will not be lost."

The duke harrumphed disdainfully. "I would never give away anything I wanted."

The sting of her father's carelessly chosen words pierced her, and she gasped. "But what about me, Papa? You were willing to give me away."

To a man you knew I didn't love.

"What?" He waved his hand as if to brush off what she said. "No. I mean, yes, of course, Gabrielle. Fathers always give their daughters away in marriage, but make no mistake. You will always be *my* daughter. And if any man dares hurt you in any way, he would have me to answer to."

Gabrielle knew that was as close as he was going to come to an endearing comment.

"What I meant was that the whole of what I promised to Austerhill and his son are worthless lands to me and useless business ventures I wanted to dispose of anyway. He is the one who had the prized lands I wanted to add to my holdings. Now, thanks to you, I won't get them."

Her father had never tried to hide his many business ventures from her, often bragging to her, and to Ellis when he was home from Oxford, about his lucrative deals. He seemed to be happiest when he was trying to lure some unsuspecting soul into selling their land, their horses, or their businesses to him.

Gabrielle walked farther into the room. "If that's the case, Papa, maybe now is the right time to bring this up. Perhaps in a few days you could suggest to Lord Austerhill and to Staunton that they might consider Rosabelle's hand in marriage so the arrangements the two families have put in place can proceed as originally planned."

"What?" The duke turned toward her, glass in hand, and laughed bitterly. "Ha! How well I would like that!

But I can assure you, Gabrielle, that neither the earl nor his weak-kneed son wants anything to do with either of my daughters now, later, or ever."

Gabrielle blinked at her father's harsh words as he put the glass to his mouth, drank heavily from it, and then turned his back on her to refill it. At least there was hope, since her father didn't know Staunton wanted to be with Rosabelle. And her father wanted the lands, so he would be agreeable. The only one to worry about would be Lord Austerhill. Surely in time, his son could persuade him to allow marriage with Rosabelle.

"But maybe all is not lost." Her father spoke more as if talking to himself than her.

"What?"

"I've already sent word to Viscount Brentwood, asking him to come see me late this afternoon."

Gabrielle tensed. "Papa, can't we just leave him out of this? I want to forget about what happened in the park."

The duke turned back toward her and harrumphed again as he walked toward his desk. "If only we could. Wouldn't that be a pretty ribbon wrapped around a boar's tail? But, no, we can't just forget about him. I have no doubt that, in time, news of your indiscretion will be tattled from the tongues of men at the clubs and whispered from the waspish mouths of every old hen and every young biddy in the ton."

"That certainly puts the situation I'm in bluntly."

"These kinds of things have a way of growing all out of proportion, but you did it, not I. Obviously, I would have considered the viscount for you, along with all the rest of the blades who were knocking on my door, had he been in Town at the beginning of the Season. I'm glad you at least had the good sense to have a tryst with a titled man."

Her father had never been one to mince his words, and she shouldn't have expected it of him now.

"But I have to say, Gabrielle, that it doesn't speak well of him that he tried to run away when he saw us coming to aid you; but then you picked him, I didn't."

"I don't know why he ran, Papa. All I remember was seeing four men charging us. That could frighten anyone."

"Harrumph," her father muttered. "I don't think it would have frightened me. But no matter the reason he ran, all that is important is Muggs stopped him before he got away."

"So what will you have me do to save face in Society? Will you banish me to one of your country homes?"

A wrinkle formed between his eyes. "Why the devil would I do that? No doubt that is what you would love, but no." He chuckled ruefully. "Life will not be so easy for you. Even after the alarming stunt you pulled, you are still much too valuable for me to hide away in a small village somewhere. Exaggerated tales of your assignation in the park with Brentwood will surface, but so be it. They will die down in due time. Thankfully, because I'm a duke, no one would dare cross me. I'm certain that if you marry quickly enough, all will be forgiven and forgotten." The chair behind his desk creaked as he lowered his broad frame into it. "So, no, dear girl, you will not be banished to our beautiful English countryside. You will be wed to the viscount."

Gabrielle looked at her father and had to bite her tongue to keep from telling him no. She wondered what had come over her. Why and how had she changed in such a short span of time? Five months ago she had readily agreed when her father told her he wanted her to marry Staunton, a man she had no feelings for whatsoever. She never once thought to disobey her father. She hardly even questioned him, but she had changed. She no longer wanted to just accept what her father wanted her to do without challenging him.

"Papa, I don't want to—"

He held up his hand to stop her. "Whatever you say will fall on deaf ears, my dear. I don't know the viscount but I'll see what kind of financial arrangements I can make with him. They won't be as lucrative as I had with the earl, I'm sure, but maybe he has something that would be worth an exchange for your hand in marriage. And, of course, I'll provide him an adequate dowry. I spoke with my solicitor before I came back home. He is already gathering information on Brentwood for me and should have it to me before the man arrives late this afternoon."

Gabrielle remembered the expression on Lord Brentwood's face when he heard she was set to be married next week, and that gave her some comfort. He was not a happy man. No matter what he'd said about willing to lie in the bed he made. If she read him right, his expression told her he would rather suffer the depths of hell than marry her.

"Since you liked the viscount well enough to meet him in the park and let him kiss you," her father continued, "I intend to see that you marry him."

Showing more confidence than she was feeling, Gabrielle took a bold step toward her father's desk, and in a strong voice, said, "I don't want to marry him."

The chair squeaked as he reached over and placed his glass on the desk. "You should have thought about that before you designed your affair with him."

Gabrielle gasped. "There was no affair, Papa."

He slammed a meaty hand down on his desk. "Then what would you call it, Gabrielle?"

"Madness," she whispered. "Utter madness." As the words passed her lips, fleeting memories flooded her. Strong, warm, and passionate arms wrapped tightly around her. Cool, soft, and inviting lips pressed against hers. A wide, firm palm pressed gently to her breast.

"Madness?" he asked and then sighed heavily before picking up his glass again. "Aptly put. Now leave me, Gabrielle, I'm tired of this subject, and I have work to do."

Gabrielle studied her father. It was clear she wasn't going to change him, but she could change herself. No, she *had* changed. She wasn't sure what had happened to her when she saw her sister and Staunton together, but she wasn't the same person anymore. She knew she'd done the right thing in keeping scandal away from Rosabelle's name, and now she had to keep from ruining Lord Brentwood's life, as well. Even though he had been kind enough to indicate he would marry her if her father insisted, she held out hope that he would come to his senses and help her convince her father that marriage between them wasn't necessary.

With no fear of reprisal, she said. "I want to be present whenever you talk to Lord Brentwood."

Not bothering to look at her, the duke harrumphed again and said, "Absolutely not."

"It's my life, Papa."

He looked up at her. "Which you have turned into total chaos, along with mine. I'd say you've done quite enough."

"Still squealing like a wild boar caught among the briars, Duke? It looks as though I got here just in time to help Gabby before you blow up like a hot air balloon."

Gabrielle whirled to see her favorite aunt standing in the doorway with her hands on her hips, a black travelling cape on her shoulders, a fancy feathered hat on her head, and cotton gloves on her hands. At the sight of her beloved aunt, Gabrielle felt as if a burden lifted from her shoulders, and she smiled.

"You know," her aunt continued, "that my dear sister would have never allowed you to talk in that tone to one of her daughters."

The duke grunted. "I see you still haven't learned the art of knocking and being announced, Elizabeth."

"Never saw the reason to, after my sister told me I would always be welcomed in her home. She said the door was always open to me, so why shouldn't I just walk right in?"

"Because you are usually butting in where you're not wanted," the duke said.

"Auntie Bethie," Gabrielle exclaimed excitedly and rushed toward her aunt. "I'm so glad to see you! I was hoping you would come soon."

"Lovely to see you, dearest," her aunt said as they hugged and kissed each other on their cheeks. "You do get more beautiful every time I see you."

"Nonsense, Auntie, let me help you with your cape."

Gabrielle's father had three sisters, and while Gabrielle enjoyed seeing them all, she had never adored any of them the way she adored her mother's only sister. Mrs. Elizabeth Potter was petite in size, but her loud and gravelly voice made her sound as boisterous as most men. Her nose and chin were sharp, and her eyes were as dark brown as the chocolate she liked to drink. She had a shock of golden-red hair that never seemed to fade or show gray. No doubt that was because of a secret solution she bought from the same apothecary where she bought her fountain of youth cream that she put on her face every evening before retiring. Gabrielle didn't know why her aunt bothered to tint her hair. It was usually hidden beneath one of her many outrageously designed hats.

"You do remember that my wife passed on more than a dozen years ago, don't you?" Gabby's father barked. "Or have you gotten so old that your memory doesn't serve you well anymore?"

"Don't be such a tyrant, Papa," Gabrielle said. "I'm thrilled Auntie Bethie is here." Gabrielle took her aunt's cape and laid it on a chair by the door.

"You would be," her father murmured, "but I'm not. She dotes on you and treats you as if you were a piece of the finest china." He looked over at her aunt and said, "I don't even know why you are here."

Auntie Bethie ignored him and smiled at Gabrielle

as she handed over her drawstring reticule. "I'm here for the wedding, of course."

Gabrielle blinked and opened her mouth to say the wedding had been canceled, but her father spoke first.

"You're early," he snapped.

"When it involves a wedding, a week is not too early to arrive. Besides, I wanted to surprise Gabrielle."

Her father picked up his glass again. "It's more like you wanted to irritate the devil out of me."

She gave him a cunning smile as she untied the ribbon of her feathered bonnet and said, "You've always been able to see right through me, Duke."

He matched her smile with a smirk of his own. "It's easy to see through shallow water, Elizabeth."

A deep, throaty laugh emerged from the small woman, and she walked farther into the room, taking off her gloves as she went. Her dark brown travelling dress swished around her ankles as she moved.

"I'm delighted I can still manage to irritate you, but by the looks of that glass in your hand, I'd say I'll have to stand in line today. I think someone has already beaten me to it this morning. It's a bit early in the day for the fish juice, isn't it, Duke?"

"You would change your Puritan ways and be drinking, too, if you'd had the morning I've had," he grumbled.

Though the subject was a serious one, Gabrielle couldn't help but smile as her father and aunt traded barbs with each other. Even though their dislike for each other was very real, always intense, and at times very caustic, they could be quite comical. For as long as she could remember, the two had never had a kind word for the other. Because of their constant bickering when they were around each other, Auntie Bethie visited them only once or twice a year. She usually stayed at least three or four weeks every time. The duke would always find a reason to leave shortly after her arrival, and she would always leave as soon as he returned.

Elizabeth stopped in front of the duke's desk, propped a lean hip against it, and asked, "Who is the lucky devil who dared to take my place of honor in your cold heart?"

Gabrielle's father lifted his glass in salute to Elizabeth. "A viscount named Brentwood."

Auntie Bethie turned toward Gabrielle. "Perhaps I'll meet him at the wedding?"

"You're too late for the wedding," her father said gruffly.

Her aunt peeled her hat off her head, tossed the feathered bonnet to Gabrielle, and then turned back to the duke. "Will you make up your mind, old man? You just told me I was early."

"Blast it, woman, you were early because the wedding was next week, and there was no reason for you to come until the day of it. And you're late now because the wedding has just been canceled."

A garbled gasp came from the doorway. "Gabby, you're not going to marry Staunton?"

At the sound of her sister's voice, Gabrielle spun toward the door. Rosabelle stood just inside the room, her bright blue eyes glistening with questions Gabrielle wasn't ready to answer.

Rosabelle rushed breathlessly into the room, her

long golden curls bouncing on her back. Her gaze searched wildly from Gabrielle to their father, to their aunt, and then back to Gabrielle. "Tell me, is what I just heard true?"

Looking at her sister's hopeful expression, Gabrielle knew that Rosabelle was brimming with love for Staunton. Earlier in the day, Gabrielle had wondered how she'd missed their love for each other, but now she knew. She simply hadn't cared enough for Staunton one way or the other to notice how he looked at any other young ladies, or how they looked at him.

The duke rose from his chair. "That is the truth."

Relief that quickly turned to hopefulness washed down Rosabelle's face. Her chest heaved with expectations, and her eyes once again eagerly searched every face in the room. But obviously reading the dire expressions of Gabrielle, her father, and her aunt, she quickly masked her happiness with a troubled, exaggerated frown of shock.

Rosabelle clutched her skirt in her hands. "Auntie Bethie, is this why you are here?" Not waiting for an answer, she turned to Gabrielle. "Gabby, this is absolutely the most dreadful news. Why? What happened between you two? When did it happen?"

Not wanting to get into this with Rosabelle or her aunt at the moment, Gabrielle said, "There is no need to go into the details about this to anyone, is there, Papa?"

"None I can see. Everything will have to be settled with Austerhill before anything concerning Brentwood need be formally announced. Though I'm sure your aunt will not rest her old bones until she knows more from you."

Rosabelle kept concern on her features. Her hands worked the fabric of her dress. "How can you bear it, Gabby? You must be so brokenhearted and distressed. I don't know why you aren't drowning in a pail of tears."

"Because she's her mother's daughter," Auntie Bethie said. "She's much too strong for that kind of nonsense."

Feeling calmer now that her aunt was here and now that Rosabelle knew the wedding was canceled, Gabrielle said, "Don't be alarmed for me, Rosa. You know that it never was a love match between us. It was all financial, so there are no broken hearts, just details that need to be handled, which Papa is already in the process of taking care of."

"Still, to have your wedding canceled a week before—I don't know what to say. You had everything planned. Your trunks are packed and ready to be delivered to your new home. What are you going to do?"

Those were little details Gabrielle didn't need to be reminded of.

"She will do nothing," Auntie Bethie said. "I shall be happy to take care of everything, all the cancellations, all the notes that must be sent, everything. I will handle it all."

"Thank you, Auntie, that would be so very kind of you."

"Consider it done."

Gabrielle was glad to see Rosabelle's attempted expression of alarm relax into a frown of real concern for her. She knew her sister hadn't deliberately set out to steal Staunton away from her.

Gabrielle couldn't blame Rosa for not telling her about the loving feelings she had for Staunton, either. After the way her father had put her through the mill with all his questions about Lord Brentwood, Gabrielle knew admitting to a wrong doing wasn't an easy thing to do.

Now that Gabrielle had had time to think rationally, she couldn't blame Rosabelle for anything that had happened. Gabrielle had read enough books and heard enough gossip from widows and dowagers to know it wasn't unusual for young ladies to fall in love with men as handsome and dashing as Staunton. Even she had fallen victim to that malady once.

For a brief time last year, Gabrielle had fancied herself madly in love with a handsome soldier she'd seen while strolling with her family through Vauxhall Gardens. He had been so powerful looking, so handsomely debonair in his uniform, with his wide leather belt strapped around his slim waist and a shiny sword hanging by his side. When he'd looked her way and smiled, her heart fluttered and felt as if it had melted in her chest. She couldn't count the nights she'd lain awake dreaming about him, hoping she'd see him again, but she never did.

"I know you are very strong, Gabby," Rosabelle said. "You're the strongest lady I have ever known; but still, you must be devastated by this turn of events."

There was no acting or faking in Rosabelle's comments about Gabrielle's strength, and she appreciated the kind words from her. But there had been several times that day when Gabrielle hadn't felt strong at all.

"Oddly, I'm not," Gabrielle said, wanting to put an end to this uncomfortable conversation. "I will just say I am not unhappy about what has happened, Rosa, and leave it at that. I'm sure there will be gossip about me in the next few days, and quite possibly for weeks to come. But I believe the scandal of a canceled wedding will die down as soon as another scandal happens to take its place. Which, knowing London Society as we do, shouldn't be too long. In any case, I'm sure the worst of it will be over by winter's end and will in no way affect you or your prospects for a good match next Season."

Gabrielle saw the love for Staunton in her sister's face. That told her she had made the right decision to sacrifice her reputation to save Rosabelle's. Her sister was in love, and Gabrielle wasn't. What she had to do now was find a way to help the young lovers be together and to keep her father from forcing her to marry Lord Brentwood.

Hopefulness etched its way back into her sister's features again as she asked, "Do you really think that?"

"Of course she does, and so do I and your father, too," Auntie Bethie said. "Now come give me a proper hug and a kiss before I start thinking you no longer care about me."

Rosabelle ran over and hugged her aunt and kissed her cheek. She then, unexpectedly, rushed over and threw her arms around Gabrielle and said, "Oh, Gabby, what will you do?"

Gabrielle's heart softened even more as her sister's

arms circled her, holding her tightly. Rosabelle's body trembled. Gabrielle knew they would eventually have a heart-to-heart talk about what happened, but she wasn't ready for that yet, and she felt Rosabelle wasn't either.

Her father looked at Gabrielle from over Rosabelle's shoulder and said, "She'll marry someone else, of course."

Gabrielle patted her sister's back, knowing she had argued with her father all she could for one day, but there was always tomorrow and the next day. Whatever had come over her in Hyde Park had changed her. She was a different person, and she wouldn't be so easily led by her father's wishes again.

But putting those new and different feelings aside for the time being, Gabrielle said calmly and without emotion, "Don't worry about me, Rosa, I know exactly what I will do."

Four

It is better to suffer wrong than to do it.

—Samuel Johnson

HELL AND DAMNATION! BRENT HAD CALLED HER NAME until he was hoarse. He couldn't find the dog.

And to top that off, he'd come home to find a tersely scribbled note from the duke, ordering him to appear at the man's house before dark. He would have liked to have responded with a terse note of his own, by saying, "When hell freezes over," but he knew better than to be that disrespectful to a powerful duke.

When Brent woke that morning, there was no way he could have imagined the hellish day he'd have. He wiped the last traces of shaving soap off his face and neck with a cloth and looked at himself in the small mirror on his shaving bureau. No doubt the Duke of Windergreen would smile when he saw the angry-looking scratch beneath Brent's eye, and his swollen bottom lip. Thankfully, the scratch didn't look deep enough to leave a bad scar.

He dried beads of water from his chest, then walked

over and grabbed his trousers off the bed, where Raymond had neatly laid out his clothing, and stepped into them.

Brent had spent all morning and half the afternoon scouring that damn park, looking for Prissy, after the duke, his daughter, and his henchmen had left him standing in the middle of the park with a torn coat, a smashed and ruined hat, and a body that was bruised and scraped. Not to mention he had been on foot for the entire search.

He'd decided against wasting time by going to his house to get a carriage or a horse to ride. But, if at the time he'd known how long he would be out there, he would have certainly gotten some kind of transportation. It was well into the afternoon before he realized he might have to leave the park without the aggravating little dog.

And it was all because of an enchanting lady who walked out of the mist and into his arms. He would dearly love to put his hands around the slender neck of the beautiful and very tempting Lady Gabrielle and scare the devil out of her cheating little heart. At just the thought of her, his lower body stirred reflexively, and Brent grunted a rueful laugh.

His brain could not fool his body. If he ever got close enough to her again to put his hands around her lovely neck, he was much more likely to slowly caress the hollow of her throat where the beat of her pulse raced, or draw lazy circular patterns with his fingertips on that exquisitely soft skin behind her ear, than he was to try to strangle her.

Over the years and through his many travels, Brent

had had many women seek his attention, but he was quite sure this morning was the first time he'd ever had such an intriguing young lady walk up to him and kiss him as Lady Gabrielle had. She had been soft, exhilarating, and heavenly. She'd smelled like spring's first rose, and she had been utterly enchanting by first taking him to task over his tone with Prissy and then by surprising the hell out of him with her seduction.

But what was she thinking? She was a duke's daughter! She must know that set her apart from most young ladies. Or perhaps, because she was a duke's daughter, she felt free to behave as she wished with no thoughts of consequences, knowing her father would make everything right for her.

Even without her being engaged to another man, what she did was sheer madness, and he'd allowed it, even welcomed it. But he never would have touched her—well, he liked to tell himself that anyway—if he'd known she was promised to another. Years ago, when Brent found out about his mother's affair with Sir Randolph Gibson, the man who had fathered her twin sons, he vowed never to touch a married or betrothed lady. He had firsthand knowledge of the havoc that kind of affair could bring. And he had kept that vow until this morning, when Lady Gabrielle seduced him with her seemingly innocent and extremely tempting undertaking.

That he hadn't immediately caught on to what she was up to irritated the devil out of him. At the time, he had been far more interested in her sweet kisses and the way she felt in his arms than he was about the reason she was so free with her affections.

Young ladies out to snare him into matrimony weren't unfamiliar terrain for him. More than one had tried a number of tactics, tricks, and offers to lure him into marriage; but so far, he'd managed to elude them all. One thing was sure, if he made it out of this misfortune with his freedom intact, he'd make damn sure he never got caught unawares by another scheming lady ever again.

But Lady Gabrielle's antics were second to a more important worry at the moment. He couldn't do anything about that situation until he met with the duke. The disappearance of his mother's cherished pet was a bigger concern, because Prissy could be hurt.

Brent never realized how big that damn park was until he started walking it, looking around trees, under bushes, and along the shoreline of the Serpentine for Prissy. Throughout the morning and into the afternoon, he'd stopped everyone he passed and asked if they had seen a small, long-haired, ivory-colored dog with a red braided collar and leash.

No one had seen her.

It was as if she'd disappeared into thin air.

He wouldn't allow himself to consider the possibility that Prissy had met her demise by a wild animal of some kind. His hope was that, because the park was so big, they were continuously missing each other's paths, or that, perhaps, her leash had caught on a rock or become entangled in some bushes and bound her, and she was still waiting to be found, freed, and fed.

Brent walked to his bedchamber window and looked out over the small garden at the back of his rented town house. Most members of the peerage owned their own homes in London, but Brent's father had sold their home in Mayfair years ago. Though he didn't like the idea, Brent would have to consider the idea of buying a place if his brothers' business venture worked out and they settled in London. He supposed he could understand their wanting to move back to England, because he certainly didn't want to entertain the idea of living in any other country. And his brothers now understood why their father wanted them to make their home across the seas.

With any luck, by the time he made it to the duke's house, he would discover that all had been worked out with Lady Gabrielle's fiancé, and the wedding would take place next week as planned. He would happily swear to the duke he would never breathe a word about what happened in the park and, of course, he wouldn't anyway. However, the earl's son might want to keep a close watch on his new bride. She obviously liked to slip out of her bed in the early hours of morning and prowl.

One of the reasons Brent had come to London was to find a wife. His intentions had been to look over a bevy of different young ladies before deciding which one should bear his name and his children. He certainly didn't like the idea of being deceptively snared by one, no matter how tempting she was.

Suddenly, Brent remembered soft, willing lips pressed gently on his, luxuriously silky hair threading between his fingers, and an enticing breast flattened beneath his palm. When she was kissing him, he would have bet a hundred shillings she was an innocent, but now he wasn't so sure. She had a fiancé, and if she had kissed Brent so wantonly, having just met him, there was always the possibility she'd gone much further with her fiancé. Not that it mattered to Brent what she'd done or with whom. He didn't even know what the devil he was doing thinking about her again.

All he wanted to do was get this meeting with the duke behind him so he could go back to the park and concentrate on the more important matter of searching for Prissy while there was still a chance she was alive. He had vowed to keep the dog safe, and he was miffed at himself because he'd let the sweet lips of a tempting lady make him forget all about Prissy.

"But what man could have resisted her seduction?" he mumbled to himself.

Brent headed toward his bed but stopped when he heard the heavy stomp of booted feet running up the stairs. He knew what all that noise meant and, quite frankly, he wasn't up to it.

The door swung open, hitting the wall with a bang. Brent's identical twin brothers strode into his bedchamber as if they owned it, just the way they always had since they were two years old. Matson, the firstborn twin, plopped onto the middle of Brent's bed and made himself comfortable by leaning against the headboard. The heels of his riding boots landed on Brent's pressed white shirt. Iverson sauntered over to the brocade slipper chair, turned it around, and straddled the seat.

Raymond, Brent's ever stiff and proper valet, walked calmly into the bedchamber behind them. "Excuse me, my lord. I explained to your brothers that you were preparing to leave for an appointment, but they insisted on seeing you immediately, and I couldn't stop them."

"No reason for you to try, Raymond. When they want to see me, they don't let anything stand in their way. Thank you; that will be all."

With all the correctness of a well-paid man, Raymond nodded once, turned around, and walked out, gently closing the door behind him. Brent would have had the fellow out looking for Prissy, too, but the man was so stiff and proper about everything he said and did, he would be completely useless combing the park.

Brent turned his attention to his brothers. They were tall, powerfully built men who wore their business success and breeding well. Even though he'd grown up with them, the only thing that made it possible for him to tell the two apart was the fact that, whether intentional or not, Iverson always wore his hair longer at the nape. And even though they were the spitting image of each other as far as looks, they couldn't be more different in personalities. Iverson had always been the one to jump to conclusions, a ready to do battle hothead, and Matson a slow-to-action reasonable thinker.

It hadn't been easy, but Brent had kept his mother's secret for ten years. At the back of his mind, he knew the time would come when the twins would want to come to London. And before that happened, he had to tell them the man they had always thought to be their father wasn't. And the man who had fathered them was very much alive and living in London.

As Brent looked at his brothers making themselves quite comfortable in his bedchamber, his mind drifted back to that stormy evening more than a month ago at his Brentwood estate.

Rain beat against the window panes, and the fire crackled and roared as Brent, Matson, and Iverson drank brandy in the drawing room, catching up on old times. It was the first time he'd seen them in the two years since their mother had died. They had come home to tell him they would be moving their shipping business from across the sea in Baltimore, Maryland, to London. Brent was getting nowhere in trying to talk them out of it.

"But why?" Brent asked for probably the twentieth time. "If your shipbuilding business is successful in Baltimore, why do you want to move it to London?"

"Damnation, Brent, why not?" Iverson said. "Only where we live will change, not the business itself."

"Besides, England is our homeland," Matson added. "We stayed in Baltimore only because our father started the business there and, for whatever reason, insisted we keep it there. Out of respect to Mama, we stayed there after he died. But she's gone now, and we're coming home. We never planned to live there a lifetime."

"And quite frankly, Brent," Iverson said, "we should have moved the company right after she passed."

Brent drained his glass and put it on the table in front of the settee. "So your minds are made up? There's no talking you out of it?"

"Not a chance in hell. We're going to London tomorrow to find places to live and to start the process of moving the entire operations of Brentwood's Sea Coast Ship Building."

"Since you both insist on settling in London, there's

something I must tell you before you go. Something our parents never wanted you to know."

Matson laughed and set his glass beside Brent's. "Why are you sounding so somber, Brent? It's like you don't want us to move back."

"Yes, why are you trying so hard to talk us out of it?" Iverson said. "We'd think you'd be glad to have us nearby. We're not children anymore, you know. Out with whatever it is you want to tell us."

"All right, there's really no other way to tell you than directly, anyway. The man you always thought of as your father is not."

"What did you say?" Matson asked.

"There is a man in London, and the two of you look just like him."

"So?" Iverson said, swirling the last of his brandy in his glass, looking as if he couldn't be less interested in what Brent was saying.

"What exactly are you saying, Brent?" Matson asked, seeming a little more intrigued than Iverson.

"When I say you look like him, I'm telling you the man is your birth father—not Judson Henry Brentwood, sixth Viscount Brentwood."

Matson leaned forward and froze his gaze on Brent. "What the hell do you mean?"

"And it better not be what I'm thinking right now," Iverson added in a cold voice and then drained his glass.

"I'm afraid it is. This isn't some slight favoring with the same color of eyes and hair. It's your build, the structure of your faces, the way you carry yourselves. You look just like the man, because he is your father. Mama admitted it to me ten years ago."

"You lie." Iverson rose and glared at him.

Brent remained calm. "No. And why would I?"

"If this is true," Matson said, "Why did she tell you and not us?"

"Isn't it obvious? She didn't want you to ever know. That one son had found out about her indiscretion was enough of a blow to her. She wanted to spare herself the shame and you two the shock of finding out, as well."

"Sit down, Iverson," Matson said. "This needs an explanation and, obviously, Brent's the only one who can give it."

Brent sucked in a deep breath. It wasn't natural for a son to talk with his mother about her affair, and he'd hated every moment of it, but so had she. And it wasn't any easier telling his brothers about it.

"The summer Papa took you to Baltimore to set up the business, I went to London. While there, I went to a ball, and that is where I saw the man. His name is Sir Randolph Gibson. I was stunned at how much you two look like him. Naturally, I came home and told Mama I had seen him. She admitted to a brief affair with the man one spring while she was in London for the Season. She had no way of knowing until years later, when you grew up, that you had been fathered by Sir Randolph. She admitted the affair to our father, and that's when he went to Baltimore to set up the shipping business for you there. His hope was you would never have reason to set foot in London. He never wanted you to hear about or to meet Sir Randolph."

"We're almost thirty, blast it, we should have been told before now," Iverson said.

"No, I'm almost thirty, and you are almost twenty-nine.

And I should have never had to live with this knowledge these past ten years, but I have. Take my word for it, if I could have persuaded you to stay away from London, I would have, but I couldn't let you go and not be aware of your connection to Sir Randolph. If you two weren't insisting on going to London tomorrow, I would have kept my bloody mouth shut until doomsday rather than have you find this out."

Matson looked at Iverson. "So what do you have to say about all this?"

Iverson shrugged, picked up the decanter, and refilled the three glasses. He looked from Matson to Brent. "I say we're going to London, and to hell with whoever this man is or the fact that we might look like him."

Matson looked at Brent and smiled. "Well, then, Brother, we're going to London."

And they had.

Brent looked at the two strapping men and said, "Please don't stand on polite ceremony, Brothers, when you can barge in with such tantalizing fanfare."

Iverson placed his forearms on top of the chair back and looked directly at Brent with his dark blue eyes. "From what we're hearing, you are the one creating fanfare."

"Me?" Brent said, pulling his shirt out from under Matson's boot. He threw a disgruntled glance toward Iverson and then pulled the shirt over his head. "You are the one causing a stir by leaving your mark on that coxcomb Lord Waldo Rockcliffe as if you thought it would go unnoticed."

Iverson shrugged. "I've not heard of him telling anyone what happened to him, have you, Matson?"

"Not a word," his twin answered.

Brent knew Iverson had a cocksure way about him that intimidated most men, and he seldom had to resort to fisticuffs to settle anything. Lord Waldo must have been blind not to have known he was pushing Iverson too far.

"Did you happen to think that might be because he doesn't have to tell anyone? Most people are smart enough to know it was either you or Matson who blessed him with the black eye, because all he's been talking about for the past week is how much you two resemble Sir Randolph. Now he's quiet as a church mouse on Sunday morning. Of course, I know you both too well to think it was Matson who left his mark on the poor bloke."

"Really?" Matson smiled. "I'm pained to know you don't think I did it. But has it ever once entered that thick brain of yours that it's quite possible some Londoners might think you were the vile creature that was crass enough, or perhaps I should say you were the one courageous enough, to knock a duke's youngest brother on his arse?"

"That might be especially believable now that we see you are also sporting a fat lip and a nasty scratch of your own," Iverson added.

Matson chuckled. "Yes, no doubt you met with someone who didn't like what you had to say, much like Lord Waldo did."

"Are you two through?" Brent grumbled as he swiped his neckcloth off the edge of the bed and slung the long strip around his neck. He walked over to the tall bureau where his shaving mirror sat and started the process of tying the blasted thing.

"Not quite, big Brother, tell us what happened."

Iverson laughed and said, "But then again, maybe he doesn't want to tell us what happened."

"Just as well, because that wasn't the fanfare we were talking about anyway, was it?"

"No, but I still want to know how he got that nasty cut on his lip and shiner under his eye."

Brent tuned out his brothers as he struggled with his neckcloth. He'd never learned how to do a decent job of tying a perfect bow. No matter how hard he tried, his neckcloth always came out looking like he hurried through it. He wasn't in a mood to make the bow look respectable today, and wouldn't except for the fact that he had to see the Duke of Windergreen, and for some reason, felt he needed to look his best.

"So, are you going to tell us, or am I going to have to beat it out of you?" Iverson asked.

He watched his brothers behind him in the mirror. "I don't know what fanfare you two are talking about, but I suppose it has something to do with the fact that I plan to ask Sir Randolph Gibson to meet with me."

His brothers' banter ceased, and they looked at each other and then back to him. "No, we hadn't heard that," Matson said.

Iverson's eyes narrowed, and his lips set in a grim line before he said, "Our resemblance to Sir Randolph has nothing to do with you, Brent. Stay out of it."

Brent had to quell his instinct to give Iverson and Matson orders and expect to be obeyed as he had when they were boys. "Of course it has something to do with me. You're my brothers. I simply want to know where the man stands concerning this."

"He stands where he's always stood," Iverson said. "We don't expect our coming to London to change him or his behavior, and we sure as hell won't let him change us or what we plan to do."

Matson added, "As far as we can tell, he's never said a word about us, and as long as he stays quiet and doesn't bother us, we won't bother him."

"If he starts talking," Iverson added, "I'll pay him a visit."

"I'm sure that won't be necessary," Matson said, and then in an unusual tone of warning, added, "and it's not necessary for you to meet with him, Brent. If it comes to the point that something needs to be done, we will do it. Now, let's talk about something other than Sir Randolph."

Brent was happy to do that since his brothers didn't know he had already been to Bow Street and had hired a runner to gather information on Sir Randolph Gibson. Once Brent knew more about the fellow, he'd arrange for a time to meet with him, whether his brothers wanted him to or not. As his mother once said, *What they don't know can't hurt them.*

"Tell us about this more pressing matter of what happened in the park this morning," Matson urged.

"Yes," Iverson added. "We've been getting bits and pieces of this outlandish story everyone insists you are involved in."

"Though, to me, it doesn't sound like anything you would be caught up in."

"Right," Matson said. "I would believe it of Iverson but not you, Brent. What's going on?"

Brent made the last loop of the bow in his neckcloth and turned to face his brothers. "Damnation, I have no idea. She's with me one moment, and the next thing I know she's crying for help. I knew something was wrong, but I couldn't get to her." Brent noticed Iverson's eyes getting bigger, and Matson rose up and swung his feet off the bed. Brent kept talking. "I searched all over that damn park and tried to find her, but I haven't seen any sign of her yet. It's dreadful to even think about it, but I can only hope a wild animal didn't get to her."

"Damnation, Brent," Matson said, "what the devil did you do to Lady Gabrielle?"

"You think a wild animal attacked her?" Iverson said. "Hell's gates, Brent, what is the matter with you? Why did you leave a defenseless woman alone in the park?"

"And what were you doing in the park with her in the first place?" Matson asked.

"I think we know the answer to that," Iverson said. "From what I heard at White's an hour ago, Brent was the wild animal who got hold of her."

"What? No, no, stop." Brent blew out a breathy laugh. "We are talking about two different females here, Brothers."

"What's gotten into you?" Matson asked. "You met with more than one woman in the park?"

"That's so unlike you," Iverson said with a wicked grin. "London must be having some kind of strange effect on you and, whatever it is, I hope I catch it."

"But what happened to your vow never to touch a betrothed or married woman?" Matson asked.

Iverson chuckled. "I guess that oath is out the window now."

Matson rose from the bed. "Brent, you know better. She's a duke's daughter and engaged to an earl's son."

Brent shook his head. His brothers could make the biggest mountain out of the smallest amount of dirt. He was determined not to let them frustrate him. He'd already been there today with Prissy and Lady Gabrielle, and he wasn't going there for his brothers. He picked up his light brown waistcoat with fabric-covered buttons and put it on over his crisp white shirt. Thankfully, the waistcoat hid the black heel mark on the front of the shirt made by Matson's boot.

"My hope is that Lady Gabrielle is still engaged to the earl's son, and my vow has not changed. At the time, I had no idea Lady Gabrielle was betrothed."

"How you talked her into meeting you in the park is what I want to know." Iverson said. "I never seem to be quite that lucky with ladies of quality."

"And who is this other woman who was crying for help and might have been attacked by a wild animal?" Matson said. "That's rather gruesome, isn't it?"

Brent sighed. Why couldn't they ask their questions one at a time? "I didn't arrange to meet Lady Gabrielle. It was quite by accident. And the other female is not a woman but a dog. Prissy was with me, but when I was—" Brent suddenly found himself reluctant to say more, so he stopped.

"When you were what?" Matson urged with a grin and sat back down on the bed again.

"When he was in the middle of the best part," Iverson said with another wicked gleam in his eyes.

"I mean no such thing, you beast. Damnation, Iverson, contrary to whatever lewd and scandalous comments you may have heard in the boisterous back-rooms at White's, nothing happened between me and Lady Gabrielle this morning. And as a gentleman I'll say no more on the matter."

"Forget Lady Gabrielle for the moment," Matson said, "because obviously she is safe at her home by now. What I want to know is where Prissy is at the moment."

Brent felt as if his stomach twisted. "I don't know where she is. Unfortunately, she ran off somewhere in the park, and I couldn't find her. I have to go to the Duke of Windergreen's house right now, and after I'm through there, I plan to take another look through the park. Somehow, I've missed finding her."

"So you are telling us you managed not only to compromise the duke's engaged daughter, you lost Prissy, as well?"

Brent picked up his dark brown coat and shoved his arms into the sleeves. "That is exactly what I'm telling you, Brothers. I sent my footman and his son out looking for her as soon as I returned. Right now would be a good time for the two of you to speak up and say you'll take a ride through the park to see if you can find her."

"Absolutely, we will," Matson said, and then looked at his twin. "If it's a good time for you. If not, I can go alone."

Iverson rose from the slipper chair. "No, I'm ready."

"Good," Brent said. "If you find the little devil, bring her back here and make yourselves at home for as long as you want. You know where the wine is kept. I go to discover my fate."

Brent turned and walked out the door.

Five

Pick battles big enough to matter, small enough to win.
—Jonathan Kozol

GABRIELLE WAITED IMPATIENTLY AS LATE AFTERNOON sunshine slashed across her bedroom window. Since leaving her father, aunt, and sister downstairs, she had tried reading and working on her embroidery, but neither pastime could take her mind off the fact that Lord Brentwood was coming to talk with her father about their marriage.

Auntie Bethie had taken charge of the house and had insisted she handle everything concerning canceling all plans for the wedding. She never once asked Gabrielle to tell her what had happened, for which Gabrielle was grateful.

The afternoon wore on, and in a fit of unrelenting frustration over her inability to control her own destiny, Gabrielle set up her easel and a small canvas by her window. She pulled her oils and brushes from their drawer and started painting a blue, blue sky. But not even the solitude of her work soothed her troubled mind as it usually did. She couldn't stop thinking about ways she might be able to persuade the duke from wanting to force a marriage between her and the viscount.

Considering the way Lord Brentwood had looked at her with such disdain when he found out she was betrothed, she had a little hope he simply would not agree to marry her. But if he acquiesced to pressure from her father, she had to come up with a plan of her own to present to Lord Brentwood.

From the loud knock and chatter downstairs, she knew when the viscount had arrived. She kept painting, adding a dark blue tumultuous ocean with crashing waves, and a lone ship with tattered and battered sails sitting in the middle of it. Though her hand continued its creation as the minutes passed, her thoughts kept wandering to what Lord Brentwood and her father were saying to each other about her future.

Would Lord Brentwood be strong enough to stand up to her formidable father? Or would he be like most people who had dealings with the duke and finally agree with everything he wanted?

A knock sounded on her door, and Gabrielle jumped. Her brush smeared a dark brown streak across the canvas, marring the hull of the ship she was working on.

"Good heavens!" she exclaimed under her breath. She had never been skittish in her life, and she didn't like feeling that way. She remained quiet and hoped whoever was there would go away.

The knock came again.

"I'm painting," she called, trying to fade the streak into the canvas. Everyone in the house knew Gabrielle didn't want to be disturbed when she was painting. Because the house was always filled with servants and family, it was the one time she insisted she be left totally alone.

The door opened, and her maid, Petra, peeked inside. "So you are in here, my lady. It was so quiet at first, I wasn't sure." She stopped just inside the room and put her hands on her slender hips. "You usually let me know when you want to paint, so I can get everything ready for you. And what's this? No apron covering that pretty pink dress you have on? What am I going to do with you?"

Gabrielle found herself smiling at Petra's softly spoken reprimand. She absolutely adored her maid. Petra was a few years older than Gabrielle and much shorter, with a thin, narrow face and huge smile. One of the things Gabrielle had liked about Petra in her first interview was she was always smiling, even as she talked.

Looking down at her dress, Gabrielle said, "Yes, you're right. It was careless of me to forget to put on my apron, but I really want to be by myself right now, Pet. So whatever it is you thought to do here in my room, could you come back later?"

Petra gave her a sad smile. "Mrs. Potter told me about your wedding being canceled and that I shouldn't disturb you this afternoon."

"And I appreciate that."

"I'm very sorry for you, my lady."

"Please, Pet, it isn't the canceled wedding that is

bothering me. You know better than anyone it was not a love match between me and Staunton. It's what's taking place downstairs right now that has me in a dither, and Auntie Bethie was right, I'm not good company for anyone, so shoo!"

Petra walked over to Gabrielle's wardrobe and pulled out a drawer. "Can't do that for you. Your papa sent me up here to fetch you."

Gabrielle tensed and laid her brush down on the paint-smeared palette. "Papa wants to see me?"

"Not exactly," Petra said, pulling out a dark wine-colored shawl trimmed with gold fringe. "I think this one will go nicely with what you have on, don't you?"

Gabrielle pursed her lips in frustration. "I'm not cold, Pet."

Petra walked over and wrapped the shawl around Gabrielle's shoulders. "You will be."

"Whatever do you mean by that?"

"I'm following His Grace's orders. He said for me to tell you Lord Brentwood is in the garden waiting to speak to you and you may have a few minutes alone with him before he leaves."

Gabrielle's shoulders sagged a little. Though she knew what that meant, she didn't want to believe it. If her father was allowing her a few minutes alone with the viscount, then another marriage contract was in the works for her.

"The sun is about to set, and the wind has whipped up," Petra said, "and it's bone-chilling out there, but this shawl should be enough to keep you warm for no longer than you will be in the garden."

Gabrielle's stomach lurched. What would she say to

Lord Brentwood? Should she apologize to him again for getting him mixed up in this debacle?

No, she was through with apologies, worries, and concern.

Perhaps if her aunt had already been here, Gabrielle would have gone to her this morning instead of the park... but there was no use thinking about what might have been. She had to think about the future. No matter what her father and Lord Brentwood had decided, she had plans of her own, and she was prepared to go forward with them.

"Where is Papa?" Gabrielle asked, hooking the ends of the shawl around her elbows.

"He said he will be in his book room, where he can look out the window and see into the garden."

"And where are Aunt Bethie and Rosabelle?"

"Lady Rosa has been in her room all afternoon, just like you, and after a long visit with your father, your aunt has been in the parlor, writing notes or letters or something."

Gabrielle's heart was suddenly filled with gratitude once again. She was glad her aunt had insisted on taking care of everything concerning canceling the wedding. "I'm so glad Auntie is here," she whispered.

"Me, too," Petra said with her usual bright smile, "because that usually means your papa leaves for a few weeks, and we all breathe easier when the duke is away."

"Petra, you are being far too fresh with your comments," Gabrielle admonished, knowing Petra was only voicing what all the servants had thought for years. Her father was a difficult man, but Gabrielle couldn't allow such freedoms from servants. "You cannot be so disrespectful of my father and your employer."

Petra's smile evaporated quickly. "I truly meant no harm."

"I'm sure you didn't, but you must never be that familiar again."

"Yes, my lady, I agree, and I beg your pardon a thousand times. I'm very grateful to the duke for allowing me to be in your service."

"I know. Now, I better get out of here before Papa thinks you are the reason I'm late."

Gabrielle left her room and hurried out the door and down the back stairs to the rear of the house. Her chest tightened as she walked. For some strange reason, she was filled with the feeling of wanting to see Lord Brentwood, yet not wanting to.

She stopped and peeked out a small window of the china-and-crystal storeroom and saw him. He sat on a bench in their small garden, one booted foot propped on his other leg. His side profile showed a high brow, straight nose, and strong chin. There was an arrogant tilt to his head, and his light brown hair fell attractively just below his collar. Gabrielle stared at him until, as if sensing someone watched him, Lord Brentwood turned his head toward the window. She quickly ducked down and flattened herself against the wall.

What was she doing spying on the viscount?

Taking a deep breath, she shored up her courage and continued on her way to the garden. At the back door, she hesitated only a moment before opening it and stepping out onto the landing.

Lord Brentwood rose from the bench. Their eyes met and held much longer than she would have wished, but for some reason, she couldn't look away.

His gaze swept lazily up and down her face, seeming to linger on her lips before settling on her eyes. After another moment, he walked toward her with a loose, lean-hipped stride that caused a breathless catch in her throat. His chest was broad and his shoulders straight. He was handsomely dressed in camel-colored trousers and waistcoat, with a dark brown coat that fit him to perfection. As he neared her, she remembered the strength she'd felt in his arms, and an unexpected heat that started at her throat rose up to flash in her cheeks and warm her against the chilling breeze.

He certainly didn't look as scruffy as he had when she last saw him in the park. The red scratch under his eye looked a little better than when she'd seen him earlier that morning, though his bottom lip was still quite swollen. But none of that detracted from his handsomeness or the attraction she felt every time she looked at him. Somehow, the injuries made him look all the more roguish, dashing, and a little bit dangerous.

Holding her shawl tightly about her as if it were a shield, she walked down the steps to meet him.

Forgetting all about a proper greeting, she asked, "What did you say to my father?"

Brent stopped, not far from her, and folded his arms across his chest. The side of his mouth that wasn't swollen lifted, forming a half grin that stirred the persistent butterflies in her stomach. Suddenly she was filled with hope once again. Would such a strong and commanding man as he agree to marry her after what she had done to him?

"What's this?" he asked, his eyes almost caressing her. "Have you no enticing greeting for me this time,

Lady Gabrielle? No sweet smiles to tempt me? No softly spoken words to draw me closer to you? No affectionate kiss to warm me? Must we get right to the cold, heartless business at hand as if our lips had never touched?"

Gabrielle's breasts tightened, and her lower abdomen clenched excitedly. She felt spellbound. It surprised her how quickly and easily those same wonderful sensations that had melted through her in the park returned. Lord Brentwood was trying to seduce her right here in her own garden, with her father looking out the window.

And he was succeeding!

She swallowed hard. "Must you remind me of my lapse in sanity this morning?"

His head tilted back as if he were questioning her. "Is that what I was doing?"

"Yes, and you know it. Furthermore, you know the way I behaved was sheer madness."

"Madness? Is that what it was?"

Yes, and that I'm feeling those same exciting sensations right now proves it!

"How can you doubt it?"

"It's easy, because I don't know you, Lady Gabrielle, but that is about to change."

She lightly shook her head, and then cleared her throat and said, "All I want to do is forget we ever met. I never meant to involve you in my troubles. I've begged my father to leave you out of this."

"You tried that argument on him this morning, and it didn't work. I think we both know it was too late for that the moment your lips met mine."

"Do you intend to remind me of that kiss every time you speak?"

That engaging half smile lifted the corner of his mouth again. "Is that what you think I'm doing?"

"Stop it. You know what you are doing."

He moved closer to her. "Then tell me, what were you doing in the park this morning? Are you just a terribly spoiled duke's daughter who was looking to have a little tryst with someone before you settled down to the drudgery of marriage?"

She blinked slowly and cautiously looked at him. She could understand why it seemed that way to him. "No, of course not."

"Then you must have been looking for some unsuspecting gentleman to waylay so you could save yourself from a marriage you didn't want."

"No, you're wrong. That's not true either."

Lord Brentwood quirked his head to the side as if to indicate he didn't believe her. "Then what is, Lady Gabrielle, because I can think of no other explanations."

She couldn't explain it to him any more than she could explain it to her father when he asked.

It was clear the viscount didn't intend to let her get the best of him again, so she simply asked, "What did my father say to you?"

"Don't you know?"

"Of course not, my lord. How could I possibly know what either of you said when I wasn't allowed to be in the room while *my* future was discussed and, I presume, settled?"

His smug expression faded, and he gave her what looked to be a reluctant nod. "I take it you do know your father was unable to talk the Earl of Austerhill into continuing with your wedding plans to his son."

Suddenly feeling calmer, Gabrielle loosened the tight hold she had on the ends of her shawl and relaxed a little. "Yes, and that suits me, but what did Papa say to you?"

"What I expected; that we must marry."

"I was afraid of that," she said. She inhaled deeply, trying to renew her strength to fight this now with Lord Brentwood. "I hope you held your ground, remained firm, and told him I was not compromised, and you have no intentions of marrying me under any circumstances."

A half grunt, half chuckle passed his swollen lip, making his smile lopsided. "No, I didn't."

He spoke so quietly she was stunned for a second. Her gaze searched his face. "But surely you don't want this marriage forced upon you any more than I do."

"No, I don't. But after long and somewhat rancorous negotiations, we finally settled on terms of a marriage contract. The conclusion is I will live by my honor, do my duty, and marry you, Lady Gabrielle."

She winced inside. He might have tried to spare her feelings by calling it his duty and honor, but she knew what that really meant. Staunton was going to marry her for financial reasons, and now Lord Brentwood was going to marry her because he was being forced. She didn't understand this honor he talked about.

"If you feel you were trapped by me, why would you agree when you know I was not compromised?" she asked.

His eyes narrowed, and he took a step closer to her. "There are a number of reasons, Lady Gabrielle, not the least of which is the fact that your father is a very powerful duke who knows the King well and considers him a friend. He is well liked and often sought out for advice by the prince. Your father is admired, respected, and feared by many throughout London."

"So you agreed to marry me because you are afraid of my father?"

Lord Brentwood snorted with derision, and a low chuckle passed his lips. His gaze held firmly on hers. "I am afraid of no man."

"You say that, yet you ran from my father and his men this morning in the park."

Suddenly, the viscount was so close she could feel his breath and almost taste his anger. "Do not doubt my courage." His words were biting. "I ran to find my mother's dog. When I pulled you into my arms, I let go of Prissy's leash. She wandered away while you held me bewitched by your charms. I heard her yelping in pain, so I ran to help her, but your father's men caught me and stopped me."

Gabrielle swallowed hard. She would have done the same thing had it been Brutus who needed help. But, obviously, if Prissy had been given the kind of training Brutus had, she would have never left her master's side.

"Oh, I see. I didn't know," Lady Gabrielle said without rancor but also without apologizing for misreading the situation. "As you know, it was chaotic after my father and Lord Austerhill arrived, and I'm sorry to say I didn't notice she was gone. What was wrong with her?"

His eyes darkened as quickly as blackness filled a room when the light was extinguished. "I have no idea. I searched for her after you, your father, and his men left, but I couldn't find her."

She lifted her chin in surprise. "You left the park without finding her? Your mother must have been beside herself when you came home without her darling dog."

He seemed to relax a little, though he stayed very close to her. "I'm sure she would have been if she were still living. My mother died more than two years ago."

And still he walked her dog.

Gabrielle softened. "Prissy seemed to be very brave. I'm sure she's fine and that she'll find her way home soon."

Lord Brentwood looked away from Gabrielle for a moment, and she saw it truly disturbed him that the dog hadn't been found. Knowing how she loved Brutus, she couldn't blame him. She felt ashamed for having as good as accused him of being a coward for running away in the park. She didn't think that was true and wouldn't have even said it in the first place had she not been at the point of madness over the entire day.

"I do hope you find her. I know how upset I'd be if Brutus were missing."

"I have no doubt Prissy will be found," he said, seeming to casually brush aside her concern. "But to answer your other question, my brothers will be moving their shipbuilding business from Baltimore, Maryland, to London in the coming weeks. Your father made it quite clear to me that, if I didn't marry you, he had many connections and would make it impossible for my brothers' business to be successful. Moving their business to London won't be easy, and I will not allow your father to add to their burden."

She knew her father would have had his solicitor find out what he could about the viscount before the day was over. When the duke wanted something, he left no stone unturned. It struck her as odd that she and Lord Brentwood were more alike than she could have imagined. She was willing to sacrifice her reputation for her sister, and he was willing to sacrifice his freedom for his brothers' success.

"So your father gets his wish, Lady Gabrielle. We will be married."

Gabrielle shook her head in frustration. "I didn't want to marry Staunton, but at least I was willing to until—"

Lord Brentwood's brown eyes narrowed and questioned her. "Until what?"

She hesitated before saying, "Until recently, but none of that matters now. I certainly don't want to marry you, and you don't want to marry me."

"Well, take heart, Lady Gabrielle, it looks as though you'll have plenty of time to get to know me, as the duke said it will likely take weeks to untangle your previous betrothal agreement with Lord Austerhill's son. As soon as that is done, we'll post the banns."

She pulled her shawl up closer around her neck and positioned herself where her back was to her father's book room window and said, "Perhaps not. I have a plan, my lord."

His eyes narrowed. "For what?"

"Us. Thankfully, Papa does have to sort out all the financial arrangements with Lord Austerhill and his son, so I propose we lead my father to believe we are in favor of this marriage and find a way to stall it even after all other matters are settled. We can then, sometime after Christmas but before the Season starts in the spring, come up with a reason to call off the wedding."

Lord Brentwood's face wrinkled into a frown, but she kept talking. "That way, come the new year, you will be free to pursue more willing young ladies. The scandal of our hasty engagement will have died down, and the gossips will have moved on to someone else's unfortunate situation. I venture to say that, halfway through the Season, no one will even remember I was once engaged to you or Staunton."

His golden-brown eyes seemed to burn into hers. A wrinkle of warning formed on his brow. "Did you not hear what I had to say about my brothers and moving their shipping business to London? Did you not hear me speak of your father's threat to assure they would have no success in their business?"

She blinked rapidly at his sudden change. "Yes, of course I heard."

"Then mark my word, Lady Gabrielle, we will be married as soon as it is legally possible. I don't know how to make myself any plainer than that."

She would have liked to tell him her father's intimidation was no more of a threat than Brutus's growl, but she would be lying. The duke would have no qualms about ruining the viscount's brothers' business in order to achieve his goals.

Lord Brentwood's gaze scanned her face, down her neck to her breasts, and back to her eyes. He gave her a lopsided grin. "Besides my brothers' plight, I'll be thirty soon, and I could do worse than to marry a powerful duke's daughter. You will no doubt know how to manage my home. And your father is making sure your dowry is quite substantial. It's time for me to take a wife and produce an heir. Judging from our short time together in the park, you should do quite nicely for that and be the perfect wife for me."

She gasped. "How dare you, my lord. That was a perfectly vulgar thing to say. That you should even suggest using me as a brood mare to bear your children sounds positively ghastly."

He leaned his head in closer to hers and hooded his eyes with determination. "You may think so now, but once I get you beneath me, I will prove to you that you are no lady, Gabrielle. I will have you in my bed, and I promise you will not want to leave it."

She shivered and hugged her woolen shawl more tightly around her. "You are being unbelievably ill-mannered, Lord Brentwood."

His gaze stayed firmly on hers. "Perhaps I'm thinking it's fitting right now for a young lady who walks out of the mist and into my arms. You are a tempting wench in spite of the fact that, for your own selfish reasons, you used me in your plan to get rid of the earl's son."

"No, no— I—" For a brief moment, she was tempted to tell him the truth.

"Yes, and now you have me, Lady Gabrielle. Before you approached me in the park, perhaps you would have done well to have remembered the old adage my mother used to say to me: 'Be careful what you wish for, because you just might get it.'"

Gabrielle straightened her backbone, his words giving her strength to continue the fight. "I never wished for you."

"Didn't you? A knight in shining armor to rescue you from what you perceived was a fate worse than death?"

Gabrielle couldn't deny that. She could only imagine that if she had married the man her sister loved, death would be welcome.

"The only thing I haven't figured out yet is if you wanted to be rescued from your father or your fiancé. Perhaps it was both."

Was that true? Did she secretly want to be rescued from a loveless marriage, from her father's tyrannical ways?

She fixed him with a determined frown. "If I had wanted to be rescued from my father, that could have been easily accomplished, my lord, because my wedding to Staunton was only a week away. But why would I have wanted to be rescued from one loveless marriage just to be forced into another with you?"

"It's your story. You tell me."

"I may be forced to marry you, my lord, but I assure you, your bed will not be an easy one. You will find it cold, hard, and empty."

His crooked smile turned into an attractive chuckle that held promises she didn't want to think about and sent her pulse racing. He thought she was lying, and that made her all the angrier.

His gaze swept up and down her face again in a way

that sent chills of anticipation storming throughout her body.

"I'm up to the challenge, Lady Gabrielle. Let's see how cold, hard, and empty that bed will be when you are like butter melting beneath my hot palm."

"You are no gentleman, Lord Brentwood."

"I don't think you were looking for a gentleman when you walked into my arms this morning. But you are the one who walked into my life, and make no mistake, there you shall live."

He took another step away from her. "I would give you the kiss your pouting lips are asking for if your father wasn't watching from that window, but there will be plenty of time for that. I'll see to it. Perhaps later in the week at a party, or maybe I'll call on you and take you for a ride in the park. For now, I will take my leave and see myself out the back gate."

Gabrielle seethed with anger. How dare he say she had pouting lips or that she would be like butter melting beneath his hands? She watched him walk away with all the confidence of the titled man he was. So he thought he was in control. So he thought a duke's daughter would do nicely as a proper wife for him.

He was in for a surprise.

She was no longer the obedient, dutiful person she was just yesterday. That person was gone for good. She rather liked herself as the lady who had the courage to kiss a stranger. And that lady wasn't going away.

Gabrielle heard the back door open, and she turned and saw her father and her aunt walking down the steps. The duke hadn't bothered to don a coat or cape, but her aunt was clutching a black shawl around her arms. Fog was stealing in with feathery wisps of mist. The cold air felt damp and threatening. Gabrielle was glad her aunt had come to London and would be staying with her for a while.

"Gabby," her father said, "now that your aunt is here, I've decided to leave for Windergreen the day after tomorrow. The Duke of Norfolk has invited me to his hunting lodge, and I will go there for a few days as well."

Her heart constricted. "But, Papa, nothing is resolved."

"As far as I'm concerned, it is. It takes time to settle a breach of contract, and there's nothing I can do here while that is being done except pray Staunton and his father will be reasonable in what they ask for. I'll spend tomorrow with my solicitor so he will know what I'm willing to do to settle this thing. Unfortunately, we can't go any further with Lord Brentwood until that is handled. Your aunt will be of more use to you in the days to come than I will be." He cut his eyes around to Auntie Bethie and gave her a disdainful look. "I'm sure she's been involved in more than one scandal in her lifetime."

Auntie Bethie laughed. "Quite true, Duke. My family never lived down the scandal of my sister's marrying you."

"Huh!" he huffed. "You best be glad she did. It has kept you in a fine lifestyle for many years." He turned back to Gabrielle. "I expect Elizabeth to look after you and not allow you out of her sight. I don't want to hear one more word of scandal concerning you, or I'll banish both of you to Northern Coast of Scotland."

"You'll have no more trouble from me, Papa," Gabrielle asserted.

"See that I don't. And I'll expect you to take care of your sister. You know how quickly her temperament can change."

Without further words, the duke turned and went back inside.

Auntie Bethie stepped closer to Gabrielle and said, "Now that the roaring bear is gone, we can talk. You don't look like you want to, but it would probably be good for you if you did."

Gabrielle slightly shook her head and turned to watch Lord Brentwood close the gate without looking back at her. "It's too difficult to explain, and even if I could, you wouldn't understand."

"You aren't giving me much credit for having gained wisdom with my advanced years."

Staring out over the garden, Gabrielle said, "I'm sorry, Auntie. It's just that I did the wrong thing this morning, which turned out to be a good thing, which then caused another bad thing."

Her aunt laughed in a low, gravelly voice. "That's easy to understand, and it makes perfect sense to me."

Gabrielle turned toward her aunt and smiled. "No it doesn't, because it doesn't even make sense to me."

"Of course it does," Auntie Bethie said, trying to convince her. "You did something you shouldn't have, which must have involved the man who just went out that gate."

"Yes."

"It turned out all right because it canceled your wedding, and you are obviously happy about that."

Gabrielle nodded. Auntie Bethie understood better than Gabrielle thought she would.

"But that something good caused a different bad thing to happen, which I'm assuming is the scandal your broken engagement is going to cause, not to mention your father is quite peeved that he'll have to settle money and probably lands, too, for your breach of contract. And I haven't quite decided where the viscount fits into all that, but something about him is bothering you, too."

Gabrielle looked at her with awe. "You did understand. That's a fairly close estimate of what has happened because of me and one mistake I can't take back."

"I understood because you sounded so very much like your mother when you were talking just now, the way you had that wistful look to your eyes. You want so desperately always to do the right thing, and if you do make a mistake, you must set everything right."

"That is how I feel, Auntie. But did I really sound like my mother?"

Her aunt nodded and smiled sadly at Gabrielle. "Oh, yes. She always wanted to do the right thing, and it tormented the fires of hell out of her when she didn't."

"Auntie."

"Well, it's the truth," her aunt said without apologizing for her indelicate language. "She was always coming to me and saying, 'Oh, Bethie, what should I do about this?' Or, 'Bethie, I did this and such, or I said that and the other, and I shouldn't have. What can I do?' She was always in a dither about something. And I would always tell her, 'Forget about it, dearie. It doesn't matter.' But she wouldn't rest until she made whatever it was right. Now me, I'm a far different person." She winked at Gabrielle and chuckled low in her throat again.

"Not so much, Auntie," Gabrielle said.

"Oh yes, I am, and Rosa is more like me. I never cared a bluebell in hell if what I did was right or wrong. I only cared to do what I wanted when I wanted."

"Shame on you, Auntie," Gabrielle said with no real admonishment in her voice. "And you know Rosa is not like that."

She gave her a curious look. "You don't think so?"

"No, of course not."

Auntie Bethie shrugged. "Everyone has their own opinion. So tell me what goes on with this handsome viscount who just left. From what little you've said and what your father told me about your being in the park this morning, it sounds to me as if Mr. Alfred Staunton is out of favor with you and Lord Brentwood is in."

Gabrielle inhaled deeply and then said, "Definitely Staunton is out of my life, and yes, Lord Brentwood is in it—for now."

"And that means?"

"That right now, Papa and the viscount want us to marry, but I'm trying to find a way to keep that from happening."

Her aunt frowned. "Why don't you want to marry him? You met him in the park."

Gabrielle didn't want to go over all that again, so she said, "I don't want another arranged marriage,

Auntie. And I certainly don't want Lord Brentwood to marry me because he's forced to."

Her aunt gave her a naughty smile. "You could always find another handsome gentleman to kiss in the park. Dare I say that would be an easy way to get rid of the viscount?"

"Oh, no, Auntie," Gabrielle said, shaking her head as she wrapped the shawl tighter about her. "I've learned my lesson about that. Once was enough for me. I must find a way out of this situation without creating another scandal. And I will."

Six

A certain amount of opposition is a great help to man. Kites rise against, not with, the wind.

—John Neal

It was blasted cold.

Brent muttered more than one curse to himself as he drove his curricle along London's quiet streets at the break of dawn. The nippy wind dried out his eyes, and his warm breath stirred the frosty air. Most of the streetlights had been extinguished with the coming light, but there were very little stirrings of life moving along the boardwalks or in the shops he passed. He seemed to be one of the few people insane enough to be on the streets at this ungodly hour.

After leaving the duke and Lady Gabrielle last evening, he'd come home to find that neither his servants nor his brothers had had any better luck finding Prissy yesterday than he'd had. But he wasn't ready to give her up as lost. He probably could have covered more ground in the park on horseback than on foot or in the curricle, except for the fact that he

wanted to carry food and water for her. Besides, if—
no, when he found her, should she be hurt, it would
be better to have a carriage for her to ride in. For some
reason, the idea had come to him that he would have a
better chance of finding Prissy at about the same time
he'd lost her yesterday.

Brent gently tugged on the right ribbon, turning
the horse and entering the park as a pinkish gray
lightened the dark sky. The fog had lifted, which was
a good sign that there might actually be a few hours of
sunshine at some point during the day. He immediately left the well-worn path the carriages usually took
around the park and cut across the expansive, uneven
ground that led to the center. He traveled a short
distance and then stopped.

He gave as loud a whistle as his swollen lip would
allow, and then called, "Pris! Here, girl. Come on; let
me hear your bark."

He listened but heard nothing other than the
bone-chilling quietness of early morn. He slapped the
ribbons on the horse's rump and continued deeper into
the park before stopping and calling for Prissy again.
The mare shuddered, snorted, and shook her head,
rattling the harness, but there was no other sound to
break the silence. Brent repeated this routine again and
again until he heard sounds of another vehicle coming
toward him. He set the brake and laid the ribbons
aside. He tightened the collar of his greatcoat around
his neck and blew his breath into his gloved hands to
warm them while he waited to see who would emerge
out of the stand of trees.

It wasn't long before he recognized the rattle of

milk containers and saw the robust lad and two young women he'd seen with their milk cart yesterday. When the youngster noticed him, he automatically slowed his steps, and the two women cautiously moved closer together.

"Hello there," Brent said, jumping down from the curricle.

As he walked closer, Brent saw the lad looked to be around twelve or thirteen, and on closer scrutiny, Brent could see the females were not as old as he'd thought yesterday. They were more the age of schoolgirls than young women. One appeared to be maybe sixteen or seventeen, and the other a year or two younger.

"Do you remember me from yesterday?" Brent asked.

The lad stopped the cart, let go of the handles, and straightened to his full height. His gaze remained steadfastly on Brent's face, clearly distrusting him. Brent couldn't blame him. With a black eye and busted lip, Brent knew he looked like a ruffian who'd been in a tavern brawl.

"Yes, sir," the young man said quietly and moved slightly to stand between Brent and the lasses. "I remember you."

Obviously, the young man's job was not only to deliver the milk but to take care of the girls with him, as well. He wasn't very tall, but he was stout and looked strong as an ox. Brent couldn't help but think Lady Gabrielle would have done well to have had such a watchful lad as he with her yesterday morning. It would certainly have made Brent's life a lot easier if she'd had.

"I am Viscount Brentwood," he said, walking closer to the trio. "You have no reason to fear harm from me."

The lad rolled his hat off his head, showing thick, unevenly trimmed brownish-red hair. He bowed and then fixed Brent with a wary gaze as he said, "I've never met a lord before."

Brent did not doubt that. "No matter. I'm just like any other man you'd meet. What is your name?"

"Godfrey."

"Very well, Godfrey, I want to ask you some questions."

"I don't rightly know how to talk to a lord, my lord. I just deliver the milk for me mum."

Sensing his fear and wanting to make him feel comfortable so he would talk to him, Brent said, "That's a very important job you have. Everyone wants their milk when they rise. Tell me, are these girls your sisters?"

The young man cut his eyes over to the two and nodded.

"That's good, Godfrey. I want you to talk to me the same way you would if you were talking to them. It's that simple, all right?"

He nodded again.

"Do you remember seeing the small dog I had with me yesterday?"

"Yes, my lord."

A snicker sounded from one of the girls, and Brent and the lad glanced their way. The younger girl held a gloved hand over her mouth while the older one fixed her with a disapproving glare.

"I… we," the young man hesitated and cut his eyes around to his sisters. "We remember the dog."

Only too well, Brent thought. The milkmaid could cover her smile and muffle her giggle, but laughter showed clearly in her youthful eyes.

"Good. Her name is Prissy, or Pris. She answers to both. She wandered away from me yesterday, and I can't find her. In your travels back and forth, have you seen her?"

"No, my lord," Godfrey said while nervously twisting and squeezing his wool hat in his hands.

"Do you always pass along the same route through the park each day?"

"Yes, my lord, but sometimes we don't."

Brent wasn't sure exactly what that meant, but said, "If you see her and can catch her, bring her to Number 12 Mayfair Lane, and I'll see to it you are handsomely rewarded." Brent reached into his pocket and pulled out a shilling and threw it to the lad. He caught it up to his chest with both hands. "There will be more if you find her."

Godfrey's eyes rounded and brightened. Surprised gasps came from the two girls. "Th-thank you, my lord."

Brent turned and walked back to his curricle. Within moments he was continuing his search for Pris. It was still too early for the sun to shine hot or bright enough to chase away the gray clouds, but it didn't feel as cold as when he first arrived at the park. When he was close to the area where he'd last seen Prissy, he once again set the brake on the curricle and jumped down.

He intended to scour every inch of ground, including

looking under every tree, bush, and shrub. Frustration mounted as he slipped on a patch of wet leaves and twisted his ankle, so it hurt a little every time he took a step. He knocked his hat off his head by a low-hanging branch, and a limb scratched the cheek that was still angry and swollen from his tussle with the duke's men. But he found no sign of the pet.

Half an hour later, he was making his way back to the carriage when he heard what he thought was a familiar voice. He stopped and stood still.

"Prissy!" he heard a lady call.

Brent's stomach tightened. Was he hearing things, or was that really Lady Gabrielle calling for his dog? He looked up at the sky and judged the time to be somewhere past eight. What the devil was she doing back in the park so early in the morn? And probably alone again, too!

He turned and started toward her voice. He heard a deep, menacing growl from Brutus, and Brent knew the dog had smelled him. He hoped that this time, Lady Gabrielle had a leash on the mammoth dog. Brent knew the mastiff to be old, deaf, and half blind, too, but not without the capability of knocking him down.

Brent walked out of a stand of trees and saw Lady Gabrielle and Brutus standing beside a two-seated open carriage, where a small, older lady sat, wearing a ridiculously fancy hat for so early in the day. A servant sat on the bench behind her. He recognized the driver as one of the men who'd chased him down and jumped on him yesterday. The man watched him warily, but he had no reason to fear Brent.

Lady Gabrielle's bright-blue eyes widened with surprise as he walked toward her. Brutus barked another warning and then started wagging his tail. Brent also noticed the animal was once again unfettered. Lady Gabrielle reached down and patted Brutus's shoulder and whispered something to him. Hopefully, it wasn't the command to attack.

Brent approached them slowly and stopped a respectful distance away from her and the dog. He took off his hat, bowed, and said, "Lady Gabrielle, I must say I'm not at all shocked to find you in the park so early in the morning."

"Nor I you, Lord Brentwood," she said, giving him the customary curtsey his title deserved. "Obviously we've found something we have in common."

He gave her a knowing smile. "I think you mean something *else* we have in common." And then, not wanting to give her time to answer, he quickly turned his attention to the mastiff and added, "And how are you this morning, Brutus?"

The dog made another woof that seemed only a little friendlier than the first. "Temperamental as ever, I see. Perhaps you don't enjoy the park on cold mornings as much as your mistress, or is it the early hour that bothers you?"

Lady Gabrielle ignored his comments to her dog and presented to him her companion, her mother's sister, Mrs. Elizabeth Potter.

He smiled and said, "Mrs. Potter, you are a brave lady to be out on such a dreary day."

"Balderdash, I'm not brave at all, I'm freezing my—"

"Auntie Bethie." Lady Gabrielle interrupted her

aunt before the last word was uttered, though Brent knew exactly what the loud-voiced lady was going to say.

While Lady Gabrielle was dressed in the same simple black-hooded cloak she'd worn yesterday, her aunt was not so restrained. Mrs. Potter wore a well-cut black coat trimmed at the neck with fur. Her hands were stuffed into a fur muffle, and her legs and feet were covered by a finely woven wool blanket. She was a small woman, and there wasn't much of her that wasn't covered in wool or fur, with the exception of a ridiculously tall, short-brimmed hat that was piled high with flowers and pheasant feathers. With sharp features, olive skin, and wide, deep-set brown eyes, she looked nothing like her much fairer and comely niece. Lady Gabrielle turned back to Brent and, with an almost shy smile, said, "My aunt is truly wonderful to indulge me as she does."

"I'm not wonderful at all," Mrs. Potter said with threads of humor lacing her lusty tone and a sparkle glinting in her dark eyes. "I'm here because I was coerced."

"Auntie!" the duke's daughter gasped. "You know I did no such thing."

"Not you, silly girl." Mrs. Potter laughed heartily in a voice that was much too deep and gruff for a woman her size. "I'm talking about your obnoxious father."

Keeping her gaze on her aunt, Lady Gabrielle asked, "What did Papa do this time?"

"What he always says he will do but never does. That he will cut off my allowance and force me to live in one of his dreadfully damp country homes if I don't keep an eagle eye on your every move. But don't worry about that, dear. He has been saying that since your mother died. As you can see, I've been saved from his gallows many times." She quickly turned her gaze on Brent and, without hesitation, said, "Not that the duke or his daughter told me all the intimate details, but I understand Lord Austerhill's son jumped the fence at the paddock and you are the new stallion."

Brent chuckled, stretching the injured corner of his mouth and wincing from the sudden pain.

"Auntie, please. You are being far too brash. You've just met the viscount. He doesn't know your nature."

"Nonsense, Gabby. Don't be so fussy. If he's marrying you, he'll learn me soon enough," she answered and then turned her incorrigible gaze on Brent again. "I understand nuptials are in the future for the two of you."

"That is the case, Mrs. Potter," Brent said to the lady and let his gaze slowly drift to Gabrielle as he added, "even though the duke doesn't want it widely known until the previous engagement matters can be resolved. As soon as they are, the banns will be posted, and Lady Gabrielle and I will wed."

"That sounds lovely," Mrs. Potter said and then turned and smiled sweetly at Lady Gabrielle. "Does that suit your gentle nature better, my dear?"

"Much," Lady Gabrielle said quite stiffly, making it clear she wasn't happy her aunt was going beyond the pale.

Brent was enjoying the conversation between the

two ladies, who were as different as night and day. The first time Mrs. Potter spoke, Brent knew she was nothing like her niece.

"No doubt you are the reason she wanted to come to the park so early this morning, so I'll allow her five minutes to talk to you while my maid pours me another cup of chocolate. But next time, Gabby, don't make up a story about a poor lost dog. Just tell me you desire to see your handsome viscount, and I'll do my best to make it happen."

Lady Gabrielle opened her mouth as if to counter her aunt's words but turned toward Brent instead when she heard his chuckle.

Brent held up his hand to stop her from speaking, and she pressed her lips together. He allowed his gaze to drift lazily over her lovely face. Lady Gabrielle let out a sighing breath. Her taut shoulders relaxed, obviously realizing he wasn't offended by her aunt.

"Don't let your aunt's comments disturb you. I find her refreshing and charming, and I don't, for a moment, believe you came to the park to see me."

"Thank you for that, my lord, it is true."

"But did you come to the park just to look for Prissy?"

A wrinkle of concern formed between her eyes. "I must admit I hardly slept a wink last night. I've been anxious about her since you told me she was missing. Have you found her?"

"Not yet, but I'm still hopeful."

Lady Gabrielle's frown deepened. "I feel responsible for her disappearance and was hoping if I came to the park that, perhaps, I could find her for you. Brutus has a very good nose. I fear she may have somehow gotten trapped or tangled up with her leash or…"

She didn't finish the sentence, though Brent could imagine what she wanted to say but had then thought better of it. He'd found himself thinking the same thing more than once. And while he would love to blame Lady Gabrielle for Prissy's running away, in truth only he was to blame.

"I'm the one who let go of her leash. I know she's prone to be a wanderer, and that's why I have never trusted any of the servants to walk her. If she can get away and explore, she will. Her disappearance is in no way your fault."

"That's kind of you to say." Her eyes searched the distance behind him. "I'm afraid the only thing I've found is this is a very big park when you are looking for a little dog."

"That's what I've found, too."

Brent couldn't help but be touched by her concern for Prissy, but knowing how much she liked dogs, he wasn't surprised.

"How long have you been out here?" he asked.

"Though Auntie Bethie would lead you to believe we've been here hours, we haven't been here that long," she said and lowered her lashes over her eyes so he couldn't see in their depths.

Brent didn't believe her. The tip of her nose and crest of her cheeks were dark pink from the cold. Mrs. Potter was shivering from the chilly wind. However, he couldn't help but be impressed Lady Gabrielle came out on this windy day just to look for his dog.

He was quite certain he had never met another young lady who would trouble herself to do that on such a cold morning.

He took a step closer, lowered his voice, and said, "I'm glad to see you are properly chaperoned this time."

She lifted her chin in quiet defiance. "I do try to never make the same mistake twice, my lord."

"That's good to know."

Their gazes held a moment longer than was necessary, and then she said, "Your injuries look better today."

He gave her what he knew was a crooked smile and shifted his hat from one hand to the other. "You think so? I thought a monster was looking back at me when I was shaving this morning."

"It seems I still have things to apologize for. I'm sorry about what Muggs and Lord Austerhill's footman did, as well."

Brent threw a quick glance to the beefy man sitting on the driver's bench as he touched the corner of his mouth with his thumb. "Don't be. It was a small price to pay for a few kisses."

"You two are going to have to speak up if you want me to hear you," Mrs. Potter called.

Lady Gabrielle glanced back toward the carriage with a smile and said, "We are only talking about the weather, Auntie."

"Ah, that's what I thought," she answered and then chuckled. "In that case, carry on."

"Your aunt is a very astute person."

"I can see she amuses you. Some people, including my father, find her crude and offensive at times."

"Everyone's nature is different."

"I know, but she has shocked most everyone in the ton at one time or another with her loose tongue."

Brent nodded. "I'm sure. Has she lived with you since your mother's death?"

"Good heavens no," Lady Gabrielle said. "Not that I would have minded. I would much rather have had her than the string of governesses we've had over the years. But she and my father can't tolerate each other for very long, and they stay away from each other as much as possible."

"But he allows her to visit."

"Yes, once or twice a year. She arrived in London just yesterday. She was going to help with last-minute preparations for the wedding."

Brent watched Lady Gabrielle's face carefully. There wasn't even the tiniest bit of disappointment or bitterness showing in her eyes or voice when she mentioned the canceled wedding. That sort of thing would have devastated most young ladies. He couldn't help but wonder why she hadn't wanted to marry the earl's son and why she was willing to elicit the aid of a complete stranger to make sure the wedding wouldn't take place. That puzzled him immensely. He'd tried to get her to tell him when they talked yesterday. She was keeping that bit of information to herself, for now, but Brent intended to find out the answer.

"When I talked to your father yesterday, he mentioned your sister. I take it that, since she's not with you, she doesn't enjoy early morning jaunts to the park like you do."

Brent watched a faraway look come to Lady

Gabrielle's eyes, as if she were remembering some private pain she didn't want to surface, and he wondered what it was about the mention of her sister that brought such a look of sadness and contemplation to her face.

"Her name is Rosabelle," she finally said. "Not even as a small child did Rosabelle want to start her day early or in a hurry. She has always wanted to stay up all night and sleep all day."

"My mother was like that until she was given Prissy. That dog changed her life. She didn't trust the servants to walk her, so she was up at dawn almost every morning to make sure Pris had her stroll."

Lady Gabrielle lowered her lashes over her eyes, as if shielding what she felt from him. He hadn't meant to bring up Prissy again.

"Gabby," her aunt called, "I do believe it's time for us to go. I'm going to catch a death chill if we stay out here any longer. Lord Brentwood?"

"Yes, madame?" he said, looking over Lady Gabrielle's shoulder at the woman.

"We are planning to be at Lady Windham's party on Saturday night. Will you be there?"

"Yes," he said at the same time Lady Gabrielle walked closer to the carriage and said, "No, Auntie."

"He just said yes," Mrs. Potter contended.

"I mean no for me. I will not be attending any parties for the foreseeable future."

The older woman's brow wrinkled, and her lip curled up curiously. "That's pure poppycock."

Lady Gabrielle glanced back to Brent before saying, "There's bound to be talk, Auntie."

"Of course there will, but you have to treat it like falling off a horse. If one throws you, you get right back on and ride him again to overcome your fear. That's what you shall do in this case. Besides, the best way to confront scandal and gossip in Society is to face it head on and dare them to breathe it to your face. I will not allow you to hide away in your house and feel as if you have been shunned by Society. No, it won't happen as long as I am here." She turned back to the viscount. "We all know gossip travels fast, don't we, my lord?"

"Yes, madame."

"I've hardly been in Town twenty-four hours and I've already heard about your twin brothers. Interesting fellows they must be."

"Society seems infatuated with them, and I must admit they are not shying away but enjoying the attention."

"See, Gabrielle. That's how you handle scandal. Will they be attending Lady Windham's party with you?"

"I've not talked to them personally about it, but they will probably be there, too."

"Good. They can help keep you out of trouble. Judging from what little I know about your rendezvous with Gabby, I believe there will be a certain amount of unflattering talk when both of you appear at the same party for the first time. You must keep your wits, she must keep her head held high, and you both must resist the urge to fight back verbally or otherwise. It will only invigorate and prolong the gossip and enlarge the scandal. It will do more harm, and I would say the two of you have done quite enough already, wouldn't you, Lord Brentwood?"

She spoke with such authority Brent was surprised the lady wasn't the duke's sister. But perhaps that was the reason she didn't get along with Lady Gabrielle's father. They were too much alike.

"Yes, Mrs. Potter, I understand," Brent said, "but I would find it difficult not to defend Lady Gabrielle's good name should it come to that."

"Understood, my lord, however you must. She is a duke's daughter, so she will be forgiven more easily than most young ladies in her current circumstances. The majority of people in Society will be respectful of her position, but there will be some who cannot contain themselves. For her, you must. Do I make myself clear?"

"Perfectly."

Mrs. Potter smiled and said, "Good. Come along, Gabby, we'll return to the park at another time to look for your phantom dog. Preferably when it's warmer and the sun is shining."

"I'll be right there, Auntie. Muggs, would you please help Brutus get into the carriage?"

Gabrielle turned back to Brent. Her blue gaze lighted on his face. She studied him as if she were trying to absorb every detail of his features, causing his lower stomach to tighten. He remembered her saying yesterday it was madness that caused her to kiss him, and he could almost believe it, because right now he was feeling a little madness himself. He was tempted to pull her to him and kiss her right in front of her aunt.

Lady Gabrielle looked deeply into his eyes for a moment before saying, "I hope you find Prissy."

He nodded once, thankful he hadn't followed his urge to kiss her. That would have been sheer, unadulterated madness.

"Do you want me to tell Mrs. Potter there is really a lost dog you were looking for?"

She shook her head. "She wouldn't believe you."

"I didn't think so. Thank you for your help, Lady Gabrielle."

Her expression changed to one of concern again, and she said, "There is always the possibility someone has taken Prissy home and is desperately trying to find her owner as we speak."

"That she is safe and warm in someone's gentle care is a comforting thought."

"Gabby, we really must go."

"I'm sure Prissy will turn up soon, Lord Brentwood. Would you mind sending me a note once you find her?"

He nodded. "Lady Gabrielle, Mrs. Potter."

The servant rushed to help her onto the carriage, but Brent stepped in front of him and held out his hand for her. Lady Gabrielle hesitated and then looked at her aunt for approval. Only when Mrs. Potter gave the nod did Lady Gabrielle accept his offer and place the tips of her gloved fingers in his before stepping into the carriage. But just that brief touch was enough to send the heat of sexual desire rushing through him. He didn't know why, but she affected him like no other woman ever had.

Lady Gabrielle seated herself beside her aunt and turned back and smiled at him with such genuine happiness that Brent's breath caught in his chest. He felt the same feelings he'd had yesterday when she'd approached him. At times like this, she utterly enchanted him.

This was the lady who had intrigued him so desperately he forgot about everything but her in his arms. When they'd first met, she appeared so capable and independent. And this was the lady who stood so confidently before him and admitted she was betrothed to another.

He watched her as the carriage pulled away. Her father was a strong, unyielding man. Obviously, he'd taught his daughter to be a strong-willed and accomplished young lady, and obviously she had learned early how to get her way. And when he was with her, enjoying their banter, it was easy to forget she'd designed to catch him in a parson's mousetrap. There could be only one reason why she had. She didn't want to marry the earl's son. But why?

Suddenly, he couldn't wait for Lady Windham's party so he could see the lovely and intriguing Lady Gabrielle again. He made a mental note that it would be five days.

He stood and watched until her carriage was out of sight before he started back toward his own vehicle. He would write up a notice for *The Times* and all the other newsprints when he got back home. Maybe offering a handsome reward for Prissy's safe return would bring results quicker than his outings to the park.

A few minutes later, when Brent neared the curricle, he noticed a man standing a short distance away, looking at his horse. "Can I help you?" Brent called.

The man turned toward Brent, and the first thing

Brent saw was a black patch covering one of the stranger's eyes. His long beard was graying and unkempt. A tattered plaid scarf wrapped around his neck. His hands and arms were huddled to his chest in an unusual position, and as Brent got closer, he could see that he cuddled something beneath his coat—and it was moving.

Prissy was Brent's first thought. He picked up his pace.

"No, sir," the man answered, turning to walk away. "I was just admiring your fine horse and carriage. I'll be on my way."

"Wait," Brent said, gaining on the man. "Are you holding something underneath your coat?"

The man stopped and faced Brent. "Yes, sir," he said in a calm voice and showing no fear of being caught doing something wrong. "But I didn't steal anything from your carriage."

Brent didn't know what the man carried but now realized it couldn't be Prissy. She would have started barking like a fiend the moment she heard Brent's voice. But he was curious as to what the stranger held.

"I believe you, but do you mind showing me what you are holding on to?"

"Don't mind at all. Got nothing to hide." The man unfastened the one large button on his coat and cautiously opened it.

Brent saw the wild black beaded eyes of a gray rabbit.

"Got yourself a pet, I see," Brent said, realizing he was disappointed the animal wasn't Prissy.

The man shook his head. "On a cold morning like this, I hold them underneath my coat to help keep me warm. I catch them in the park and sell them to taverns, inns." He shrugged. "I sell to anyone that's buying. Are you interested in it for your supper?"

"Not today," Brent said, and climbed up on his curricle and headed out of the park.

Seven

Experience is not what happens to a man; it is what a man does with what happens to him.

—Aldous Huxley

SHE COULDN'T GET HIM OFF HER MIND.

It was frustrating for Gabrielle that most of her waking moments she was thinking about Lord Brentwood or his poor dog. It had been several days since she'd seen the viscount, and she hadn't received a note from him saying Prissy had been found. She had managed to drag her aunt to the park twice more to look for the dog, with no luck. She hoped with all her heart the Pomeranian was back home and the arrogant viscount had just failed to notify her. She would make a point to ask him about Prissy tonight.

Every time Gabrielle thought about seeing Lord Brentwood at Lady Windham's party later in the evening, her stomach would quiver excitedly. She didn't understand why her attraction to him was so great. She only knew she had never felt this way about any other man.

Gabrielle stood near the fireplace in the drawing room, sipping her second cup of afternoon tea. Brutus lay on his big pillow, so deep in sleep he was snoring, and other than the sound of the crackling fire, the house was quiet.

Too quiet.

Her aunt was spending the afternoon with a friend. Her father, knowing his solicitor was working on dissolving her first engagement and planning the particulars for her second, had left for his hunting trip, thus continuing his tradition of never being in residence when Auntie Bethie was visiting.

Gabrielle had probably thought more about Lord Brentwood in the past five days than she had about Staunton the entire six months she was engaged to him. It had crossed her mind that she could quite possibly see Staunton at Lady Windham's party tonight. It wouldn't bother her one bit to see him and talk to him. She had wondered why he hadn't done the expected thing and approached her father about marrying Rosa, but it could be that his father had put a stop to that.

Should she let him know she knew about him and Rosabelle, and she would help them in any way she could in dealing with their fathers? Though at present she had very little clout with her father and absolutely none with Staunton's, so her help might be limited.

When Gabrielle wasn't thinking about the dashing Lord Brentwood and his dog, her sister was on her mind. Rosabelle hadn't come out of her room since the morning she came running into the book room to ask if what she'd heard about Gabrielle's broken engagement was true. Gabrielle had tried several times to talk to her, but she would either pretend to be asleep or pull the covers over her head and say she was too ill to talk.

And while Gabrielle had enjoyed having her vivacious aunt all to herself since their father left, she knew it wasn't good that Rosabelle was avoiding her. Gabrielle had a feeling it was because her sister was riddled with guilt. Even though there was only thirteen months difference in their ages, Rosabelle had always seemed much younger.

Rosa was highly emotional and way too impetuous at times. Gabrielle knew she had to take some of the blame for that. Since their mother died, they had been raised mostly by governesses, and Rosabelle had often let her fears and insecurities surface. Gabrielle always took up for Rosabelle and sometimes even took punishments for her.

Perhaps their lives would have been different if their mother had lived or even if Auntie Bethie could have spent more time with them. But neither their aunt nor their father had wanted that. Auntie Bethie had tried to persuade Gabrielle's mother not to marry the duke. The duke never forgave Elizabeth for her intrusion.

Gabrielle knew she couldn't let Rosabelle continue to brood in her room. Her sister was carrying a heavy burden, and Gabrielle had to lighten it for her. She cared too much not to. And she needed to tell Rosa about Lord Brentwood before she heard about him and Gabrielle from someone else. So if Rosabelle wouldn't come to her, Gabrielle would go to Rosa.

She placed her tea cup on the silver tray and looked over at Brutus. If she tiptoed out of the room, maybe she could get out without waking him. He could no longer make it up the stairs, and she hated for him to wait for her at the bottom rather than on his comfortable pillow by the fire.

Gabrielle went up to her sister's room and entered without knocking. Rosabelle turned from the window by her bed where she stood still dressed in a white long-sleeved night rail in the middle of the afternoon. Her long blonde hair didn't look as if it had been combed in days.

Her red-rimmed eyes searched Gabrielle's face, and she blinked rapidly for a moment. It struck Gabrielle that her sister seemed frightened. Her gaze suddenly bounced erratically around the room, like a mouse cornered by a cat. She was looking for a place to run but couldn't see how to get past Gabrielle.

"I didn't hear you knock," Rosabelle said in an accusing tone.

"That's because I didn't."

"You should have. That wasn't very mannerly of you."

"I know, but I knew if I announced myself, you would either pretend you were sleeping or tell me you didn't feel up to seeing anyone, as you have claimed for the past five days."

Her sister's shoulders and chin lifted in a show of courage, though her face was marred by fear and anguish. "I'm not pretending, Gabby. I haven't been feeling well."

"If you need a doctor, I will get one."

"No, no, it's not that serious. I'll be fine."

"When? Later today? Tomorrow? Next week?"

Rosabelle's bottom lip trembled. "I-I don't know. Don't press me about this."

Gabrielle walked farther into the room and shut the door. "It's so unlike you to be ill for so long and to spend so much time in your room. I'm worried about you, Rosa."

Her sister turned back toward the window. "Don't be. I just need for you to leave me be."

Rosabelle had always been one to run from her problems rather than face them, deal with them, and get over them. This time, Gabrielle couldn't allow her to do that. Rosa had to admit what she'd done so she could begin to forgive herself and move past it.

"The time for leaving you alone is over," Gabrielle said firmly. "I'm not going away until you tell me what is wrong."

"Oh, Gabby, I can't tell you. I've done something absolutely wretched, and I'm dreadfully sick about it. You're the last person I want to know about this."

"Tell me. I can help."

Keeping her back to Gabrielle, Rosabelle rubbed her arms as if she were chilled. "No. I can't. I don't even know how to explain it so you would understand."

Gabrielle's heart broke for her sister. She knew exactly how Rosa was feeling, because she had felt the same way when her father kept asking her why she was in the viscount's arms. Some things just couldn't be explained. They could only be felt.

Gabrielle took hold of her sister's arms and forced her to turn and face her. Fresh tears brimmed out of Rosabelle's eyes and rolled down her cheeks.

"What do you mean I wouldn't understand? Have you ever known me not to?"

"But this is different. You don't know what I've done."

Gabrielle led Rosabelle over to the slipper chair and gently sat her down. Gabrielle knelt down in front of her and took Rosa's cold hands in her own. It was difficult to see her in this much pain. It would be so easy to just tell her she knew what she had done, and she forgave her, but somehow Gabrielle knew that wasn't the right thing to do. Rosabelle needed to confess what had happened between her and Staunton.

"Look at me, Rosa. Have I ever given you reason to think you can't trust me?"

She sniffled. "No."

"Am I such an ogre to have caused you to think you can tell me things and I wouldn't understand?"

"No, but if you knew, you would hate me, and I couldn't bear that."

Gabrielle squeezed her hands. "Didn't I understand when we were younger and you pushed me into the pond and I got soaking wet and I caught a chill? Didn't I understand when you failed to finish your schoolwork and I gave you mine so the governess wouldn't punish you?"

Fresh tears left the pool in her eyes. "I can't, Gabby. This is so different from childhood pranks or silliness. Don't make me tell you."

"I must. You cannot continue to hold this inside and let it fester, or you will continue to be sick."

"But what I did is unforgivable."

Another tear fell from the edge of her eye. Gabrielle reached up and wiped it away with her thumb. She smiled. "No, it's not. Whatever has happened, or whatever you've done, you are my sister, and nothing could keep me from loving you. Nothing is unforgivable."

"I-I love Staunton, and he loves me," she blurted out, and then jerked away from Gabrielle's grasp and hid her face behind both her hands and sobbed brokenheartedly.

Gabrielle gave a quiet sigh of relief. Now she could say, "I know, Rosa."

Rosabelle took in a deep breath and let out another sniffle. She slowly took her hands away from her damp face. Her wet blue eyes were wide with surprise.

"You know?"

Gabrielle nodded.

"How? When? Did Staunton tell you? He promised he wouldn't say a word to anyone."

"No, he said nothing to me. I only recently found out, and how doesn't matter."

"We tried to keep it from you and our fathers. I didn't mean to fall in love with him, Gabby. We didn't want it to happen; it just did, and I didn't know what to do. I've tried to stay away from you these past few weeks so you wouldn't see in my eyes how much I loved him."

"I knew you were withdrawn but thought you were just sad because I was leaving to have my own home. Thank you for telling me the truth. All three of us would have lived miserable lives if the marriage between Staunton and I had taken place. I never should have let Papa arrange it for me in the first place, but at the time I thought it was the right thing to do. I knew I had no loving feelings for him, but I thought perhaps they might develop after we married."

Rosabelle's eyes widened. "I don't know how you kept from loving him, Gabby. He's the most handsome and dashing man in London! We didn't fall in love until after you were engaged. Once we did, I was so miserable, but I didn't know what to do."

Gabrielle smiled and touched Rosa's cheek with the palm of her hand. "I can understand that. All that misery is behind you now. You and Staunton can bide your time through the winter and, when the Season arrives next year, you two can meet fresh and make your plans to wed."

"Do you think our fathers will let us marry?"

"Why wouldn't they? They both had reasons for wanting a union between the two families, and those reasons haven't changed. I'm sure Staunton will tell his father you are the lady he wants to marry, and it will be handled."

Concern etched its way into Rosabelle's features. She raked the backs of her hands across her cheeks and dried them. "I had thought I would have a note from him by now, but I haven't heard a word from him."

"I'm sure it's just that he doesn't know what is going on in this house, and he's waiting until things settle down. He doesn't know I know about you two. And, Rosa, no one will ever hear about it from me. He probably doesn't want to contact you for fear someone would find out about the two of you."

Rosa threw her arms around Gabrielle's neck and

hugged her tightly. "That's what I thought, too. Oh, Gabby, you are the most wonderful sister a girl could have."

Gabrielle pulled away and looked at Rosa while she brushed her hair away from her face. "And you are a wonderful sister, too; don't ever forget that."

"I won't. I don't know what I would do without you."

"There's something else I need to tell you."

"Oh, please tell me something wonderful, Gabby. I want to hear some good news."

Gabrielle rolled her shoulders and cleared her throat as she thought about what she needed to say. "No, it's not wonderful news, but you need to know, anyway. A few mornings ago I was in the park and had a chance encounter with Viscount Brentwood."

"I recognize that name. The Brentwoods are twins, right?"

"Yes, but they also have an older brother who is a viscount. Anyway, I was walking Brutus, and he had his dog. The short of the long story is because we were seen together in the park, our names are now being linked together."

Rosa's brows drew together in confusion. "Linked together as in possible matrimony?"

"Yes, there is that possibility for my immediate future."

"So that is why your wedding to Staunton was canceled?" Her brows drew together as if she was confused and then suddenly widened in shock. Her mouth fell open. "You were with another man while still engaged to Staunton."

Gabrielle lifted her chin and said, "It wasn't a planned meeting but, yes, that's what happened."

"Gabby, how could you do that to Staunton?"

A rueful chuckle passed Gabrielle's lips. She would have loved to say, "Because, my dear, I saw Staunton kissing you." But she couldn't find it in herself to be that cruel and tell Rosa everything that happened that morning was because Gabrielle had seen her and Staunton in a passionate embrace.

"And now I know you and Staunton love each other, I see how it has worked out for the best. Don't you agree?"

"Yes, of course."

"So don't be bothered if you hear rumors about me and Lord Brentwood. We are handling everything quite well." Gabrielle rose to her feet and inhaled deeply. "Now, Auntie Bethie and I are going to Lady Windham's party tonight. I would love it if you felt up to joining us."

"A party tonight? Oh, no, I couldn't. Please don't ask it of me. I'm ghastly tired, as I haven't slept in days." Her eyes welled with tears again.

"All right, but if you don't feel like attending the party, at least come help me decide what I should wear."

"How can you do it, Gabby?"

"What?"

"Be so strong. Be so sensible about everything. I would never go in public again if my wedding were canceled or if I thought there would be rumors about me."

"At first, I didn't want to go, either. Auntie Bethie told me I had to treat the canceled wedding as if I were riding a horse. When a horse throws you, you are supposed to immediately get back on and ride him. She said I must go out again, and the sooner the better. I know she's right. I would be much happier to just stay inside or flee to the country until next spring, when I could start all over, but that would only put me running away from my problems, not facing them. I don't want to run away from anything."

As Gabrielle said those words, she realized for the first time they were true.

She had made a horrible mistake in kissing the viscount, but she wasn't going to let that one lapse in judgment keep her from going forward with her life. Her father had left London, so she could no longer work on persuading him that she and Lord Brentwood shouldn't marry. That left Lord Brentwood, whom she hoped would be an easier target than her father.

Since he would be at Lady Windham's tonight, she would put her plans into action. She had only a few weeks at most to convince him she was not the lady he wanted to marry.

Eight

Do not look back in anger, or forward in fear, but around in awareness.

—James Thurber

A NERVOUS FLUTTERING ATTACKED GABRIELLE'S stomach as she entered Lady Windham's house with her aunt later that evening. The spontaneous jitters had nothing to do with her dreading cold stares or unflattering comments whispered about her or her broken engagement. This wouldn't be the first time she was the topic of conversation. People felt a certain familiarity that came with being the daughter of a powerful duke. Some were not only comfortable but believed they were justified in talking about her. Gabrielle had never minded.

Her fluttery feeling was because she knew she would see Lord Brentwood again tonight. She had paid special attention to her appearance, selecting a long-sleeved, high-waisted velvet gown of the palest pink that went perfectly with her golden-colored hair. A single strand of pearls circled her neck, and a delicate teardrop-shaped pearl dripped from each ear. Her hair was swept up into a loose chignon and circled by a band of pearls.

Lord and Lady Windham's house was bright with the yellow glow of candles and oil lamps. Their home was one of the largest in Mayfair, and any event hosted by them was a grand affair. They spared no expense with food, drink, or the guest list whenever they gave a party. The house was buzzing with the constant strum of lively music, raucous laughter, and the chatter of conversations.

In the large foyer, the attendant helped Gabrielle and her aunt take off their velvet cloaks. From where she stood, Gabrielle could see into the drawing room and down the corridor. She quickly scanned the area to see if she could catch a glimpse of Lord Brentwood. When she saw no sign of him among the crush of people spilling into the rooms, she relaxed a little.

"Tell me, dearest, how are you feeling now that you are here?" Auntie Bethie asked her.

Gabrielle turned to her aunt, who was dressed in a puce-colored gown adorned with three flounces on the skirt and the sleeves. An elaborate necklace of gold and garnets was fastened around her neck, and large garnets were clipped to her ears. In her red hair, she wore a comb that had been festooned with ribbons and short-cropped pheasant feathers.

Long ago, Gabrielle had learned how to adapt and to accept whatever situation she was in at the time, so she gave her aunt a smile of confidence and said, "I feel exceptional, Auntie."

Her aunt's dark brown eyes gleamed with happiness.

"That's what I wanted to hear. You are doing the right thing, my dear, by coming out to the parties. When a person shies away from Society, it's natural for people to think it's because they have something to hide."

Gabrielle pursed her lips and thought on that. "I suppose you are right."

"I know I'm right. Now, who are those two young ladies I see standing over by that clock, trying desperately not to let me know they are trying to get your attention?"

Gabrielle laughed softly as she caught sight of her two friends motioning for her to join them. Fern Crenshaw was a lovely red-haired young lady who had married right after the Season ended and was blissfully happy with her new husband and the baby that was expected next spring. Babs Whitehouse was a voluptuous golden-haired beauty and an outrageous flirt who had turned down more than three offers for her hand this past Season. She was constantly admonishing Gabrielle for her prim and proper ways.

"No doubt they are eager to hear what has been happening in my life."

"I'm sure they've heard the gossip their parents have brought home to them, and they are ready to hear the truth from you, should you decide to divulge more of it to them than you have to me."

"Never, Auntie," Gabrielle said with a sly smile.

Her aunt winked at her. "Go to them. I'll be watching you from one of the chairs around the dance floor. Enjoy yourself, and I'll find you whenever I'm ready to leave."

Gabrielle leaned over and kissed her cheek. "Thank you, Auntie. I don't know what I would have done without you these past few days."

"You would have managed and done the right thing. You always do. Now, remember what I said about holding your head high, and go have a wonderful evening. You deserve it."

"Auntie, there's only one thing I'm concerned about."

Her gaze searched Gabrielle's with concern. "What's that?"

"I haven't talked to Staunton since our marriage was canceled. What should I say to him if he is here? Should I apologize to him?"

"For what?" her aunt asked a little too loudly.

Gabrielle quickly put her finger to her lips and whispered, "Not too loud, Auntie. It seems to me that might be the proper thing to do, since I was in the park alone with Lord Brentwood."

Auntie Bethie gave her a gentle smile, and in a softer voice said, "And just like your mother, you always want to do the proper thing. She would have been so proud of you. Tell me, are you the one who called off the engagement, or did he?"

Gabrielle thought about that. "That might be up for debate. I believe it was actually his father, Lord Austerhill, who called it off, but as you know it was because of what I did."

Her aunt pursed her lips for a moment. "Hmm, in that case, I'm going to counsel you the way I think your mother would have had she been here instead of me, because I would probably say to you never apologize." She laughed softly for a moment and then said,

"But I can remember your mother once saying to me, 'My dear Bethie, there are two things that are never out of line, out of place, or out of time—an apology and a thank you. You can never go wrong saying I'm sorry or thank you.'"

Her aunt's remembered words from her mother brought a happy sadness to Gabrielle, and she smiled. "Thank you, Auntie. I think I know what I need to do."

Babs and Fern didn't wait for Gabrielle to reach them. When they saw her heading their way, they ran to meet her, excitedly throwing questions at her without giving her time to answer any of them.

"Is it true your wedding to Staunton has been canceled?" Babs asked.

"Gabby, you must tell us what happened," Fern said. "We feel as if we've been sitting on pins and needles, hoping to get to see you so we could find out what happened."

Fern's eyes widened. "I overheard Papa tell Mama you had been caught in the park in a state of *dishabille* with one of the Brentwood twins. And Staunton has challenged him to a duel. It's so romantic to have two handsome gentlemen fighting over the right to your hand in marriage."

Gabrielle gasped, looking from one friend to the other. How in heaven's name did events in the park get so far from the truth?

"Tell us it's not true," Fern said.

"No, tell us it is true," Babs said with a mischievous smile. "Tell us all about your secret lover. It's so naughty of you to keep something like this from us, Gabby. How could you? We are supposed to be your dearest friends."

"When did you meet him?" Fern asked. "Was it love at first sight?"

Babs added,. "Mama said she would have believed it of me before she would have believed you were meeting a lover in the park."

"Please, please," Gabrielle said, taking both their hands and moving them away from listening ears. "Both of you must talk more softly so no one will hear you. People are looking at us. Come. Let's walk calmly to the punch table, and absolutely no more questions until we are where no one can hear us."

Gabrielle smiled pleasantly, held her head high, and led the way, weaving her friends through the throng of people crowding the house. She nodded to some, spoke to others, and curtseyed to a countess as she made her way to the back of the drawing room where the punch table had been set up. With every step, she felt questioning eyes and icy stares. From her peripheral vision, she saw hands cover mouths and fans cover faces. The roar of laughing and talking ceased as she approached and started up again as soon as she passed.

She and Auntie Bethie had talked about what might happen tonight, and she knew shunning by some members of Polite Society was a very good possibility, but Gabrielle wasn't bothered by that. If it happened, so be it. She still didn't know why she had kissed Lord Brentwood, but she was glad she had, and she wasn't going to be ashamed of it.

After the three ladies were served a cup of punch, they moved away from the well-attended table to a far corner in the crowded room.

Gabrielle looked at her friends' eager faces and

took a sip of the fruit juice. She wouldn't wish all the different feelings she'd gone through the past few days on anyone. But how much should she tell them? Not everything that happened, for sure.

"How long do you intend to keep us on the point of this needle?" Babs asked. "Tell us what happened!"

Gabrielle smiled understandingly. She would have no peace if she didn't tell them a little, and it was quite clear they expected to hear something salacious. She would have to disappoint them on that. There wasn't much she hadn't shared with her friends over the past couple of years, but she didn't want to tell them about how the viscount made her feel. It was personal, intimate, and it was glorious. It wasn't something she wanted to share with anyone.

She looked around to make sure no one was close enough to hear them and then softly said, "First, let me assure you I was not with one of the Brentwood twins."

"Then who?" Babs asked.

Fern clasped a hand to her chest and said, "Or was it all a horrible lie, and there wasn't a gentleman with you at all?"

"No, there was a gentleman," Gabrielle admitted, "but most of what you have heard is not true. I was in Hyde Park with Lord Brentwood, the twins' older brother, but we didn't plan to meet there. It was quite by accident."

"Oh, the viscount," Fern said in a softly whispered voice.

"I saw him and his brothers at a party last week," Babs said, "but I haven't been introduced to any of them. How and when did you meet him? And why did you agree to a secret rendezvous in the park with him? And what did Staunton have to say about all this?"

"It must have been love at first sight," Fern said.

"I haven't talked to Staunton," Gabrielle readily admitted, "and my meeting with Lord Brentwood was not a secret affair."

"If you didn't go to meet him or someone else, why were you in the park alone?"

"Oh, I wasn't alone, Brutus was with me. I hadn't been able to sleep, and I was troubled about my upcoming marriage. I decided to dress and take a walk."

Gabrielle continued the story, sticking to the facts when she could, but being careful. The last thing she wanted to do was mention anything about Rosabelle's secret or the passionate kiss she shared with Lord Brentwood.

"So you were just standing there in the park, talking with him, when your father and Lord Austerhill found you?"

Leave it to Babs to ask for more details than Gabrielle wanted to share.

"Well, we were talking about our dogs," Gabrielle said, feeling a little guilt at skirting the truth, or at least the timing of it.

"Oh, I've heard about Lord Brentwood's combing the park every day for his dog," Fern said. "And just tonight I heard that some people think Lord Pinkwater's ghost picked up the viscount's dog and is keeping her for himself."

"Some people actually think a ghost has Prissy?" Gabrielle asked.

"Forget the ghost and the dog," Babs said. "After

all I've heard, I was hoping for a more scandalous story than you were helping Lord Brentwood look for his dog. Especially since all the gossips had your cloak lying on the ground and your dress hanging off your shoulders!"

Gabrielle gasped. "Babs, no such thing occurred."

"How can you even suggest that?" Fern said, turning to Babs with a firm expression. "Shame on you for even repeating such rubbish. You know how tightly Gabby is laced."

Gabrielle was a little taken aback by Fern's strong defense.

Babs frowned at Fern. "No, obviously we don't know that. But I do know how quickly and easily a handsome, sweet-talking gentleman can sweep a lady off her feet, no matter how tight her stays!"

"The only thing I know for sure—" Gabrielle stopped as two elderly ladies walked very close to her. As they passed, one of them said quite loudly, "In my day, when a young lady was involved in a scandal, she didn't show her face in public for years."

"If ever again!" her companion added haughtily.

"And it didn't matter if she was a duke's daughter."

"The nerve of those ladies," Fern whispered.

"It was all gossip meant to ruin her," Babs called after the ladies. "She was in the park looking for her dog."

One of the ladies turned around and said, "I'll make sure you three are never admitted into Almack's again."

"You can try," Babs returned.

"Babs, please, don't antagonize those ladies," Gabrielle said. "I don't want you getting into trouble because of something I did."

"Why not?" She smiled mischievously at Gabrielle. "What kind of friend would I be if I let you have all the pleasure of being the most talked about young lady in London?"

"You are much too self-assured for your own good," Gabrielle said with a smile. "And it wasn't my dog that was lost. Brutus would never run away from me. It was Lord Brentwood's dog."

"Excuse me, ladies."

Gabrielle's breath caught in her throat at the sound of the viscount's voice. She turned, and her gaze fell on a broad chest covered by a crisp white shirt and a black tufted waistcoat. She saw wide, straight shoulders that fit perfectly into a black cutaway jacket. Her gaze continued up a strong, cleanly shaved neck, sailed over a smooth, slightly square chin, and lingered on sculpted masculine lips, before resting on intriguing golden-brown eyes that seemed to reach down into her very soul and softly greet her there.

Her heartbeat faltered and then raced. Lord Brentwood was a magnificent-looking man. He stood perfect in stature and impeccable in dress, letting her stare at him. And she did so without guilt, shame, or hesitation. Everything about him awakened and stimulated her senses like no other man ever had.

Lord Brentwood bowed, then picked up her hand and kissed it. Her breath caught in her throat at the excitement that coursed through her at seeing him. His fingers boldly caressed the inside of her palm. Even through her gloves, she felt the heat of his fingers. A shiver of something wonderful skittered through her fingertips and exploded inside her. His gaze fluttered intently down her face, lingering on her lips before lifting back to her eyes again.

He smiled. "I believe you promised the next dance to me," he said.

Nine

What must be shall be; and that which is a necessity to him that struggles, is little more than a choice to him that is willing.

—Seneca

IT WAS ON THE TIP OF GABRIELLE'S TONGUE TO SAY TO Lord Brentwood that she never promised him anything, but she stopped herself before speaking. It was brash of the viscount to assume she would play along with what was so obviously not true, rather than call his hand.

"I, ah, yes, I believe I did," she said, deciding she didn't want her friends to know Lord Brentwood was being brazenly forward, because she hadn't agreed to a dance.

He took her punch cup from her hand and placed it on a table behind him. "I haven't had the pleasure of meeting these two lovely ladies. Perhaps you would like to present them before we leave."

"Yes, please," Babs said and curtseyed.

"Yes, of course," she said, and then taking a deep breath, she presented Fern and Babs to Lord Brentwood.

A roguish grin made its way across Lord Brentwood's lips, intriguing Gabrielle so much she couldn't take her eyes off him. It was then she realized the scratch under his eye and cut on his lip had healed. In the deepest recesses of her abdomen, a quickening started and shuddered all the way up to her breasts and lingered there before moving on to her throat, tightening it. Would this man always make her feel this way every time she saw him? By the heavens, could he possibly know she had been completely enchanted by him since the moment she first saw him, and she was desperately trying to fight it?

Gabrielle had to find the strength to deny those wonderful feelings he always sparked inside her and plant her feet back on solid ground. If Staunton, who had been her fiancé for almost six months and had kissed her on more than one occasion, couldn't make her feel these wonderful sensations, how in heaven's name could the viscount?

After a few moments of chatting with Fern and Babs, Gabrielle and Lord Brentwood excused themselves and headed in the direction of the room that had been cleared of furniture and readied for dancing.

As soon as they were far enough away from her friends, Gabrielle looked over at the viscount and said, "I'm certain I didn't promise you a dance, my lord."

He glanced over at her and smiled. "No?"

She shook her head.

"Well, you should have. I'm a very good dancer. Besides, it's only a matter of time before your father returns and our engagement will be formally announced. Perhaps it's best I stake my claim on you now."

His choice of words stung. Why couldn't Lord Brentwood want to marry her because she made him feel all the wonderful things he had made her feel, and he wanted to feel them over and over again?

"The way you said that makes me sound like a piece of land, my lord."

"You are far more valuable to me than land, Lady Gabrielle."

It was clear he still thought that, as a duke's daughter, she would make him a perfect wife. She was going to do her best to change his mind about that. And if he considered himself a very good dancer, she might as well begin her plan on the dance floor.

"Ah, that's right," she said. "How could I have forgotten that as a duke's daughter, my dowry is considerable, and more important, I am the key to your brothers' business success, right?"

"All that is true, but as we discussed in your back garden, there are certainly many things that will make you an excellent choice for my wife."

Wanting to change the subject, she said, "I had hoped to receive word from you this week concerning Prissy's safe return home."

"I had no news to report. I would have sent you a note, as I promised, if I had."

That wasn't what Gabrielle wanted to hear. She knew how much he adored the little dog and, sadly, if she hadn't been found in a week, she probably wasn't going to be. It was best to change the subject again.

"I'm glad your face has completely healed since I last saw you."

He chuckled ruefully and touched the side of his

mouth with the back of his hand. "Yes, I now recognize myself when I look in the mirror."

She tried not to look at anyone as they walked side by side through the drawing room and into the music room where the dancing was to take place. But she couldn't completely shield her eyes from everyone. Though she was well aware the whispers behind the fans and hands were about her, she hoped no one would be ill-mannered enough to say anything about her while she was with the viscount, as the ladies had when she was with Babs and Fern.

They stopped at the edge of the dance floor, as the call to assemble on it hadn't been announced. Wanting to avoid the awkwardness of standing in silence, she said, "I don't know much about you, Lord Brentwood. I looked in copies of old newsprint for some mention of you in the Society Column and found none. I find that odd."

He smiled. "You admit you wanted to find out more about me?"

She eyed him curiously. "Yes, of course. Why shouldn't I?"

"You could have just asked."

"There has been precious little time for that when we've been together."

His lashes lowered, and his gaze fell to her lips. "I agree. We've always had other pressing matters to discuss, haven't we?"

Gabrielle's abdomen tightened. She refused to let her attraction to him overtake her again. She inhaled deeply, focused on remaining calm, and asked, "Is this your first visit to London?"

His gaze lingered for a moment longer on her mouth and then swept back up to her eyes. "Not the first, but I don't come often. There is much to keep me busy at my estate in Devonshire. On the whole, our lands are fertile, sheep and cattle are plentiful, and there are several surrounding villages. Certainly there are enough people, parties, and dinners to keep a much busier social life than I care to participate in."

"On occasion, I have traveled throughout England, Wales, and Scotland with my father, but I don't think I've ever been to your part of Devonshire."

"In that case, I'll look forward to showing it to you after we are married."

Suddenly, she could hardly wait to watch that cocksure attitude of his crumble. "I love London, my lord, and doubt I would ever be happy living in the country. With my father such an important figure in Parliament and advisor to the prince, we've never spent much time at any of our country homes. I'm sure I would get dreadfully lonely away from the shops, the plays, the opera, even the street lamps. I don't know what I would do if I couldn't take a walk in one of London's parks."

Lord Brentwood regarded her thoughtfully for a moment with his golden-brown eyes. "Nonsense. The Brentwood estate is surrounded by nature that is much more impressive than Hyde Park, St. James, or any of London's other parks. And believe me, Lady Gabrielle, you won't have to wade through all the people, horses, and carriages for your strolls. You won't see the street vendors, milk carts, or the traveling minstrel shows and carnivals that put up their tents around the parks. All you have is the beauty of nature, peace, and tranquility without the trappings of civilization."

The picture he was painting for her sounded divine, but she didn't want him to know that, so she gave him a queer look and offered, "But I want all that in my life, my lord. I enjoy civilization. I like seeing people and talking to them. I love to attend carnivals, circuses, and all the traveling shows that come to London."

The assembly was called while she was still speaking, so Lord Brentwood took hold of her hand and led her out onto the dance floor. "You will get used to the quietness of country life."

The old Gabrielle would have simply acquiesced to his statement and remained quiet, but she was no longer willing to be agreeable or dutiful simply for the sake of being the way others thought she should be. She said, "I don't want to get used to it, my lord. I want to be free to make my own decisions about where I shall live as well as whom I should marry."

"That decision was taken away from you when you were found in my arms, Lady Gabrielle."

She scoffed at his comment. "No, my lord. That decision was taken from me the moment I was born the duke's daughter."

They fell silent as other dancers took the floor and surrounded them. A short introduction was played, and Gabrielle realized they would be dancing the waltz. She would have much preferred the quadrille or an even faster dance, where there wouldn't have been the constant touching. But perhaps all was not lost. She would take this opportunity and use it to show him why she would not be a good wife for him.

He took her hand in his and then placed the other on her back, while she lifted hers and laid it on his broad, strong shoulder. The music started, and on the proper note, Lord Brentwood took a gliding step forward. Gabrielle purposefully didn't move her foot in time, and he stepped on her toes. He tried not to put his weight down on her and almost tripped himself trying to keep from hurting her.

"Ouch," she whispered, not realizing it would hurt so much to have him land on her foot.

"I'm terribly sorry," he said.

"No, no. It was my fault," she said and quickly missed another step, causing the viscount to step on her toes again.

"Nonsense," he said, trying to be polite. "I'll take smaller steps."

As soon as he said the words, she stepped on his foot. "I'm sorry," she said and then took a huge step backward and deliberately bumped into the couple behind her.

Lord Brentwood quickly guided her away from the middle of the dance floor and to the outer edge of the dancers. "I just assumed you would know how to waltz," he said.

She had to bite her bottom lip to keep from smiling when she saw the confused look on his face.

"I do," she said honestly. "Perhaps I'm simply not as good at it as you are. I used to be a very good dancer, but tonight I seem to have two left feet."

"Don't give it another thought," he mumbled. "We'll muddle through."

And so they did. Trying not to dance properly

wasn't as easy as Gabrielle thought it would be. She had been dancing since she was a young girl, and it was second nature to her. She could waltz as gracefully as anyone, so she had to pay close attention to the beat of the music so she could deliberately miss steps. At one point, she started forward rather than stepping back. She remembered how irritating it was once when she danced with a young man who counted the steps under his breath, so she whispered, "One, two, three, four, one, two, three, four," in time to the beat of the music.

She knew her constant mumbling had gotten to him when he said, "Lady Gabrielle, if you will just concentrate on following me, there will be no need for you to count the steps."

"Oh," she said and gave him a sheepish smile. It made her feel positively wonderful to be in control of the dance and to cause him a few moments of frustration.

By the time the music stopped, her toes were hurting from being mashed by Lord Brentwood's much larger feet, and she was certain her beige satin pumps would be beyond repair; still she smiled. All in all, it was a small price to pay if it helped the viscount see that she would be far from a perfect wife for him.

Lord Brentwood bowed, and she curtseyed before they left the dance floor.

When she looked into his eyes, a warm, tingling sensation washed over her, and that made her feel a bit guilty for having deceived him, even though it was necessary. "I'm sorry I didn't waltz very well."

He studied her face for a moment before he leaned forward just a fraction, lowered his voice, and said,

"Not a problem, Lady Gabrielle, I'll see to it you have a few more lessons after we marry, and soon you will be outdancing even the most accomplished dancer."

That wasn't what she expected to hear. Suddenly a charming light glinted in his eyes. There was something about the way he looked at her that led her to believe he might know she had only been pretending not to know how to waltz.

"I see my brothers have arrived at the party. Do you mind coming with me to meet them?"

Gabrielle looked in the direction of his gaze and saw the two tall and powerfully built men entering the drawing room. They were the epitome of identical twins, from their same height, coloring, and features, to every detail of their evening clothing being exact in color and style.

"Not at all," she said. "Your brothers are very handsome."

A queer expression settled on his face. "You think they are handsome?"

"Very much so, don't you?"

He laughed. "I suppose I do."

"They look so much alike, how do you tell them apart?"

"In appearance, even I have trouble telling them apart sometimes unless one is wearing his hair longer than the other, as they are now. If you'll notice, Iverson's hair is a little longer in back than Matson's."

"Thank you for telling me the difference," she said, studying the two men. "But I do believe what others are saying to be true. From this distance, they look nothing like you."

"Really? I always thought I was a handsome blade, too."

Gabrielle gasped. "Oh, I'm sorry. That's not what I meant. You are quite handsome, too. I meant they—"

His eyes sparkled with laughter, and he said, "I know what you meant. My brothers take after our mother's side of the family instead of our father's."

"Yes, I'm sure," she said, grateful he hadn't taken offense at her offhanded comment and seemed more than willing to laugh off her reference to the fact the twins looked nothing like their older brother.

He stopped and looked at her for a moment before they reached the gentlemen. "One thing I would ask of you. My brothers don't know of your father's threat to ruin their business. I want to keep it that way."

"If you wish, but why is it so important to you?"

"Because if they knew, they would move heaven and earth to prove your father wrong and make their business prosper. I would rather not get a war going between your father and my brothers, and I don't think you want that either."

"Heavens, no."

"Then we are in agreement that it won't be mentioned."

"Absolutely, and just so you know, I never planned to mention it."

He grinned and said, "And I didn't think you would, but I had to be certain."

The viscount presented Mr. Iverson Brentwood and Mr. Matson Brentwood to her. It wasn't just the longer length of Iverson's hair that made him different from Matson. She sensed something about his air of nonchalance that immediately told her this man was a rogue of the highest order. Mr. Iverson Brentwood looked her directly in the eyes and lifted his chin slightly, as if to challenge her to try to figure him out, but she had no desire to do so. She greeted him pleasantly and then turned her attention to the more affable Mr. Matson Brentwood. The last thing Gabrielle wanted to do was to match wits with another roguish Brentwood.

"I've heard a lot about you, Lady Gabrielle," Mr. Matson Brentwood said with a much more engaging smile than his twin.

Gabrielle returned his smile. "Would that be from Lord Brentwood, the gossips, or from the scandal sheets?"

He chuckled. "All three."

She smiled. "Judging by some of the gossip I've heard about myself tonight, I can only imagine the kind of wagers that must be going on at White's and other clubs about me and Lord Brentwood."

Matson gave a quick glance to Lord Brentwood, as if to ask if the subject was acceptable, before he answered. "It's true there are quite a few, but Iverson and I are not strangers to scandal ourselves. Perhaps you've heard some of the gossip about us."

"Yes, more than once, but I never put stock in gossip." She looked over at Lord Brentwood and said, "Besides, now that I've gotten a closer look at the two of you, I can tell that both of you look just like Lord Brentwood."

Matson lifted his eyebrows and quirked his head slightly to the side. "Really?"

Iverson added, "If true, you are the first to think that." He looked over at Brentwood and asked, "Does she wear spectacles when she's not at parties?"

Lord Brentwood grinned. "Perhaps that is why I have such a difficult time getting her to see things my way."

While his brothers laughed at his remark, Gabrielle smiled and took the time to look each of them in the eyes before she answered Mr. Iverson Brentwood with, "How could you not favor? All three of you are tall, powerful-looking, and handsome."

Lord Brentwood and his brothers laughed again, and Gabrielle was suddenly aware of how natural it seemed for her to be so at ease with these three gentlemen.

"There you are, Lord Brentwood, I've been looking for you. I simply must speak with you about a pressing matter."

Gabrielle turned to see the Earl of Snellingly walking up to them, holding a lace handkerchief in one hand and a small leather-bound book in the other. The points of his collar were so stiff and high, his head was cocked back in an odd-looking position. His neckcloth looked to be tied in a fancy triple bow with wide ends that flared and covered a good portion of his dark pink waistcoat. The cuffs of his shirt had so many layers of lace, his fingertips were barely visible.

After proper introductions to the twins, who promptly excused themselves, Lord Snellingly turned to Gabrielle and, taking her hand in his, said, "Every time I see you, you remind me of a slice of warm sunshine on a cold and dreary day."

He bent and kissed the back of her gloved hand.

Gabrielle worried he might choke himself, because his collar looked so tight.

"Thank you, my lord," Gabrielle said as she slowly pulled her hand from his grasp.

Lord Brentwood eyed the earl warily and moved closer to Gabrielle. "What was it you wanted to see me about, Snellingly?"

"Oh, yes," Lord Snellingly said and then sniffed into his handkerchief as he took a step closer to the viscount. "Pardon me for interrupting your tête-à-tête with the most charming Lady Gabrielle, my lord, but her beauty made me forget my sorrow for a moment. I thought perhaps you could help me, as we have the same troubles."

Lord Brentwood's eyes drew together with curiosity. "What's that?"

"My darling little spaniel, Josephine, ran away from me yesterday morning, and I haven't been able to find her. I heard you have been walking the parks and streets for a week, annoying everyone, trying to find your dog. I thought perhaps you might have seen her."

The viscount's eyes darkened and narrowed. His shoulders shifted. "Did you say I've been annoying everyone?"

"Annoying? No, no." The earl's eyes widened, and he sniffed again. "Well, yes, I might have said that, but forgive me. I'm sure I meant to say asking everyone. You've been asking everyone, and no, surely not everyone, but some people. Again, forgive me, my lord, as I'm overwrought because Josephine hasn't returned home yet. Please tell me you have seen her."

Lord Brentwood took a step back. "Naturally I've seen several stray dogs in the park, but I don't recall seeing a spaniel."

Lord Snellingly rolled his eyes up and put his hand to his forehead. "Oh, it pains me to hear you say that. Are you quite sure? Her coat is an exquisite shade of cream with a smattering of golden-brown spots on her back and a large one that circles down the side of her face and over her left ear. She has a good disposition, seldom barks, and is sweet and loving to everyone she meets."

"I'm sure she is. I haven't seen Josephine, but if I do I'll catch her and bring her to you."

"Thank you. You don't think it's true what some people are saying about Lord Pinkwater's ghost, do you? Do you think he has stolen our dogs and is keeping them for himself?"

Lord Brentwood shifted his stance restlessly and cleared his throat before saying, "I can assure you that is not the case with Prissy, Lord Snellingly."

"Then what has happened to them?" he asked, a nervous twitch attacking one of his eyes. "It's as if they've simply disappeared into thin air. I think it could be true. I've heard Lord Pinkwater was quite fond of dogs when he was alive. I don't think I could bear it if I knew my sweet little Josephine was living with a ghost and couldn't get back to me."

Lord Brentwood glanced at Gabrielle with an expression that seemed to be asking, "Where did this fop come from?" Lord Brentwood was clearly not interested in having the ghost conversation with the earl. Gabrielle knew it was time to direct the conversation in a different direction.

"Perhaps there is a dog thief in town, Lord Snellingly," Gabrielle said. "Perhaps someone is taking the dogs."

The earl frowned and looked from Gabrielle to Lord Brentwood. "For what purpose would they? The only thing I can think of is if they wanted to use them for such dastardly deeds as experiments for some insane alchemist or depraved physician, or perhaps to be fed to other animals."

Gabrielle's eyes widened in shock at the earl's inappropriate comments. She glanced over at Lord Brentwood, whose frown had deepened to anger.

She quickly said, "No, my lord, such things as that never entered my mind. I meant someone who wanted to love the dogs and care for them, of course. Dogs such as the quality of your Josephine and Lord Brentwood's Prissy are highly sought after as pets. Surely you know that."

"Yes, yes, of course, pardon me, my dear." Lord Snellingly sniffed into his handkerchief and took the book he held in the other hand and placed it over his heart. "It's just that no one could love Josephine as I do. No one. I've written a poem about her. Since you are both so fond of dogs, I'll recite it for you."

Without giving either Gabrielle or Lord Brentwood time to object or retreat, Lord Snellingly looked up toward the ceiling and said:

"With shining black eyes and fast dancing feet
My beloved Josephine is no longer mine to greet
Take my wife, take my wine
I shall never once repine

Take my breath and all sunshine
Take my health and my wealth
But not my darling Josephine's yelp
My yearning is deep, intense, and fatal."

Gabrielle gasped and interrupted him. "Surely you don't mean fatal, Lord Snellingly?"

He looked down at her. "Oh, not as in death, of course not." He sniffed in his handkerchief again. "But I don't know how I shall live without my sweet little companion. I thought perhaps coming to this party tonight might cheer me, but the only thing that really helps is my poetry. Shall I recite another for you?"

"Excuse me, Lord Snellingly," Lord Brentwood said. "I see someone I must speak to before they leave. But please do recite another poem for Lady Gabrielle. I have it on good authority she adores poetry almost as much as she loves dogs." He turned to Gabrielle with a mischievous grin, and in a low-pitched voice that sounded far too intimate and much too cocky, he said, "Lady Gabrielle, thank you for the dance; now enjoy the poetry."

There was no way in hell Brent was going to listen to another word from that sniveling fop. He wanted to get as far away from the man as he could, but Lady Gabrielle deserved to listen to more of the obnoxious man's dreadful poetry. Brent loved the look of shock on her face when he turned away.

He chuckled when he heard:

"Happy bark, wagging tail..."

Brent smiled to himself as he made his way through the crowd in search of drink or his brothers, whichever came first. He couldn't imagine what had made Lady Gabrielle pretend she couldn't dance. Her feet must be killing her. He must have stepped on her toes at least five or six times.

Ah, but she was beautiful. The moment he saw her tonight, he wanted to pull her into his arms and kiss her. She was stunning in that pink velvet gown. When he'd brought her into his embrace for the waltz, it took all his willpower not to pull her up close and hug her to his chest. He watched her lips when she talked, and all he could think was that he wanted to kiss her until she surrendered to his will.

Someone tapped Brent on the shoulder, and he turned around just in time to see a fist heading straight for his face. He tried to duck, but the punch was so unexpected, he didn't have time to react fast enough. The fist landed on the corner of his mouth that had just healed. Brent stumbled backward and bumped into someone, who gasped. Somehow, he managed to catch his footing and didn't hit the floor. In his younger years, Brent had been in one or two fights at tavern brawls, and he'd matched his fists against others at notable boxing salons, but he couldn't ever remember being caught off guard.

Brent's right hand closed tightly, and his arm flew back, ready to take on his attacker. He stopped short when the irate man was quickly grabbed by a couple of other men. He was held back when he lunged forward at Brent again. Brent's fist clenched nervously, tightening, itching to knock the man's teeth down his throat, but Brent couldn't hit a man whose arms were being held behind his back.

"Let go of me," the stranger yelled. "I want to hit him again!"

"No, Staunton!" said one of the men holding him. "Stop this madness."

The name Staunton reverberated in Brent's ears as his breaths came fast and hard.

Lady Gabrielle's former fiancé.

Now Brent knew why the man had attacked him. Brent's fist relaxed a little, and he lowered his arm. He supposed he'd be fighting mad, too, if their situations were reversed, but Brent doubted he would have waited a week to punch any blade who dared to touch his fiancée. And he sure as hell wouldn't have resorted to such a cowardly strike to an unsuspecting man.

With his thumb, Brent wiped blood from the corner of his mouth and fixed the man with a cold stare. "I suppose I deserved that."

"You're bloody right you did," Staunton said, struggling to free himself from the men who held him. "You deserve to be run through with a sword for what you did."

Brent looked at Staunton. He seemed to be close to Brent's age but not nearly as tall or as big. To engage someone almost twice his size, the man had to be either courageous or have a whole jug of whiskey in his stomach. A crowd had gathered around them and was quickly growing larger by the second.

"Perhaps," Brent said calmly, "that one makes us even, but if you want to try your hand at getting ahead, I'm ready. Let's take this fight out of Lady Windham's house and into the park."

"No, he's through," said the oldest man who held Staunton.

"I'm not," Staunton said bitterly. "I insist on meeting him in the park."

"You can't. Your father will disinherit you if you have another fight. You've had too much to drink, and you're not thinking properly. Now come on, and let's get out of here before you cause more trouble for yourself and everyone else."

Staunton jerked free of the men and pulled on the tail of his coat before walking past Brent, deliberately knocking against Brent's shoulder as he did. Brent started to grab the man and give him the fight he was looking for, but as his arm drew back, he saw Lady Gabrielle forcing her way through the crowd with Iverson right behind her. In that split second, he knew the last thing he, Lady Gabrielle, or his brothers needed or wanted was more scandal. And certainly Lady Windham didn't deserve an all-out brawl in her drawing room.

"My lord, what happened?" Lady Gabrielle asked, stopping in front of him.

"Nothing worth talking about, Lady Gabrielle," he said, knowing he needed to say as little as possible and leave with even less fanfare, as his brothers would say.

"Are you all right?" Iverson asked, scowling as he moved to stand beside him.

Brent nodded.

"You are not all right," Lady Gabrielle said, her features marred with concern. "Your lip is bleeding. Tell me what happened to you."

"I'll tell you," someone called from the crowd. "Mr. Alfred Staunton punched him in the mouth."

Her eyes rounded with horror and concern. "Did he?" she said. She stepped closer to him and whispered, "Did you provoke him, my lord?"

A half laugh passed his aching lip. He wanted to say, *Yes, Lady Gabrielle, I provoked him by taking you in my arms and kissing and touching you so thoroughly that still I cannot get the taste of you off my tongue, the scent of you from my nose, or wash the feel of you from my hands.* But that wasn't the kind of thing a gentleman said in front of a crowd that was getting larger by the second.

He couldn't continue standing there, talking to Lady Gabrielle or his brother, and feeding the gossips.

"All is well, Lady Gabrielle," he insisted firmly, wiping blood from the corner of his mouth with the back of his hand. "I'll pick you up for our afternoon ride in the park on Wednesday as planned."

Her brow wrinkled. "We planned no—"

"As we planned," he interrupted in a low voice. "Now, if you'll excuse me, I need to bid our hostess farewell."

Ten

There is delicious scandal brewing in London as more than feet hit the dance floor at a well-attended soirée last night. It was told that Viscount Brentwood and Mr. Alfred Staunton met for the first time and, before the party was over, one of them left seeing fireworks behind his eyes and the other being helped out the door by his friends. And Lady Gabrielle left without a word.

—Lord Truefitt, *Society's Daily Column*

WOULD THE SCANDALS NEVER STOP?

Brent wadded the newsprint and threw it at the draperies. Hell and damnation to the beast who wrote that rubbish. Brent would like to get his hands on whoever the hell Lord Truefitt was, and wipe up the dance floor with him. Brent had been in London less than two fortnights, and either he or his brothers had been in that blasted scandal sheet every morning since they arrived. It was no wonder his mother never allowed any of London's newsprint in the house. And if Truefitt was really a lord, a titled gentleman of Polite Society, he wouldn't stoop to write such drivel.

He didn't even know why he bothered to look at it, other than he started looking at the column as a way to keep up with what the gossips were saying about his brothers. Brent had wanted Truefitt to stop writing about his brothers, but he never thought he'd be the latest scandal to take their place.

Brent pushed his chair back from the breakfast table and walked over to the buffet. He had very little appetite for the scrambled eggs, large pieces of ham, and fresh baked bread that filled the silver platters. Since he returned home from Lady Windham's house last night, only two things had been on his mind: Staunton and Lady Gabrielle. He spent half his sleepless night wanting to smash Staunton's face with his fist and the other half dying to kiss Lady Gabrielle again. How could he have become so bewitched by her and so quickly?

The slam of a door and the commotion of boots stomping on floors and chatter alerted Brent that his brothers had arrived. The twins made their way over to have the morning meal with him three or four times a week. He wasn't up to their banter this morning. No doubt they wanted to talk about what happened last night. But Brent wouldn't be talking.

He heard their heavy footfalls on the hardwood floors of the corridor and watched the doorway as first Matson and then Iverson appeared.

"Are we interrupting your breakfast?" Iverson asked as he leaned against the doorjamb.

"Not at all. I was expecting you, and you're late," Brent said and dipped into the eggs. "I'd decided you weren't going to come today, so I started to eat without you."

"We can't have that," Matson said, walked over to the buffet, and picked up a plate. Iverson headed for the silver coffeepot and poured himself a cup.

When their plates were full and all were seated at the table, Matson asked, "How's your lip this morning?"

"Hurts like the devil," Brent said, cutting into his ham. "But I'll live."

"What are you going to do about Staunton waylaying you at the party?" Iverson asked.

"Nothing."

"Why?" Iverson asked as he spread fig preserves on his toast.

"Because the man's a coward," Brent muttered. "And I have no use for cowards."

"I agree with that assessment," Matson said. "If Staunton had wanted to fight you, he should have called you out like a gentleman for a fair fight, not ambush you like a thief in the night."

"Right," Iverson said. "He's an earl's son and should act like one."

"Maybe Brent feels the retaliation from Staunton was justified; after all, he did steal his fiancée away from him."

"And now that we've met both of them, I can understand why you had no qualms about doing it. She's lovely and charming and surely doesn't deserve a sniveling coward."

Brent smiled to himself and kept quiet while he buttered his bread. If they only knew he'd had no choice about that meeting in the park with Lady Gabrielle. She had enraptured him the moment she walked out of the mist. But there was no reason to tell his brothers what happened that morning.

"There is something good that has come from this," Matson said.

"I'd like to know what it is," Brent argued and then winced as he tried to open his mouth wide enough to bite into the thick piece of bread.

"Oh, not for you, for us." Iverson grinned, reached down, and picked up the wadded newsprint from the floor. "You usurped us in Lord Truefitt's society column."

"And I feel slighted," Matson added.

"Like hell you do," Brent grumbled.

Iverson threw the wadded newsprint over to Matson. "He's an ungrateful blade, isn't he?"

Matson and Iverson laughed, and they ate in silence for a while until Matson said, "Lady Gabrielle has much to recommend her. She's beautiful, intelligent, and not without good humor."

"Mmm," Brent said, thankful his mouth was full. If it hadn't been, he might have been tempted to add that she was also enchanting, seductive, and very, very passionate.

"From all the eligible young ladies I've seen at the parties so far, you have picked the loveliest one."

She picked me.

And Brent still wanted to know why. One of the men who held the earl's son last night indicated that

Staunton had been in more than one fight. Men who couldn't control their rage turned into beasts and would strike out at anyone. Brent couldn't help but wonder if the man had ever harmed or threatened to harm Gabrielle. That thought twisted Brent's stomach, and he pushed his plate away. It would certainly explain why she would risk kissing a stranger and getting caught in order to keep from marrying him.

"Why do you always suddenly get so quiet when one of us mentions Lady Gabrielle?" Iverson asked.

Because a gentleman never tells.

Brent ignored the question and said, "It's true Lady Gabrielle is the loveliest young lady in London, but keep in mind, Brothers, that many families are not even in Town at this time of year. By far most of them have retired to their country homes and estates to spend the winter and Christmas. They will only come back to Town in time for the Season next year."

Iverson looked up from his plate. "So there will be more delectable young ladies to choose from come spring?"

"They will be buzzing about like bees after flowers," Brent said.

"Another reason to hurry spring," Matson said and then added, "I suppose you would have told us immediately if there had been any good news about Prissy."

Brent looked up at his brother. "You know I would. There hasn't even been a response from the newsprint notice."

"Tell me," Matson asked, "did you hear about Lord

Snellingly's missing dog and that he actually thinks a ghost might have taken it?"

"Believe me, I heard more than I wanted to from that man," Brent said and couldn't keep the smile from his face as he remembered the shocked look on Lady Gabrielle's face when he left her with the earl. That should keep her from ever pretending again she didn't know how to dance.

"There was also talk that there might be a particularly vicious animal prowling the darkness of Hyde and St. James," Matson continued. "Perhaps a wild boar. They can grow quite large."

"But they don't usually bother dogs," Iverson added. "Still, strange occurrences happen from time to time. Some of the men have discussed getting a hunting party together."

Brent didn't want to think about the possibility of Prissy's meeting a wild boar. That impish dog had no fear and would challenge an animal of any shape or size.

Iverson added, "I also heard the carnival that set up camp on the south end of Town last month hasn't moved on like it usually does. Someone thought perhaps one of their big animals might have escaped."

"If that was the case, everyone in London would be in danger, not just small dogs," Matson said. "I can't see anyone hiding something as dangerous as that. Besides, isn't it late in the year for traveling carnivals and fairs to still be around?"

"Seems to me it is, but you never know what makes them linger. I suppose they have to winter somewhere and make a little money. Someone was going to pay the owner a visit and see what they could find out about their menagerie."

"Enough about the gossip and last night, Brothers," Brent said, not wanting to dwell on what might have happened to Prissy. He'd heard more than enough from Lord Snellingly last night. "Tell me how it is going for you two on finding a building space near the docks to house your business."

Matson laid down his fork and pushed his empty plate aside. "We've found a couple of places we are interested in, but there's one problem."

"A big problem," Iverson added.

"What's that?" Brent said warily.

"No doubt they've all heard the rumors about you and Lady Gabrielle."

Brent didn't need to hear more but said, "And?"

"We think they are waiting to see what the duke has to say about you, and apparently he is out of town."

"How much time do you have?"

"Not much," Matson said. "As soon as we arrived in London, we sent a letter to our man in Baltimore and told him to load up all our equipment, machinery, everything, including any of the workers who wanted to leave America, and set sail."

"But we aren't letting anything stop us from securing a place to house our business," Iverson said. "We'll find something, and we'll be ready when the ship gets here."

Brent picked up his coffee cup and sipped. He had believed the duke when he'd told him he could keep his brothers from having a successful business in London, and throughout England for that matter.

Brent had never doubted Lady Gabrielle's father, but now his brothers had just given him proof.

❧

The rain came down at a steady drizzle and so did Gabrielle's thoughts of Lord Brentwood. Neither had stopped all day. Even though the fireplace was lit, there was a cold chill to the house as she sat by the drawing-room window, her needlework in her still hands and Brutus snoring heavily on his pillow.

She had worried herself silly wondering what had been said between Lord Brentwood and Staunton and couldn't wait until tomorrow so she could ask the viscount. She had wanted to stay at Lady Windham's and hear what everyone had to say about what happened between the two men, but her aunt, sensing more scandal in the making, had hurried her out of the house. Fern had sent her a note, saying she heard Staunton had punched the viscount in the mouth, but that the viscount was a perfect gentleman and had refused to be drawn into a fight in Lady Windham's house. Gabrielle already knew that much.

She was considering the possibility of confronting Staunton and letting him know what a hypocrite she thought him to be. He had some gall to attack Lord Brentwood for being alone with her when he had been guilty of doing the same thing with her sister.

And when she wasn't worrying about the tussle between the two gentlemen, she was smiling over the fact that Lord Brentwood had the audacity to leave her with the insufferable Lord Snellingly. She should be furious he had the nerve to smile at her after he told the earl she would love to hear more of his dreadful poetry, but she wasn't. She was amused the viscount was so clever. She certainly hadn't wanted Staunton to hit Lord Brentwood, but it had been useful in getting her away from the pompous earl.

Just thinking about Lord Brentwood made Gabrielle smile. He was such a striking figure in his formal evening coat, slim-legged trousers, and buckled shoes. And she couldn't help but be impressed that no matter how many times she missed steps on the dance floor, he never once became annoyed with her. She couldn't imagine her father or Staunton being so accepting of a lady who couldn't dance.

Gabrielle looked out the foggy windowpane and continued her dreams of Lord Brentwood. She remembered how eagerly she had anticipated seeing him, how fast her heart beat at the sight of him, and the feeling of those wondrous sensations low in her abdomen and across her breasts when his hand touched hers as they stepped onto the dance floor. She loved the feel of his strong embrace as he guided them through the steps of the complicated waltz. And as much as she hated to admit it to herself, she could hardly wait for the day of their afternoon in the park.

"There you are, Gabby," Rosa said, hurrying into the room. "I didn't see you at first. What are you doing over here in the corner?"

Gabrielle smiled, picked up her embroidery from her lap, and held it up. "Does this give you a hint?"

Rosa looked down at it and said, "Oh, yes. Nice stitches. Would you take the time to read this and give me your opinion?"

Gabrielle laid her work on the table by the lamp, took the sheet of foolscap from Rosa, and read:

> *My Dearest Staunton,*
> *I have missed you and long to see you.*
> *Where and when can we meet?*
> *I wait for word from you.*
> *Your forever love*

A feeling of dread settled over Gabrielle. She looked up into Rosabelle's young, eager eyes. She saw a raw desperation in her sister's face that worried her.

"Rosa, I don't think you want to send this note."

Rosabelle's mouth tightened. "Of course I do."

Gabrielle knew she had to be careful with what she said. "What if it falls into the wrong hands?"

An irritated wrinkle formed on Rosa's brow. "What if it does? I didn't sign it. Staunton will know it's from me, but no one else will."

Gabrielle rose from her chair. "True, but it is very risky for you to suggest the two of you should plan to meet in secret."

"Yes, but it can be done."

Treading lightly, Gabrielle asked, "Has he contacted you?"

Rosa bit down on her bottom lip and then said, "No, I haven't heard from him in over two weeks, and I don't know why. I think I'll go completely mad if I don't see him soon."

"You might well, but this secrecy is not the way to see him. Auntie and I will be going to Mr. and Mrs. Cuddlebury's dinner party on Saturday night. Staunton will probably be there too. I think you should plan to attend with us and see him there, as is proper."

"What? That's almost a week away, Gabby. I can't wait that long. I won't wait that long." Rosabelle snatched the note from Gabrielle's hand. "I should have known you wouldn't understand, and you wouldn't want me to see him."

Her belligerence startled Gabrielle. "Rosa—"

"No, don't say it," Rosa demanded. "You always say you understand, but you never do, Gabby. You have always been jealous of me, and now you are jealous of Staunton's love for me."

Gabrielle was speechless for a moment. "That is simply not true. I'm happy you have found true love."

"Then why don't you want me to see him?" she asked petulantly.

Gabrielle was trying to hold on to her patience. "I don't care if you see him. I want you to see him. Just not in secret. I asked that you go with us to Lady Windham's last night. Staunton was there, and you could have seen him the proper way."

Rosabelle's eyes widened, and her face instantly changed from peevish resentment to eager delight. She grabbed Gabrielle's hands in hers and asked, "What did he say, Gabby? Did he ask about me? I know he did. Oh, I could just scream at myself! Why didn't I go?"

"Rosa, settle down. I saw him only from a distance as he was leaving. I didn't speak to him."

"Did the poor dear look absolutely miserable, like me? He's probably pining away for me. I must see him soon or I shall die."

"And you shall see him, Rosa, but it has to be under the proper circumstances. You cannot meet him in secret."

"Of course I can." She dropped Gabrielle's hands as if they were a hot poker. "You've done it. You met with Lord Brentwood in the park while you were still engaged to Staunton, so I don't think I need any lectures from you."

Gabrielle's shoulders stiffened. "I told you that was a chance meeting and not by design."

"But no one believes you, including me."

Her words angered Gabrielle. "That's not true, Rosa."

"Of course it is, but it's all right. I've met with Staunton in secret before and no one caught us. I will do it again if I so desire. It's time you realize, Gabby, that you are not my mother. I don't need you telling me what I can or cannot do. Furthermore, I'm old enough to make my own decisions without your help."

Rosabelle turned and started to run from the room, but stopped short and looked back at Gabrielle. "And if you dare tell Papa about me and Staunton," she said, "I will never speak to you again as long as I live."

Gabrielle gasped again as Rosa stomped from the room.

What was she going to do? The last thing Gabrielle wanted was for Rosabelle to have to endure rude comments and outrageous rumors from stuffy old

ladies. Was it finally time for her to confess everything
to her father? No, her father would not understand
Rosabelle's behavior at all.

But it was time for Gabrielle to have a talk with
Staunton. He was older and wiser than Rosa, and
he would have to make her see that they could not
continue to meet in secret. If he truly loved her,
he had to know how impetuous she was and how
dangerous it was for the two of them to have an affair.
Since he didn't seem to know what the sensible thing
was for them to do, she would tell him. He must stand
up to his father and hers and demand that the two of
them be allowed to go ahead and be married, or at the
very least be engaged.

But when to talk to him was the problem.

Should she wait until the Cuddlebury's party next
week and try to talk to him there? No, even if he
attended there would be too many opportunities for
interruptions, prying ears, and more gossip. And it
might be too late. Rosabelle had a bee in her bonnet,
and there was no time to waste.

Gabrielle would send her own letter to Staunton,
but unlike Rosa, she would sign her letter. She left
her needlework on the table, went to the secretary in
the drawing room, and sat down. She opened a drawer
and took out a quill, ink jar, and a sheet of vellum,
and wrote:

> *Staunton,*
>   *I find it is necessary that I should talk to you*
> *about an important matter as soon as possible. I*
> *would be most grateful if you would please respond*

*with a date and time that would be good for you so
we might meet in Hyde or St. James Park. I await
your answer.*

With all regards,
Gabby

❧

Brent stepped out of the pouring rain and into the
warmth of the Harbor Lights Club. A stiff-looking
attendant approached him, staring at the swelling
on the side of Brent's mouth. No doubt he wasn't
used to seeing many gentlemen coming into the
establishment with a fat lip. Brent ignored his scrutiny
and handed the man his wet coat, hat, umbrella,
and gloves, and explained who he was and that he
wasn't a member of the club but was to meet Sir
Randolph Gibson in the taproom. When Brent
said he was Viscount Brentwood, the man's attitude
changed immediately, and at the mention of Sir
Randolph's name, the attendant's face lighted with
a smile.

The man handed Brent's soggy garments off to
another person, and then he led Brent down a dimly
lit corridor. They passed more than one room where
he heard loud talking, laughter, and billiard balls
smacking together. For a small club, it seemed to
have a lively atmosphere. The man stopped in the
doorway of the taproom and pointed to a finely
dressed gentleman who was seated at a table by the
front window that opened to the busy street.

He'd seen Sir Randolph at a couple of different
parties over the past month, and there was no

way Brent wouldn't have known the man. Matson and Iverson's resemblance to him was stunning. Sir Randolph had been presented to Brent at a party, though they hadn't really spoken, other than the perfunctory greetings that civility required. Unlike his meeting with Mr. Alfred Staunton, both Brent and Sir Randolph had behaved as gentlemen, and neither had said a word about what was really on their minds. The man had readily accepted when Brent sent him a note suggesting they meet.

Brent could understand his brothers' wanting to ignore the fact they looked just like the man and simply get on with their lives. That's what Brent wanted for them, but he also wanted more. He wanted to see where Sir Randolph stood with the twins. It wasn't that Brent didn't think his brothers could handle any situation that might come up; it was mainly his vow to his mother that he would keep up with them and, if need be, help them.

Sir Randolph Gibson was staring out the window, though Brent had no idea what he might be looking at. The rain was now pouring down in torrential sheets, and no one was on the walkways. When Brent had been out, it was too gloomy and murky even to see the coaches as they passed him on the streets.

Brent remained where he was for a moment, watching the man. From what he'd learned from the runner he'd hired from Bow Street, Sir Randolph was in his sixties, though he hardly looked a day over fifty. He was a tall, robust, handsome fellow, with a thatch of silver hair that most men his age would envy.

Apparently there were three gentlemen, cousins in fact—a duke, a marquis, and an earl—who watched after the old man and had saved him from losing his wealth to such risky ventures as a hot air balloon travel business and a time machine. Earlier in the year, the old man had even been involved in some kind of boxing match over a spinster's honor. The runner couldn't find out much about that, but said shortly after the fight—which somehow the old man had won—the lady and her brother had left London.

The runner said Sir Randolph inherited his considerable wealth. His father had struck it rich in the shipping business when England was still trying to maintain control of its colonies across the sea. The war that followed made the old sea merchant a wealthy man, and it all went to Sir Randolph when his father died.

Brent didn't know any of the three gentlemen who watched over Sir Randolph. No doubt the man's substantial estate and no legitimate heirs were the main reasons the cousins, who had no blood relation to him, were so eager to step in and take care of him when needed.

The most interesting thing he'd been told was that over the years, Sir Randolph Gibson had been constantly sought after by ladies young and old, widows, innocents, and spinsters, too, all wanting to better their station in life by becoming his wife. But according to the runner, no one had ever caught his fancy enough for him to propose matrimony. According to rumor, Sir Randolph held solidly to the fact that the deceased Lady Elder, who was married four times but never to Sir Randolph, was the only woman he'd ever loved. But obviously she wasn't the only lady he'd ever made love to. Matson and Iverson were testament to that.

With that thought, Brent entered the room and headed toward the table by the window.

Sir Randolph rose from the table and bowed. "My lord."

"Sir Randolph," Brent said, pulled out the chair opposite the man, and sat down.

"What are you drinking?" Sir Randolph asked as a server approached.

"Ale will do," Brent said and waited for the server to walk away before adding, "I suppose you are wondering why I wanted you to meet me today."

Sir Randolph shook his head as he folded his arms across his chest. "No, I didn't wonder at all. I figured I knew."

"My brothers," Brent said.

Sir Randolph nodded.

"I'm afraid they are not as worried as I am by the fact they look so much like you."

A sparkle lit in his brown gaze and he quipped, "Would it help if I shaved my head and grew a beard?"

Liking the twinkle of humor in the old man's eyes, Brent smiled. Only a few words out of his mouth and already he had disarmed Brent. It was no wonder Sir Randolph had caught his mother's attention. Brent would have to be careful around the distinguished-looking dandy. Clearly, the sly old goat was cunning and clever enough to know how to win over his enemies.

Trying not to let Sir Randolph know that, so far, he was impressed with him, Brent said, "I think it's a little late for that, don't you?"

"I suppose it is," Sir Randolph answered, some of the sheen fading from his eyes. "I guess that would have worked only if I had known the twins were coming to Town."

"So you knew about my brothers?"

Remaining unflustered, Sir Randolph nodded again and said, "Of course. I knew your parents had three sons."

"Did you know two of them look like you?"

"I had never seen them until they arrived in Town a few weeks ago."

Brent shifted in his chair and said, "Have you kept up with my brothers over the years?"

Sir Randolph's gaze stayed steady on Brent's. "That wasn't my place to do, my lord."

He was cagey, answering every question but giving little information. Brent started to ask, *But did you know they were your sons? Did you and my mother or my father ever talk about the fact that they are your sons?* But Brent held his tongue, not knowing if he really wanted to know that much about what went on with his parents and Sir Randolph.

The server approached, and Brent waited until he'd placed his drink on the table and turned away, before saying, "What I really want to know, Sir Randolph, is if there will be more scandal coming."

A genuine look of puzzlement wrinkled the dandy's forehead, narrowed his eyes, and tightened his lips. "I'm not sure I know what you mean by that comment."

Brent picked up his ale and took a sip. The tankard hit his bruised lip, and he stifled a wince. Every time it pained him, he thought about how good it would feel to pummel Mr. Alfred Staunton's face into the ground.

"Then let me be forthright with you, Sir Randolph," Brent said, placing his ale back on the table. He looked the man coldly and directly in the eyes, wanting to make sure there would be no misunderstanding as to what he had to say. "I do not want to wake one morning and find you have blabbed to every scandal sheet and gossipmonger in the ton about your clandestine affair with my mother almost thirty years ago, because if you do, I will pay you a visit."

Sir Randolph jerked back as if Brent had struck him. Wide-eyed surprise quickly turned to a deadly glare. It didn't surprise Brent that the man wasn't cowed by his strong words.

Sir Randolph's hands jerked to the table, and his fingers white-knuckled the edge as he leaned in closer to Brent. "By your words, my lord, it's clear you don't know me, so I'll forgive you this once for questioning my honor and not take offense at what you just said. I have only one and will always have only one thing to say about your mother to you, Society, or anyone else in London. She was a fine and virtuous lady, and I'll take up my sword, my pistols, or my fists against any nobleman, gentry, or servant who dares to say differently about her. And, my lord, that includes her sons."

Brent sat back in his chair and slowly nodded. He

couldn't have said that better himself. "Then we're in agreement, Sir Randolph."

Eleven

Has fortune dealt you some bad cards? Then let wisdom make you a good gamester.

—Francis Quarles

GABRIELLE WAS TREADING ON UNFAMILIAR GROUND. She hated to be late for anything. It went against her nature. It worried her if anyone had to wait for her, no matter for how short a time. She had fought the urge to race downstairs to meet Lord Brentwood the moment he was announced. Instead, she had paced in her room, making him wait for over an hour before gathering up her pelisse, bonnet, and gloves to make her way below stairs. From what she could tell, stepping on his toes and making him step on hers hadn't seemed to do much to deter his desire to marry her. He took her bungling of the waltz in stride the way a perfect gentleman should. If she hadn't been so stunned by his calm acceptance, she would have laughed when he said all she needed was a few more lessons. That was not what she'd wanted to hear. But since that little episode hadn't worked at all, she had been thinking up new ways to annoy the viscount.

From her father, she knew that few gentlemen could abide a lady who was habitually late. She was hoping her tardiness would add another unacceptable trait to the list he must now be forming about her. But just in case, Gabrielle had more than one card up her sleeve. She wasn't leaving anything to chance. She was going to add as many uncomplimentary things about herself as she could while they waited for her betrothal to Staunton to be dissolved.

It wasn't easy for her to play the part of a twit, but she had to believe if she annoyed Lord Brentwood enough, he was sure to give her up as unredeemable and insist to her father that he couldn't marry a young lady who was so inept at so many things.

She smiled as she slipped her velvet drawstring reticule over her hand. She had written some dreadfully long and uninspired poetry and had it tucked in her purse, ready to pull it out at the most inopportune time and read it to him. Considering the extreme look of anguish she saw on Lord Brentwood's face when he'd heard Lord Snellingly recite his poetry, her attempt at verse should have the viscount running for the country to get away from her.

Much to her surprise and puzzlement, when she made it to the bottom of the stairs, she heard talking and laughter coming from the drawing room. She had expected to find him extremely annoyed or, at the very least, to hear Lord Brentwood pacing from sheer boredom as she had been doing in her room. She hurried down the corridor and, when she rounded the doorway, she saw Lord Brentwood and her aunt in delightful humor, playing a game of cards across the small table that sat between the two settees.

He certainly wasn't in the dither she'd hoped to find him. Far from it. He looked as if he was actually enjoying himself with her aunt. Gabrielle was the one who felt flushed, out of breath, and annoyed that he wasn't. Obviously, being late wasn't going to provoke him as long as Auntie Bethie was around to amuse him.

"I beg your pardon, Lord Brentwood, for taking so long," she said, walking into the room.

Lord Brentwood laid his cards on the table, rose, and let his gaze linger on her face, causing a shiver of awareness. She saw appreciation in his eyes for the way she looked, and she liked that he let her know. She wore a dark beige carriage dress with a dark brown velvet pelisse covering most of it. She held a matching bonnet in her hand, and her brown velvet reticule dangled from her gloved wrist.

The viscount looked amazingly handsome in a dark blue jacket over a pale blue waistcoat adorned with ivory-colored buttons. His slim-cut, fawn-colored trousers were stuffed into shiny black boots that had decorative silver buckles at the ankles and emphasized his long, powerful legs. She swallowed hard when she noticed the jagged cut and swelling at the corner of his mouth where Staunton had hit him. The injury made him look all the more handsome, roguish, and unattainable. But she was most captivated by how relaxed and casual he seemed in her home, playing cards and conversing with her aunt.

Gabrielle had the unusual urge to stomp her foot in frustration. Why wasn't he upset and irritated that she was so late? Her father would have been red-faced with anger and pacing at the bottom of the stairs, shouting for her to hurry. Obviously, she was going to have to try harder in order to displease the very likable Lord Brentwood.

"Your tardiness wasn't a problem for me, but the wait was made better when fortune smiled on me. Mrs. Potter came along and saw me sitting here alone. We started talking about cards."

"Yes," Auntie Bethie said, picking up the story. "And Lord Brentwood was kind enough to show me a few pointers."

"Nonsense, Auntie," Gabrielle said with a smile and then reached down and kissed her aunt on the cheek. "You may have fooled Lord Brentwood for a time with your cunning ways, but you know you cannot fool me. You are an excellent card player and need no instruction from anyone."

"I can always learn a thing or two from a handsome gentleman."

"Not at cards." Gabrielle smiled. "No doubt you were trying to win some blunt off him, and if you did, you must give it back right now."

"Never, my darling. The money I won is all mine." Her aunt laughed, reached up, and patted Gabrielle's cheek affectionately. "And if that is the kind of disrespect you are going to show your favorite aunt, you can put on your bonnet and leave for the park straightaway."

"Perhaps we should, before you have the viscount

thinking you are a helpless lady in need of rescuing."
Gabrielle turned to Lord Brentwood. "Shall we go?"

"I'm ready," he said to Gabrielle and then turned to
her aunt. "Thank you for a lovely visit, Mrs. Potter."

"Remember, if you're not back in two hours, I'll
come looking for you," her aunt called in a friendly
tone as they left the room.

"We certainly don't want that, Auntie," Gabrielle
threw over her shoulder.

Lord Brentwood paused at the doorway and said,
"Don't worry, Mrs. Potter, we won't be late."

"See that you aren't. I'm growing quite fond of you
and I don't want that to change."

Gabrielle and Lord Brentwood stopped in the
vestibule to pick up her parasol, cape, and gloves, and
his coat, hat, and gloves. While he donned his outer
clothing, Brutus came walking down the corridor.
Her heart went out to the lumbering old dog as she
tied the ribbon of her rush-brimmed bonnet under
her chin.

On impulse, she turned to Lord Brentwood and
asked, "Would you mind terribly if Brutus came
with us?"

Lord Brentwood looked at Brutus and then back
to Gabrielle. She saw the corner of his lips twitch
just a bit as he hesitated before answering. She held
her breath.

She could see it was on the tip of his tongue to deny
her request, but instead he put a smile on his face,
looked down at the dog, and said, "Of course not.
Brutus and I are old friends now, aren't we?"

Gabrielle let out her breath and gave him a grateful

smile. "Thank you, my lord. He won't be any trouble at all."

When they reached the carriage, which was parked on the street in front of her house, he helped her step up and into the curricle. While she seated herself, he looked down at Brutus and said, "Come on, boy, you're next. Up you go."

"Oh, I'm sorry, my lord," Gabrielle said with concern. "Brutus is too old to climb steps without a boost. I'll go get Muggs to help him into the carriage for us." She started to rise.

"No, no," he said, holding up his hand to stop her. "Sit back down, Lady Gabrielle. No need to disturb your footman. I'm perfectly capable of helping Brutus get into the carriage."

As if knowing exactly what to do, Brutus immediately put his front paws on the first step of the curricle, looked back at Lord Brentwood, and gave a short woof. The viscount reached down and gently grasped him under the stomach with one arm and, with the other, cupped the back of his hind legs and carefully lifted the dog. A passing phaeton slowed and the driver asked if Lord Brentwood needed help, but he shook his head and called out, "I've got it handled."

It was a bit of a struggle for him at first, but he managed to get Brutus onto the floor of the small carriage, where he slowly lay down.

With a teasing smile, Lord Brentwood brushed dog hair from his coat and said, "Did I mention that you have a big dog?"

When the viscount was so charming, she had to

remind herself he was being forced to marry her, and she didn't want that for him or for herself. She must remember her plan and do all she could to convince him she would not be a good wife. But looking at him now, she knew that would be hard to do.

Gabrielle laughed lightly to cover the good feeling that washed over her from simply looking at him. She smiled and patted the panting dog on the head.

"But he is such a darling, and I know it pains him to be so much trouble to everyone."

"You are obviously a good master," Lord Brentwood said as he carefully climbed into the carriage, trying not to step on the dog's large paws. "But I don't think darling is the word I would use for the mastiff, Lady Gabrielle. He cares not for trouble. He's just happy to be going along for the ride."

The viscount sat down beside her on the padded bench. She immediately felt the heat of his body as his thigh settled brazenly against hers. She knew she should move away and give him more space on the seat, but there was something intimately comforting about the slight touch from him, and she didn't want to deny herself his warmth.

"You know you can't keep doing this."

His eyes narrowed, and he seemed puzzled for a moment. "What's that?"

"You said I had promised you a dance when I hadn't, and you said we had planned to go for a ride today in the park, yet you had never asked me to go with you this afternoon."

His eyes narrowed further. His gaze settled gently on her face and he questioned, "Really?"

Gabrielle watched as Lord Brentwood reached for a wool blanket from underneath the seat. All his hand found was dog. The small curricle was not the carriage he needed if Brutus was going to join them. He finally caught an edge of the blanket, pulled it out, and laid it over her lap.

"Yes, and you know it," she admonished with a soft smile. "You cannot continue to just assume we have made plans and I will go along with whatever you say."

He smiled, and she noticed it was a little crooked from the swollen corner. "It's worked for me so far. Why mess up a good plan?"

Gabrielle suddenly felt wistful and said, "Because I would like to have a say about my life, about what I do. I want to be in on making the decisions that affect me, the decisions as simple as where we go together."

"All right, it's your turn. Tell me what you would like for us to do after this outing."

Though he sounded genuine, Gabrielle wasn't sure she trusted him. "You will let me decide?"

He gave her a curious look, as if he wondered why she questioned his sincerity. "Yes, of course. What do you want to do?"

His insistence that she could choose surprised her. "Well, I don't know yet. I will have to think about it."

He clicked the ribbons on the horses' rumps and the carriage took off with a jerk, rattle of harness, and clopping of hooves.

After he had safely maneuvered them into the street behind a hackney, he threw a smiling glance her way, and said, "Fine. You can let me know when you've decided. You have approximately two hours to think about it."

Gabrielle settled comfortably into her seat and opened her brown ruffled parasol. The rain and dreary weather of the past few days had lifted. A light blue afternoon sky was filled with puffy white clouds. The air felt cold and breezy, but with the bright sunshine and Lord Brentwood's thigh next to hers, Gabrielle felt very warm. She wasn't sure why, but an exciting sense of awareness bubbled up inside her. Something told her it was going to be a splendid afternoon.

She looked down to see if Brutus was settled, and her breath stalled in her lungs. The dog's mouth was poised over Lord Brentwood's feet. Brutus's drool and slobber from his exertion of getting into the carriage was dripping onto the toe of one of Lord Brentwood's highly polished boots.

As she tried to decide if she should tell the viscount to move his feet, or simply try to shift the big body of the dog, Lord Brentwood asked, "Is everything all right?"

Gabrielle turned and looked up at the same time Lord Brentwood bent his head to glance down. The edge of her parasol hit the brim of his hat and knocked it off his head. The strong wind caught the top hat and sent it flying like a kite through the air and over the curricle behind them. He pulled hard on the ribbons to stop the horses. She and Lord Brentwood looked back in time to see his hat land crown-up in a wide mud puddle on the other side of the road. He set the brake and turned to jump down but stopped as a shiny painted barouche passed by, the wheels splashing black muddy water all over the hat.

"Oh, no!" Gabrielle gasped. "I'm so sorry, my lord."

She expected him to start yelling at her how it was his favorite hat, or how expensive it would be to replace it, as her father would have done, but that didn't happen. Instead of anger, Lord Brentwood was merely looking with detachment at the soiled hat floating in the puddle.

"I'll get it for you," she said, starting to remove the blanket covering her legs.

"No," he said, placing his hand on top of hers to still her.

She looked down at his black gloved hand lying over hers. There was no shake or quiver of fury in his touch. No anger. Her father would have been furious at her.

"But, my lord, I can see it was an exceptional hat. Perhaps I can have it cleaned."

"It's no matter, Lady Gabrielle. Look over there." He pointed to a street urchin not far away who was wistfully eyeing the hat. "Let him have it. Maybe he can salvage it and make a shilling or two off it. I have others."

"That's very kind of you."

Lord Brentwood turned away and released the brake, picked up the ribbons, and started the horses to moving again. She hadn't wanted to ruin his hat, but with any luck, he'd add it to the growing list of things that would one day make him realize she was not the wife for him.

They were both quiet the rest of the short ride

to the park. She had no idea what the viscount was thinking, but she knew she was quickly counting up all the things that made Lord Brentwood different from her father.

There were only a few people in the park as they entered from the east side. That was to be expected, since it was windy, cold, and a weekday. Lord Brentwood took his time and searched for just the right place to stop, which was a level stretch of land not too far from the Serpentine. There was a crop of trees to break the wind but still sunny enough to help keep them warm.

He set the brake on the curricle and jumped down. He first helped Brutus make it down the two steps and then reached back to help Gabrielle.

She closed her parasol and laid it on the seat before taking his hand. "I don't think I'll need this."

He grinned. "And I might be safer if you don't have it with you."

Gabrielle laughed as she took his hand and stepped down.

Lord Brentwood took the blanket that had covered her legs and spread it on the ground, and then he walked back to the carriage to get the food basket from underneath the seat. "I hope you like what my cook prepared for us. Warm—" He stopped mid-sentence when he glanced back and saw that Brutus had staked out his claim right in the middle of the small blanket and was making himself comfortable.

But without missing another beat, Lord Brentwood looked at her and said, "Warm chocolate, bread, cheese, and fig preserves."

Gabrielle started to tell Brutus to move and would have, except on second thought, she knew her dog's antics were working right into her plan to make the viscount see how unsuitable she was to be his wife. It was best he know that wherever she went Brutus went, and the dog always got special treatment.

"It all sounds wonderful to me," she said to him and walked over to the blanket.

She gave Lord Brentwood her hand, and he helped her to sit on a corner. He lowered himself on the opposite side of her, leaving the food basket as a barrier between them. She slipped her reticule off her wrist and pretended not to see him looking curiously at the toe of his boot that Brutus had christened with his slobber.

After taking off his gloves and scarf and unbuttoning his overcoat, the first thing he did was to pull out a flask and pour warm chocolate into a delicate china cup and hand it to her. She sipped the drink and watched in silence as he laid pieces of bread and containers holding butter and preserves onto the napkin the cup had been wrapped in.

"Mmm, this chocolate is wonderful, my lord, but has a strange taste to it."

"That might be because it's laced with a little brandy. I thought it might help keep you warm."

"I've never had chocolate with brandy, and it does make my cheeks feel warm."

"It also makes them turn a lovely shade of pink."

"Really?" she said, touching her cheek.

Gabrielle set the cup aside. She felt wonderful sitting on the blanket under a tree with the viscount.

She felt so happy and so free, she did the unthinkable and took off her gloves and laid them beside her.

She broke off a piece of bread and buttered it with the small knife he'd brought. "Will you tell me what happened between you and Staunton?"

Lord Brentwood popped a piece of bread loaded with fig preserves into his mouth and swallowed before saying, "There's nothing to tell. There were very few words spoken between us."

Gabrielle thought for a moment. Staunton had always been a man of few words. She'd actually had very few conversations with him during their engagement. When they had first become engaged, he'd often sought her out, always wanting her to take walks with him in the garden, or if they were at parties, to go out on the terrace with him. It hadn't taken her long to realize all he wanted to do was kiss her, and that held no appeal to her, so she'd stopped going anywhere with him. He'd soon stopped asking. And that was obviously when he started noticing her sister and fell in love with her.

"Is it true he just walked up to you and hit you?"

The viscount gave her a crooked smile. "You know, Lady Gabrielle, I have only one thing to say about my encounter with Mr. Staunton. I might have hit a man, too, if I thought he'd stolen my fiancée from me. In fact, I might have done more than he did."

"But Staunton didn't want to marry me because—" Gabrielle caught herself before she revealed the truth about Staunton and Rosabelle. She quickly popped a piece of bread in her mouth.

"Staunton didn't want to marry you because of what?"

She struggled to come up with something, but words

were failing her. She needed to say something that would make herself sound like a dreadful person. Without thinking clearly, she quickly blurted out, "Because I have a nasty temper, and I've been known to throw things."

"At Staunton?"

She hesitated. "No, others," she said, sensing Lord Brentwood didn't believe her for a moment, and she was only digging the hole she was standing in deeper. "Believe me, no man should have to abide a woman as ill-tempered as I."

He sipped his chocolate and looked at her thoughtfully. "Did Staunton ever tell you that?"

She looked at Lord Brentwood. He was still waiting for an answer, so she said, "No, not in those words exactly. But take my word for it: he did not want to marry me."

"All right," he said calmly. "I'll believe you." He added more chocolate to their cups. "But what about you? Why didn't you want to marry him?"

Gabrielle hesitated. How had she allowed them to get this far into a conversation about Staunton? She immediately started looking for a way out of it.

"I didn't object at first when my father told me he'd picked Staunton for me. I'm sorry he hit you and cut your lip again."

A half laugh blew past his lips and he shrugged. "Yes, it wouldn't have been so bad if Staunton had caught me on the other side, but his fist landed where my lip had just healed."

Her eyes searched his. Suddenly, everything around them was very quiet. On impulse, Gabrielle reached over and touched the injured side of his mouth with the pads of her fingers. He took hold of her hand and kissed the back of it while his gaze searched her face.

"The care and concern I see in your eyes isn't necessary," he said. "It's almost well and doesn't hurt anymore."

"But it was because of me that Staunton hit you."

He gave her a half smile. "A small price to pay for such sweet kisses." His gaze stayed steady on hers. "Do you mind if I kiss you right now?"

Her heart rate soared, and she felt hot, even though a cool breeze chilled the air. Why was he asking? Staunton had kissed her often and he had never once asked if he could. He would always just pull her into his arms and kiss her without any warning. But then, she had never wanted Staunton's kisses.

Did she mind? She was eager for this man to kiss her.

"No," she whispered.

Reaching over the basket, Lord Brentwood bent his head and lightly brushed his warm, moist, and pliant lips over hers. She tasted the sweetness of the jam he'd just eaten, and a quickening tightened her abdomen. The viscount's kiss was gentle and satisfying, much more pleasant than Staunton's kisses had been. She wanted it to go on forever, but it ended far too quickly.

She moistened her lips and asked, "Why did you ask permission for a kiss?"

"That's what a gentleman is supposed to do the first time he kisses a lady."

"But we've—" She stopped.

"I know," he said, as if reading her thoughts.

"We've kissed before, but it was you who initiated our first kiss, wasn't it?"

She nodded again and lowered her lashes over her eyes, embarrassed by how brazen she'd been that morning in the park.

"I didn't mind, you know," he said.

"Didn't you think it made me seem a very loose lady to have done that?"

"Very," he said with a slight grin as his arms tightened about her.

"And being loose makes me completely unacceptable as a titled man's wife, doesn't it?"

His expression turned serious, and his eyes darkened. "No. You can kiss me again any time you want to. I will never rebuff you, and wanting to kiss me will never make you unsuitable as my wife."

Exasperation settled over her. If that didn't make her undesirable as a wife in his eyes, she didn't know what would. She should be furious he wanted her to be so fresh and free. Until she had met him, she had lived a life above reproach and had never been anything but circumspect in the company of a man. But all that was forgotten whenever Lord Brentwood was near her. She had found far too many things to like about him.

Gabrielle looked deeply into his eyes and remembered the breathtaking embrace they'd shared that morning more than two weeks ago. The memories of his tempting kisses fused with what she was feeling now, and she wanted him to kiss her again as he had that day. The desiring look in his hooded eyes left her no doubt he wanted to kiss her that way again too.

And that was not a good idea. She couldn't examine her feelings for him beyond her intense desire to keep this man from being forced to wed her. She had to put a stop to the way he was making her feel, and she had to do it quickly. She reached behind her and grabbed her reticule off the blanket and fumbled inside it, finally drawing out her sheet of poetry.

She found it difficult to steady her cold fingers as she unfolded the paper. "Since you seemed to enjoy Lord Snellingly's poetry so much a few nights ago, I thought perhaps I'd read you some of mine.

"In the shadows of a cold night, my fragile dreams…"

Lord Brentwood reached over and slipped the foolscap out of her hands and dropped it to the ground behind him. "I don't think so, Gabrie."

"No?" she whispered.

"No," he answered with a smile. "We'll let the wind read it."

He shoved the food basket out of his way so suddenly it knocked over her cup and disturbed Brutus's slumber. He growled, a low woof sound.

"Stay out of this, Brutus," Lord Brentwood said and moved closer to Gabrielle.

He positioned his legs in the opposite direction from hers and pulled up his knees so she could rest her side against his thighs. He slid his arms around her, pulling her close.

"I can think of a far better way to spend our time in the park than reading poetry. Tell me how you like this."

His hold on her was possessive as he lowered his head to hers. Gabrielle instinctively closed her eyes.

His lips pressed against hers and moved languorously over them. She parted her lips, allowing his tongue to slip inside and probe the depths of her mouth. The kiss was generous and glorious. At times she heard short, gaspy breaths, and sometimes she heard long contented sighs, but had no idea if the sounds came from her or Lord Brentwood. She loved the way his lips roved expertly across hers, loved the taste of brandy and chocolate that lingered on his tongue.

He raised his head and looked down at her with his crooked smile and asked, "Well?"

"I do believe you are right. Kissing is much better than reading poetry."

Lord Brentwood chuckled, and with all thoughts of verse fading from her mind, Gabrielle slipped her arms inside his coat and around his waist. His body was warm and inviting. She drew him closer to her. There was something decidedly rebellious and thrilling about being in his arms and kissing him in the bright light of sunshine, and suddenly she was aware of nothing but the ecstasy she felt in his arms.

His hand found the ribbon under her chin and he untied it. He gently pulled the bonnet off and set it aside. She felt his fingers at her throat as he pulled on the bow of her short velvet cape and let it fall away from her shoulders. With ease, he unfastened her velvet pelisse and opened it, exposing her scooped-neck carriage dress. His lips left hers and kissed their way down the column of her throat to the part of her chest that was exposed by the neckline of her dress. The touch of his warm lips on her cool skin excited her.

He rested his open palm on her breast over her

heart, and she wondered if he could feel the constant pounding that sounded like a loud drum in her ears. She knew what she was allowing him to do was beyond the pale, but she had discarded all caution and reasoning the moment his lips met hers. She had no inclination to stop him until, in the distance, she heard the sound of carriage wheels.

Startled, she tried to pull out of his arms.

"Wait," he whispered.

Without letting go of her, Lord Brentwood leaned forward and carefully peeked around the trunk of the tree directly in front of them.

"Don't be alarmed," he whispered, brushing aside her concern and scooting even closer to her. "The carriage is far away and not coming in this direction. I can see around the tree and I will keep watch. I will not let anyone catch me kissing you."

When he looked down at her, she touched the side of his mouth again and said, "Didn't it hurt to kiss me so passionately?"

He smiled and outlined her lips with the tip of his finger. "It didn't hurt at all." He placed his lips on hers again and whispered against them, "Your mouth is so soft, sweet, and gentle, it could never hurt me to kiss you."

Her mouth opened and met his once more. She didn't know why, but she felt an inexplicable feeling of urgency. His kisses bruised over hers hungrily, and she matched his furor. His arms wrapped tightly around her back, crushing her to him. Her tongue filled his mouth, and it pleased her when she heard him swallow soft gasps of pleasure.

His hand skimmed over her breasts, causing her breathing to be erratic. There were the sounds of men talking in the distance, and Gabrielle stiffened in his arms once again. Lord Brentwood looked up and leaned forward.

He gazed down at her and, with the pad of his finger, drew a line from her lips down to the hollow of her throat, and let his finger rest there. "We are safe here, Gabrie."

She took in a deep, relaxing breath and settled more comfortably against his legs. She smiled her pleasure at being so close to him and so free to be able to enjoy all the wonderful sensations he created inside her with just a touch and a kiss.

"That's the second time you've called me Gabrie."

He nodded as his hands moved over her breasts, up to her face, where his fingers drew circles and patterns around her lips, on her cheeks, down her neck, and over to her earlobe, where he softly caressed it. She could hardly concentrate on what she wanted to say for the wonder of all she was feeling.

"My family nickname is Gabby," she finally got out.

His eyes and forehead formed into a frown as his fingers trickled down to her chest and rested on her breast again. "And I think it's fine for them to call you Gabby, but I like Gabrie, and that is what I will start calling you."

"It would be forward of you to do that in front of anyone, my lord."

"Indeed, but I think I like being forward. I want you to call me Brent. I don't want to hear you say 'my lord' to me anymore."

"That's extremely improper, and I know my father wouldn't approve of that, and certainly not of the kisses and intimate caresses we are sharing now."

He smiled and bent his head toward hers. "No, he wouldn't approve, but right now I don't want you proper. I don't care about what the duke thinks. I am Brent, you are Gabrie, and we are going to kiss. Understand?"

No matter how delicious his kisses were making her feel, she had the presence of mind to know that enjoying his embrace was not part of her plan to convince him she would not be an acceptable wife for him. She had to do something to break the spell of desire he'd cast over her.

Taking a long breath, she moistened her lips and said, "Did I ever tell you madness runs in my family?"

His eyes narrowed, his forehead wrinkled into a frown, and he leaned back as if to get a better look at her. "Where did that come from?"

"Oh, from my father's side of the family. There have been many relatives, and going back for several generations."

His gaze searched her face curiously. "No, I meant why did you bring it up now?"

Gabrielle moistened her lips again. Telling prevarications wasn't as easy as she'd thought, and obviously what she'd always heard was true. If you tell one, you'll most assuredly have to tell another to explain the first.

"I felt I needed to warn you before you thought further on marriage with me."

His lips slowly eased into another smile, and she knew he didn't believe her for a moment.

"Oh, I see," he said. "I'll keep that in mind to think on later, but for now, I'm going to kiss you."

And he did.

His lips lowered to hers again, and this time he kissed her softly at first but then deeply and passionately. His lips moved from hers, across her cheek, and over her jawline, to the delicate spot behind her ear. He breathed in deeply. Her skin pebbled with delicious goose bumps. He kissed the lobe of her ear on his way down to the hollow of her throat, swirling his tongue in its shallow depths and lingering there to tease, taste, and moisten her skin. His hand gently massaged her breasts, and she moaned softly.

Gabrielle was hardly breathing. She felt as though her insides were twisting, folding, and floating into a wonderful and exciting knot of desire. His touch was thrilling. Through the fabric of her dress and stays, he palmed her breast, lifted it, and closed his fingers around it, squeezing gently yet firmly.

She didn't understand why she had no inhibitions when she was in his arms. Shivers of delight bolted through her at breakneck speed at his touch. She was amazed at how much enjoyment she received from the caress of his hands. She couldn't let her hands be still, either. She was eager to explore and enjoy everything about him, from the silky feel of his hair to the expensive fabric of his coat beneath her hands. She was succumbing to a brand new world that she had never experienced before.

Some of their kisses were soft and warm, while others were fierce and passionate. For the first time in her life, she knew what it was like to want a man to desire her, love her, and it was an exhilarating feeling. She boldly slid her tongue deep into his mouth again, and he muffled a groan.

"If I could remove your dress, I know your breast would fit perfectly into my hand," he whispered passionately against her lips. "I would warm it with my mouth."

He raised his head and looked into her eyes, as if considering the possibility of undressing her, and God help her, she was considering the possibility of letting him.

All of a sudden, his head jerked to the side and he said, "Did you hear that?"

"What?" she whispered from the fog of passion. "Is someone coming toward us?"

Then she heard it, the bark of a small dog. Gabrielle noticed Brutus had roused his head and was looking in the direction of the barking, too.

"That sounds like Prissy," she said and shoved out of Lord Brentwood's arms.

Twelve

The intelligent man finds almost everything ridiculous, the sensible man almost nothing.

—Johann Wolfgang von Goethe

Brent jumped up and then helped Gabrielle rise. "I don't know if it's Prissy, but that is a small dog we hear. Let's go."

Gabrielle quickly turned to Brutus, who was struggling to rise. She pointed her finger at him and said, "Stay. Stay."

"He won't, you know," Brent said and took hold of her hand.

She threw Brent a worried glance. "But he can't run anymore. He can't keep up."

"No, but he can catch up with us, and he will. Let's go."

They took off toward the barking. After they passed the stand of trees that had been their shelter, in the distance they saw an old woman pushing a small cart that was covered by a lumpy canvas. They headed in her direction. The woman must have heard them running toward her, but she paid them no mind and kept walking.

As they approached her, Brent could see that her dark gray coat was soiled and worn. A frayed woolen scarf was wrapped around her head, covering her neck and chin. The dog, hidden by the canvas, continued to yelp and scratch, but she made no attempt to stop and see about it.

Brent and Gabrielle slowed their steps a few yards from the woman. "Don't be frightened, madame," Brent said, breathing hard as they walked alongside her. "We mean you no harm."

The woman kept walking and didn't bother to even glance his way as she said, "Didn't think ye did. Not done nothing to ye. Got no reason to think ye'd 'arm me, 'ave I?"

"No, of course not," he said. "Do you mind if we have a moment of your time."

At that, she looked over at them and stopped. "Don't mind at all."

Brent saw that her gaze suddenly sailed past them and froze on something behind them. Concern etched its way into her lined face. Brent knew she must have caught site of Brutus. He glanced back and confirmed his suspicion. The large old dog was slowly lumbering toward his mistress.

"Don't worry, madame," Gabrielle said in a friendly voice as Brutus came up beside her, panting heavily from trying to keep up with them. "He's big, but he won't hurt you."

"'E's old," the woman said as the dog under the canvas continued to bark and scratch, clearly wanting to be free.

"Yes." Gabrielle reached down and patted Brutus's shoulder. "He doesn't see or hear as well as he used to, but age has given him a quiet and gentle nature."

The woman wasn't convinced. Apprehension about the dog didn't leave her face. She said, "What can I do for ye? I don't 'ave a thing a fine fella like you or a fancy-dressed lady like her would want."

Brent smiled and nodded once. "I understand that. I was hoping you wouldn't mind telling me what you have under that canvas in your cart?"

At first she looked at him as if he was daft, and then she gave him a happy, toothless smile. "I 'ave me dog under there. Can't you 'ear?"

Brent gave Gabrielle a hopeful glance and then turned back to the woman. "Why do you have her covered up?"

"It's a 'e, not a she."

At hearing the dog was male, Brent's anticipation faded and disillusionment flared.

Stepping closer to the woman, Gabrielle asked, "Do you mind if we ask why you have him covered in your cart?"

The old woman looked at Gabrielle as if she didn't have a brain in her head. "Don't mind at all. It's cold today if ye 'adn't noticed. I'm trying to keep Sir William warm."

"I'm sure he likes the kind treatment," Gabrielle said. "I adore little dogs. Do you mind if I see him?"

She looked at the mastiff again. "I guess it will be all right. 'E's not going to stop barking 'til 'e sees who you are, anyway." The woman reached down and peeled back the canvas, revealing a covered basket.

She took the lid off, and a small black-and-white dog of undetermined breed jumped out and into the cart, barking like a banshee at the mastiff. Brutus never uttered a woof.

"Sir William is a fine-looking animal," Brent said. "Thank you for showing him to us."

"Yes, thank you," Gabrielle said, and then she, Brutus, and Brent turned and headed back in the direction of the curricle.

As they walked in silence, Brent knew it was time he stopped searching for Prissy. He didn't want to, but it was ridiculous for him to take off running every time he heard a small dog bark. It was time to accept that Priss was gone and not coming back. He had to put her memory to rest.

Halfway to the carriage, Gabrielle touched his arm, and they stopped. Her eyes were soft and full of compassion. It was as if she knew what he'd been thinking. When she looked at him with so much concern, Brent's stomach tightened with desire. The strong wind had blown strands of her golden blonde hair from the chignon at her nape, and they caressed her cheeks. Her lips were moist and inviting. All he could think was he wanted to pull her to him and kiss her again, but they were no longer shielded by trees, and it would be too risky. Besides, Brutus stood between them, too. He couldn't help but think maybe the mastiff was a good watchdog after all.

"I'm sorry the dog wasn't Prissy," Gabrielle said.

"So am I," he said, not wanting to share with her that he'd come to the conclusion Prissy wasn't going to be found.

"Do you think there is any connection to Prissy's disappearance and Lord Snellingly's dog?"

"I do not believe in ghosts, Gabrielle."

Her eyes brightened as if she'd just had an amazing thought. "Oh, I do. They are real."

He laughed. "And I'm sure one or two of them visit you from time to time, and yes, after we are married, your ghosts can continue to visit you."

She folded her arms across her chest and gave him an annoyed look. "You are laughing at me."

"Yes," he said, and with great effort he wiped the smile off his lips. He cleared his throat, and they started walking again. "I don't see how there could be a connection between our two dogs. Snellingly's dog ran away from him at his house in Mayfair, not here in Hyde. If there is a large wild animal roaming the park, as some believe, I'm sure someone would have spotted him by now, especially if he was roaming the streets of Mayfair, too."

"I suppose you're right. I just don't want you to give up hope of Prissy's return, my lord."

I must. Starting now.

His brows drew together as he looked down at her with an exaggerated frown. "I didn't hear you say my lord, did I?"

She gave him an apologetic smile. "Excuse me, Brent."

"Much better," he said as they started down the slope toward the blanket and carriage. "I don't want to give up hope, but it's been almost three weeks now."

"I don't consider three weeks such a long time," she argued.

Brent glanced over at her. "You don't? What if Brutus had been missing for more than two weeks? Would you consider it a long time then?"

She wrinkled her nose at him, and it was so engaging, he laughed.

"All right, yes, I suppose I would think three weeks were forever."

"I'll keep the notice running in *The Times* for now, but other than that, I've done everything I know to do. It's time."

She kept her gaze straight ahead for a few moments and then turned to him and asked, "Will you be at the Cuddlebury's party next week?"

"I don't know. I was thinking perhaps I should stay out of the social scene for a while."

Her brow furrowed. "Why? As my aunt would say, the disappearing act won't make the rumors about us and your brothers go away."

"I wasn't thinking about that at all. I was thinking about Staunton. I fear if he approached me again and wanted to fight, I wouldn't have the good sense to walk away a second time."

"Meaning you would never let him hit you again without retaliating."

"That's exactly what I mean, Gabrie." For some damn reason, Brent felt Staunton deserved throwing that one punch, even though it was never Brent's intention to kiss another man's fiancée.

Gabrielle gave him a nod of understanding as they made it back to the blanket. She picked up her bonnet and settled it on her head. "I've made up my mind."

He gave her a quizzical look. "About what?"

"About what I would like for us to do at our next outing. Remember you said I could decide. You aren't going back on your word, are you?"

He found it odd she thought he'd go back on his word. "No. It's your choice. What would you like us to do?"

She buttoned her pelisse. "I think you should join me, Auntie Bethie, and Rosa for church on Sunday."

"Church?" Brent was certain he was unable to hide his surprise. He didn't suppose he minded going to church with her; he just hadn't done it very often in recent years.

"Yes, Auntie adores singing in church. She has such a strong and beautiful voice."

Gabrielle smiled so prettily at him, his stomach did a slow roll and then tightened. He picked up her short cape and settled it around her shoulders, taking his time tying the satin bow. What he really wanted to do was indulge in his desire for her and pull her to him and kiss her again.

"I don't doubt Mrs. Potter has a beautiful voice, but it's been a while since I've been to church, Gabrielle."

"Oh, but I go to church every Sunday, Brent, and after we marry, I would expect you always to go with me."

Something about how hard she was trying to convince him made him think the opposite of what she said was true. He was getting the same feeling he had when he realized she was only pretending not to know how to dance, fibbing about madness in her family, and that she had a nasty temper. He didn't know why she was playing this game, but for now it seemed harmless enough.

"Church every Sunday?" he asked, playing along with her.

"Well, almost every Sunday," she said innocently, tying the ribbon of her bonnet under her chin.

"All right, Sunday at church it is." He bent on one knee and started putting their things in the basket. He took the leftover bread and gave it to Brutus, who finished it off in two bites.

He handed Gabrielle her gloves and reticule, and then wrapped his scarf around his neck. "I don't see your poetry here. I think the wind must have blown it away while we were otherwise occupied."

"No matter," she said with a teasing smile. "I have plenty more. I try to write a few lines of poetry every day. After we're married, I shall read poetry to you every morning when we wake and every evening when we sit before the fire."

"Church every Sunday and poetry twice a day would make me a blessed man indeed," Brent whispered under his breath as he closed the lid on the basket and took it to the carriage.

Gabrielle picked up the blanket and shook it. "And there's one other thing," she said.

He could hardly wait to hear what nonsense she was going to come up with next. "What's that?" he said, taking the opposite ends of the blanket and helping her to fold it.

"Perhaps after church you would be kind enough to take me to the fair I've heard about. Papa never had the time. It's on the south side of Town. I've heard they have an albino hawk, an Indian juggler, a tiger from Bengal, and all the acrobats' feats are exceptional as well."

Brent chuckled to himself as he laid the blanket in the carriage. She was the exceptional one, surprising him with talk of going to church one moment, madness and ghosts the next, and then reading poetry and wanting to go to exotic events at a carnival.

"I think I can manage that."

"That would be lovely."

He took her hand and lightly squeezed her fingers as he helped her into the carriage. "Come on, Brutus, your turn."

It was a bit of a struggle, but with lifting the old dog's hind legs and pushing, Brent finally got Brutus into the carriage. Brent jumped up beside Gabrielle, leaned his thigh next to hers, and then picked up the ribbons.

He looked at her, and she smiled so sweetly at him he almost dropped the ribbons and kissed her.

"Auntie Bethie absolutely adores fairs," Gabrielle said, her eyes sparkling with anticipation. "She will be thrilled to hear you are taking us."

"So Mrs. Potter will be joining us, and I assume your sister, too, since she will be with us at church."

"You don't mind, do you?"

Brent looked at Gabrielle and suddenly it was as clear as a blue sky to him what she was doing. She was trying her best to annoy him and to make herself seem an unsuitable match for him. But what she didn't know was the harder she tried to make herself unappealing, the more appealing she became.

He reached over and kissed the tip of her nose. "It's your outing, Gabrie, you may invite whomever you wish."

He released the brake handle and clicked the ribbons on the horses' rumps. The carriage took off with a jolt and a rattle of harness.

Thirteen

None are so fond of secrets as those who do not mean to keep them.
—Charles Caleb Colton

GABRIELLE AND BRUTUS WALKED INTO THE HOUSE after a brief good-bye to Brent at her front door. Brutus didn't stop but continued down the corridor. Gabrielle knew he was heading for his pillow by the fireplace. She took her time removing her bonnet, cape, gloves, and pelisse. She was more confused than ever.

The problem was she had enjoyed every invigorating moment with the viscount. She enjoyed looking at him, talking to him, and kissing him. She found it stimulating to match wits with him, frustrating to try to astonish him, and humbling to commiserate with him over Prissy's disappearance.

Her hands stilled when she caught sight of herself in the mirror that hung over one of the side tables in the vestibule. She was smiling, smiling because being with Lord Brentwood made her happy. He had many good qualities to recommend him. He was handsome, dashing, and pleasant. She had never enjoyed her time with Staunton. The earl's son was handsome, but Gabrielle couldn't ever remember smiling with him over a shared pleasure, lying awake at night and longing for his kisses, or praying some turn of events would happen so she could see him before the day was over.

Lord Brentwood was exciting and very appealing to all her senses. And already she missed not being with him.

It would be so easy for her to just accept the fact her father wanted her to marry him. Because the truth was she wanted to be with him, and she had wanted to be with him since the moment she saw him standing in the mist. It was as if fate had said to her, *This man is yours for the taking. Take him.* But Brent had not chosen her. By her actions that morning, she had forced all this on him, and now she had to do her best to give him back his freedom to choose his own wife.

Slowly her smile faded. She could easily allow herself to fall in love with him, if only he wasn't merely fulfilling his obligation for being caught kissing her.

When she laid her things on the table, she noticed a letter addressed to her on the silver calling card plate. "Staunton," she said, quickly picking it up. She had been waiting to hear from him. She broke the seal and read.

> *My Dearest Gabby,*
> *If you should find yourself taking in the sights*

*of St. James tomorrow afternoon, perhaps our paths
will cross.*

> *I am with kindest regards,*
> *Staunton*

It wasn't the friendliest of correspondence, but
at last he'd finally answered her. She needed to find
Auntie Bethie immediately to see if she was free for a
ride in the park.

Gabrielle walked down the corridor and looked into
the drawing room. Auntie Bethie was reading in a chair
by the fireplace. Brutus greeted her with a woof and
wagged his tail but didn't try to rise from his pillow.

"Good afternoon, Auntie," she said, walking over
and giving her aunt a kiss on her cheek, and then over
to Brutus to pat his head and scratch his ears. Thanks
to Brent, her old companion had had a wonderful
time in the park.

"How was your afternoon?" Auntie Bethie asked,
closing her book and laying it in her lap.

There was no way Gabrielle could keep a big
smile off her face as she said, "It was quite enjoyable,
Auntie."

"I thought it would be. Lord Brentwood is
certainly handsome enough to look at for an entire
afternoon."

"Most definitely," Gabrielle said, holding her hands
in front of the low-burning fire to warm them.

"Sit down and tell me all about it. I want to hear
everything."

Gabrielle made herself comfortable on the settee
and took her time telling about the day. She went into

great detail about the viscount losing his hat because of her bumping him with her parasol, about Brutus slobbering on the glossy shine of Lord Brentwood's Hessians, and about the woman with the dog they had chased down. But she left out all references to the few exciting and satisfying minutes she spent in Brent's arms.

When their laughter over the afternoon's events had died down, Auntie Bethie said, "I've been thinking about something for a long time, even before I arrived in London, and it's time I told you about it."

Gabrielle moved to the edge of the settee. "Yes, tell me."

"I've decided to leave Southampton and find a place here in London to lease."

"Oh, Auntie, that is wonderful news! You know how I have always wanted you to be close by so we could see you more often."

Her aunt's eyes took on a sheen Gabrielle had never seen in them before and, for the first time she could ever remember, her aunt was close to tears.

"Yes, I know, my dear, but your father has never wanted that, and I have been somewhat at his mercy financially, as you know, for many years."

Gabrielle rose from the settee and knelt in front of her aunt, taking hold of her hands. "I'm sorry my father has always treated you so atrociously."

She lightly squeezed Gabrielle's fingers. "No, my dear, he hasn't. How can I think that when he has provided exceptionally well for me all these years because of his vow to my dear sister? And he has allowed me to visit you and Rosa a couple of times each year, so I can't be too harsh on him. I have been very frugal, and because of his generosity, I've been able to save a good portion of my yearly allowance from him. I've made one or two investments that have paid me well. I now have enough that even if he stops my monthly allowance, I will live comfortably in London for the rest of my days."

Happiness surged inside Gabrielle. "Stay in London, Auntie. You know I would never let you go without anything you needed."

Her aunt's eyes cleared, and she laughed in the deep, throaty voice Gabrielle loved to hear. "Thank you, dear. It makes me very happy to know you want me to live close by."

"I have an idea, Auntie, why don't we start looking tomorrow for places for you to lease?"

"Tomorrow?"

"Yes, we have no idea when Papa might return, and you should have something ready. We'll get started early in the day and then perhaps in the afternoon we can take a drive through St. James Park."

A knowing smile lifted the corners of her aunt's lips. "A ride through St. James; now why doesn't that surprise me? Of course we can, and we'll insist Rosa join us. She spends entirely too much time in her room."

"Ah, no, Auntie, please, not tomorrow," Gabrielle said, rising. She ran her hands down the side of her skirt and felt Staunton's note. She hadn't expected her aunt to include her sister. That would never work. "Do you mind so terribly much if it's just the two of us tomorrow?"

Auntie Bethie frowned. "I suppose not, as long as she doesn't ask to join us. I would hate to tell her no."

"Oh, I agree," Gabrielle said, knowing if Rosa wanted to join them to look at houses, she would have to send a note to Staunton telling him they would have to meet at another time.

Later that night, Gabrielle's eyes popped open, and she jerked upright in bed, at first not knowing what had disturbed her sleep. She propped herself up with her elbows and scanned the dark room and listened. Nothing appeared out of place, but for some reason she was certain what she'd heard was footsteps. It would be unusual for one of the servants to be on their floor in the dead of night. Perhaps her aunt or Rosa couldn't sleep and had decided to go downstairs for a cup of chocolate.

Pushing the covers aside, Gabrielle rose from the bed and quickly put on her heavy velvet robe and shoved her feet into her slippers. She lit the candle she kept by her bed, and then hurried to her door and opened it. The corridor was cold, quiet, and dark except for a small slice of light under her sister's door. Rosabelle often read late at night, so at first she wasn't alarmed; but remembering the footsteps she heard, Gabrielle decided to go to Rosa's room. She slowly turned the knob and quietly opened it and peeked inside.

Rosa was standing in front of her dressing table, combing her hair.

She gasped and turned toward Gabrielle. "Good heavens! You frightened me! What are you doing sneaking into my room? And with that candle in front of your face like that? It looks eerie!"

"I wasn't sneaking," Gabrielle said and blew out the candle as she walked into the room, closing the door behind her so their voices wouldn't wake Auntie Bethie. "I heard footsteps and came out to see who was up. I saw your light and wanted to check on you."

"Check on me? I'm no longer a little girl, Gabby. I don't need you checking on me during the night like you used to."

"And I don't usually. I haven't for a long time. You know that. Where were you?"

"Oh, I couldn't sleep, so I was downstairs, getting some milk."

Gabrielle feared she already knew what Rosa had been doing. "And you decided you needed to dress before going downstairs for milk?"

Rosabelle looked at her clothing.

Rosa opened her mouth to speak, but before she could, Gabrielle said, "And before you come up with another feeble excuse, remember I saw you earlier tonight and you were already in your night rail."

Rosa turned back toward her dressing mirror and huffed. "You are mistaken, that's all. I never dressed for bed tonight."

"I am not mistaken, Rosa. Did you slip out of the house to meet Staunton?"

She whirled back to face Gabrielle. "So what if I did meet him in the garden for a few minutes? We hadn't seen each other in weeks. We were dying to see each other."

Anger at Staunton rose up in Gabrielle. How dare he continue to put Rosa's reputation at risk. "That is what parties are for, Rosa. I've tried to impress upon you the jeopardy you face if you continue to meet Staunton in secret. You simply must not sneak out of the house again for any reason. That can only lead to trouble."

"As you know so well, Gabby," Rosa threw at her sister. "Tell me why it is perfectly all right for you to sneak out to meet Lord Brentwood, but it's not all right for me to go out and meet Staunton. Don't you think that's a little hypocritical of you?"

"It may seem that way, but, Rosa, I've told you I didn't go to Hyde to meet the viscount. We met quite by accident that morning."

"And you expect me to believe that?"

"Yes, and even though it was an accidental meeting, it has led to disastrous consequences for both of us."

Rosa walked over to the bed and picked up her sleeping gown, putting her back to Gabrielle. "Your situation really doesn't matter to me at the moment, Gabby. I'll just have to make sure you don't catch me next time. Now if you don't mind, I would appreciate your leaving my room. I'm ready to put on my night rail and sleep so I can dream about Staunton."

Frustration with Rosa burned inside Gabrielle, and she grabbed her sister's arms and turned her around. Rosa's foolishness and impulsive behavior had gone too far. "I cannot allow you to be this flippant about your reputation. I will have to tell Papa and ask him to send you to one of his country estates where you will never see Staunton again."

Rosa stiffened. "You wouldn't."

"Of course I will," Gabrielle said coldly, thinking only about how much she detested Staunton for preying on Rosa's affection for him.

Her sister's blue eyes sparkled with apprehension, and her bottom lip trembled. "Please tell me you won't tell Papa about me and Staunton. I promise never to meet him in secret again."

Within seconds, Rosa went from a self-assured young lady, determined to get her way, to looking and sounding like a frightened child begging not to be punished. For a moment, as Gabrielle stared at her sister, she was tempted to give in and agree she wouldn't tell the duke. But Brent came to her mind, and Gabrielle knew she couldn't. She had given up too much already in order to save Rosa's reputation. She would not let Staunton ruin it now.

"If I even suspect you are slipping out again to meet Staunton, or anyone else, I will not even tell you I know. I will go straight to Papa and let him deal with you."

Gabrielle turned and walked out, knowing she couldn't wait to have a talk tomorrow with Mr. Alfred Staunton.

❦

Gabrielle watched Auntie Bethie shiver as the carriage bumped along the uneven terrain of St. James Park. They had spent several hours touring homes for lease in different areas of London, but her aunt wasn't ready to make a decision to settle on any of them. There were few carriages in St. James, so Gabrielle had hoped to spot Staunton quickly, but there had been no such luck. They'd been riding the carriage path for almost an hour with no sign of her former fiancé. Gabrielle was beginning to think they had missed him or he'd decided not to meet her.

"Why must I suffer through another cold ride around this dreary park?" her aunt complained as Muggs allowed the horses to plod along slowly.

Deciding to be truthful, Gabrielle said, "If you must know, Auntie, I'm looking for someone."

"Oh, fiddle faddle, Gabby! I know that. Why can't you just invite the viscount for afternoon tea? It's much warmer in the drawing room than out here. The damp air is threatening rain."

"It's not Lord Brentwood I am looking for this time," Gabrielle admitted.

"Oh," her aunt said, sounding surprised. "Has another young blade caught your eye?"

"No, no, Auntie, not this one for sure, but you must believe me when I tell you what I'm doing is very important."

"I do believe you, dearie. I just don't know why you want to conduct your affairs in the parks so blasted often. It's not summer, you know. It's not even spring, and it is damn cold out here."

Gabrielle pulled the blanket farther up her aunt's chest and tucked it around her neck. "Oh, Auntie, I would be happy to ride alone if I could, but you know I can't, so I must bring you with me. We'll stay only a few minutes more, I promise. Shall I pour you more chocolate?"

"No, I feel like I will float away if I drink any

more before I find a chamber pot!" Auntie Bethie laughed at her remark and huddled down into the folds of the blanket.

Gabrielle joined her aunt's laughter as they rounded a bend on the west side of the park. When Gabrielle looked up, she saw Staunton sitting on his horse not far away. His back was ramrod straight and his chin lifted in an arrogant tilt.

"It's about time," she spoke softly under her breath, feeling relief he'd arrived.

She leaned up to Muggs and said, "That's Mr. Alfred Staunton ahead of us. Please stop when we get near him and help me down."

As she settled back in her seat, her aunt said, "So I now see who you wanted to meet, but I have no idea why. You don't intend to apologize to him after the way he attacked Lord Brentwood at Lady Windham's party, do you?"

Gabrielle kept her eyes on Staunton's proud figure. "Absolutely not, Auntie. I will not be apologizing to him for anything, I assure you. No, it's quite a different matter I need to discuss with the earl's son." Gabrielle looked over at her aunt and patted her fur muff. "Thank you for being patient with me and for being so willing to put up with my strange habits. I don't know what I would have done if you had not come and Papa had not gone away."

Her aunt reached over and gave her a rare kiss on the cheek, and Gabrielle gasped with delight. "What was that for?"

Auntie Bethie's eyes softened. "For all the times I've wanted to be there for you and couldn't. Now go, talk to this man and say whatever you must. I will shiver right here until you return."

Gabrielle's heart swelled in her chest, and she gave her aunt a heartfelt smile. "Thank you, Auntie."

Muggs helped Gabrielle down from the carriage as Staunton dismounted and, holding his riding crop, sauntered up to the carriage.

"Lady Gabrielle." Staunton stopped in front of her, took off his hat, and bowed rather stiffly. He then placed his hat under his arm. "It's nice to see you. I must say your loveliness brightens an otherwise gloomy day."

"Thank you, Staunton. You remember my aunt, Mrs. Potter, don't you?"

"Of course I do. How could I forget such a lovely lady? You are looking as beautiful as ever, Mrs. Potter. I trust you are well."

"Quite well, Mr. Staunton. Thank you."

Gabrielle looked at Staunton and said, "Perhaps you'll take a short walk with me. You don't mind, do you, Auntie?"

"Not as long as you don't get out of my sight and you don't take too long."

"I promise not to do either, Auntie."

Gabrielle and Staunton walked away from the carriage. It was the first time Gabrielle had ever noticed that although Staunton was broad in the shoulders, he wasn't much taller than she was. With his light blue eyes and sandy brown hair, she'd always thought him attractive. She had easily agreed with her father when he'd said there was much to recommend him. And it was true that his station in life and handsome face made him a sought-after match for many young ladies.

But looking at him now, Gabrielle knew she'd never felt any womanly desire for him. She had never felt that all-consuming, breathless excitement of wanting. She had that feeling the first time she caught sight of Brent. And it hadn't gone away. If anything, her feelings for him had only grown stronger.

It pained her to have to continue to find ways to make herself unattractive to Brent, when all she really wanted was to make herself so appealing to him he would forget about the way they had met. She wanted him to forget her father threatened to ruin his brothers' business. She wanted him to feel for her all the things she felt for him.

But she knew from experience life was seldom so accommodating.

"How are you, Staunton?" she said after they were well out of her aunt's hearing.

"I suppose I'm as well as can be expected, considering all I've been through."

"Well, you are looking quite fit."

He smiled. "Thank you," he said and then added, "It's truly been quite hellish the past couple of weeks, but I've withstood the jokes and damning wagers that are cropping up all over London. I do believe the gossip is easing now."

She wanted to say she was sorry for what he'd been through but couldn't find it within herself to do it. "Thank you for coming to meet me, Staunton."

"I rather expected I would hear from you sooner or later."

Obviously Rosa had told him she knew about the two of them. "Good. That should make what I have to say easier."

"Easier?" He laughed. "No, Gabby, I'm pleased you came to your senses and wanted to meet with me to discuss what happened and what will happen now, but you need to know I am not of a mind to make it easy for you. Why should I, after the stunt you pulled in the park with the viscount and the extreme embarrassment you caused me?"

Her brows drew together quizzically. That sounded odd. Did that mean he was going to fight her father about having their engagement annulled?

"But this isn't about me, Staunton."

"Isn't it? Your behavior was shameful. An apology about now would be appropriate."

Gabrielle pursed her lips and hesitated as she stared at his smug expression. Apparently he wanted an apology to soothe his bruised self-esteem before he would talk about Rosa. She really didn't want to say she was sorry, because she wasn't. She was happy they were no longer engaged, and he should be too.

However, she remembered Auntie Bethie telling her that her mother had said an apology is never out of line. Obviously, Gabrielle wasn't as good as her mother because she didn't feel one was necessary, considering the fact Staunton was in love with Rosa and seeing her behind Gabrielle's back.

But for Rosa's sake, Gabrielle was willing to forgive, forget, and apologize.

She cleared her throat and forced herself to say, "I'm sorry for any anguish my mistake caused you."

He sneered. "That's all?"

Exasperated, she said, "I apologized. There's nothing more that need be said, so could we please get on with the matter at hand?"

Staunton huffed and moved his hat from under one arm to the other. "Very well, I suppose it will do. And yes, I'm willing to accept you back and carry on with our wedding plans at a later date."

Gabrielle stopped walking and looked at him with uncomprehending eyes. Did he say what she thought he had?

Surely not.

He moved closer, and she instinctively stepped back. "But you have been very naughty." Suddenly he smiled. "You must first show me how contrite you are about the way you misbehaved."

A shiver of dread skimmed her spine and gooseflesh pebbled her skin, even though she was wrapped in her heavy woolen cape. Something wasn't right.

She moistened her lips. "I'm afraid I don't understand."

"Then let me explain it to you. With our first engagement, you held all the cards, and why shouldn't you? Being the eldest child of a duke, you had been taught you had certain rights and expectations. But that won't be so, this time."

This time?

Was he really talking about salvaging their engagement? Why? When he was supposed to love Rosa?

Apparently unaware Gabrielle was confused, Staunton kept talking.

"I've decided to take you back as my betrothed. And, Gabby, when I want to kiss you, my dear, I will kiss you. You will not pull away from me and plead innocent as you have in the past. You will not tell me you will not join me in the garden for a late evening good-night kiss. You will be at my beck and call, and I will call you often."

He stood so proud and confident before her that Gabrielle could only stare at him in silence. He was not saying what she had expected him to say.

"What on earth are you talking about, Staunton? I didn't come here to ask you to renew our engagement."

His brow wrinkled. "What?"

"I came to talk to you about Rosa."

He shifted his hat again, and the corners of his eyes twitched guiltily. "What did she tell you about us?"

"That you love each other."

"She's a foolish young girl who obviously has fantasies I don't begin to understand."

Gabrielle gasped. "I know you have been slipping around to see each other. I came here to tell you that must stop. If anyone finds out, her reputation will be in shreds."

Red splotches broke out on his face. "Something like your reputation, I suppose. You seem to be doing all right after your little affair in the park."

Gabrielle's jaw went slack and then tightened. She was so caught off guard by what he was saying she hardly knew how to respond.

"I am handling the gossip in the newsprint and the whispers at parties, but Rosa would find it very difficult to do. If you want to marry her, you must do the right thing by her and tell your father and hers to post the banns and marry immediately."

Staunton chuckled. His earlier nervous twitch was gone; his confidence had returned. "Marry her? Where did you get—did she tell you that?"

Gabrielle was beginning to understand Staunton, and she didn't like what she was discovering. Her gloved hands made fists inside her muff, and her throat felt tight and restricted.

"Yes, of course. She told me you loved each other and you want to be married. I know this to be true, because I saw you two kissing. I saw the passion between you. I saw—"

He stepped in closer to her and snarled. "You saw what you obviously wanted to see, you little spy."

She gasped. "Spy?"

"Yes, that's what you are. And yes, there was passion between us, because she is not afraid to be kissed and touched like you are."

"Are you telling me you don't love Rosa?"

"Love her?" He shrugged in a nonchalant manner. "I love that she is passionate. That she enjoys being in a man's arms. She likes to be caressed and told how beautiful she is. Things you never wanted me to do or say. So what else was I to do when she sought me out and offered herself to me?"

"No," Gabrielle whispered, not wanting to hear any more from him.

"Yes! Why shouldn't I accept her kisses and caresses when I couldn't get my fiancée to allow me one little kiss?"

"That's not true. Staunton, you know I allowed you to kiss me."

"You gave me chaste little kisses that meant

nothing and didn't have enough fire in them to stir passion in either of us. And I had to ask myself, how could Rosa be so hot-blooded when you were always so timid and cold? Every time I tried to kiss you, you rebuffed me as if you were too special for me to touch."

Gabrielle felt breathless and light-headed. "No, that's not true," she said but knew her words rang false.

She stared into his confident blue eyes and realized he had gone after Rosa when he didn't get what he wanted from her.

She had never wanted to marry Staunton. She wanted only to obey her father, because that was expected of her. She had never felt passion when she was with Staunton but had expected it would come after they married. But now that she had tasted desire from the lips and touch of Lord Brentwood, she knew the passion Staunton wanted from her would have never come.

"Of course it is, and now I know why you didn't want to marry me. You wanted a title. The youngest son of a wealthy earl was not good enough for you, so you went out and snared a viscount for yourself."

Is that really what he thought about her? Gabrielle inhaled, breathing the cold air deep into her lungs, clearing her head and her throat.

"Staunton, hear me well," she said calmly but firmly. "As you said, I am the daughter of a duke, a powerful duke, and I'm not afraid to use his power or his influence. Stay away from my sister, or I will see to it you will not find a mama in London who will let you come near her daughter."

His eyes narrowed and twitched. "Are you threatening me, Gabby?"

She smiled. "Yes, I am. And, Staunton, it's *Lady Gabrielle* when you are speaking to me."

Gabrielle turned and started walking back toward her aunt. Her legs were shaky, but inside she felt strong knowing Staunton was wrong. She was filled to overflowing with passion. Brent had proved that to her.

And Gabrielle knew just whom to speak to about Staunton if he dared try to see Rosa in secret again. She'd heard Lady Windham took to her sick bed after her last party because Staunton had dared cause a scene in her home. Lady Windham was already predisposed to be wary of him, and if Gabrielle told her he was enticing young ladies into ruination, no doubt she'd be happy to spread the word to the pushy mamas in London.

But how would Rosa take his absence? Would she write him another note and try to see him in secret even though she had promised not to?

There was no way Gabrielle could watch Rosa every minute. Gabrielle would ask her maid, Petra, to help her keep an eye on Rosa's whereabouts.

Fourteen

Jealousy is the only vice that gives no pleasure.

—Anonymous

THE CUDDLEBURY'S HOUSE WAS FILLED TO OVERFLOWING with elegantly dressed ladies and dapper-looking gentlemen chatting, laughing, and dancing under a brightly lit chandelier. Perhaps the lively mood of the gathering was because December was only a few days away and everyone was feeling the need to celebrate the festive season early. The music hadn't stopped all evening, and from her aunt's side at the far end of the dance floor, Gabrielle hadn't stopped watching Rosabelle. Her sister seemed to be having a delightful time. She had already danced with three different gentlemen. But every once in a while, Gabrielle would catch Rosa watching the entrance to the room.

Her sister had been eager to come to the party and had spent the entire afternoon getting ready for the affair, Gabrielle knew, in hopes of seeing Staunton. If he arrived, she was determined to see he didn't sneak into the garden with Rosabelle.

Gabrielle had worried over what to do since her egregious meeting with Staunton yesterday afternoon. She had vacillated too many times to count on whether she should tell Rosa that Staunton didn't love her or remain quiet but watchful. She had wondered how Rosa would react if she did. Would she fly into a rage, slip into a depression, or do something crazy like go see him? But in the end, she didn't tell Rosa because she feared Rosa wouldn't believe her. Gabrielle came to the conclusion there was no use in expecting Rosa to give up her dreams of marrying Staunton; Staunton would have to give up Rosa. And if he didn't do that soon, Gabrielle knew what she had to do.

"Gabby," her aunt said, "I don't think you've moved from my side since you got here. You are not a wallflower, a spinster, or an old woman like me. Now go out in the midst of that crowd and enjoy yourself."

Gabrielle looked down at her aunt. "I am having a good time watching everyone else dance."

"Not good enough. Tell me, are you waiting for that handsome viscount to arrive?"

"He told me he's not coming, Auntie."

"Why not?" Auntie Bethie rose from the chair to stand beside Gabrielle. "I've seen both his brothers here."

"After what Staunton did at Lady's Windham's, Brent thought it best he not attend any parties for a while. He didn't want to be the cause of any more trouble."

"Hmm, that means if Staunton wanted a fight, next time he'd oblige him."

Gabrielle nodded.

"That's admirable of him."

"I thought so too," she answered, but knowing his reasons didn't keep her from feeling empty inside.

"Look, I see your friend Miss Whitehouse heading this way. Go spend some time with her. How will I ever get a wealthy young bachelor to notice me if you are always around?"

"Auntie!"

Her aunt laughed and turned away as Babs walked up.

"Gabby," her friend said, giving her a quick hug. "I saw you standing over here when I was on the dance floor."

"And I saw you, too, dancing with Mr. Iverson Brentwood."

Delight lit Babs's eyes, and she smiled. "I did. How did you know which one I was dancing with? I can't tell the twins apart."

"I'll give you a clue about their differences. The one named Iverson has longer hair than his brother."

"Really? I didn't notice it was."

"It's not obvious. There's only a slight difference, and it requires a keen eye."

"I will pay close attention the next time I see the two of them together."

"All right, come with me to get a drink," Gabrielle said. "I want to ask you something."

"I hope you want to know something deliciously scandalous so I can tell you something sinfully naughty," Babs said as they made their way over to the punch table.

Gabrielle laughed as they threaded a path through the crowd. "No more scandals. I'm through with them, but I do need your help. I've done everything I can think of to appear unacceptable as a wife to Lord Brentwood, but he seems completely unaware of all my efforts."

Babs gave her a quizzical look. "First, I must ask, why do you want to be unacceptable to him? He's titled, handsome, and dashing."

"All that and more."

"That's what I mean. I've heard of making a gentleman want to chase you, but why would you want to chase one away? Why do you want to appear unacceptable to such a worthy catch?"

Gabrielle pulled her bottom lip into her mouth for a moment and then released it. "I'd rather not go into details right now, Babs."

"All right. I can see this is serious for you, so tell me what you've done."

"I've tried the things I knew my father would absolutely hate. I've pretended not to know how to dance, insisted he go to church with me, told him I believe in ghosts, and forced him to help me with Brutus." She stopped and sighed. "There have been other things, too, but nothing has worked."

They stopped in front of the drink table, and the servant handed each of them a cup of punch.

"Oh, I know something my father positively abhors," Babs offered. "He says he can't abide piano recitals, and he told my mother he would never attend another."

"Oh, yes, my father feels the same way about them. And since he is still gone, and my aunt is here, I can have a recital in my home and invite a few friends and Brent."

"Brent?" Babs asked in mock horror. "That sounds rather familiar, don't you think?"

"Yes, well, anyway," Gabrielle said and cleared her throat. "I know just the pianist to invite. Mr. Michael Murray."

"Oh, yes, I remember him from last year." Babs laughed. "He's so uninspiring; he'll bore everyone to tears."

"Hopefully none more than Lord Brentwood," Gabrielle said excitedly. "Mr. Murray will be perfect. I'll talk to Auntie Bethie about it right now, and we'll start planning the recital."

Gabrielle gave Babs a hug and started threading her way back through the crowd.

"Excuse me, Lady Gabrielle."

Gabrielle stopped and turned to see the Dowager Countess of Owensfield. She curtseyed and said, "Yes, my lady?"

"I couldn't help but overhear your conversation with Miss Whitehouse. I think it would be highly improper for you to have any kind of gathering in your home at this time and expect people to attend."

"Countess," Gabrielle said, trying to remain calm as she looked at the woman's wide, flat face. "I had no idea anyone was listening to my private conversation."

"Obviously I didn't do it on purpose. You shouldn't even be here tonight. But because you have no mother to advise you, and your father has left London from what I can only assume is the shame you brought to his house, I'll take it upon myself to instruct you on what is proper. After what you did, you should not even show your face in Society, and if you do, you should be shunned. It is not acceptable for a young lady who has been caught in the park alone with a man to mingle in Society with decent, circumspect people. Especially if the lady was engaged to another man! That was shameful, and your kind is not wanted with our kind."

Gabrielle had grown more rigid with every word the dowager spoke. Her voice barely above a whisper, she said, "I was invited here."

The dowager huffed, and her heavy bosom heaved. "Yes, and I'm sure Mrs. Cuddlebury sent your invitation long before she knew of your scandalous indiscretion. I'm sure your attendance is an embarrassment to her, and you should hang your head in shame and march yourself out of this house immediately."

Gabrielle started to tell the dowager she was completely out of line and she had already spoken to Mrs. Cuddlebury, who was delighted she had come. But at that moment, Gabrielle saw Rosa and Staunton walking out of the drawing room together, and what the countess said no longer mattered. She had to stop them.

"Thank you for your observation, Lady Owensville. Please explain all your grievances to my father when he returns, and perhaps he will listen to you. I don't care to hear any more of what you have to say. Now if you will excuse me."

Gabrielle lifted her chin, her shoulders, and the hem of her skirt and walked away without so much as another glance toward the huffing dowager.

Gabrielle headed in the direction she saw Staunton and Rosa disappear. She waded through the crowd as fast as she could without causing a stir. She rubbed elbows, knocked shoulders, and bumped backs as she hurried along.

Staunton would not get Rosabelle alone if Gabrielle had anything to say about it. She caught sight of them about to walk out a side door and picked up her pace. She reached them in time to grab Rosa's arm and swing her around.

"There you are, Rosa," she said breathlessly. "I was just looking for you."

Rosa's astonished expression at being caught quickly turned to a look of fury, but Gabrielle paid her no mind. She turned to Staunton, smiled sweetly, and said, "And how are you this evening?"

He looked her up and down stiffly and said, "Well, Lady Gabrielle, and you?"

Rosabelle looked at her as if she wanted to scratch her eyes out and pulled her arm from Gabrielle's grasp. Gabrielle left a sweet smile on her face as if nothing were wrong.

"Did you just arrive, Staunton, or were you just leaving?"

He looked at her curiously. "Just arrived," he said.

"Oh, that's such a shame, as Rosa and I have to leave."

Rosabelle glared at her and said curtly, "No, we don't."

"I'm afraid we must, Sister. Auntie Bethie isn't feeling well and asked me to find you so we can leave."

Gabrielle had never told an untruth until recently and, suddenly, she was telling far more than she was comfortable with. All the ones she'd told to Brent had bothered her, but telling this prevarication to Staunton didn't bother her at all.

"We can ask someone to see us home," Rosa argued. "We shouldn't have to miss the evening because Auntie isn't feeling well."

Keeping her false smile in place, Gabrielle said, "Surely we can't allow Auntie to go home alone. Now I'll go tell her I found you and you'll meet us at the front door in two minutes. That should give you two plenty of time for a chat. Have a nice evening, Staunton." Gabrielle turned away.

When Gabrielle made her way back to Auntie Bethie, she was talking with another lady but excused herself when Gabrielle motioned for her to come.

"What is it?" Auntie Bethie asked.

"I fear I have put you in a most untenable position, Auntie, and I hope you will forgive me."

The corners of her eyes wrinkled in worry. "What's wrong?"

"I found Rosa about to take a walk in the garden with a gentleman I know she shouldn't be with, so I told her you were not feeling well and she was to meet us at the front door in two minutes. Are you angry with me?"

"Angry?" Her aunt laughed heartily. "Heavens, no! I trust your judgment about the man, and I've been ready to go since we got here."

"Good. That makes me feel somewhat better about my prevarication."

"Nonsense. It wasn't a prevarication. At my age, I always have an ache or a pain somewhere in this body. You can always use my ailments as an excuse."

Gabrielle hugged her aunt tightly and whispered, "I'm so glad you will be staying in London. It looks like I'm going to need you."

"And I'm glad," her aunt said, patting her shoulder. "There's nothing I'd rather do than help you with a sister who is one minute so happy she's on top of the world and then the next feels like her world is crumbling beneath her feet."

The servant walked up with Gabrielle's cloak. Thank goodness she had her aunt to lend a hand with Rosa, because Gabrielle had her hands full with Brent.

∽

Brent walked into White's and handed his coat, hat, and gloves to the attendant. He was in need of something strong to get his mind off Gabrielle. If not for Staunton's foolhardy stunt, he could be at the Cuddlebury's house, talking and dancing with Gabrielle. Instead, he had to settle for a few hands of cards or a game or two of billiards to fill the hours in the night. He spoke to a couple of gentlemen on his way to the taproom, where he walked up to the bar and leaned against it.

A roaring fire added warmth to the dimly lit room. It looked as if every chair was filled with men talking noisily. The scent of burned wood and candle wax hung heavily on the air. Brent stuck his finger down his collar, trying to loosen it, while he ordered a glass of brandy. Perhaps a sip or two of the amber liquid would lift his spirits and put him in the mood to win big at the gaming tables.

As he waited for his drink, Gabrielle came to his mind. The truth was she seldom left his thoughts. And he didn't know why. She had played him for a fool when they first met, but after getting to know her, it had been easy to forgive her for that. She had her reasons, and one day he'd find out what made her walk out of the mist and into his arms.

It wasn't her fault her father had threatened to ruin his brothers' business if he didn't marry her, and she certainly hadn't let that stop her from making it perfectly clear she didn't want to marry him. She had gone to great lengths to make him not want to marry her. He chuckled to himself, remembering the afternoon she hoped to read poetry to him. He'd tried to make it clear to her she couldn't do anything that would dissuade him from marrying her, especially now that he had tasted her passion.

He closed his eyes and remembered how soft and pliant her lips were when he'd kissed her under that tree. He remembered how her breasts were firm yet soft beneath the palm of his hand.

"Lord Brentwood?"

Brent's eyes popped open. He turned and saw Lord Waldo, the Duke of Rockcliffe's youngest brother, standing beside him. After his altercation with Iverson, Brent was surprised the man spoke to him.

"Evening, Lord Waldo."

The duke's brother asked the server for a tankard of ale before turning back to Brent. "I don't know if you've heard, but my brother's dog is missing." The man was as nervous as a hen staring at a fox. His big blue eyes twitched and he blinked rapidly.

Brent straightened. "No, I hadn't heard."

"My brother doesn't know Tulip is gone yet, as he's been away. I'd like to find her before the duke returns. I was wondering if you might be able to help me."

First Snellingly approached him and now Lord Waldo. Was everyone who lost a dog going to come to him for help now?

"I don't suppose I'd mind, Lord Waldo, but I don't know how I can. I've not yet found my mother's dog."

"I'm sorry about that. I was hoping you had. It would have given me more hope. I know you've been searching the parks and streets for your dog, and I was hoping maybe you'd seen a small beige terrier. She answers to Tulip or Tooley."

Brent thought about the little dog he'd seen with the old woman in the park. It couldn't have been the Duke of Rockcliffe's dog because that one was black.

There was no use in telling the man he was no longer looking for Prissy. He knew from personal experience that all Lord Waldo wanted was hope, and he didn't mind giving the man that. "I haven't seen the duke's dog, but I'll keep my eye out for her and certainly try to catch her if I do."

"Thank you. I suppose you've heard some think maybe Lord Pinkwater's ghost is snatching up the dogs for his own pleasure."

The server set a glass of brandy in front of Brent, and he pulled it toward him. "I've heard."

"I'm not one who believes that," Lord Waldo said, "in case you're wondering."

"I wasn't."

"Some others are thinking there might be a wild animal roaming in the parks and streets."

"I've heard," Brent said, though he had his doubts

about that as well. He was beginning to believe it was a two-legged animal who was taking the dogs, but who and for what purpose? But as nervous as Lord Waldo was acting, there was no way Brent was going to tell him he thought the possibility of finding the duke's dog was very slim.

The server put a tankard in front of Lord Waldo, and he picked it up with a shaky hand and took a long drink before saying, "I'm working on organizing a group of gentlemen to go on a night hunt through the parks. I'd be pleased if you would join us. It's all right if you don't want to," he added quickly. "I asked Lord Snellingly and he declined. He said he's not much of a hunter."

Brent could believe that of Snellingly. He couldn't imagine that fop sitting a horse in the dead of night, as cold as it was this time of year.

For whatever reason, it appeared to Brent that Lord Waldo was trying to make amends for his disastrous meeting with Iverson. Brent needed to buck up and meet the man halfway. He didn't know what was happening to the dogs, but whatever it was, he was damn sure it had nothing to do with a ghost.

"Let me know when and where to meet and I'll be there."

Lord Waldo smiled gratefully. "Thank you, my lord. You can count on it."

Brent picked up his brandy and headed down the corridor that led to the gaming rooms. He stopped to look in the billiard room and saw that games were in progress at both tables. He started toward the card room when he caught sight of Sir Randolph

Gibson, and immediately an idea popped into his mind. Brent leaned against the door frame. He sipped his brandy, deciding to watch for a while and think on his idea. His brothers wouldn't like it, but it wouldn't be the first time he did something they didn't like.

When Sir Randolph's game ended, he put his cue stick in the wall bracket and walked over to Brent. It was past midnight, and some men were beginning to show signs of being brandy-faced, but the old man appeared as dapper as he looked at midday.

Sir Randolph bowed. "My lord."

"Sir Randolph, may I buy you a drink?"

He hesitated. "I was on my way home. It's late for an old man like me."

"I won't detain you long."

"In that case, I'll have a glass of whatever you're drinking."

They walked back into the noisy taproom and found a table that had just been vacated. Brent asked the server to bring two glasses of brandy, and then he sat down opposite Sir Randolph.

"I understand your father was in the shipping business during the war with America."

Sir Randolph folded his arms across his chest and nodded. "That's right."

"You sold the business years ago."

He nodded again.

Obviously Sir Randolph was a man of few words. He wasn't going to offer any information that wasn't specifically asked for. "Did you know my brothers have a shipbuilding business in Maryland?"

"I've heard that."

The server put their drinks in front of them, but neither man offered to pick up his glass.

"Then I'll get right to the point. They are moving the business to London and are looking for space at the docks to lease, but they keep running into trouble."

The older man's eyes narrowed, and he unfolded his arms. "What kind of trouble?"

"It seems that all the owners who have space available are holding it until the Duke of Windergreen decides whether or not he will need it in the future."

"There aren't too many people who would go against a duke. I'm sure if he asked them to hold the space for him, they will."

"Yes, that's the problem. I thought perhaps because your father was in shipping you might have knowledge of existing space that wasn't being held for the duke."

Sir Randolph picked up his glass and sipped, keeping his gaze on Brent the entire time. After he set his glass down, he said, "I might."

Encouraged by that, Brent asked, "Do you think it might be available for my brothers to lease?"

The old man's crafty brown eyes never wavered, and his hands stayed steady. "I could check into that for you."

"And if there were such space, would my brothers have to know you had anything to do with finding it for them?"

"Not as far as I'm concerned."

Brent relaxed a little. "And how might they go about finding this space?"

Sir Randolph picked up his drink thoughtfully and took a slow sip. "I'll see that someone finds them."

Fifteen

He is most free from danger, who, even when safe, is on his guard.
—Publilius Syrus

CHIMES DINGED AND BELLS CLANGED AS BRENT, GABRIELLE, and Mrs. Potter walked down the church steps on a cloudy midday Sunday. A slight breeze added a chill to the gray day. Brent settled his top hat on his head, and the ladies opened their parasols, even though there wasn't a slice of sunshine to be seen anywhere in the sky.

"It was a lovely service," Gabrielle said, "don't you think?"

"Absolutely," her aunt answered quickly.

"What about you, my lord, what did you think?" Gabrielle asked him.

He glanced over at her and, with a smile, said, "I thought it divinely inspired."

Mrs. Potter laughed heartily as they strolled down the walkway toward the row of carriages and drivers waiting for their owners. "In case you don't know, Gabby, that means he was utterly bored to tears."

"Nonsense, Auntie," Gabrielle said with a sly smile.

"Every time I looked over at Lord Brentwood, his eyes were closed, and I saw no tears whatsoever. He must have been praying."

"Praying! Ha!" Her aunt belted a hearty laugh. "If he was praying, he was asking the Good Lord to let the service be over quickly!"

"Auntie, I'm sure that's not true."

Brent chuckled. He found Mrs. Potter charming and her ribald comments witty. "My eyes were closed only when I was sleeping," Brent said.

"I've noticed that a lot of gentlemen always seem to doze when in church," Gabrielle's aunt said.

"But I never closed my eyes while you were singing, Mrs. Potter. You have a lovely voice."

Mrs. Potter's dark brown eyes sparkled with humor. "Thank you, my lord. I do love it when a handsome young gentleman flatters me."

Brent stopped in front of his landau and reached for Mrs. Potter's hand. "It wasn't sweet talk. It's the truth. Should I have my driver put the top on the carriage? It doesn't look as if the day will get any warmer."

"Oh, no, not for me," she said. "I'm sorry to say I won't be joining you and Gabby today, so you must keep the top off." She turned and pointed farther down the street. "Muggs is right over there. I told him to wait for me when he dropped us off this morning."

Concern etched its way across Gabrielle's face. "But Auntie Bethie, you wanted to go to the fair. You've been looking forward to it all week."

"Of course I have, and perhaps I'll have the chance to go another time, but not today. I don't feel good about leaving Rosabelle alone for so long, especially since she isn't feeling well."

"Oh," Gabrielle said. "You're right. I should skip the fair as well, and go home with you."

"You will do no such thing, young lady," Mrs. Potter admonished. "Don't be silly. It doesn't take two of us to watch over her. Besides, I don't think there is anything seriously wrong with her, and I don't believe you do either. It's certainly nothing a little time can't cure. You two run along and enjoy yourselves. I'll take care of Rosa."

"Thank you, Mrs. Potter; that is exactly what we shall do."

"You will check on her often, won't you?" Gabrielle asked her aunt.

"More than she would want, for sure."

Keeping his distance from Gabrielle's parasol, Brent reached for her hand and helped her step into the carriage.

"Don't leave her alone for one second, my lord," Mrs. Potter said. "There are always unsavory characters at fairs and carnivals."

"You have no cause to worry about that. She shall not leave my sight."

"Good. I'll expect you back before dark."

"You can count on it," Brent said.

Brent looked at Gabrielle. Her gorgeous blue eyes sparkled despite the dreary day. She wore a beige dress sprigged with tiny blue flowers. Her black cape and matching bonnet were trimmed with a white-and-black—corded braid. He couldn't help but think how damn lucky he was that the lady who caught him in a parson's mousetrap was the most beautiful and fascinating lady he'd ever met.

Brent wouldn't have minded Mrs. Potter going with them. She was a fascinating lady, too, and always in a good humor. But if Mrs. Potter had gone with them, there would have been no chance he could kiss Gabrielle's delectable lips. He smiled to himself as he climbed onto the carriage and settled himself beside Gabrielle. Yes, he wasn't the least unhappy the lady had decided to spend the afternoon with her other niece.

Brent gave the driver the signal to go as he tucked a blanket around Gabrielle's legs. The first thing Brent noticed was she was not sitting as close to him, because the seats were longer in the much-bigger landau than they were in the curricle they used a few days ago. He missed feeling the warmth of her skirts. The second thing he noticed was her beige parasol with the fancy blue trim wasn't as big as the one she carried on their last outing, so hopefully his hat would remain on his head. He had lost two very expensive hats because of Gabrielle. The first was ruined the morning he met her, when it was stepped on by her footman after he wrestled Brent to the ground, and the second on his last outing with her. It was hard to believe it was now more than a month ago since he met her.

The driver guided the two mares out of the queue in front of the church and into the busy traffic as Gabrielle waved good-bye to her aunt. Sunday was the one day of the week when most Londoners didn't work, and there were always a lot of carriages, wagons, and horses on the streets.

"I see your lip has healed once again," Gabrielle said as the driver fit the landau in between a black shiny barouche and a low chaise.

Brent scooted a little closer to her, relaxed against the back of the seat, and said, "Yes, at last."

"You know what they say, don't you?"

He glanced at her. There was a twinkle of mischief sparkling in her eyes. "No, what do *they* say?"

"That things come in threes. So that means you can expect one more cut on the lip before the next new moon."

He hoped not. He didn't want to lose another hat either. "I do believe I have heard that, Gabrielle, but I can assure you I won't take kindly to whoever takes a swing at me the next time. And from now on, I'll be doubly wary if anyone taps me on the shoulder from behind."

"Then I'll make sure it's not me."

He smiled at her. "You are in no danger from me."

Her eyes softened. "I have no fear of you, Brent."

"Maybe that is true." He quirked an eyebrow at her. "I noticed you don't have your bodyguard with you today."

"My body—" She stopped and laughed. "Oh, you mean Brutus."

Brent tried to remain serious when he said, "Yes. I suppose he gets bored and falls asleep in church, too."

Gabrielle picked up on his teasing and continued it with, "Oh, yes, I had to stop bringing him because his snoring would drown out Auntie Bethie's singing."

They laughed, and Brent found himself slipping a little closer to her once again, and he made sure his thigh rested against hers. It pleased him that she didn't shy away from him.

"If I didn't know better," Gabrielle said, "I would think you are happy my precious dog is not with us today."

"To that, I'll only say that Brutus and I are becoming friends. I'm looking forward to seeing him when I attend the piano recital in your home on Thursday evening."

"I'm glad you're coming, and I know Brutus will be happy to see you, too."

With a deep contented breath and a smile, Gabrielle turned away from him and looked at the sights along the streets as the carriage rolled along at a lively pace.

Lady Gabrielle was the most difficult person he had ever tried to figure out. At times it seemed as if she was trying her best to keep him from being attracted to her by pretending she couldn't dance, pulling out poetry to read to him, or trying to make him believe she had a hellish temperament, and several of her ancestors had gone mad. But then there were other times, like the first time they met in the park, when she intrigued him by telling him to speak gently to Prissy. And times like now, when she was just so delightful he couldn't wait to get her alone so he could pull her into his embrace and kiss her for as long as he wanted.

It didn't matter which lady she decided to be, she was always desirable, and if he'd had the opportunity to pick a wife of his own choosing, he was beginning to think he certainly couldn't have done any better than Lady Gabrielle.

"Oh, I forgot to ask you," Gabrielle said after they

had ridden in silence for a while, "did you hear about the Duke of Rockcliffe's dog, Tulip? She is now missing, too."

Brent slipped his arm over the top of the bench and eased it around her. "I heard a day or two ago that she went missing, but I don't know any details and I didn't ask. How and where did the dog disappear?"

"She was with the duke's youngest brother, Lord Waldo. The duke is actually with my father and the Duke of Norfolk and several other gentlemen on a hunting jaunt in Kent."

"I've not met the Duke of Rockcliffe, just his younger brother," Brent mumbled, remembering his brief conversation with Lord Waldo a few nights ago.

"The duke is a very somber man, much like my father," Gabrielle continued. "But Lord Waldo is really a pleasant man. He was enjoying an afternoon in Hyde Park with Miss Alice Peyton when Tulip wandered off and never came back."

Brent grinned and then chuckled softly. "I wonder if they had as much pleasure in the park as we did. As I recall, I enjoyed myself immensely, didn't you?"

Her eyes widened, and pink flamed in her cheeks. "Well, ah—of course, but I really don't know what they were doing in the park."

Brent laughed again. She was enchanting when she was embarrassed and flustered.

She straightened her back, lifted her chin and shoulders, and very properly said, "However, I do know that Lord Waldo had the duke's little dog with him and while he wasn't looking, Tulip wandered away and now can't be found."

"Hmm," Brent said, pretending to be in deep thought. "It sounds like maybe they *were* in the park doing what we were doing."

Gabrielle huffed. "I'm trying to be serious, and you are making it very difficult."

"Sorry. I couldn't resist a little teasing. Forgive me."

They hit a huge hole in the road, and the carriage nearly bumped them off the seat. They laughed, and Brent took the opportunity to press even closer to Gabrielle. The tip of her nose was turning pink from the wind, and already a golden strand of hair had escaped the tight fit of her short-brimmed velvet bonnet. Brent loved looking at her, and it was very satisfying being so close to her he felt the warmth of her body.

"So tell me about this dog," he said.

"I really don't know very much about Tulip. I just found it remarkably odd that another dog has gone missing. I can't ever remember a time when I've heard of three dogs missing in little more than a month."

"I agree," Brent said. "Something like this doesn't happen unless something or someone is making it happen."

"Some ladies and I were talking about the same thing before you arrived at the church today."

"Really? I chatted with two gentlemen before the service started, and no one mentioned it to me."

"I'm sure that's because everyone knows how distraught you've been because you haven't found Prissy."

Brent's brows drew together, and he frowned. "Distraught? Is that what people are saying about me?"

"Not so much now, of course, but when you were

searching the park for Prissy, I might have heard that term used once or twice."

"Might have?" he grumbled.

Her eyes softened gently. "Well, you were distraught that your mother's dog is missing, and there's nothing wrong with that."

Brent knew White's had a wager going about whether or not Prissy would be found by Christmas, and then there were wagers about whether she'd be found dead or alive. For the life of him, he couldn't figure out why Londoners found such perverse pleasure in mocking someone's trials... but they did.

"She's gone, Gabrie. I told you I've accepted the fact Prissy is gone and will not be returning."

Her blue gaze fluttered down his face, and she gave him a compassionate smile. "You know, all the ladies—young, married, and widows—think it makes you the most dashing of gentlemen because you care so much for your deceased mother's pet."

Brent wasn't sure that was how he would choose to be thought of by any lady. "No, I didn't know that."

"But perhaps I shouldn't have brought up dogs at all."

He put his hand over her muff and tried to find her hand beneath the fur. "No, I'm glad you did. And you are right. I, too, find it odd that three small dogs have now gone missing. It gives some credibility to the fact a large animal is on the prowl."

"Yes, I've heard that. What do you think is happening to them, Brent?"

"I don't know." And he didn't. "But I'm joining some other men, and we're going to scour the park to see if we can find a beast."

"I hope you do."

They rode the rest of the way to the fair in silence.

"Oh, look," Gabrielle said with a sparkle in her eyes and excitement in her voice. "I can see the tents. We're almost there."

The fair was bustling and lively with people and noise as the driver maneuvered the carriage to the parking area. Loud pianoforte music mixed with the chatter of talking and laughing. The scents of burning wood, cooked food, and animal waste lingered in the chilly air.

After the brake was set on the landau, Brent jumped down and reached back for Gabrielle. He settled his hands around her waist and lifted her from the top step of the carriage and swung her around twice before setting her on her feet.

She laughed breathlessly and said, "That was completely uncalled for, my lord."

"But highly enjoyable, was it not?"

Her gaze stayed, and the pleasure he saw in her face made his stomach tighten. "Yes," she said, "very much so."

"Should I get your parasol?"

She shook her head and took her muff off and tossed it into the seat. "With so little sun out, I shall be fine without it."

He smiled. "All right, what do you want to see first?"

Her eyes lighted with happiness. "I want to see everything, of course. Whatever we come to first, we will stop and see what is going on."

He took hold of her hand. "Let's go."

The afternoon flew by for Brent. Even though the air was crisp and their hands must have been tight from cold, the acrobats managed to do amazing feats of tumbling, twirling, and swinging from ropes. They watched a man twist his body into odd and what looked like painful positions. A juggler kept five balls in the air at one time and never missed catching any of them.

With awe, they stared at a young woman dressed in what Brent could only classify as her unmentionables, which in itself was a spectacular thing to do because of the chilly air. She defied gravity by walking on a thick rope that was stretched about three-houses high, between two poles that had been erected and with nothing beneath her to catch her should she fall. They spent time watching a tiger, which Gabrielle didn't think was very impressive at all. She said he didn't look fierce, lying so calmly in his cage. Some youngsters walked up beside them and yelled to the big cat. They wanted him to lift his big head and growl at them, but the tiger was more interested in his nap.

Late in the afternoon, when Brent knew they must soon leave, he found a place for them to sit down near a booth that was serving hot tea and warm biscuits dusted with finely ground sugar and cinnamon. Brent could hardly eat his own biscuit for watching Gabrielle, who had removed her gloves and was daintily licking sugar from her fingertips. He was sure she had no idea how enticing she looked doing that. When his body could take no more of watching her, he knew it was time to head for the carriage and get her home. But first he intended to steal a few kisses from her tempting lips, and he had already seen the perfect place to do that on the way back to the carriage.

"There is one more thing we need to do before we go," Gabrielle said, fitting her black gloves back on her hands.

Brent swallowed the last of his tea. "I thought we had seen and done it all," he said.

"No, I saw the booth earlier and resisted its lure until now."

"I'm intrigued. What haven't we seen?"

"The fortune-teller booth."

Brent folded his arms across his chest and eyed her warily. "You aren't serious."

"Of course I am." She smiled. "Don't you want to know what your future holds?"

"Not particularly," he said. "I have no interest in such folly."

"Oh, I do," she said quickly. "I absolutely adore having my fortune told, and I believe everything they say will come true."

He studied her and said, "Do you now?"

"Oh, yes. My father believes in what fortune-tellers say, and my sister, too. And we all consult them often."

Brent smiled. He didn't believe a word of what she was saying. The second she heard he had no interest in fortune-tellers, she was suddenly very intent about it.

"All right, Gabrielle, let's go and see what your future holds."

The cramped booth was painted black with small, shiny red stars. A woman sat behind a counter. She was dressed in all black with a sheer lace netting covering her face.

"Welcome, gentleman and lady," she said in a

heavy Italian accent. "I tell both fortunes for one shilling, no?"

Gabrielle looked at Brent. "You will do it, won't you?"

"Only for you."

Brent paid the woman, and she asked Gabrielle to take off her glove and hold out her hand, palm up.

"It's all right I touch your hand?" the woman asked.

Gabrielle nodded. The fortune-teller lightly traced the lines in Gabrielle's hand as she hummed. After what seemed like a dreadfully long time to Brent, she looked up and said, "I see that recently in your life there has been a major change, and that has troubled you."

Gabrielle nodded and glanced at Brent. He shrugged.

"Ah, but I see great happiness in your future. But first"—the woman paused for another long time as she seemed to study Gabrielle's hand—"first something more will trouble you and cause you pain. You have very strong men in your life, and they all want to choose for you."

Gabrielle frowned. "Choose what?"

"That I cannot say, but when it comes, you will remember I was the one who told you it would happen."

"Thank you," Gabrielle said and pulled her hand back. She turned to Brent and said, "Now it's your turn."

Brent took off his glove and, as he extended his hand to the woman, out of the corner of his eye, he caught sight of a man walking by. Something about him seemed very familiar. It took a moment or two for Brent to realize it was the black patch over his eye that jogged his memory. This was the man Brent had seen in the park a month or so ago, who had a rabbit under his coat. Brent turned and looked behind him. The man was carrying a lumpy, dirty canvas sack over his shoulders.

Brent's senses went on alert, and he jerked back his hand from the fortune-teller. Brent remembered the talk going around Town that not only the remains of horses and cattle were fed to beasts at fairs, but strays, too.

He wanted to follow the man and find out what he had in that sack he carried, but what could Brent do with Gabrielle? He quickly glanced around him. There was no place safe where he could leave her unattended at the fair. There were too many disreputable people milling around. But he had to do something quickly. The man was getting farther away.

He grabbed Gabrielle's and said, "Come with me."

"What's wrong?" she asked, almost running to keep up with his long strides. "What about your fortune?"

"Later," he said, searching the people in front them and trying to catch up with the man before he lost him in the crowd.

"Brent, what is wrong? Where are we going in such a hurry?"

"Look ahead of us to the left. You'll see a man in a gray coat. He has a sack thrown over his shoulder."

"Yes, I see him."

"I want to follow him to see where he is going, and I don't want him to know we are doing it."

"Why? What has he done?"

Brent glanced over at her and wondered if he was doing the right thing by bringing her along with him. He could understand her curiosity, but he didn't have time to explain to her what he was doing. He wished like hell he didn't have Gabrielle with him. He couldn't leave her alone, though he wasn't sure she was any safer with him following this man. Brent had to know what was in that bag.

"I'll tell you later. Just stay close beside me and do whatever I tell you to do."

"All right."

"And that means without questioning me, Gabrielle."

"I understand, my lord," she said, squeezing his hand to let him know she understood the gravity of what they were doing.

Gabrielle held tightly to his hand and stayed close to him as they weaved through the throng of people. Near the far end of the booths and tents, the crowd thinned and it was clear the man was heading to the back of the main attractions, to where there were several large tents and four large covered wagons. Off to one side, children played with a ball. Not far from there, several women sat around a large pot that had a fire going underneath it.

Brent tried to keep his mind from racing with possibilities, but why would a man who said he caught rabbits in the park to sell to the taverns and inns be so familiar with the back area of a traveling fair? Unless he also sold what he caught to the owners.

Brent slowed and looked around when the man turned a corner and headed to one of the tents behind a roped-off area. He needed to stop him before he entered the tent. He led Gabrielle over to a booth.

Brent put his finger to his lips and said, "Shh. Stay here. Do not follow me."

Without further thought, Brent hurried past the

rope barricade and called out to the man. He turned, saw Brent, and started to run. Brent rushed the man from behind, caught him, and pushed him up against the wagon, pinning him against it with his body. The man reached back with his fist and knocked Brent's hat to the ground. Brent caught the man's flailing arm and pulled it behind his back, stretching it up toward his shoulder.

"I don't have any money, nothing of value," the man managed to say as Brent pressed his face against the wagon.

"I have no need of your money or anything else. I simply want to know what you have in the sack."

"Squirrels. You can have them. Take them if you want. They're yours."

Inhaling deeply, Bent relaxed and blew out a disappointed breath. He let go of the man and stepped away.

The man turned to face Brent. His wide eyes seemed frozen in shock as he held out the bag to Brent with a trembling hand.

Brent took the sack and looked inside. Dead squirrels. He closed it and handed it back to the man. "You told me you sold the animals you caught to tavern and inn keepers."

The man nodded. "I do, my lord, but I also told you I sold to whoever is buying. And sometimes I sell to the people here. Their money spends just as good."

"Have you ever picked up stray dogs and brought them here for the animals?"

The man's eyes widened, and Brent could tell his throat constricted as he swallowed hard. "Not lately, sir."

"But you have?"

He nodded. "Nobody's ever cared."

Brent's stomach turned over. "Did you pick up a small, fluffy dog in the park a few weeks ago and bring it here?"

"I swear I didn't, my lord." His lips trembled, and his voice shook. "I'd never pick up a well-fed animal. Only pick them up if they are old, sickly, or starving. Sometimes it's hard for the owners of places like this to get the leavings at the slaughterhouses. Strays are easy to catch, a lot easier to catch than a rabbit or squirrel. All you have to do to get a stray to come to you is offer him food or a bone, and he'll come right to you. But believe me, sir, I like dogs. I wouldn't ever sell a healthy dog to anyone."

"Did you know that several small dogs have gone missing in London?"

The man shook his head. "Can't read and don't have time to listen to folks talking on the streets."

Brent didn't know why, but he believed the man. He pulled a coin out of his coat pocket and gave it to the man. "If you hear anything that might help me find out what is happening to the dogs, find me. I'll reward you for it."

The man attempted a nervous smile and nodded.

Brent picked up his hat and dusted it on his leg as he headed back toward Gabrielle.

"Brent," Gabrielle said, rushing up to him. "What was all that about?"

He took hold of her hand and kissed it. It calmed him and settled him just to be able to touch her. As they headed back to the main part of the fair, in as little detail as possible in order to spare her sensibilities, Brent told her why he was questioning the man.

"It's positively gruesome to even think about what you suspected the man of doing."

"I know, but something is happening to the dogs, and I'm not going to rest until I find out what it is."

"Wait," she said, suddenly pulling on his arm. "The fortune-teller booth is right there. You paid for your fortune. Don't you want to know what it will be?"

Her eyes sparkled, and her lips looked so moist he knew he could go no longer without kissing her. "I prefer to make my own fortune, Gabrie."

He led her around to the back of the booth and pulled her into his arms. He leaned her against it, and his lips came down on hers with an urgency he didn't know he was capable of. He didn't want to think about anything—not dogs, not marriage, not where they were. He just wanted to kiss Gabrielle and touch her. He wanted to indulge himself and satisfy his thirst for her.

His desire was instant, intense, and eager. She opened her mouth and accepted the deep thrust of his tongue. In the coolness of the day, her mouth was warm and tasted of sweet sugar and cinnamon. His arms slid down to her hips, and he pulled her up against the hard bulge in his trousers. Her body was soft and inviting. He groaned into her mouth as his pelvis started a rhythmic motion against her.

As his lips passionately devoured hers, his hand moved up from her waist and slid beneath her cape to cup her breast. He felt her breath quicken, and it excited him all the more. His palm flattened against her breast and gently massaged it, enjoying the gratifying feeling of touching her, wishing he could remove the barrier of her clothing. His kisses moved to her cheek. She arched her head back, giving him freedom to kiss her neck and explore the soft skin behind her ear before he moved up to brush her lips once again.

A soft moan of pleasure wafted past his ear, and he smiled against her skin. It pleased him greatly to know she enjoyed his touch so much. His body ached, and he was desperate to possess her. His hands clutched at her skirts, gathering the bountiful fabric and pulling it up her legs.

He heard the snort of a horse behind them and quickly, breathlessly, hid Gabrielle's face in his chest while an old man leading two horses walked past them, but thankfully never looked their way.

Trembling from unreleased desire, he lowered his head to the top of hers and tried to calm his breathing. He was angry at himself for wanting her so desperately he was willing to take her where anyone might happen upon them. It didn't matter how much he needed her right now, how delicious she felt in his arms, or how willing she was to accept his loving; this wasn't the place to touch her. And he had to gain better control of himself where she was concerned.

"That was close," she whispered against his chest.

"Too close. We should go," he whispered, pulling away from her.

She looked up at him with questioning eyes. "Brent, why is it that whenever you kiss me I seem to lose my good common sense?"

He snorted a half laugh. "I can't answer that, Gabrie, because I find I lose mine as well. So come, let's get you home right now while I still have a tenuous hold on my common sense."

Sixteen

There are few wild beasts more to be dreaded than a communicative man having nothing to say.

—Christian Nestell Bovee

GABRIELLE STOOD AT THE DOORWAY TO THE MUSIC room of their Mayfair town house and smiled. It had taken her and her aunt two days to get the house ready for the recital and finally everything was in place. The pianoforte had been situated in the far corner, where the pianist could look up and appreciate his audience. Lighted candelabras, placed on tall Corinthian column pedestals, stood on both sides of the piano. All the furniture in the room had been removed, and small straight-back chairs were lined tightly together in rows for the thirty guests who had been invited.

With the help of Babs's and Fern's delicate hand-writing skills, all the invitations had gone out the day after the Cuddlebury's party. Rosabelle had been eager for the party when Gabrielle first told her about it, but her mind had changed quickly. She refused to help with anything concerning the recital and vowed not to come out of her room the entire evening because she couldn't convince Gabrielle to invite Staunton.

The response to the event had been better than Gabrielle expected, considering the short notice and her less-than-spotless standing in Society. She had remained firm against her aunt's insistence that she must at least add a flutist or violinist to the pianist or the guests would become quite bored. She didn't want her aunt to know, but that was exactly what Gabrielle wanted.

This entire evening had been set up so she could impress upon Lord Brentwood that she didn't know the first thing about the proper way to give a party. Surely he wouldn't want a wife who didn't know how to adequately entertain or maintain his household. Though, in truth, she was the complete opposite. She had helped her father plan and manage parties since she was sixteen. She was more than efficient with every social occasion and knew all the proper dos and don'ts. She was sure her knowledge of what was expected, and always doing it, was the reason she was having such a difficult time trying to prove to Lord Brentwood she wouldn't make an acceptable wife. Trying to change one's natural abilities wasn't as easy as she thought it would be.

She had been very select in choosing the guests. She had invited Lord Snellingly and several other members of the Royal Society of Poets. Those gentlemen would probably send Brent running for the door the moment they opened their mouths about verse. Lord Waldo Rockcliffe had responded that he would be in attendance. That should make Brent very uncomfortable, since most everyone in London suspected that Lord Waldo and one of Brent's brothers had been less than civil to each other.

She had also invited the extremely showy, pious, and well-decorated Count Vigone, who had recently returned from Italy with more stories about how great he was than anyone wanted to hear. That count had a propensity for irritating the most patient of gentlemen. She had invited Brent's brothers and the youngest and silliest of the past Season's debutantes who hadn't already made a match. If all these misfits didn't make Brent see she would have no idea how to pair guests and host a party for him if they married, she had added one more gentleman to the evening. Sir Randolph Gibson had to be Brent's biggest nemesis. With almost everyone in London thinking the dapper old gentleman was his brothers' real father, surely Brent would never forgive her for inviting that man to the recital.

This simply must work. Not only was Gabrielle finding it very difficult to resist Brent's romantic attentions, she was running out of time. She knew any day now she would hear from her father that he was returning home. Once that happened, she knew he would be calling on his solicitor and checking with Brent about setting a wedding date.

"I've made the rounds one last time," her aunt said, coming up behind her. "Everything seems to be in place."

Gabrielle faced her aunt. "Oh, good."

Auntie Bethie rubbed the back of her neck. "I have to say again, Gabby, I'm not happy about making the guests come inside and immediately sit down to an hour of music before we give them a sip of drink or bite of food."

Gabrielle knew it was the epitome of bad taste to do so, but she was getting desperate. "I know what I'm doing, Auntie."

"Then why in heaven's name couldn't we at least add a violinist, a cellist, or a flutist? Piano music can become tedious for those who are not trained in music."

"I know you don't understand, Auntie. But you must trust me that this is the way I want it."

She knew desperation made people do strange things. She'd certainly done that the morning she'd met Brent in the park and she was still trying to make amends for her rash behavior.

"I've been trying to work out in my mind why you want tonight to be a disaster, but I'm puzzled."

Gabrielle remained silent. She hated the thought of disappointing her aunt, and for a moment wondered if she had gone too far. But what other choice did she have? Her father was away. She couldn't try to dissuade him. There was nothing left for her to do but discourage Brent.

"You know you don't have to tell me what is going on in that busy mind of yours," her aunt said. "I just hope it accomplishes what you want."

Gabrielle hugged her aunt. "You don't know how much I appreciate your saying that, Auntie."

"Well, you certainly chose your dress well," her aunt said, admitting defeat again and changing the subject. "You look stunning tonight, dearie."

"Thank you," Gabrielle said and looked down at

her gown, a plain, cap-sleeved, high-waisted dress of pale yellow. Over the shift, she wore a long-sleeved, golden-colored tulle that flowed gracefully down her body. Around her neck hung three long strands of delicate pearls, and matching earrings that had belonged to her mother. Her hair had been swept up into a loose chignon with pearls woven throughout the bun.

"Oh, that was the doorknocker," Auntie Bethie said. "Let's go greet the first guest."

More than two painful hours later, Gabrielle had finally had enough. As the guests had arrived, she had shown them straight into the music room and had them sit down. When Brent arrived, looking dapper in a black evening coat with an ivory-colored waistcoat, she asked him to sit on the front row and save her a seat beside him.

After it appeared that all the guests had arrived, she announced the pianist, Mr. Michael Murray. She had heard him before and knew him to be an uninspired pianist who played long, tiring scores. When she had asked him to do the recital, she had told him to feel free to play as long as he wanted. He reminded her that he sometimes played for hours without stopping. That gave her a moment's pause, so she then told him to play until she rose from her seat and went to stand beside him.

Everyone had remained alert and attentive during the first hour, but when it stretched far into the second, she started hearing coughs, clearing of throats, and scooting of chairs. Still she didn't rise. Beside her, Brent remained the perfect gentleman, seldom moving, and listening as if he was enjoying every moment. Occasionally, she would glance over at him to see if he were sleeping, because someone near her was snoring. When she couldn't take the boredom any longer, she rose and went to stand by the pianoforte, waiting for Mr. Murray to finish the score.

She started clapping, and all her guests rose and started clapping joyously, too. After Mr. Murray took his bow, she asked her aunt to lead everyone into the dining room for the champagne and the buffet. Brent was the only one who didn't exit the room quickly. He waited patiently until Mr. Murray had finished talking to her and left the room, leaving them completely alone.

Brent stood in front of her and looked as if he was holding back a smile. That didn't bode well. She had hoped to see anger, or at the very least strong annoyance at having to sit through such a dreadful recital. Her father would have been steaming with rage.

She clasped her hands together under her chin, smiled, and said, "Did you think he was divine, a true master at the pianoforte?"

Brent walked a little closer to her. "Did you think so?"

Not wanting to add another fib to her long and growing list, she took a step back and answered, "Don't you?"

"I've heard better pianists, Gabrie," he said and advanced on her again.

Gabrielle took another step back and hit the side of the pianoforte. She was trapped. "There was much applause. I'm certain everyone loved Mr. Murray's interpretation of so many of their favorite scores."

"I'm certain the reason they clapped so long and loud was because it was finally over and they could stand up and get something to eat and drink."

"I'm sure you are unjustly embellishing everyone's reaction."

He bent his head closer to hers and said, "No, Gabrie, I'm not."

She looked at his lips and had the urge to moisten her own. Whenever he was close to her, she always wanted him to kiss her. "Perhaps we should join everyone else for the buffet."

"Oh, yes," he said with a knowing smile and moved his face even closer to hers. "I'm quite eager to go into the dining room and greet everyone. You've managed to invite some of my favorite people—the insipid Lord Waldo, the crafty Sir Randolph, and the braggart Count Vigone. I'm surprised you didn't invite Lord Snellingly, too."

"Oh, I did," she said quickly. "But he didn't come."

"No doubt he was the only one who'd heard the pianist play before."

"But I also invited your brothers and several young ladies for them to meet and have wonderful conversation with them."

"The young ladies who are here are so charming, my brothers are probably already hoping they will never be on one of your guest lists again."

He was so close, her breathing became choppy. She desperately wanted him to kiss her, knowing it would be madness for him to do it here in her home where anyone could walk in at any time. She searched his eyes and couldn't read their depths, but she wondered why there was no real anger in them. Why couldn't she seem to do anything that made him fiercely angry or even mildly upset with her?

"Are you chiding me or teasing me, my lord?" she asked.

"Neither. I'm thinking about kissing you. After what you just put me through, I believe I deserve a kiss or two, don't you?"

She spread her arms out to her sides, grasped hold of the pianoforte, and leaned her weight against it. Oh, yes, that was what she wanted from him.

But she said, "You can't do that. Someone might walk in and see you, and there would be more scandal."

He placed his fingertips under her chin and tilted her head back, lifting her lips to his, and whispered, "I have no fear of that, Gabrie. Your guests' throats are dry, their stomachs empty, and their rumps tired of sitting. I'm sure they are devouring the buffet, swilling the champagne, and praying they won't see you so they don't have to lie to you and tell you they enjoyed the evening."

She swallowed hard. "Please don't feel you have to spare my feelings, my lord."

He smiled. "I don't have to. You knew exactly what you were doing, just as I'm more than willing right now to take my chances on another scandal."

Suddenly Gabrielle craved to feel his lips on hers. Brent must have felt the same, because his eyes darkened and his lips parted slightly. He bent his head so close to hers she felt his breath. Gabrielle's breathing became short and rapid in anticipation.

Instead of kissing her, he gently placed the tips of

his fingers on her forehead and let them trickle down the bridge of her nose, over her lips and chin, and then down the slender column of her throat, to stop where her bosom heaved beneath her dress. He watched the trail of his light touch. His lace cuff tickled her skin, and she smelled the clean scent of shaving soap on his hand. His intense gaze moved back up to her eyes. He then flattened his hand, pressing hard as his hand slid between her breasts, down her midriff, past her stomach to rest at that most intimate spot between her legs.

Gabrielle gasped at the thrill of desire that shot through her. Her heart was beating so fast she thought she might faint.

She knew she should slap his hand away, yet she didn't want to. She wanted him to touch her. She wanted to feel the delicious tingles she was feeling. His palm cupped her and pressed against her. She gasped again as she lifted her lower body to him, straining to get closer to his warmth. Their eyes searched. Their breath mingled. She didn't know what he was doing to her, but it was making her knees weak, her breaths jerky, and her body moving in rhythm to the pressing of his hand. He moved his face even closer to hers. She parted her lips to accept his kiss.

Loud laughter sounded from the corridor, and Brent spun away from her, putting distance between them. Gabrielle straightened and tried to control her breathing.

They both stared at the doorway, but no one came into the room.

Finally Brent looked at her and said, "I won't be staying for the buffet."

She cleared her throat and huskily whispered, "Why?"

"Lord Waldo asked me and my brothers to go hunting with him and some other men later tonight. I need to go home and change for that."

"Lord Waldo?" she questioned.

"Yes. We have one thing in common, remember? Our dogs are missing. We'll search the parks."

"Oh, I see."

She wanted to ask when she would see him again, but knew that was the last thing she needed to say.

"I'll walk out first," he said. "You can follow me in a few minutes. You need to give the blush time to leave your cheeks."

Brent turned and walked out. Gabrielle's hands flew to her face. Her cheeks were hot, and no wonder! Whatever it was he was doing to her had her completely in his control. She was failing miserably at her vow to be an unacceptable bride and resisting his charm.

A few minutes later, Gabrielle walked into the drawing room and was surprised to see Brent still there and that Lord Snellingly had arrived. The earl was talking excitedly to the small group that surrounded him.

She walked up beside Brent and said, "What is going on?"

Without looking at her, he said, "Lord Snellingly found Josephine."

"No!" she whispered in surprise. "I mean, oh, how wonderful for him that he found her. Where was she?"

"He's not sure. He said a young man brought her to his door late this afternoon, and that's why he's just now getting here. He had to spend some time with Josephine before coming over."

She touched his arm, and he turned to her. "I'm thrilled for Lord Snellingly, but I'm also sorry it wasn't Prissy who was found. Will you still go on the hunt tonight?"

His gaze brushed down her face, and she had the feeling he was telling her he wanted to kiss her.

"I've told you I've settled my mind about Prissy, but if I can help find the other dogs, I'm willing to do what I can." He nodded to her and turned away.

Gabrielle watched Brent walk out, and her hands tightened into fists as her heart broke for him. She would give anything if he could find Prissy.

"Gabby," Auntie Bethie said, taking her arm and ushering her away from the crowd. "That was the longest and the worst performed piano recital I have ever been to."

"I know."

Her aunt's brow wrinkled. "Did you know that several people didn't even stay for a drink? The Brentwood twins, Count Vigone, and Lord Waldo have already left, and I just saw Lord Brentwood walking out the door, too. I think they were afraid you would call them back into the music room for an encore. You don't plan to do that, do you? For if you do, I'll take my leave now as well."

"No, of course not, Auntie." Gabrielle smiled. "Mr. Murray played quite enough for one evening."

Her aunt tilted her head and inquired, "So do you think your attempt to give the worst party of the year was a smashing success?"

"Yes," Gabrielle said somberly, wishing she'd never attempted the ill-fated party, because while the viscount was quite bored along with everyone else, he seemed to be once again willing to overlook her shortcomings. She was beginning to think she would have to give up on Lord Brentwood and accept that her hope rested in changing her father's mind when he returned.

As if finally sensing her mood, Auntie Bethie said, "What's wrong? I thought you'd be happy the evening went as you'd planned. There's hardly anyone left here but the members of the Royal Poets Society and some chaperones for those young ladies, who are over there in the corner giggling because they drank their champagne too fast. Isn't that what you wanted?"

"Yes, I'm pleased the evening went so very well." She stopped and gave a sad smile. "That is I'm glad it was as boring as I planned. It's just that I feel so sorry for Lord Brentwood because Lord Snellingly has found his dog, Josephine, and Brent's dog, Prissy, is still missing."

Auntie Bethie sighed. "Oh, my, yes. That would put a damp cloth on anything. But maybe after he's had time to think about it, he'll feel encouraged that since Lord Snellingly's dog was found, his will be too."

"Maybe," Gabrielle said.

"What's wrong, dearie? There's something more wrong than the missing dog, isn't there?"

Gabrielle looked at her aunt, who had such concern in her features. "Yes, Auntie," Gabrielle said, realizing she wanted to speak the truth. "I think I've fallen in love with Lord Brentwood. And I'm so afraid that, because of my feelings for him, I will weaken my resolve, give in, and let my father arrange a marriage to Lord Brentwood."

A look of compassion settled on her aunt's features and she asked, "Why would that make you sad? I should think you would welcome these feelings, since your father wants you to marry him."

Gabrielle felt an ache in her heart. "He doesn't want to marry me, Auntie. My father is forcing him. How could I ever find any happiness living with a man my father forced to marry me?"

Seventeen

A great wind is blowing, and that gives you either imagination or a headache.

—Catherine the Great

It was a seldom-seen, beautiful, late November afternoon in London. Gabrielle stood in front of her father's book-room window, looking out over the barren garden. Auntie Bethie had talked Rosabelle into joining her to look at town homes, so the house was quiet. All but two servants had the afternoon off, and Gabrielle was thrilled to have some undisturbed time to think, to daydream, and to paint. She would have at least two, or if she were lucky, maybe three hours before the house became busy again.

Petra had set up Gabrielle's easel, canvas, and paints before she left. The double set of windows in the book room faced west, and the bright sunshine made that area of the house a perfect place to paint. Gabrielle had covered her hair with a white scarf and donned a freshly pressed but paint-stained apron over her simple pale blue day dress.

Earlier that day, Gabrielle had received a letter from her father stating he would be returning to London within the week. That meant she had some serious thinking to do about Brent.

When she thought about the way he made her feel when he kissed her, the way he was constantly in her thoughts, the way she yearned to see him again, she knew it would be so easy to simply marry him. But every time that crossed her mind, she remembered he was being forced to marry her to save her reputation, and to save his brothers' business. How could he ever come to love her or even fully accept her as his wife, thinking she had tricked him that morning in the park? She didn't want the man she loved feeling trapped.

But what else could she do? She'd tried everything she could think of to make him say no to her father's demands. Well, there was one thing she hadn't done. She could let Brent catch her kissing another man. But the thought of that was so distasteful to her she cringed inside. Besides, if she did that, she would only be doing to another man what she'd already done to Brent.

That idea was definitely out.

The possibility of joining a convent had entered her mind. Her father would never give his permission for that, so she would have to slip away from the house without anyone knowing. But she wasn't sure she wanted to spend the rest of her life never being kissed again. She had enjoyed Brent's kisses and caresses. Gabrielle gently closed her eyes and continued to stand at the window, letting the warm sunshine melt against her face. She remembered Brent's smile, his touch, his laughter, and his passionate embraces, and knew for certain a convent wasn't the right plan for her either. A nun was not supposed to dream about kissing a gentleman or to think herself in love with a man.

She opened her eyes and turned away from the window. Maybe if she submerged herself in her painting, she could keep thoughts of Brent at bay. She looked at the blank canvas. What should she paint this lovely afternoon? Landscapes, flowers, fruit, or Brent—she smiled to herself. She wasn't good with portraits, or she might be tempted to paint him.

Gabrielle walked behind her father's desk to look over his bookshelf in hopes of seeing something that might spark an interest of what to paint. Her fingers sailed along the spines as she read titles from history, science, plants, and poetry, but nothing she saw gave her any new ideas. A three-drawer mahogany chest covered about three feet of the last four rows of books. Gabrielle looked at the chest and realized she had no idea what was behind it. Curiosity got the best of her, and with great effort she pulled it away from the shelving and pushed it aside. The hidden shelves were stacked with books covered in what must be years of dust.

She lifted her skirts, dropped to her knees, and continued her search of the book titles. One of the first books she looked at was on botany. She took it off the shelf, blew the dust off it, and thumbed through the pages, hoping to discover the sketch of a rare plant or flower, but found nothing. She coughed from the dust and fanned the air in front of her nose before putting the book back in its place. Another book showed diagrams of the constellations and for a moment she thought about the possibility of painting the night sky and filling it with stars. She laid that book on her father's desk as a possibility and continued her search.

Gabrielle skimmed every title until she made it to the very last book on the bottom shelf. There was no title on the spine. That seemed odd. She took it off the shelf and opened it. The cover had been wrapped with some type of heavy canvas. Thinking it must be a very old and rare book, she carefully opened it to the first page and read, *The Art of Being a Most Pleasing Mistress*.

"Hmm," she said aloud. "A book that could be beneficial when I become mistress of my own house." She laid it on her father's desk beside the constellation book and rose, leaving the chest where it was so the housekeeper could have the area cleaned.

There was very little inspiration from her father's bookshelves, but a night sky filled with stars was something she'd never thought about painting. She would do that. She walked over to the window and picked up a small box of paints. Making the entire backdrop midnight sky was the first thing she needed to do. While that dried, she would look at the sketches and decide which constellations she wanted to put in her sky. She found the jar of dark blue oil and spread it on her palate. She swirled her brush in the paint and then started making wide, sweeping strokes across the beige canvas. But it wasn't long before Brent's face came to her mind, and she smiled as she brushed.

Thoughts of him always made her stomach tingle. She wanted to remember and recapture what she felt every time he kissed her, caressed her, or breathed against her skin. Softly she laughed to herself and turned to look out the window to the clear blue sky. How could she want to paint anything dark on one of the warmest and most beautiful afternoons she'd seen in weeks?

Gabrielle laid the brush back on the easel and walked over to her father's desk. She picked up the book about being the mistress of a home. Maybe if she curled up in the settee and read about running a kitchen and keeping housewares in good order, she could keep her mind off the viscount.

She opened to the first page and read:

Being a mistress is not for every woman, but it can be very satisfying, yes, even quite rewarding for the few elite women who choose to become one. There were no books, no friends, no one to offer help to me when I became a mistress, so I write this book in hopes that someday I will find a company brave enough to publish this valuable guide, bookshops brave enough to sell it, and ladies or gentlemen brave enough to buy it and use it.

Having been a successful mistress for more than thirty years, I am well qualified to write this compendium of most useful and even helpful hints. It is my honor, and I believe it is my duty, to pass on the knowledge I have acquired in the art of pleasing and satisfying a man. No well-heeled gentleman of any station in life should be without a mistress to take care of his bedchamber desires. Every well-bred gentleman knows, duly expects, and deserves to have a wife who is too sheltered, too delicate, and too timid to master the art of sexually pleasing him, and he would, of course, never have the inclination to teach or force her into doing what a well-trained mistress already knows how to do.

Gabrielle looked up from the book. *Sexually pleasing?* She felt hot and cold all at the same time, and her heart started to beat faster than it should. Surely this sort of pleasing didn't mean what she thought it did. Could it?

She looked down and continued reading.

The first thing a mistress must do is to make herself pleasing to the eye of the gentleman. At all times she must be enticing. A gentleman always desires a woman of beauty. She should keep her hair styled, her lips and cheeks rosy, her skin sprinkled with perfume, and dress in the latest fashionable clothing.

Gabrielle's gaze was riveted to the pages as she continued to read. Suddenly it dawned on her. This book wasn't about being the mistress of the house. This book was about being a *kept* mistress!

A courtesan!

She glanced guiltily around the room to make sure no one witnessed what she was reading.

"Oh, my," she whispered and slammed the book shut. Dust flew into her face, and she sneezed.

Her mind whirled. Her breaths came short and quick.

"I can't read this," she said to herself.

What was this book doing on her father's bookshelf? What was it doing in his house? Did he even know it was there? Perhaps it belonged to her grandfather or someone else. Who could have hidden it there? Clearly the book hadn't been touched in many years.

Gabrielle worried her lower lip. What she had read sparked her curiosity. She had no idea what mistresses could do that was too difficult and too delicate for wives. And should a properly brought-up young lady like herself even know?

Without further thought, she bent down to the

bottom shelf and stuffed the book back in its slot. She leaned her weight against the chest and quickly shoved it back in place. She hurried from behind the desk to the center of the room and stood there, looking from the chest to the door.

Would anyone ever know she'd found the book? Would anyone ever know if she had read it?

Of course not! How could they?

Her aunt and sister were out for the afternoon. The servants knew not to bother her when she was painting.

So...

She could read the book and no one would ever know. But did she want to?

"Heavens yes!" she exclaimed.

Gabrielle ran over to the chest again, pushed it out of the way, and grabbed the book. She walked over to the broad-striped settee that stood in front of the lit fireplace and settled down onto the cushion. She opened the book and continued to read about the things a mistress should do for a man but a wife was not supposed to do or even know about.

As she read, a thought niggled at her mind, but each time she shook it away. She wouldn't even think of that possibility.

Soon everything was forgotten except the hypnotic words written on the pages. She kept reading page after page, sometimes scanning the details because she was simply too embarrassed to let her eyes read the words.

"Lady Gabrielle."

Gabrielle slammed the book together so hard and fast as she jolted up from the settee that dust rose in a puff.

"Yes, Mrs. Lathbury?" she said breathlessly, her heart beating so fast she thought she might faint.

"Lord Brentwood is here to see you and insisted I tell you he is here."

The idea she had tried to keep at bay sprang back to mind with the speed of lightning and the fury of a fierce wind. And just when she thought her heartbeat might settle down, it started thudding crazily again.

"Lord Brentwood? Here?" she asked, trying to calm the storm that had so suddenly erupted inside her. "Are you sure?"

"Yes, my lady."

Scandal was the only thing she had thought might finally make Brent see she wasn't an acceptable wife for him. What if she did something to him only a mistress would know how to do? Surely that would give him reason enough to say it didn't matter about his honor, his brothers, or anything else. How could he marry a lady who knew the ways of a gentleman's mistress?

But could she play the part?

She had to. There were no other options.

"Give me a couple of minutes, and then send him in."

"Yes, my lady. Will you be wanting me to serve tea?"

"No, thank you, Mrs. Lathbury, we won't need refreshment, and I'll see Lord Brentwood out when he is ready to leave. That will be all."

The housekeeper nodded and walked away. Gabrielle's mind suddenly went blank. She opened the book again and read:

The first thing a mistress must do is to make herself pleasing to the eye of the gentleman. At all times she must be enticing. A gentleman always desires a woman of beauty. She should keep her hair styled, her lips and cheeks rosy, her skin sprinkled with perfume, and dress in fashionable clothing.

Gabrielle looked down at her paint-stained apron and the simple blue day dress she wore. There was no time to change into a finer dress. She laid the book on the settee and quickly untied her apron and took it off. Looking around for a place to hide it, she stuffed it in a tall urn that stood by the fireplace. She yanked the white scarf off her head and sent it the way of the apron.

Remembering she had read that gentlemen loved long, flowing locks, she tumbled the pins out of her hair and shook it, letting the tangled curls fall around her shoulders. She bit her lips and pinched her cheeks to make them rosy, while she looked around the office to see if there was anything to perfume her skin; but of course there was nothing in the book room.

Her fingers trembled as she picked up the book again and thumbed through it. Of all she had read, what could she do to make Brent think she was too knowledgeable in the ways of a mistress to be his sheltered, timid, and delicate wife?

She remembered reading something about gently fondling a gentleman's golden orbs with her hands. Fondling? Orbs?

She quickly turned the pages, looking for the correct one, so she could read it again and get it right. There was something about how to hold them in the palm of your hand while your fingers lightly squeezed.

Gabrielle shook her head and mumbled to herself.

She couldn't find it. She had always thought of eyes as being orbs, but she couldn't imagine how anyone would fondle eyes. Which left only ears. Odd? But what did she know about the ways of a mistress?

The sound of footfalls in the corridor made her heart leap into her throat, and she closed the book with a nervous snap. Her quarry was on his way.

With no time to make it across the room to the shelf, she shoved the book behind an embroidered pillow just as Brent walked into the room.

She swallowed hard, curtseyed, and said, "My lord."

"Lady Gabrielle." He smiled and bowed.

"This is a surprise."

He looked at her with a curious sparkle in his eyes. "Yes, I can see I should have sent a note around. I must have caught you at a bad time. You look flustered."

"Me? No."

"Your cheeks are flushed and your lips pink and your hair is, well, perhaps I will just stop at that."

She brushed a strand of hair away from her face and said, "Yes, perhaps that is best... Please sit down."

He motioned for her to sit first, and she did, making sure she put her back against the pillow that covered the book.

He took the opposite end of the settee and said, "I had news I wanted to share with you, and I didn't stop to think it might not be convenient to drop by."

"No, really, this is a fine time. I was painting." She pointed to the easel by the window.

He looked at the canvas that was half-painted dark blue and hid a smile behind clearing his throat. "Yes, that's very nice. Shows talent."

She started to explain it was a midnight sky but stopped herself. She had more important matters to deal with. If she was ever going to play the part of a mistress, she had to do it now, before she lost her nerve.

"What did you want to tell me?" she squeaked, then cleared her throat. "My lord," she added, hoping she sounded sufficiently sultry.

Brent looked at her oddly. "Are you sure you are all right?"

"I'm fine," she tried to coo. "Better than fine. How are you?"

He gave her a questioning look and said, "I heard that Lord Waldo's dog was returned to him today."

"Oh, that's wonderful news!" she blurted, every ounce of sultry evaporating into the room. "When? How?"

"Lord Waldo said a young man showed up at his door with the dog," Brent said. "I talked at length with him about who found Tulip, and then I went to see Lord Snellingly. After talking with both of them, I'm fairly certain it must have been the same lad who found both dogs and, of course, both men had paid the young man handsomely."

"That's amazing the lad found both dogs," she said.

"Quite, and I think it's very curious, too."

"Do you?" she said without really thinking about what she was saying. She was concentrating too hard on the shape of his ears and wondering how she was going to touch them.

"Yes, and I think I know who he is."

Her gaze swept from Brent's ears to his eyes. "You do? Who?"

"A young man named Godfrey," he said. "He and

his sisters travel Hyde Park each morning to deliver milk into Mayfair. I'm going to the park tomorrow morning and following him home."

"You think he has Prissy?" she asked.

"Maybe, maybe not," Brent said. "But he certainly knew how to find the other dogs, and now that I've heard Lady Windham's prize-winning pet has gone missing, this has gotten to be more than just peculiar. Right now, Godfrey's the only lead I have."

"Tell me what time you will be in the park, and I will meet you there."

Brent shook his head. "Oh, no, Gabrie. I must do this alone."

Gabrielle took a deep breath and scooted down the settee closer to him. "But you said he had his sisters with him. I might be of some help if you need to talk to them."

He seemed to consider her suggestion. "The girls do seem frightened of me."

She swallowed past a dry throat, reached up, and went for an orb. With a trembling hand, she lightly traced his outer ear with her fingertips. Softly, she said, "Then it's settled; I'll come."

His brow wrinkled into a frown and his lips set in a grim, or perhaps confused, line. The news of another dog returned to his master while he was still missing Prissy obviously had him tense.

"All right. I should think they'll be back through the park between nine and ten o'clock, after making their deliveries, so we should meet at the west gate before nine just to make sure we don't miss them."

Gabrielle continued gently touching him, letting

her fingers move to the back of his ear and then skimming down his neck to the top of his neckcloth and back up again to draw lazy circles on the smooth, warm skin behind his ear.

All of a sudden he grabbed her wrist, kissed the back of her hand, and said, "Gabrie, what are you doing?"

Her gaze met his and held. "Touching you," she whispered.

There was a passage where it said a man liked for a mistress to straddle him and sit on his lap. That was a very daring thing to do, but maybe she should try that. It was certainly unladylike and would surely make him see that she knew how to do things she shouldn't know. Besides, it would make it easier for her to fondle both ears at the same time.

Her breathing was labored. Her chest felt tight, but she was beyond thinking about anything but what she had to do. And she had to do it now. Rising from the settee, she quickly lifted her skirts and straddled his hips with her knees. His eyes widened, his hands grabbed her waist, and he groaned as she settled her bottom onto his lap.

"What the devil do you think you're doing?" he asked huskily.

She reached up and cupped both his ears with her hands and caressed them.

Looking deeply into his eyes, she countered, "Do you like that?"

His hands settled around her hips, and he pressed her harder onto his body. "Immensely, but do you know what would happen if your aunt came in and saw you sitting here on me like this?"

"She and my sister are out for the afternoon."

"Thank God, but what about your servants?" he asked, his breaths coming faster and louder.

"There are only two in the house this afternoon and they know not to bother me when I'm painting."

He leaned his head back against the settee. "You are not painting, Gabrie, you are seducing me, and for the life of me I can't figure out why."

"Do you like it?" she said softly as she moved her hands across his broad chest. She bent and kissed the corner of his eye, letting her lips softly trail down to his cheek and over to the corner of his mouth. She felt his lower body move beneath her, and Gabrielle gasped at the wonderful sensations that flooded her body.

"Very much, too much," he whispered huskily before pulling her to him so his lips could claim hers.

Her mouth clung to his in an eagerness she didn't want to deny or control. His kisses were rough and demanding. His tongue probed deeply into her mouth over and over again, filling her with the sweet taste of his surrender. She yielded to his strength as he pressed his lower body up to hers time and time again. Fire shot to the area between her legs, and Gabrielle moaned as she wiggled against the hardness beneath his breeches.

His hands found the front opening of her day dress and he pulled it apart, dragging it and her shift off her shoulders, laying bare her breasts to his view. He covered one nipple with his mouth and the other breast with his hand. The wanton sensations crashing through her were staggering as she cupped his head to her breasts and moaned with sweet, satisfying pleasure.

Suddenly he tumbled her back onto the settee. Her back hit the sharp end of the book, and she cried out and flinched.

He jerked away. "Did I hurt you?"

Gabrielle froze. The book. "Ah, ah, no. I'm fine."

"Something hurt you," he said and reached behind her and found it.

Gabrielle gasped and grabbed for the book. But Brent was too fast for her.

She felt as if her blood ran cold as she fastened the front of her dress. "Let me have that," she whispered.

"Why?"

"I-I, nothing," she said, thinking quickly. "It's just a book. Throw it down and kiss me, Brent."

He still leaned over her, so she reached up and placed her lips to his. She felt him respond involuntarily and, for a moment, he melted into the kiss. She smiled against him.

All of a sudden he rolled away from her and rose from the settee. He opened the book as she lunged at him.

"No!"

He grasped her wrist as she grabbed for the book that he held just out of her reach. "I knew something must have been going on when you started touching me. Why don't you want me to know what you are reading?"

He let go of her wrist and opened the book. Heat flamed in her cheeks as he read out loud, *The Art of Being a Most Pleasing Mistress.*

His brow wrinkled in surprise. "You were reading this?"

"No, no." She blinked rapidly.

The corners of his mouth lifted in a smile. "Yes, you were."

How dare he be so amused by her horror? "All right, yes," she said haughtily. "If you must know, I was reading it."

He flipped through a few pages. "And what did you learn?"

If he could find her situation amusing, she would be damn if she'd be embarrassed about it. She lifted her shoulders and her chin. "I learned that men like to have their golden orbs rubbed when they are tense, so I was trying to please you by rubbing them."

His smile turned into a wide grin. He nodded as if he understood, but when he saw she was not amused, he cleared his throat and said, "What exactly are my golden orbs, Gabrie?"

The look on his face could only be called predatory, heated. Primal. And she felt a decidedly inappropriate need to do more than fondle his orbs.

She pulled her shoulders back. "Your ears, of course."

That heated look mixed with surprise before he burst out laughing.

Gabrielle huffed in exasperation. "Why are you laughing? You are being most unkind when all I was trying to do was please you."

He faced her again, trying his best to contain himself. "You do please me, Gabrielle."

"That is the real problem," she blurted. "I have been trying to make myself unacceptable to you as a wife. I don't want to please you. It says in this book a gentleman doesn't like for his wife to do these things, like squeezing and fondling his golden orbs, but it is okay for his mistress to do it."

Laughter was bright in his eyes and on his lips again, but he managed to say, "You want to be my mistress?"

"No, of course not," she said, completely shocked by the suggestion. "I thought if I did something only a mistress knew how to do, you might be angry enough that you wouldn't want to marry me."

He chuckled low in his throat. "Oh, no, Gabrie, that is not going to happen." He took the book and placed it back in her hands. "By all means, keep reading this and learn all you can. It will be my pleasure for you to show me all you have learned after we are married."

Her shoulders dropped in defeat.

"And as far as the golden orbs you were reading about—they are not ears. You will learn exactly what they are on our wedding night."

He turned and walked out.

Eighteen

Always do right; this will gratify some people and astonish the rest.
—Mark Twain

GOLDEN ORBS!

Brent smiled and his body tightened every time he thought about his encounter with Gabrielle yesterday afternoon, and that was often. She had bewitched him. If she hadn't been sitting on his lap, caressing his ears with such tenderness, tempting him with her kisses and touches, he would never have agreed for her to meet him in the park and come with him to follow Godfrey. It was really something he should be doing alone, but given the circumstances of what she had been doing at the time, how could he have denied her anything she wanted?

Brent chuckled to himself. *Golden orbs!*

She was unbelievable! And oh, so tempting. After yesterday, he could hardly wait to make her his wife.

But his yearning for her was more than just his attraction to her. He loved not knowing what she was going to come up with next to try to get him to free her from the bond of marriage to him. He hoped her father returned soon so all the financial paperwork could be finalized. A few weeks ago, he would never have thought it, let alone admitted it, but now he could say fate chose well for him. He was besotted with Gabrielle. Thoughts of her smiling at him, laughing with him, and even being outraged by him played through his mind.

Oh, yes. He was very happy to be marrying her. He didn't want to think about the possibility of her not belonging to him.

He heard a conveyance approaching and looked up to see Muggs driving up in a closed carriage. The man always looked wary of Brent, but there was no reason for him to. Brent wasn't one to hold a grudge. Besides, the man had attacked him only after the duke had ordered him to.

When the carriage rolled to a stop, Brent took off his hat and walked over to open the door. He wanted to take hold of Gabrielle's waist and swing her around as he helped her down, but since Muggs was already glaring at him, Brent politely took her hand and let her step down on her own. He started to shut the door, but Gabrielle touched his arm.

"I hope you don't mind, my lord, but I brought Brutus with me."

Yes, he did mind. He stepped close to her so Muggs wouldn't hear everything he said. "Gabrie, this is not a good time to have him along."

She stuck her hands in the black velvet muff she carried. "But, my lord, he looked so forlorn when I started to leave. You know how much he enjoys the park. I couldn't say no to him."

"We will be following two girls and a lad pulling a milk cart. What if he barks at a squirrel or another dog and tips the young man to the fact we are following them?"

She looked at him aghast. "You know Brutus doesn't bark at squirrels," she admonished. "He is very well behaved and he minds me instantly. I will not let him reveal to anyone what we are doing. So do not worry; he will not hamper our mission."

He looked at her bright eyes and hopeful expression and knew he couldn't deny her.

"All right," he said and settled his hat back on his head. Reaching back into the carriage, he helped Brutus move his hind legs so he could step down. "Come on, boy, we don't have much time. I don't want to miss Godfrey."

The sky was gray and the air chilly but not bitter as they walked to the area Brent had already picked out, where they could hide behind a stand of trees. He had a fairly good idea of which path Godfrey took each day, and it was simply a matter of waiting until he emerged from the park. All they had to do was stay out of his sight as they followed him. And Brent kept thinking it would have been a whole lot easier to do that without Gabrielle and Brutus.

Once they were seated behind the largest tree, Gabrie said, "Explain to me once again why you think Godfrey is the dog thief. I'm afraid I had my mind on other things when we were talking yesterday."

Brent's lower body stirred. "Gabrie, let's not discuss right now what your mind was on yesterday." He grinned. "But at another time, I'd be most interested in finding out what other things you learned from that book."

Heightened color rose in her cheeks. "You have heard all you are going to hear from me about that book, Brent. I put it back where I found it, shoved the chest up against it, and I don't intend to look at it ever again."

"Pity," he said and hid a chuckle behind his gloved hand and a cough. "Now, regarding your question about Godfrey, at first I didn't think there was a connection, and I'm still not certain of my suspicions. Prissy and Tulip went missing in the park and Josephine in Snellingly's neighborhood. But yesterday it dawned on me that Godfrey travels through both every day of the week. So I went to see Snellingly and Lord Waldo and asked about who had returned their dogs. They both gave the same description of a red-haired, strapping lad of about twelve to thirteen years of age. That fits Godfrey. It just seemed too much of a coincidence to me that he found both dogs. Especially now that Lady Windham's dog is missing. I thought it might not be a bad idea to know where he lives and then to talk to him."

"In case more dogs go missing and are mysteriously found and returned by him."

He smiled. "Exactly."

"But if he is the dog thief and returned their dogs, why wouldn't he have returned Prissy first, since she was the first to go missing?"

Brent looked into her concerned eyes, and a calm feeling settled over him. "I don't know the answer to that. I'm hoping to find out today."

Brutus lifted his head and looked straight in front of him as if he heard something. A few seconds later, Brent heard the rumbling of wheels and rattle of milk cans.

"I hear the cart," he said, peering around a tree. "Make sure Brutus remains quiet."

"He will not make a sound," Gabrielle assured him as she patted the dog's head and rose on her knees to watch.

When Brent considered the lad and the two girls a safe distance ahead of them, he, Gabrielle, and Brutus rose and followed them. Godfrey was obviously well versed on where he was going and the shortest route to get across the city. Within a few minutes, he left the shopping district of London and was maneuvering his way across the back streets and through narrow alleys. Brent stopped trying to remember the route they were taking, deciding it would be best to hire a cab to take them back to Mayfair as soon as their mission was complete. It was easy to stay out of sight and keep up with Godfrey because of the rattle of milk cans and the squeaking of the cart's wheels.

Occasionally the lad would stop and talk to someone, or he and the girls would wave to a passing rig or wagon, but they kept a steady pace of winding farther and farther into an area of town where Brent would have rather Gabrielle not be. But there was no going back now.

Brent often looked over at her. She and Brutus had no trouble keeping pace with him. And by the expressions on the faces of some of the people they passed, no one was going to come near them with Brutus walking between them.

Brent estimated they had been following Godfrey for a couple of hours when they came to a neighborhood of rundown tenant houses. The skies had turned dark and thunderous, but not a drop of rain had fallen. He knew better than to leave his house without an umbrella, but his mind had been too busy with other thoughts when he'd walked out the door. He hoped the rain would hold off until after he talked to Godfrey.

A few minutes later, Godfrey stopped in front of what looked to be a small barn. Brent heard him tell the girls to go on home and that he would put the cart away and wash the milk cans. The girls skipped a couple of houses down the street and disappeared.

Brent turned to Gabrielle and said, "You and Brutus stay here. I want to talk to Godfrey alone."

"Talk to him?" she asked, taking her hand out of her muff and laying it on his chest.

He liked the warmth of her touch. "That's why I followed him, Gabrie."

"Isn't that dangerous? I thought you just wanted to find out where he lived."

Brent could see she was concerned. "I need to ask him a few questions. I want to talk to him about where he found the dogs. You and Brutus stay here, and don't worry."

Godfrey was coming back to the cart to get more cans when Brent was close enough to say to him, "Godfrey, I'd like a word with you."

The lad looked up and saw Brent only a few feet away. He grabbed a can off the cart and threw it at Brent. Brent ducked and then sidestepped the tumbling can. The lad took off running.

"Stop!" Brent yelled and managed to get close enough to grab the back of Godfrey's coat, stopping him. When the young man swung around, he surprised Brent with a fast, hard fist to the side of his mouth, snapping his head back. Brent's hat flew off his head and he staggered. A moment later he heard Gabrielle yell, "Brutus, no!"

Brent struggled to regain his footing as Godfrey quickly bent low and rammed his shoulder into Brent's stomach and pushed him backward. Brent stumbled over a milk can and fell to the ground. He grunted and looked up in time to see Brutus's big front paws land on Godfrey's chest and pummel him to the ground.

"Get him off me!" Godfrey screamed, trying to squirm away from the large dog, who growled, slobbered, and held him pinned to the ground with two saucer-sized paws. "Help me!"

"Stop fighting him, and he won't hurt you," Brent said, rolling to his feet. "Off! Brutus, get off!" The dog looked at Brent but didn't move. "Off, Brutus," he said and grabbed him by the neck scruff.

Panting, Brutus growled his complaint but hobbled off Godfrey.

Gabrielle ran up to them and dropped to her knees and hugged Brutus around his big shoulders and neck. When she looked up at him, Brent was surprised to see tears brimming in her eyes.

"He hasn't been able to run for months," she said with a tremulous smile. "I couldn't stop him. He wanted to help you."

A lump formed in Brent's throat. "I know," he said

and tried to tell Gabrie with his eyes he understood what she was feeling. He knew what it took out of the old dog to help him. Brent patted the dog's head with one hand and wiped blood from the corner of his mouth with the other. Godfrey had hit him on the same side of the mouth as his previous injuries, and it hurt like hell. He looked around for his hat and spotted it flattened into the ground. Brent didn't know if a can had rolled over it or if Brutus had stomped on it, but it was definitely ruined.

Brent looked at Godfrey, who was backing away from the dog. "Get him away from me," Godfrey shouted again.

"First, tell me… where is my dog?"

"He's standing right beside you," Godfrey said, fear and fury flashing in his eyes.

"No, that's her dog." Brent pointed toward Gabrielle.

"What dog are you talking about?"

"Don't play dumb with me, Godfrey. You know the small dog I'm talking about. I paid you to be on the lookout for my Pomeranian. I know you returned Lord Snellingly's and Lord Waldo's dogs, so where is mine?"

"I'll tell you."

Brent turned and saw one of Godfrey's sisters standing a short distance away. The misting rain fell on her white mobcap and straight shoulders. Brent didn't know when it had started to rain.

"You stay quiet, Emily," Godfrey said. "You don't have anything to say."

The girl didn't even look at her brother. "Just don't let the big dog hurt him again, and I'll tell you what you want to know."

Gabrielle rose to stand beside Brent and said, "Brutus didn't hurt him and will not hurt him. He only wanted to stop Godfrey from running away. He's big but a gentle dog."

"Don't say anything, Em," Godfrey ordered. "This doesn't involve you."

The slender brown-eyed girl walked closer. "Yes, it does. We all took the dog that day. No one ever knew. It was easy to keep all the dogs quiet in the wagon. We just kept putting milk in a bowl for them. Your dog is inside the house with our mother."

Relief washed through Brent like water rushing over stones in a brook. Prissy was alive.

Gabrielle grabbed his arm and squeezed it as she leaned against his side. "Thank God," she whispered. "You've found her."

"You can't have her back," Godfrey spat at him.

"We'll see about that," Brent muttered. He turned to the girl. "Where is your mother?"

"Wait, Brent," Gabrielle said. "Why don't you talk to him first and let him tell his story."

Gabrielle had pulled the hood of her black velvet cloak over her bonnet, and looking at her, Brent saw the intriguing, gorgeous, and tempting young lady he met in the park weeks ago, who said to him, *"You talk softly to dogs just like you do to people."*

She pulled a handkerchief out of her muff and handed it to him. He looked from Godfrey to the girl, and then back to Gabrielle as he pressed her handkerchief to the corner of his mouth. He supposed with his adventures with Gabrielle, he was destined to lose his hats and have a cut lip.

Brent turned toward Godfrey and said, "Tell us why you took the dogs."

The lad nervously wiped rain from his face, and Brent was reminded how young he was.

"It wasn't my fault you lost her," he said belligerently. "She was just wandering around in the park that morning when we were heading home. She started following us, so I put her in the wagon. We planned to take her back to the park the next day, but me mum thought I'd brought the dog home for her, and I couldn't tell her I didn't."

"She's sick," the girl said.

"What is wrong with her?" Gabrielle asked.

The girl shrugged and shook her head.

"It don't matter what's wrong with her," Godfrey said angrily. "She fell in love with that dog the moment she saw it. I couldn't take it away from her."

"What about the other dogs?" Gabrielle asked. "Why take them?"

Godfrey looked at Brent and pointed his finger at him. "He gave me money just to look for the dog and said there'd be more if I found it. I was thinking maybe other lords and gentlemen would pay me for finding their dogs, too. I took them so I could return them."

"So you decided to start yourself a little business of stealing dogs," Brent said, finding it difficult to feel sorry for the lad.

"We're trying to get enough money to pay a doctor to come see our mum," Emily said.

"I told you to hush up, girl," Godfrey snapped.

"Godfrey," Gabrielle said, stepping forward. "That

is no way to speak to your sister. Can we go inside and see your mother?"

"No," he said, walking closer to them for the first time. Fear returned to his eyes. "Don't tell me mum what I did. I'll find a way to pay back the money."

"How?" Brent asked. "By stealing more dogs or maybe stealing something else next time?"

"I'm not a thief," Godfrey said, tears pooling in his eyes. "I gave the dogs back. I couldn't give yours back."

"Godfrey, one way or the other, we're going in to see your mama whether or not you want us to."

The lad swallowed hard and then suddenly hung his head and said, "Come on."

Brent, Gabrielle, and Brutus followed Godfrey and Emily down the street to one of the small houses. Gabrie told Brutus to stay outside. As soon as Godfrey touched the door, Prissy started barking. They stepped inside a one-room house. Prissy ran toward Brent, barking like the hounds of hell were after her.

Brent bent down and the little dog jumped up into his arms and started licking his face. He patted and rubbed her head and hugged her to him as he laughed. "How've you been, girl?"

"Godfrey, son, why in God's name have you invited these nice-looking people into our home? You know I'm not receiving guests."

Brent looked past Prissy and saw a woman who didn't look much older than he, sitting up in a bed that stood in the far corner of the room. She was wrapped in a heavy cloak, and several blankets lay across the bed. The woman was pale and frail-looking. Her long, graying hair hung limply on her shoulders. Emily joined her other sister in a corner, and Godfrey immediately started putting more wood on the fading fire.

"Please excuse us, Mrs....?" Gabrielle said.

"Jones," she said weakly. "I'm Mrs. Carlton Jones, but my husband is no longer with us. He died almost two years ago now."

"I'm very sorry to hear that," Gabrielle said.

"Prissy acts as if she knows you," the woman said, looking at Brent. "Godfrey told me that was her name. He's the one who gave Prissy to me. The name suits her, don't you think so?"

"Yes, it does," Brent said, tucking the little dog under his arm.

"But I've never seen you before. Em, go heat some water and make these nice people some tea. Godfrey, stop poking that fire and pull the chairs over so they can sit down and tell me why they've come."

"No, no, please don't trouble your daughter for us," Brent said, rubbing Prissy. "We can't stay long enough for tea."

Pris squirmed, whined, and wanted to get down, so Brent set her on the floor. She ran back over to the woman and put her front paws on the bed. The woman reached down and lifted Prissy up on the bed with her. Brent watched in surprise as Prissy made herself comfortable in the woman's lap.

"Well, that's a shame. What can I do for you, Mr....?"

"Brentwood, madame," he said, not wanting the woman to know he was a viscount. "Just call me Brentwood, and this is Lady Gabrielle."

The woman's eyes rounded in surprise. "A real lady?" She looked at Gabrielle and then brushed a tangled strand of hair away from her shoulder and straightened her bed coat. "Godfrey told me he was working for someone who paid him well." She stopped and looked at Brent. "It's you, isn't it? He also told me he was working for a man who gave Prissy to him. Are you the kind man who did that?"

Brent cleared his throat. "No, madame, I did not give Prissy to him."

"Oh," she said, surprised, and started rubbing Prissy's back.

Gabrielle touched Brent's arm. "May I talk to you? Alone."

"No, Gabrie. I know what you are going to say, and no."

Gabrielle smiled at the woman and said, "Would you excuse us, Mrs. Jones? We're going to step outside for a moment. We'll be right back."

The sickly woman looked puzzled. "All right."

Brent opened the door for Gabrielle, and she stepped outside into the rain. Brutus came walking over to stand between them.

"I know what you are going to say, and just don't do it," Brent argued before she even opened her mouth.

"I will say it. Brent, you can't tell that woman what Godfrey did. You are not an uncaring person, and you can see she is far too ill to hear that about her son on top of your taking Prissy away from her."

"What are you saying? I have to tell her, Gabrielle. He stole dogs and extorted money. That's against the law."

Gabrielle blinked rapidly, as if she didn't understand him. "But he was trying to get enough money for a doctor to help his mother. It might have been the wrong thing to do, but it was for a very good reason."

"That doesn't make it right. If he isn't punished for doing this, he might do it again, or do something worse next time."

She moistened her lips. "I agree he needs some type of punishment, but that doesn't mean his mother has to know. He said he would pay back the money, and that can be his punishment."

"Pay it back with what, Gabrie?" Brent said, exasperated as the chilling, misting rain fell on his hatless head. "He has no money."

"You can give him a job and let him work it off."

"Me?" She was unbelievable! "Me, give a job to the wretched little thief who stole my dog?"

"All right, I'll give him a job. He not only needs to pay back Lord Snellingly and Lord Waldo, but once he gets enough money for a doctor to see his mother, I'm sure he will need money for some type of medicines or tonics or something."

"Fine, you give him a job," Brent said a little too sharply, and she flinched at his harsh tone. Brent took a deep breath. He didn't like arguing with Gabrielle. "You give him a job," he said in a softer tone. "I'm going to get Prissy and go home."

Gabrielle lowered her lashes over her eyes. "I'll wait out here with Brutus."

He walked back into the house. The woman's eyes were filled with tears and her lips trembled. "I'm sorry, Mr. Brentwood, Godfrey just told me he found the dog in the park and she is your dog and you have come for her. I understand."

She picked Prissy up off her lap and sat her down on the floor. Now Brent felt like a wretch. Why did the woman have to be sick?

"Come, Prissy." The Pomeranian just looked at him. Pris had always been stubborn. "Come on, girl, let's go." Prissy barked once and started toward him. He bent down to scoop her up, but she quickly barked again and then turned around and ran back to the bed. She lifted her front paws on the bed and barked at the woman.

"Shoo—Prissy. Your master has come for you. Shoo now, you must go with him."

Brent stared at Prissy, who was begging the woman to pick her up and put her on the bed, and for a moment he saw his mother. That was exactly how Prissy used to demand his mother put her on the bed. Brent's heart softened. He thought about all the times the dog had gotten him up early, barked at the moon, and scratched on his door. Had he kept Prissy only because of his mother? He had missed the little mutt when she first disappeared, so he must have some feelings for the dog.

It hardly mattered anymore. Prissy was making her choice. She wanted to stay, and he was going to allow it. Somehow, he knew his mother would want this woman to have Prissy.

"You keep her, Mrs. Jones. She seems quite taken with you."

A hopeful expression rounded her dark-circled eyes. "Oh, I couldn't take her from you. I'm just happy we were able to keep her safe until you found out where she was." She looked at Prissy. "You stop holding up your master. Now go."

Brent walked over and picked up the little dog and gave her a hug. Prissy licked his face again and barked. He then placed the dog in Mrs. Jones's lap.

"No, Mrs. Jones, she's your dog now. You've taken excellent care of her. I'll keep up with her through Godfrey."

Mrs. Jones smiled gratefully and lovingly stroked Prissy's back. "I don't know how to thank you."

"Get better so you can continue to take good care of her." Brent looked at the two girls who hadn't moved from the corner. "You will help your mother take care of Prissy, won't you?" The girls nodded. "All right then." Brent looked at Godfrey and pointed toward the door. "I'll see you outside."

The lad followed Brent. Brutus growled at Godfrey, and the lad backed up. Gabrielle rubbed the mastiff's shoulder and calmed him. Brent could tell the temperature was dropping. The misty rain felt icy to his hatless head. He wrapped his scarf tighter about his throat and hoped they didn't have to walk too far before finding a cab to hire.

Gabrielle gave him a questioning stare, but he turned to Godfrey and said, "There's still the problem of what to do about your taking money from Lord Waldo and Lord Snellingly."

Godfrey ran a hand through his damp red hair. "I know it was wrong, but me mum gets worse every day. She hasn't the strength to get out of bed anymore. We don't know what's wrong with her. I've got to get her help."

"I understand, but the best way to help your mother is to make an honest wage, Godfrey. I'll see that a doctor comes around tomorrow to examine her."

Grateful tears brightened Godfrey's eyes again.

"Do you have Lady Windham's dog or any other dogs?"

He nodded before lowering his head. "Two. They are in a pen behind the milk shed."

"All right. The first thing you are going to do this afternoon is take back the dogs you have, and do not accept any money for their return. Understood?"

Godfrey nodded again.

"Then tomorrow you are going back to Snellingly's and Lord Waldo's houses to give back the money they gave you."

His eyes widened and he raked the back of his hand under his nose. "But how will I pay for the doctor you will send if I give back their money?"

"I'll take care of the doctor for now. In return, you will deliver fresh milk and eggs to my house every day until spring. That should just about pay me back. Do you have any problems with this?"

"No, my lord," he said and pulled his coat tighter about his neck.

"If you stay faithful to your deliveries each day, I'll see to it your mother has whatever medicines, tonics, or elixirs she needs, but it all depends on how dedicated you are."

Godfrey's shoulders lifted. "I won't neglect my duties to you, my lord. I won't miss a day."

"See that you don't." Brent turned toward Gabrielle. Her eyes shimmered with tears of happiness. She was smiling at him, letting him know she approved of how he had handled Godfrey, and suddenly that meant everything to him.

"My lord."

Brent turned back to Godfrey.

"Thank you for giving Prissy to me mum."

Brent nodded once and watched the lad go back into his house.

"Thank you," Gabrielle said.

He tried to smile at her and realized his lip had swollen from where Godfrey had hit him. He grunted a laugh. He'd lost three hats and had his lip cut three times since he'd met Gabrielle, and he didn't give a damn. She had been worth it.

He touched the small of her back. "Let's go see if we can find a hackney and get out of this weather." They looked around for Brutus and noticed he was struggling to get up.

"Come on, boy," Brent said. "I know it's difficult to get the legs going when it's cold and wet. I'll help you." Brent helped Brutus to lift his back legs. The dog coughed, shuddered, and shook off the rain.

Brent and Gabrielle walked in silence, and Brent was thankful. He needed to think about his feelings for her. He didn't know when or how it had happened, but she'd filled a part of him no other woman ever had. He realized now that she had found that spot inside of him where love was hidden. She had watered it, tended it, and made it grow. And he had to find a way to tell her.

Giving Prissy to Mrs. Jones had made him realize a few things about Gabrielle he had avoided even thinking about. But now it was time to do just that.

They were quite a far distance from Godfrey's house when Gabrielle said, "I know it was very hard for you, Brent, but you did the right thing."

He glanced over at her, but her hood covered the side of her face so he couldn't see her. "You think so?"

She nodded. "I do."

"I hope the lad has learned his lesson. After the lecture from you, I couldn't do anything but help his mother and give him a job so he could work off the money he had to repay."

"You would have done the right thing concerning his mother had I not even been here. But I wasn't talking about Godfrey. I was talking about Prissy. I'm sure it wasn't easy for you to give up your mother's cherished pet."

Brent wondered if he should tell Gabrielle it was easier than he thought it would be. And the truth was, he and Prissy had only tolerated each other the past two years.

But all he said was, "Mrs. Jones obviously pampers Prissy as much as my mother did, and I'm sure the dog is delighted not to be leaving the woman. I'm content knowing Pris is well cared for."

Brent touched Gabrielle's arm, and they stopped. Her heavy velvet cloak had absorbed about as much rain as it could, and her hair and clothing must be getting wet. With the temperature as cold as it was, it wouldn't take long for her to get chilled. Her face was damp, but her eyes sparkled invitingly at him. He knew she was cold, and he needed to find them a cab, but he had to say what was on his mind before he lost his nerve. He was afraid if he waited until they found a carriage or until he got her home, if he waited until he had more time to think about it, he'd change his mind, do what suited him, and never tell her.

"I've come to another conclusion, Gabrielle. I'm not going to marry you. I'm giving you the freedom you want."

Her eyes widened and blinked rapidly. Her mouth fell open, and a surprised gasp passed her beautiful lips.

"I realized if I could allow Prissy to make the decision about who she wanted to live with for the rest of her life, I could certainly let you be free to decide who you would spend the rest of your life with."

Her eyes searched his face. "I–I don't know what to say. What about your brothers and my father's vow to ruin their business if we don't marry?"

The rain started coming down harder. "That's no longer an issue. I recently did something I'm sure my brothers won't like if they find out the truth, which I'm sure they will; but I did it anyway."

"What?"

"I went to see Sir Randolph Gibson. I knew his father made his money in shipping, and I thought he might know some people in that business or in some way be able to help them. And it appears he did. They told me yesterday that they have leased the space they need to get their business started."

"That is good news for them."

He nodded. "And when your father returns, I'll tell him any negotiating he and I had started before he left is canceled. I'll be going back to Brentwood without you."

Her eyes searched his. "You're leaving London?"

"I came to see my brothers settled. I've done that. Anything else I planned to do in London can wait for some other time."

Brutus made a coughing, gagging sound, and they both looked at him in time to see him slowly sink down and roll over on his side.

"Brutus!" Gabrielle exclaimed and dropped down beside him.

Brent knelt on the other side of the big dog. His breathing was labored and his eyes were closed.

"What's wrong with him?" Gabrielle asked frantically, rubbing his neck and shoulders as the old dog struggled to breathe.

"I don't know. He must be chilled." Brent unbuttoned his coat and took it off, holding it over the dog like an umbrella.

"What can we do?" Gabrielle said, tears mixing with rain on her cheeks. "We've got to get him home and do something for him."

"Stay calm. We will."

Brent looked up and down the street but already knew this was not the kind of neighborhood that had cabs for hire. In fact, there were no carriages at all on the street. He would need to go several blocks over for that. But this also wasn't the kind of neighborhood where he wanted to leave Gabrielle alone.

"I'm going to pick him up and carry him until we find a carriage."

Gabrielle looked at him as if he were a madman. "You can't pick him up; he's too big."

"Nevertheless, I will try. I'm not leaving the two of you alone on this street while I go for help."

"Brent, you must," she said desperately. "There's no other way."

"I won't, Gabrielle," he stated firmly and handed his coat to her.

Brent planted his feet solidly on the ground and bent at his knees. He slid his arms under Brutus's large body and lifted.

Damnation, the dog was heavy.

The muscles in his arms burned, and his legs trembled as he struggled to stand with the dog that probably weighed as much as he did. He had to give up and settle the dog back down on the ground again.

"I'm going to help you," Gabrielle said.

He put his hand on her arm. "No, I can manage," he said, unwilling to doubt his strength to do so. "I need to get a better grip on him."

Gabrielle pulled on Brent's arm. "He's my dog, Brent. I will help lift him and carry him to safety."

Brent looked at her lovely, emphatic, and worried face, and knew he couldn't deny her anything.

"All right then, on the count of three. One. Two." In the distance, Brent heard a familiar sound and glanced behind him. Out of the foggy rain he saw Godfrey walking toward them, pulling his cart.

Brent gave a heaving sigh of relief and whispered, "That boy is about to earn his first pay."

Nineteen

Grief can take care of itself, but to get the full value of joy you must have somebody to divide it with.

—Mark Twain

SHIVERING, GABRIELLE FLUNG OPEN THE FRONT DOOR to the town house. "Auntie, Rosa, Mrs. Lathbury, somebody quick! Come help us!"

Brent and Godfrey hurried in behind her, struggling to stay in step as, between the two of them, they carried the mastiff into the house. Gabrielle led them down the corridor toward the drawing room. The three of them had done their best to warm Brutus after they had found a hackney to bring them home, but it was difficult to do, as none of them had a dry thread in their clothing.

Gabrielle didn't know what they would have done if Godfrey hadn't happened upon them. He and Brent had lifted Brutus into his cart. They had raced across streets and taken shortcuts down alleyways until they found a carriage for hire.

Thankfully, a fire was lit in the drawing room.

Gabrielle pulled Brutus's giant pillow close to the fire, and they gently laid the dog down. His eyes were closed, but he let out a low, strangled woof. Her heart squeezed. She knew he was letting her know he was glad to be home.

Gabrielle rushed back to the corridor and almost ran into Mrs. Lathbury. "We need blankets," Gabrielle said, peeling off her wet gloves.

The woman scampered away. Gabrielle hurried back to Brutus, untying her cloak with one hand and her bonnet with the other as she went. She flung the saturated garments aside and knelt on the floor beside her dog.

Brent rose and handed Godfrey a few coins. "There is enough here to pay the driver for bringing us here and to take you back to your cart. The rain has stopped, so I'm depending on you to get those other dogs returned to their owners before the afternoon is over."

"You can depend on me, my lord."

Gabrielle looked up at the wet young man and said, "Thank you, Godfrey. I don't know what we would have done had you not helped us. Brutus is such a big dog."

"That he is, my lady," Godfrey said, "but I don't need any thanks. I'll be off now unless there is more I can do."

Gabrielle looked at Brent. She didn't like the look of concern that etched the corners of his eyes and mouth.

"Brent, perhaps we should send him after the veterinarian Papa uses for his horses when one is down. Maybe he can help Brutus."

Brent's expression was strained but his voice tender

as he said, "I don't think you need to do that, Gabrie. Brutus knows he's at home, safe and warm now. That's what he wanted. I don't think he wants to be looked at or bothered by a stranger right now."

Gabrielle knew what Brent was trying to tell her, and all she could do was deny the truth of his words by shaking her head and looking at her beloved dog. She heard Godfrey leave and felt Brent kneel down beside her, but she kept her gaze on Brutus, willing him to open his eyes and raise his head.

"Tell me Brutus is going to be all right," she whispered.

Brent tenderly placed his warm hand over her cold hands. "I can't do that, Gabrie. I don't know. Don't lose hope."

"Gabby, what's wrong?" Auntie Bethie said, rushing into the drawing room. "And who was that strange young man I just saw walking out the front door?"

"He helped us with Brutus, Auntie," Gabrie said, looking up at her aunt, trying to hold back the tears that surfaced in her eyes and clouded her vision. "We got caught in the rain, and he collapsed. He's so big we couldn't lift him, we couldn't find a cab, and the icy rain just kept pouring down on us."

Auntie Bethie looked down at Brutus and then over to Brent. Gabrielle winced with soul-shattering pain because she knew what their exchanged glances meant. She wanted to cry so bad her throat ached, her chest heaved, but somehow she managed to control her emotions and not let them spill over into weeping.

"But he's home now, dearie," her aunt said, placing a comforting hand on Gabrielle's soggy shoulder. "He's on his big pillow by the fire, his favorite place to be. He'll be all right now, no matter what happens."

Mrs. Lathbury came rushing in with the blankets and Brent helped Gabrielle tuck them around Brutus. He hadn't opened his eyes since he collapsed, and Gabrielle knew that was not a good sign.

"Gabrie," Brent said softly, "you need to go to your room and get out of your wet clothing."

She shook her head and rubbed behind Brutus's ears. "I'm not leaving him until I know he's going to be all right."

"Be sensible, Gabrie," Brent said. "If you catch a chill, you won't be able to look after Brutus."

"You are just as wet as I," she said without looking up at him.

"But I am a strong man, and you are a gentle lady. I will stay right here and not leave Brutus until you return. Mrs. Potter will stay too, right?"

"Of course. I will do anything."

Gabrielle shook her head again. She glanced at Brent and appreciated the concern he had for her and for Brutus. Unwanted tears pooled in her eyes but somehow, once again, she kept them from spilling. "I'm not leaving him. Don't you understand I'm afraid he might die while I'm away, and I couldn't bear it if I wasn't here with him?"

"Oh, dearie," her aunt said in an unusually soft voice. "Here, at least get out of that soaked pelisse and step out of those wet shoes. You, too, Lord Brentwood. This is not the time to stand on ceremony. Out of that wet coat you're wearing so your shirt can dry. You're both going to catch a chill. Hand them to me, and I'll hang them before the fire.

"Mrs. Potter," Brent said, handing her his coat and waistcoat, "why don't you have someone prepare her hot chocolate with a little brandy in it? That should warm her up quickly, don't you think?"

"Indeed, it will," Auntie Bethie said in a stronger voice. "I'll see to it right now."

"No, Auntie, please," Gabrielle said, handing off her soggy pelisse. "I really couldn't put anything in my stomach right now."

"All right, dearie, we'll wait a little while."

"Oh, Gabby, there you are," Rosabelle exclaimed, hurrying into the room. "I thought I heard you calling me. I didn't think you would ever get home. Where have you been?" Rosa skidded to a stop beside her aunt. "My lord." She curtseyed to Lord Brentwood and quickly turned back to Gabrielle. "I must talk to you alone. I have something to share with you that you simply won't believe. Let's go to my room."

Lord Brentwood rose and said, "Lady Rosabelle, now is not a good time for your sister. Brutus is not well. Perhaps you could hold off with whatever you wanted to talk to her about until she can see to Brutus."

Rosabelle's gaze darted from Lord Brentwood down to Brutus. She frowned. "Oh, my, yes, of course." She backed away. "He doesn't look good, does he? What's wrong with him?"

"We're not sure," Brent said.

"It appears he's sick." She stared down at Brutus. "I don't think he's breathing."

Gabrielle sucked in a loud breath, wanting Rosa to go away. She couldn't deal with her right now.

"He is breathing," Brent said tightly.

"Oh, well, I'm sure you know about that better than I do. I'm just going to leave you alone, Gabby. You know I simply can't bear situations like this."

"Rosa," Auntie Bethie said, "I was just going out. I've decided which house I'm going to lease, and I need to let the owners know. Why don't you go with me to make all the arrangements?"

"Yes, Auntie, I believe I would like that. We'll talk later, Gabby, after Brutus is better." Rosa quickly fled the room.

Gabrielle looked up at her aunt and mouthed a "thank you."

Her aunt turned to Brent and said, "You'll be here with Gabby, won't you, my lord? I think it best if I get Rosa out of the house for a while."

"So do I," Brent agreed. "And don't worry, madame, I'm not leaving Lady Gabrielle."

"Good. I'll tell the staff you're not to be disturbed, and I'll entrust her to your care."

Gabrielle heard her aunt leave the room, but she couldn't take her attention off Brutus. Beneath the blankets, she could see his breathing was slow and labored. She wanted him to rise and look at her. She wanted him to bark, sniff, and lick her hand as playfully as he had when a puppy, but all he did was lie there so still. She would give anything to help him right now. She wanted to give him back his youth, to turn back the clock so he could be the fierce protector he once was, but all she could do was stay by his side and stroke his head.

For a moment, she was angry that the warmth of the room and the fire had heated her body and already had her clothing drying. She was angry that Rosabelle was so happy and her aunt was leasing a house. It seemed so unfair that life was moving on, going forward, and her Brutus wasn't.

"He's not in any pain, is he?" she managed to look over at Brent and ask without her voice breaking.

"No," Brent said, adding some wood to the fire and then stoking it before glancing back at her with caring eyes and a sympathetic expression. "He's peaceful."

"Good. I wouldn't want him to be in pain." She paused for a moment and then added, "I don't know what I will do without him."

Brent took hold of her hand again and squeezed it as his gaze swept down her face with compassion. "Don't think about what might happen; just keep good thoughts."

She smiled gratefully at him. A few minutes later, she heard Rosa and Auntie Bethie chatting in the front hall, and then the front door open and shut. It was then, knowing they were alone, that Brent pulled her into his arms. She melted against him, resting her cheek against his damp shirt as she continued to stroke Brutus's head and rub behind his ears.

"Thank you for staying with me."

He kissed the top of her damp hair, sighing heavily. "I wouldn't leave you, or Brutus, right now, Gabrie. I know it's my fault Brutus collapsed. I'm sorry. I wouldn't have had it happen for anything."

She raised her head and looked into his warm

golden-brown eyes. She wasn't sure she could talk, but she managed to say, "This wasn't your fault. If anyone is to blame, it's me. You told me it wasn't a good time to bring him and I forced you to do it."

"No, he was fine until he ran to help me when Godfrey hit me. Brutus's big old heart just couldn't take the exertion. It was too much for him."

In that moment, Gabrielle was filled with so much love for Brent it swelled in her chest and throat, and she didn't know if she could contain it.

"Neither of us asked him to do it. You were good to him, and he wanted to protect you."

"Even at his age, he was fearless."

Brent's words were so touching, Gabrielle had to hide her face in his warm chest again, needing and drawing strength from the consolation he was so generously giving.

"And I've known for a long time that his days were short, but I've not wanted to accept it. He's lived well beyond most dogs his size. My heart aches for him," she said against Brent's chest, not knowing or caring if he could understand her muffled words. "I just want to turn back the hands of time and renew his youth."

"But life doesn't work that way for any of earth's creatures," he whispered against her cheek. "It's all right if you want to cry, Gabrie."

"No," she answered, finding such comfort in his embrace it was almost too much to take in. "I don't want to."

Gabrielle sat quietly while Brent held her, half of her face hidden by Brent's strong chest but one eye staring at Brutus. She kept her gaze on her dog until his chest slowly stopped moving beneath the blankets and his lids stopped twitching.

Pushing out of Brent's arms, she whispered, "He's gone."

Brent threw the blankets aside and bent over Brutus. He laid his head to the mastiff's chest and listened. He raised his head and looked at Gabrielle.

"I'm sorry."

She couldn't bear the sympathy she saw in Brent's face. A breathy sigh of despair pushed forth from her aching lungs and she could no longer hold in the tears. All she could think was that she wanted to run away from the pain of loss. She stumbled to her feet. Brent called her name and tried to grab her arm, but she broke free and fled the room.

"Gabrielle," he called again.

The sound of running feet echoed behind her, but she didn't stop. She needed to get to her father's book room so she could hide and cry as much and for as long as she wanted to. She slammed the door shut and fell onto the floor in front of the settee and laid her head on the seat cushion. Burying her face in her hands, she poured out her heart through wracking sobs and endless tears.

She didn't know how long she cried, and she never heard the door open, only felt a warm masculine arm go around her back. She recoiled from Brent's touch, but he caught her to his chest and held tightly. She struggled to get free, demanding to be let go, but he put his hand to the back of her head, cupping her to his chest and forcing her to be still and accept the comfort of his embrace.

"I'm not leaving you alone, Gabrielle," he whispered, hugging her close.

Brent kept whispering he wouldn't leave her. But he was. He'd told her he was going back to Brentwood. He was leaving her, leaving London. She had lost Brutus, and Brent too. Her heart was so broken she did the only thing she could do. She buried her wet face in Brent's neck and wept again.

She cried for Brutus and for herself. She cried for the loss of a mother she never got to know. She cried because her father had never really learned how to love her. And she cried because she knew, even though she had tried desperately to push Brent away, what she really desired was for him to love her and to want to marry her. He had given her what she said she wanted—her freedom and his to marry whomever they wished. But now she knew Brent was the man she would choose to be her husband.

Brent laid his cheek against her hair and ran his hand soothingly up and down her back, over her shoulder, and around her neck as they sat on the floor in front of the settee. He patted her arm, kissed the top of her head, and brushed his fingers along the side of her face. In a husky voice, he caressed her with comforting words and gave her protection in his strong embrace.

As her sobs faded and her tears dried, hearing the steady beat of his heart against his chest consoled her weary and distraught mind.

Slowly, her strength returned.

Gabrielle lifted her head. After a long intake of breath that ended on a shaky sigh, she noticed the fire burned low, giving peaceful warmth and a golden glow to the afternoon shadows that filtered through the windowpanes. She caught Brent's expression and saw he was filled with pain, too, and in that moment she knew he needed to be in her arms as much as she needed to be in his. All the emotions swirling around inside her were impossible to fathom, so she didn't try. She didn't know why, but in her grief she wanted this intimate contact with Brent. For some reason, she had a strong desire to feel alive.

Gabrielle touched the injured corner of his mouth where Godfrey had hit him. It was the third time his lip had been cut in that spot since she'd known him. "Does it hurt?"

"Like hell," he said with a lopsided grin. "But I can take it."

"Good." She smiled and then whispered, "Kiss me."

Brent looked down into her eyes as he brushed her hair away from her face. "I don't think that's a good idea, even though I locked the door when I came in."

"No one will bother us." Gabrielle pleaded again, "Kiss me, Brent."

He slid a hand to the back of her neck and cupped it. "Don't ask this of me, Gabrie. You've been through a lot today. This is not the time for me to be showing you how much I want you."

She moistened her lips and swallowed hard. "But don't you understand, Brent? I need you right now. I desperately need your strength and your touch."

"Damnation!" he whispered and covered her mouth with his. His kiss was fierce but much too short.

She wound her arms around his neck as his lips

found hers and moved tenderly over them. He cupped each side of her face with his hands and kissed her nose, her cheeks, and her closed eyelids. He kissed her lips again and again before letting his burn a trail down the slender column of her throat and back to her face. She entwined her arms around his neck and pulled him closer, lifting her chest up to his and drawing strength from the passion he gave.

Their tongues swirled in each other's mouths as their bodies strained to get closer. Without really knowing why, she started pulling the tail of his damp shirt from the waistband of his trousers. All she knew was she wanted to feel his skin beneath her hands.

"Yes," she heard Brent murmur into her mouth as her fingers found the warmth of his body. She splayed her hands and shot them up the length of his gloriously muscular back. She loved the power she felt in his firm, broad shoulders.

Their kiss deepened and turned desperate as he captured her lips with his again. His tongue explored inside her mouth with eager yet soothing strokes. Brent's hands moved up her rib cage to fondle her breasts. His fingers searched for and found her nipples hidden beneath the layers of her clothing. At his touch, they puckered and rose. Ripples of desire tightened across her breasts and shot pleasure down her body to settle into her most womanly part.

Gabrielle moaned softly.

A few moments later, his lips left hers. Brent's hands stilled. He sighed and let his forehead lean against hers as he fought to control his labored breathing.

"This is going way too far, Gabrie," he mumbled.

"I'm not such a beast as to be so insensitive as to take advantage of you at a time like this."

Her heart lurched with love, with wanting. He had always been a gentleman with her, and she shouldn't expect any less of him now.

"You aren't," she whispered earnestly. "Earlier today you told me you were giving me the freedom to choose whom I wanted. And I've known for some time now I want you."

"Don't tease me. You have been doing your best to make me walk away from you for weeks now."

"I know, but that was because I've always been ashamed of how forward I was that morning we met, ashamed you were humiliated and treated like a common footpad, ashamed my father forced you to say you would marry me. You deserved your freedom as much as I wanted mine."

"None of those things mattered to me. They never did, because the harder you tried to push me away, the more I was determined you would be mine. Don't you know the reason you couldn't get rid of me is because I've fallen irrevocably in love with you? And because I love you so much, I had to give you the one thing you wanted from me, your freedom to choose whom you wanted to marry."

Gabrielle gasped.

Had he said he had fallen in love with her?

Yes! He loves me!

Her love for him, knowing he loved her, welled up inside her. Gabrielle felt as if her heart burst open like spring's first rose. She loved him for never getting angry with her for all the ridiculous things she put him through. She loved him for helping her with Brutus and never once complaining. She loved him for telling her he wasn't going to force her to marry him.

"If I am free to choose, I choose you. I love you, my lord, and I want only you. Don't deny me the comfort of your love right now, Brent."

"Gabrielle, this is not the time to tempt a desperate man. Do you really want to be mine for the rest of your life? There will be no going back if we go further right now."

She smiled. "I love you, Brent. Make me yours."

She slid her hands back under his shirt and moved them up his rippled ribs, brushing over his smooth, tiny nipples. She heard Brent's hissing intake of breath, as if she caused him pain, and stilled her hands.

"Does that hurt too?" she asked.

"No, my lady, but it is torture for sure. If you want to touch me, please touch me wherever you wish." He quickly untied his neckcloth, wound it from around his neck, and slung it away. He yanked the rest of his shirt out of his trousers and pulled it over his head, sending it the way of the neckcloth.

Gabrielle's breaths quickened at the sight of his strong chest. Firm muscles filled out his skin. A patch of light brown hair showed low on his stomach just above the waistband of his trousers. She looked at his broad shoulders with awe and touched him again.

She smiled at him. "You are magnificent."

He chuckled softly, and she gazed into his warm brown eyes, enjoying the delight she saw in their depths.

He reached over and covered her mouth in a

brief but passionate kiss. "You must play fair, Lady Gabrielle. I must look at you, too."

She turned her back to him. He kissed her nape and across her shoulders as he quickly made short work of unlacing her bodice. His lips on her back sent chills of pleasure skipping along her spine. She faced him and helped him slide the long velvet sleeves off her shoulders, down her arms, leaving the fabric to puddle around her waist. They did the same with her sleeveless shift.

"We don't have enough time for me to completely undress you. I want to give you lingering kisses, loving touches, and sweet words, but your aunt will be—"

Gabrielle stopped him by putting her finger to his lips. "I know. Just kiss me, touch me, and whisper to me. Show me what it is I've been wanting since I first saw you standing in the mist."

"With pleasure," he whispered. He gently reached into her stays and lifted first one breast and then the other out of the fabric, letting them billow above the undergarment. A tremor of expectancy shivered through her as he looked at her with appreciation in his gaze.

"You are beautiful," he said huskily, letting his fingertips glide easily from one side of her chest to the other, from the gentle swell of one breast to the other, and down to her very sensitive nipples. "Your skin is smoother than silk or satin."

"Thank you," she whispered and gasped as he bent his head and kissed the hollow of her throat, teasing her skin with his tongue. He palmed both breasts and lightly squeezed them, filling her with wonderment.

Her head fell back and her chest arched forward. He kissed her shoulders, her neck, and her chest before finally letting his mouth cover her breast. She sighed contentedly, knowing she had wanted him to share this intimacy with her. His tongue circled her nipple, bathed it, and then gently drew it fully into his mouth. Gabrielle felt the most wonderful sensation bloom and blossom inside her, and her senses reeled in delight.

"Mmm," he mumbled. "I love the scent and taste of your rain-washed skin."

Her breasts tightened and her abdomen quivered with anticipation. Tremors and shivers tingled along her spine again, down her abdomen to settle and gather between her legs. She wound her arms around his neck and head, hugging him to her, and gave herself up to the exquisite feeling he was giving her.

"I never knew I could feel this way," she whispered.

He raised his head and sought her lips. "Just wait," he breathed into her mouth. "There's more, so much more. I wish I had the time to show you all I want to, my darling."

He gently laid her on her back on the softness of the rug. He stretched his warm body beside her. He rose on his elbow and let his gaze drink her in. He looked into her eyes for a long moment before his gaze drifted down her face and lingered over her breasts before sweeping back up to her eyes again.

"There's still time to say no. We can wait until we are married."

She smiled as she reached up and ran her hand

across his muscular chest. "I don't want to say no. Just kiss me, my love."

And he did.

Brent rose over her and seared his lips to hers. He propped himself up with one hand while the other slowly inched her skirt and shift up her legs, bunching the cloth around her waist. He found the waistband of her drawers, and on instinct she lifted her hips and helped him slide the garment to her feet to kick away. Suddenly his hand found the warm spot between her legs and he cupped her.

Startled, she jerked.

He stopped kissing her and gazed down into her eyes. "Do you want me to stop?"

This was the man she loved and wanted to marry. She touched his cheek with her fingertips. "No." In answer, she lifted her hips and pressed into his hand. "I don't know what you are doing to me, but I don't want you to stop."

"It might hurt the first time," he said as his hand and fingers continued to fondle her, stroke, soothe, and excite her all at the same time.

She sank her teeth into her bottom lip and nodded, but wondered how such heavenly sensations could turn into pain. "I've heard that."

"And you're sure you want to go forward?"

"Have no worries on that, my love."

Brent smiled and lowered his head and caught the rosy tip of her breast into his mouth. With his tongue, he sampled her heated skin over and over again, and she delighted in every touch and each new and building sensation.

Her hands roved over his back, his shoulders, down his buttocks, and back up again. She eased her hands around to his chest, to his nipples again, where she teased them by raking her thumb across them. She explored his narrow hips and firm, rounded buttocks. With eagerness, she then moved her hands down to the front of his trousers and was amazed by the hardness she felt beneath them.

Brent murmured his delight. "I love the feel of your hands on me," he whispered. "Unbutton my trousers. Slide them off my hips."

She slipped the garment past his lean, warm hips.

Gabrielle smiled and gave herself up to the worshipful way he caressed her, kissed her, and treated her. She savored every sensation, every tender caress. The gentle, gliding movements of his hand on her body thrilled her, and she never wanted him to stop. Suddenly, Gabrielle gasped and arched into his hand with a jerking motion. She buried her face into his shoulder as waves of explosive sensations tore through her with gripping speed before fading into pleasant, languid ripples.

"Brent." She whispered his name softly before collapsing back down onto the rug with no breath left in her lungs, no strength in her muscles.

With no time to catch a breath, Brent settled his body over the length of her as his mouth covered hers. His lips were moist, hot, and demanding. He kissed her deeply, roughly, crushing her body and her lips beneath his. With his knees, he opened her legs and then pushed inside her.

Gabrielle jerked and gasped loudly, not expecting such sharp pain. She trembled and twisted beneath him.

"It's all right," he whispered against her lips. "Remember, you knew it might hurt the first time." He kissed her gently and moved slowly. "Stay with me, Gabrie, and it will get better. I promise."

And it did.

He made love to her with gentleness that overwhelmed her. His movements were slow, sensual, and reverent. He kissed her, stroked her body, and moved so gently on top of her that, before she knew what was happening, she once again gave herself over to an indescribable pleasure that kept mounting between her legs.

She joined the hungry rhythm of his hips meeting hers, his body moving in and out of her with long, sure strokes that grew stronger, fuller, with delicious sensations, until she stopped and cried out, breathless with exquisite gratification.

She heard Brent's breath quicken, felt him tremble, and she gloried in pleasing him in this way. Brent covered her mouth with his in a bruising kiss. As her body shuddered, he slid his arms under her back and cupped her to him.

He lay still and heavy upon her, breathing deeply. Her hands made a slow trail over his back, down to his buttocks and up to his shoulders again. She wanted to hold him forever in this moment but knew she couldn't.

Gabrielle was the first to stir. "I've never felt such extraordinary feelings," she said on a contented sigh. "It was so much more than I expected."

"For me, too, my love," he answered. "And all I can think right now is I want to enjoy the same feelings over and over again. But we can't. Your aunt and sister will return soon."

She cupped his cheek with her hand. "I know."

He rose on his elbows and looked down into her eyes. "Are you all right with what we did, Gabrie?"

She smiled. "I'm very much all right."

He nodded and rolled away from her and started straightening his clothing. Gabrielle sat up and started the task of tidying her clothes as well. They worked quietly until he saw her trying to tighten the lacing at the back of her bodice and he said, "Let me do that."

"Thank you," she whispered and turned her back to him.

"While you repair your hair, I will get Muggs to help me with Brutus."

Instantly, fresh tears flooded her eyes. A lump formed in her throat. Reality returned. She faced him and said, "Thank you."

"Is there a special place you would like for us to take him?" Brent asked.

She tried to swallow, but it was too difficult. He reached for her hand and helped her to stand. "There's a place in the back garden Brutus was fond of and he can rest at peace there. I'll show you and Muggs. I should like to have a short service for him. Will you come back tomorrow morning? Maybe just before noon?"

"I'll be here." He lightly squeezed her fingers. "Gabrie, we need to talk about us."

She nodded. "We will, but not now, please. First I need time to bury Brutus."

"I understand."

Brent walked over to her father's sideboard and poured brandy into a glass and brought it back to her.

"Drink this while I get Muggs," he said. "Drink another before you go to bed tonight. You will sleep more easily. I'll see you tomorrow. This will be the last time I see you alone tonight, since Muggs will be with us, but remember I love you, Gabrielle."

She had such an overwhelming tenderness for this man she loved so deeply. He had given all she had asked for, all she needed—love, passion, and consolation during her grief. She would never make him sorry he put his trust and love in her.

Twenty

There is no instinct like that of the heart.

—Lord Byron

"I DON'T THINK I'VE BEEN TO A SERVICE FOR A PERSON that was any sweeter than the one you had for Brutus, Gabby," Auntie Bethie said, taking off her gloves as she walked into the drawing room.

Gabrielle and Brent followed her aunt into the room while the servants, who had attended the short ceremony Gabrielle had prepared for her long-time companion, dispersed to do their daily duties.

Gabrielle had cried off and on throughout the night and she had been weepy most of the morning, but now that Brutus was at his final resting place, her healing had begun. The few words she spoke over him came more easily for her than she had expected.

"I agree with you, madame," Brent said. "Whenever it's my time to meet My Maker, I hope whoever conducts the service makes it as short and sweet as Gabrielle did for Brutus."

Gabrielle gave him a grateful smile but made no

comment. She would tell him one day soon how much it had meant to her to have him with her yesterday, to have him love her as he did at the time she needed it most. He hadn't wanted to at first, and she understood that. But his loving had helped her cope with losing Brutus. She had felt so lost, so alone and abandoned, that his touch, his kindness, his loving her had somehow grounded her and lifted her above her grief to a thankfulness she'd had Brutus with her for many years.

"And I agree with you, Lord Brentwood," her aunt responded. "Now, what do you say to a glass of port to warm your bones?"

"I say: Shall I pour or will you?"

Auntie Bethie laughed. "Sit down, and I'll get it. How about you, Gabby. Will you have a glass with us?"

"Of course," she said with a heavy heart. "I think lifting a glass in celebration of Brutus's life is fitting."

"That we will," her aunt agreed as she busied herself at the sideboard. "I do have to say I'm not surprised Rosa didn't make it down to join us. In fact, I'm glad. She was quite fidgety yesterday afternoon, talking as fast as a shooting star across the night sky one moment and quiet as a church mouse on Sunday morning the next."

"I tried to speak to her last night before I went to bed," Gabrielle said, "but she wouldn't even let me in her room."

"She has no constitution for things that do not center on her and what she wants, that's for sure." Auntie Bethie brought over a small tray with three glasses on it, and they each took a glass and sipped.

Gabrielle started to take a seat on the settee when she heard a commotion at the front of the house.

"Someone's at the door," her aunt said.

As soon as the words were out of her mouth, Gabrielle heard her father's booming, grumbling voice and his heavy footsteps coming down the corridor. Gabrielle glanced at Brent.

His brows lifted. He angled his head and asked, "Did you know your father was coming back today?"

"Today? No, I had a letter earlier in the week telling me to expect him soon but not when."

The duke walked into the drawing room and stopped in the doorway, looking at the three.

"Welcome home, Papa," Gabrielle said, immediately wanting to run into his arms, bury her face in his chest, and pour her heart out to him about Brutus. But instead, old feelings of trying to please him pushed those thoughts aside and she greeted him the way she knew he wanted her to. With a bright smile and a low curtsey, she said, "I hope your trip was pleasant."

"Thank you, Daughter, it was," he said, walking farther into the room. "My lord," the duke added and nodded his head toward Brent. "Looks like you've been in another fight."

"Your Grace." Brent touched the corner of his lip before he bowed. "Trouble seems to follow me."

"Mmm," was all the duke said and turned his attention to Auntie Bethie. "Mrs. Potter, you can pour me a glass of whatever it is you have in your hand, and then start packing."

"Papa!" Gabrielle exclaimed.

Auntie Bethie winked at Gabrielle and laughed low in her throat as she walked over to the sideboard. "Pay him no mind, Gabby. I certainly don't. I started packing the moment you told me he was coming back."

"Glad to hear it," the duke replied.

"I won't be gone for long this time, Duke."

"What is that supposed to mean?" he grumbled.

"I'll tell you at a later time. You just got in, and I'm sure you want to hear all the latest from your daughter."

"Yes, I'll hear from her in due time, too, but it does seem it's my good fortune you are here, Brentwood. I want to talk to you and Gabrielle."

Gabrielle tensed. She glanced over at Brent, who gave her a questioning look and moved to stand closer to her.

The duke took the glass of port from Auntie Bethie. "Earlier this week, I received a letter from the Earl of Austerhill. The old chap came to his senses. He wrote to say he has decided to forgive Gabrielle for the sake of our financial plans and let Staunton marry her."

"No," Brent and Gabrielle said in stunned unison as they looked at each other.

"Yes, so you are off the hook, as they say, Brentwood, and Staunton is back on."

Brent set his wine glass on the mantel. He gazed deeply into Gabrielle's eyes and asked, "Do you want to marry him, Gabrie?"

Her gaze didn't waver from his. "No," she said, stepping closer to him. "I will not marry him. I've never wanted to marry him. I was only trying to please my father until I found out—"

"Found out what, Gabrie?" Brent said. "Now is the time to tell what you have been reluctant to say all these weeks."

"It doesn't matter," the duke said. "You'll do as I say, Daughter."

"No, Your Grace, she will not," Brent said, taking a step toward her father. "Gabrielle loves me and I love her. We've already—"

"Had this discussion," Gabrielle interrupted, suspecting he was going to admit they had already anticipated their wedding night. "It's time I told the truth, Papa. I could never marry Staunton because Rosa loves him. She admitted it to me after I saw them in a passionate embrace."

Brent's eyes narrowed in comprehension. "That's why you were walking in the park with Brutus the morning we met."

Relief at finally admitting what happened slid down her as cool and cleansing as a spring waterfall. "Yes, I was trying to figure out how I was going to get out of marrying Staunton without compromising Rosa's reputation."

"So you decided to save hers and ruin your own."

There was no accusation in Brent's voice, only understanding; still she worried he might be angry at her. She took a hesitant step toward him. "I swear it wasn't intentional, Brent. And I swear I wouldn't have been so bold with anyone else, but I knew there was something different about you the moment my eyes met yours. Something inside me was drawn to you. I think I fell in love with you the moment you told me you were walking your mother's dog."

She saw him swallow hard. Her name was the only word he got out before her father spoke up harshly and said, "Are we back to that, Gabrielle? Love? Forget about that and tell me more about Rosa. Where is she?"

Gabrielle was trembling with her need to be alone with Brent. She wanted to explain everything to him without her father and aunt listening to every word.

"Excuse me, Your Grace," Mrs. Lathbury said from the doorway. "I hate to disturb you, but Lord Austerhill is here to see you. He says it's about an important matter that can't wait."

"Well, bring him in," the duke barked.

Brent looked down at Gabrielle and smiled. "Don't be frightened, my love. Your father cannot change our plans. We will be married."

Gabrielle stared into Brent's eyes and marveled that he could be so confident against her father, and she loved Brent all the more.

Austerhill walked in, pulling on the front lapels of a coat that didn't quite meet around his bulging middle. "Your Grace." He bowed to the duke. "My lord, Lady Gabrielle, and Mrs. Potter."

Everyone politely greeted him in return.

"I must say," the portly earl uttered, "I didn't expect to see the four of you calmly drinking port at a time like this."

"We are drinking, Austerhill," Brent said, "but not calmly at the moment."

"I should think not," he barked and then turned to the duke. "I assume you've sent someone after them too."

Her father blew out an exasperated breath. "What are you talking about, Austerhill?"

The earl's gaze darted to each one in the room. "Don't tell me you don't know yet that Staunton and Lady Rosabelle have eloped to Gretna Green."

A collective gasp of "no" sounded around the room.

"Has anyone seen Rosa this morning?" the duke asked.

"No one is ever allowed to disturb Rosa until after noon," Gabrielle answered.

"I'll go check her bedchamber," Auntie Bethie said and hurried from the room.

"Papa, we've got to stop her," Gabrielle said, rushing over to him. "Staunton doesn't love her. She'll never be happy with him."

"I've already sent my oldest son to try to overtake them and bring them back," Austerhill said.

Her father drank heavily from his glass, and then, with no emotion in his voice, asked Gabrielle, "Why should I go after them? If Rosa has been so foolish as to run off with Austerhill's son, so be it. You obviously don't want to marry him. She does. I don't see this as an outrageous turn of events. I'll do nothing to stop them."

"You are content with their marriage?" Austerhill asked, seeming surprised by the duke's laissez-faire attitude about their children's elopement.

Gabrielle watched in stunned silence as the duke walked over and added wine to his glass. He then poured another glass and handed it to the earl. "As long as you are, my lord."

"Well, Your Grace, er—" The earl blustered for

a moment. "We'll have to renegotiate the marriage contract, you understand. There has to be consideration because Staunton will no longer be marrying, or that is, married to your eldest daughter."

"Of course, I agree we will have to make some changes in the contract, but I think we'll be able to work everything out satisfactorily, don't you?"

Auntie Bethie came rushing back into the room. "Rosa's bed hasn't been slept in. Here's a note addressed to Gabrielle."

She handed the note to Gabrielle, and she opened it and read aloud:

> "I wanted to talk to you yesterday because you are at times so sensible about things that make no sense. But you were too consumed with your precious dog, and later when you came to my room, it was too late to talk. I had already made my decision to accept Staunton's offer to elope and take the decisions about our lives out of our fathers' hands. We can't trust our fathers to allow us to marry, so we must do this on our own. Be happy for me, Gabby. This is what I want. I will see you when I return."

A peace settled over Gabrielle. This was what Rosa wanted, and Staunton had admitted to Gabrielle that he found passion in Rosa's arms. How could she be unhappy for them?

"That child has always had a mind of her own," Auntie Bethie said.

"Here," the duke said, pushing his half-empty glass

toward Auntie Bethie. "As long as you're still here, you might as well fill my glass again."

"With relish, Duke. Now that I've decided to move to London, I will often be here."

"What? What do you mean, Elizabeth? You know I won't allow that."

"What about a new marriage contract?" the earl asked.

"Yes, yes, we'll get to that in a moment," her father said.

Gabrielle and Brent smiled at each other. "Let's take a walk in the garden, shall we?" he said.

"I'll lead the way," she answered, knowing Lord Austerhill and her aunt would keep her father busy for a long time.

As soon as they stepped outside and Brent closed the door behind them, he pulled her into his arms and kissed her. The air was cold, but his lips and embrace were warm. She felt heavenly.

When he broke from the kiss, she said, "I'm sorry I didn't tell you about Rosa. I didn't want—"

"Shh." He silenced her with another kiss. "There are only two things I want to know, all right?"

She nodded.

"Do you love me?"

Gabrielle smiled. "Yes."

"Do you want to marry me as soon as I can get a special license?"

"Oh, yes," she said, entwining her arms around his neck.

"That is all I need to know, my love. Now kiss me again."

Brent claimed her lips for his own, and Gabrielle thrilled to his touch.

Epilogue

I am my beloved's and his desire is toward me. Come, my beloved.
—Song of Solomon 7:10-11

"Gabrielle?"

She felt light, feathery kisses on her cheek, her forehead, and her eyes. Was she dreaming?

"My sweet love. It is time to wake."

Gabrielle opened her eyes only for a second and then closed them again and turned over. She wrapped her arms around her husband's neck.

He kissed her long and thoroughly. "Are you ready to wake up, my darling wife?"

"No, not yet," she said, keeping her eyes closed. "Perhaps you should kiss me some more."

"I promise I will later, but not right now. Sit up. I have something for you."

She opened her eyes and stretched her arms up in the air. "You are already dressed?"

"I had an errand that needed to be done first thing this morning, and while I was out the mail coach came. You have a letter from London, from your sister's address."

"Oh, from Rosa? She's finally answered one of my letters."

Gabrielle sat up in bed, brushed her hair away from her face, and straightened her long-sleeved night rail across her shoulders while Brent settled himself on the edge of the bed beside her.

Taking the letter, she opened it and read aloud:

> *"Dearest Gabby, I have the most wonderful news to share with you. I am expecting a babe. I knew you would be thrilled for me and Staunton. When are you coming to visit so we can talk?*
> *Your loving sister"*

Excitement filled Gabrielle, and she looked up at Brent and smiled. "Rosa is going to have a child."

"That means you will be an aunt."

"And you an uncle."

He grinned. "I think I will be all right with that. How about you?"

"Oh, I hope I can be as delightful an aunt as Auntie Bethie."

Brent laughed. "There will only ever be one Mrs. Potter, dear wife, but I have no doubt you will find a way to be a special aunt to Rosa's child."

"I'm so glad we are going back for the Season. I want to see Rosa, Auntie, Papa, and of course you will get to see your brothers."

"Yes, I think it will be a good idea for me to be there and keep an eye on them during their first Season in London. But before we talk about that, I have something else for you. Stay right there." He went to the bedchamber door, opened it, and stepped out into the corridor. "Okay, let her come up the stairs."

For a moment, Gabrielle thought her sister was downstairs and was on her way up, until she heard the bark of a dog. Someone must have let one of Brent's hunting dogs in the house. But before she could say anything, a big mastiff puppy came loping into the bedroom and bounded up on the bed with her. The dog jumped on Gabrielle and starting licking her.

Gabrielle squealed with delight.

Brent laughed and joined them on the bed. "It's a little too early for your birthday and a little late for Christmas, but she's yours."

"Oh, Brent, how did you know I wanted another dog? I've never said a word."

"You didn't have to."

The dog jumped down and started exploring and sniffing the room.

"How did you find a mastiff that looks so much like Brutus?"

"It wasn't easy, my love, but she looks like him because she is from Brutus's bloodline."

Gabrielle's heart fluttered. Her chest tightened and her eyes teared. "You can't know that, can you? How?"

"I asked Muggs to help me track down all the people who had puppies sired by Brutus through the years. We kept looking until we found a man who could trace this dog's lineage back to Brutus." Brent reached into his pocket and gave her a piece of paper. "She's only four months old so you'll have her for many years."

Gabrielle threw her arms around Brent, laughing and crying at the same time. "How can I ever thank you? This is the greatest gift you could have given me."

"I'll do anything for you, my love, because you have made me the happiest man in the world."

She kissed him with all the love she was feeling, until she felt a jump on the bed. The mastiff wanted to play.

"What is her name?" Gabrielle asked, scratching the dog between the ears.

"She's your dog, so it's up to you."

She looked at Brent. "Would you mind if we named her Prissy?"

Brent laughed. "Not at all."

Gabrielle fell into Brent's arms and pushed him down on the bed and rolled on top of him. "Thank you, Brent. You have made me happy beyond my dreams."

"That's all I want to do. And remember that heaven is the place where all the dogs you've ever loved come to greet you."

"I believe that. So now, why don't I just show you how much I love you?" The dog bounced back onto the bed again and barked at her. She was ready to play.

Brent and Gabrielle laughed.

"Why don't I take Prissy below stairs first, and then you can show me how much you love me."

"I think that's a wonderful idea, my love," Gabrielle said and bent and kissed him softly on the lips.

About the Author

Amelia Grey grew up in a small town in the Florida Panhandle. She has been happily married to her high school sweetheart for more than twenty-five years.

Amelia has won the Booksellers Best Award and Aspen Gold Award for writing as Amelia Grey. Writing as Gloria Dale Skinner, she has won the coveted Romantic Times Award for Love and Laughter, the Maggie Award, and the Affaire de Coeur Award. Her books have been sold in many countries in Europe, in Russia, and in China, and they have also been featured in Doubleday and Rhapsody Book Clubs.

Amelia loves flowers, candlelight, sweet smiles, gentle laughter, and sunshine.

Read on for more from Amelia Grey

A Dash of Scandal

Available October 2011 from
Sourcebooks Casablanca

One

"Something is rotten in the state of Denmark" and in London, too. The Mad Ton Thief has struck again. It is reported that with more than one hundred guests in attendance at an elegant soiree in Earl Dunraven's home, the robber made off with a priceless golden raven.
—Lord Truefitt, *Society's Daily Column*

"IT WAS A DARK AND STORMY NIGHT AND ALL THE TON—"

"No, no, no, Millicent," the bruised woman said in a soft voice. "That would be the most dreadful way possible to open Lord Truefitt's column. A gossip column must start something like… 'It was a starry night for an elegant soiree.'"

"But it was raining," Lady Millicent Blair reminded her aunt.

The elderly woman, lying against several pillows on her bed, groaned and patted her chest with a hand-painted fan. "That doesn't matter at all, dearie. Society doesn't expect the truth. They want gossip, and they want it surrounded by beauty."

Millicent lifted the hem of her simple white gown and started to sit on the bed, but a low growl from the golden-haired spaniel curled at her aunt's feet stopped her just in time. Millicent backed away.

Hamlet was a friendly, adorable little dog except when reposing on his mistress's bed. At those times the mild-mannered pet became a devoted watchdog. Aunt Beatrice was recovering from a terrible fall, and any sudden movement brought her excruciating pain. It distressed Millicent to see her father's sister in such a pitiful state.

"Oh, Aunt Beatrice, I don't want to overtire you. Can't you see I'm trying to point out why I can't possibly do what you're asking of me? This proves I know nothing about writing a gossip column."

Millicent could have added once again that because of her own mother's heartbreaking experience with the scandal sheets she didn't think she should learn. But Millicent had tried the truth when she arrived in London yesterday morning and learned why her aunt had sent to Nottinghamshire for her. All she had succeeded in doing was making her aunt cry and call for her medication. Millicent couldn't bring herself to upset the badly injured woman again.

Her Aunt Beatrice Talbot was Lady Beatrice to her friends and members of the ton, but to thousands of readers she was the never-seen Lord Truefitt, notorious gossip columnist for the London newspaper *The Daily Reader*.

Beatrice shifted against the pillows and moaned again. Her heart-shaped face twisted in pain. One side of her mouth and chin was horribly discolored and swollen. The poor woman had tripped over her droopy-eared dog and fell, hurting her leg and breaking one of her arms, plus covering herself from head to toe with bumps and bruises. She wasn't able to do much more than feed herself.

After the accident her ladyship's servants had begged her to give Hamlet away so there would be no chance of repeating the terrible fall. Beatrice would have none of that and had shamed them all for even suggesting she abandon her beloved pet.

Emery, Beatrice's sturdy maid, walked into the room carrying a small cup on a silver tray. The buxom woman was the only person Hamlet would let near the bed.

"Oh, good," Beatrice murmured gratefully and slowly batted the lashes of her puffy eyes. "Finally, something to ease the pain. I thought it would never be time to take that wretched-tasting tonic again."

The maid stirred a spoon of restorative powder into a cup of tea and helped Beatrice drink it before retiring to a chair at the back of the room. Emery seemed the perfect person to take care of her aunt. She spoke in gentle tones and was careful not to jar the bed or her employer.

"You must do this for me, dearie," Beatrice whispered in a voice and expression meant to appeal to Millicent's softer side. "I'm loath even to say it again out loud, but I must. The money I'm paid for writing the column is what I live on. Without it, I would be in the poorhouse before I was able to walk again."

"Lord Bellecourte wouldn't let that happen."

"Oh, botheration," she murmured. "He would.

He might be my nephew and your half brother but when it comes to his money he is wound tighter than a William Clement clock."

"But I'm reluctant to stand in for you, and you know why I feel this way."

"Yes, yes, but you must overcome all that." She fanned herself again. "Besides, it won't be for long. Just until I'm able to walk again and attend the parties myself. It's a simple task, really. And you won't be without my help and the assistance of my longtime friends Viscount and Viscountess Heathecoute. The three of us have been around Society long enough that between us we know everyone in Town. We've already secured a voucher for Almack's, as well as invitations for you to attend all the best parties of the Season."

"Aunt Beatrice, if Lord and Lady Heathecoute are such dear friends, why can't they write the column for you?"

She rolled her puffy eyes upward and sighed heavily. "Oh, the viscountess would like nothing better. She absolutely loves gossip. I fear if I allow her to do the job it will never be mine again. She has recently suggested it might be time for me to hand the column over to her. She is a bit younger than me, you understand. But, not only do I enjoy what I do, I must have that income."

Millicent felt her resolve wavering. Writing a gossip column? Would it be like an adventure after living quietly in the country all her life?

Shaking those intrusive thoughts away, she tried to boost her argument by saying, "But Mama and I thought I was coming to London to be your companion and help you while you recover from your accident."

"Goodness. What foolishness. What could you do for me? I have Emery and Phillips to take care of my physical needs. What I need from you is your eyes and your ears. You, dearie, have the most important job. Keeping me out of the poorhouse."

"But scandal sheets?" Millicent whispered more to herself than her aunt. She shook her head wondering how she would ever explain this to her mother should she find out. "I never dreamed you wrote tittle-tattle or that you would want to engage me in your profession."

"Don't make it sound so contemptible, Millicent. Heavens, someone has to do it and it has to be someone who's accepted by the ton. Take my word for it, if Society didn't want to read gossip, the newspapers wouldn't print it." Beatrice looked past Millicent to her maid. "Now, Emery, please ask the viscount and his lady to join us."

"Oh, Aunt Beatrice, I didn't mean any disrespect to you or what you do."

"It's truly no more than writing down a few facts and making them sound much more fascinating than they are."

"Facts? I thought most of what was written was considered rumor and speculation."

"Well, maybe sometimes, but enough of that. Remember, what is most important is that what you are doing has to be kept a secret. No one can know that you are listening to their conversations." With puffy slits for eyes, she looked at Millicent's dress, her face, and her hair. Her aunt slowly shook her head.

"Oh heavens, you are too beautiful. All the beaux will want to dance with you. We must do something."

Millicent looked down at her gown. Her father had provided well for her and her mother before his death and twice a year they had new clothes made that were suitable for the county social affairs held in Nottinghamshire. Her gown was the latest fashion and the unadorned, high-waisted design suited her well. The delicate flowers in her headpiece were chosen especially to show off her golden hair and light brown eyes.

Beatrice had told her she must not stand out at the parties. "You mustn't appear so pretty that the young bachelors seek your attention, or so unattractive you are singled out and talked about as a wallflower."

"What should I do?" she asked, not wanting to displease her aunt further.

"I have just the thing. Look over there on my desk and you will find my spectacles."

Millicent's shoulders reared back and her eyes rounded in rebellion. "No, Aunt Beatrice, that's going too far. I don't need spectacles."

"Of course you don't need them, but they will help keep the young bucks from falling over themselves to dance with you and come calling. Place them in your reticule and put them on when you get there. These are wonderful parties and there is no reason you can't enjoy yourself while you're there, but remember, you are attending the parties to obtain information. Not to be pursued. And do smooth those lovely curls away from your face, dearie. You must try to look a little plainer."

Millicent brushed the sides of her hair and for the

first time admitted to herself that she was not going to get out of doing this for her aunt. She picked up the spectacles and tucked them into her lacy drawstring purse but never expected to actually use them.

"What a delight you would be to all the bachelors if you could attend the Season as a debutante," Beatrice said proudly. "You would be a diamond of the first water."

"Thank you, Aunt Beatrice."

For a moment Millicent thought she might blush over her aunt's unsolicited praise, but she quickly reminded herself that she was far too sensible for something like that.

Millicent shook her head in disbelief. Was she truly going to do this for her aunt? Surely there was some way she could get out of it. She had to think of her mother and what she had been through years ago.

Millicent was the only child born to the middle-aged earl of Bellecourte and his young wife, Dorothy. The earl already had a grown son and two married daughters by his deceased wife when he married Dorothy, at the request of Dorothy's father, his longtime friend. Earl Bellecourte married Dorothy after her reputation had been ruined by a scandal in London.

When Millicent was twelve her father died suddenly, leaving his wife with a jointure more than sufficient to cover her own and her daughter's needs. Dorothy was an attentive mother and saw to it that Millicent was educated in a manner befitting the daughter of an earl.

She was given everything except a London Season.

Dorothy expected her daughter to marry a local vicar, or some suitable gentleman of means. Much to her mother's distress, at age twenty, Millicent had already refused three offers of marriage.

Her mother had left London in shame twenty-one years ago vowing never to return. When Beatrice's frantic plea came, Dorothy was reluctant to let Millicent go up to London, but having always been fond of her deceased husband's sister, she agreed Millicent would be the perfect companion to Beatrice while she recuperated.

Millicent understood why her mother had never wanted her to go to London, but her mother had no cause to worry. Millicent didn't plan to fall in love with a scoundrel and ruin her reputation.

Thinking of her mother prompted Millicent to try once more to talk her aunt out of involving her in this scheme. "I don't see how I can listen to conversations, then come home and write about them."

"Oh, heaven's gates, Millicent, don't be so puritanical. Everyone in the ton loves the gossip columns. They can't wait for the Society pages to come out each day so they can read what has been said about the parties of the night before and the people who attended."

Millicent bristled at the inconsiderate attitude of her aunt. "It was that very same kind of gossip that forced my mother from London in shame."

"Oh fiddle-faddle. That was years ago, and it was the best thing that could have happened to her. The last I heard the man she was caught with in the garden has never married. He wanted a conquest, not a wife, and your mother was foolish enough to believe every lie he told her. But, because of that scandal she married my dear departed brother, and was, by all that I could see, very happy." Beatrice offered her a slight smile from swollen lips.

Millicent nodded, knowing that her mother and father had been devoted to each other, but her mother had paid a terrible price for the good life she'd had with her husband.

"And best of all, dearie, they had you. My brother often wrote to me what a joy and comfort you were to him."

"My father was a fine gentleman, but I'm not sure that makes up for the humiliation my mother suffered from Society when she was declared an outcast and shunned."

"True, my dear." Beatrice grimaced in pain. "Your mother had a compromising, but, I understand, not a consummated relationship with a gentleman who later refused to marry her. Society is unforgiving of such things. But it was all for the best. I know if your father were alive he'd want you to help me in my hour of need."

Millicent looked down at the vulnerable lady before her. Aunt Beatrice had finally found Millicent's soft spot. Millicent had always adored her father. Would she be honoring him by doing what Aunt Beatrice asked? Millicent wasn't shy or retiring. She knew she would be able to do the work, she just didn't like the idea of deceiving people.

"Now, before my medication puts me to sleep, let's go over who you will most likely see and hear about tonight one more time. Start at the beginning."

Resigned to her fate, Millicent said, "Lord and Lady Heathecoute will be my chaperones and make introductions for me. I am to slowly walk around the room and listen to conversations and make mental notes of all I hear. I will accept if a gentleman asks me for a dance, but I am not to show interest or give encouragement for another dance or an afternoon call."

"Good. Now, what are the names of the people who are of special interest?"

"The notable young ladies are Miss Bardwell, Miss Donaldson, and Miss Pennington. The widows are Lady Hatfield and Countess Falkland."

Aunt Beatrice tried to smile again, but her swollen chin and cut lip made it impossible. "Perfect. You are a quick learner. I knew I did the right thing in sending for you. I should have done it two days ago. Now, who are the Terrible Threesome?"

"Chandler Prestwick, the earl of Dunraven; Andrew Terwillger, the earl of Dugdale; and John Wickenham-Thickenham-Fines, the earl of Chatwin. They have been inseparable friends since Oxford."

"Splendid. The ton simply thrives on anything about those three bachelors. There are many others, of course, but none more popular with Society. So unusual, too. All three of the gentlemen lost their fathers and became earls at a young age. Perhaps that is why they are such delicious rogues and easy targets for gossip." Her lids drooped. "I do hope Emery hurries. My medicine is making me sleepy, and I must introduce you."

"Would you like me to fluff your pillows?" Millicent started to reach for the pillows, but Hamlet's head shot up in warning and she stopped.

"No, dearie. I find that no movement is best. Oh, and remember, anything you hear about the

Mad Ton Thief is noteworthy. The ton and all of London are simply in a passion wanting news and information about that criminal. The thief robbed Lord Dunraven's house two nights ago." She made an attempt at a smile. "I'm sure that put his lordship in a dither. You must try to find out something about that so we can mention it again in the column. I do hope Emery returns soon with—Oh, here they are."

Hamlet stood on his short, feathered legs and barked as Millicent watched the viscount and viscountess enter the room.

"Don't make such a fuss, Hamlet," her aunt cooed to the little dog. "Be polite. You're acting like you've never seen the viscount and his lady before." Hamlet trotted up to Beatrice's uninjured side. She patted his head affectionately and he curled down beside her.

Lord and Lady Heathecoute walked directly to the foot of Lady Beatrice's bed, but no closer, and greeted her warmly. Obviously, they knew of Hamlet's protectiveness of his mistress.

The viscount was tall and lanky, but superbly dressed. His graying tufts of hair were thin and cut fashionably short. He held his chin at such an elevated level and his neckcloth was tied so high, Millicent was certain his back must be in a continuous strain.

She was surprised to find his wife was as tall as the viscount. Few women could boast such a height or such a girth. The viscountess was more than a little plump. Her rounded face was flat but pretty and attractively framed by a row of tight dark curls. She wore a green high-waisted gown that hid most of her bulk and was becoming on her large frame.

"May I present Viscount Heathecoute."

Millicent curtsied when the viscount turned to her. "It's my pleasure, Lord Heathecoute."

"Delighted to meet you," he said as stiffly as he carried himself.

"And Lady Heathecoute, who has been a dear friend these past few months," Beatrice said.

Millicent curtsied again. "How do you do, ma'am?"

"Splendid, my dear. Very splendid." Her voice was loud and throaty. Her widespread brown eyes looked Millicent over carefully. "I think the gown you have chosen for this evening is good for you, the touch of embroidery around the hem sends just the right touch of elegance. Not too elaborate to gain attention, but certainly adequate so that you won't be out of place among the ton." She looked back to Lady Beatrice.

"She will be perfect for you."

"I'm glad you approve, and I'm indebted to you for watching after her for me."

Lady Heathecoute looked over at her husband and said, "We will take very good care of her, won't we, my lord?"

"Indeed, we shall." The viscount lowered his narrow light green eyes to look at Beatrice when he spoke to her, but his head remained erect. He seemed to have a pinched look to his face even when he was smiling. "The only thing you need to do is rest and get well."

"I know you will get on together. Millicent has such a pleasing disposition that she won't tire you." Beatrice cut her weary eyes around to Millicent. "They will make all the right introductions for you. Have no fear, and they will be there to assist you all evening."

"Thank you, Aunt. I shall be fine." Millicent was glad her voice sounded strong and confident, even though it was the exact opposite of how she felt.

"Excellent. And remember, dearie, young ladies like to talk in the retiring room when they think no one is around, and at the supper table. You must not encourage a gentleman to become enamored of you. I hope you are clear on all this?"

"Yes, Aunt Beatrice."

"Good. Now go on to the parties while I sleep, and I will help you write the column when you return."

She followed the Heathecoutes out the door and down the staircase with unexpected excitement growing inside her. She tried to tamp it down, but it was impossible. She had always wanted to attend a ton party in London. She just never dreamed she'd be going as a gossip writer.

Millicent determined she wouldn't look at what she had to do as if she were spying on people concerning their personal lives. She wouldn't think about how her mother would feel if she ever found out Millicent had participated in this scheme.

She was going to look at this as if she were writing a general news column for *The Daily Reader*. She would find a way to make the column uplifting and never negative if she had any say about the final writings.

As she stepped out the front door an idea struck her that she was sure would be perfect. She would include a little Shakespeare in Lord Truefitt's column. Everyone loved the master storyteller. That should give a new dimension to the "Society's Daily Column."

NEVER A BRIDE

BY AMELIA GREY

HER NAME IS ON EVERYONE'S LIPS...

When he left for America six years ago, the handsome Viscount Camden Brackley never suspected that he would return home to England to find his lovely fiancée embroiled in the scandal of the decade. The woman he planned on making his wife has been kissing every man in London...except him!

BUT SCANDAL DOESN'T MATTER IN SEARCH OF THE TRUTH...

Engaged and then abandoned, Lady Mirabella Wittingham is determined to find the man who drove her cousin to suicide, even if it means ruining her reputation and disgracing herself in the process...

When her plans go awry, Mirabella has no choice but to turn to her long-lost fiancé for help. But can she trust the man who deserted her so many years ago, or is he destined to fail her yet again?

ISBN: 978-1-4022-3978-6 • $7.99 U.S./$9.99 CAN/£4.99 UK

A *Duke* TO *Die For*

BY AMELIA GREY

THE RAKISH FIFTH DUKE OF BLAKEWELL'S UNEXPECTED AND shockingly lovely new ward has just arrived, claiming to carry a curse that has brought each of her previous guardians to an untimely end…

Praise for Amelia Grey's Regency romances:

"This beguiling romance steals your heart, lifts your spirits and lights up the pages with humor and passion." —Romantic Times

"Each new Amelia Grey tale is a diamond. Ms. Grey…is a master storyteller." —Affaire de Coeur

"Readers will be quickly drawn in by the lively pace, the appealing protagonists, and the sexual chemistry that almost visibly shimmers between."
—Library Journal

978-1-4022-1767-8 • $6.99 U.S./$7.99 CAN

A Marquis to Marry

by Amelia Grey

"A captivating mix of discreet intrigue
and potent passion." —*Booklist*

"A gripping plot, great love scenes, and well-drawn
characters make this book impossible to put down."
—*The Romance Studio*

The Marquis of Raceworth is shocked to find a young
and beautiful Duchess on his doorstep—especially when
she accuses him of stealing her family's priceless pearls!
Susannah, Duchess of Brookfield, refuses to be intimidated by
the Marquis's commanding presence and chiseled good looks.
And when the pearls disappear, Race and Susannah will have
to work together—and discover they can't live apart...

Praise for *A Duke to Die For:*

"A lusciously spicy romp." —*Library Journal*

"Deliciously sensual... storyteller extraordinaire Amelia Grey
grabs you by the heart, draws you in, and does not let go."
—*Romance Junkies*

"Intriguing danger, sharp humor, and plenty of simmering
sexual chemistry." —*Booklist*

978-1-4022-1760-9 • $6.99 U.S./$8.99 CAN

AN Earl TO Enchant

by Amelia Grey

He's determined not to be a hero…

Lord Morgandale is as notorious as he is dashing, and he's determined no woman will tie him down. But from the moment Arianna Sweet appears on his doorstep, he cannot resist the lure of her fascinating personality, exotic wardrobe, and tempting green eyes…

Arianna never imagined the significance of her father's research until after his untimely death. Now she is in possession of his groundbreaking discovery, one that someone would kill for. She can't tell Lord Morgandale her secret, but she knows she needs his help, desperately…

Praise for Amelia Grey

"Bewitching, beguiling, and unbelievably funny."
—Fresh Fiction

"Witty dialogue and clever schemes…Grey's characters will charm readers." —Booklist

"A gripping plot, great love scenes, and well-drawn characters…impossible to put down."
—The Romance Studio

978-1-4022-1761-6 • $7.99 U.S/$9.99 CAN/£4.99 UK

THE HEIR

GRACE BURROWES

AN EARL WHO CAN'T BE BRIBED...

Gayle Windham, Earl of Westhaven, is the first legitimate
son and heir to the Duke of Moreland. To escape his father's
inexorable pressure to marry, he decides to spend the summer
at his townhouse in London, where he finds himself intrigued
by the secretive ways of his beautiful housekeeper...

A LADY WHO CAN'T BE PROTECTED...

Anna Seaton is a beautiful, talented, educated woman, which
is why it is so puzzling to Gayle Windham that she works as
his housekeeper.

As the two draw closer and begin to lose their hearts to each
other, Anna's secrets threaten to bring the earl's orderly life
crashing down—and he doesn't know how he's going to protect her from the fallout...

A *PUBLISHERS WEEKLY* BEST BOOK OF THE YEAR

"A luminous and graceful erotic Regency...a captivating love
story that will have readers eagerly awaiting the planned sequels."

— *Publishers Weekly* (starred review)

978-1-4022-4434-6 • $6.99 U.S./$8.99 CAN/£4.99 UK

My
UNFAIR
Lady

BY KATHRYNE KENNEDY

A WILD WEST BEAUTY TAKES
VICTORIAN LONDON BY STORM

The impoverished Duke of Monchester despises the rich
Americans who flock to London, seeking to buy their way
into the ranks of the British peerage. Frontier-bred Summer
Wine Lee has no interest in winning over London society—
it's the New York bluebloods and her future mother-in-law
she's determined to impress. She knows the cost of smooth-
ing her rough-and-tumble frontier edges will be high. But
she never imagined it might cost her heart…

"Kennedy is going places." —Romantic Times

*"Kathryne Kennedy creates a unique, exquisite flavor that
makes her romance a pure delight page after page,
book after book."* —Merrimon Book Reviews

*"Kathryne Kennedy's computer must smolder from the power
she creates in her stories! I simply cannot describe how awesome
or how thrilling I found this novel to be."*
—Huntress Book Reviews

*"Kennedy is one of the hottest new sensations
in the romance genre."* —Merrimon Reviews

978-1-4022-2990-9 • $7.99 U.S./$9.99 CAN

Lessons in French

BY LAURA KINSALE
New York Times bestselling author

> "An exquisite romance and an instant classic." —
> *Elizabeth Hoyt*

HE'S EXACTLY THE KIND OF TROUBLE SHE CAN'T RESIST...

Trevelyan and Callie were childhood sweethearts with a taste for adventure. Until the fateful day her father drove Trevelyan away in disgrace. Nine long, lonely years later, Trevelyan returns, determined to sweep Callie into one last, fateful adventure, just for the two of them...

"Kinsale's delightful characters and delicious wit enliven this poignant tale...It will charm your heart!" —*Sabrina Jeffries*

"Laura Kinsale creates magic. Her characters live, breathe, charm, and seduce, and her writing is as delicious and perfectly served as wine in a crystal glass. When you're reading Kinsale, as with all great indulgences, it feels too good to stop." —*Lisa Kleypas*

978-1-4022-3701-0 • $7.99 U.S./$8.99 CAN

Uncertain Magic

BY LAURA KINSALE
New York Times bestselling author

A MAN DAMNED BY SUSPICION AND INNUENDO

Dreadful rumors swirl around the impoverished Irish lord known as "The Devil Earl." But Faelan Savigar hides a dark secret, for even he doesn't know what dark deeds he may be capable of. Roderica Delamore, cursed by the gift of "sight," fears no man will ever want a wife who can read his every thought and emotion, until she encounters Faelan. Roddy becomes determined to save Faelan from his terrifying and mysterious ailment, but will their love end up saving him… or destroying her?

978-1-4022-3702-7 • $9.99 U.S./$11.99 CAN

MIDSUMMER MOON

BY LAURA KINSALE
New York Times bestselling author

"The acknowledged master."
—*Albany Times-Union*

**IF HE REALLY LOVED HER,
WOULDN'T HE HELP HER REALIZE HER DREAM?**

When inventor Merlin Lambourne is endangered by Napoleon's advancing forces, Lord Ransom Falconer, in service of his government, comes to her rescue and falls under the spell of her beauty and absent-minded brilliance. But he is horrified by her dream of building a flying machine—and not only because he is determined to keep her safe.

"Laura Kinsale writes the kind of works that live in your heart." —Elizabeth Grayson

"A true storyteller, Laura Kinsale has managed to break all the rules of standard romance writing and come away shining."
—*San Diego Union-Tribune*

978-1-4022-4689-0 • $9.99 U.S./$11.99 CAN

THE
PRINCE
OF
MIDNIGHT

BY LAURA KINSALE
New York Times bestselling author

"Readers should be enchanted."
—*Publishers Weekly*

INTENT ON REVENGE, ALL SHE WANTS FROM
HIM IS TO LEARN HOW TO KILL

Lady Leigh Strachan has crossed all of France in search
of S.T. Maitland, nobleman, highwayman, and legendary
swordsman, once known as the Prince of Midnight. Now
he's hiding out in a crumbing castle with a tame wolf as his
only companion, trying to conceal his deafness and desperation. Leigh is terribly disappointed to find the man behind
the legend doesn't meet her expectations. But when they're
forced on a quest together, she discovers the dangerous and
vital man behind the mask, and he finds a way to touch her
ice cold heart.

"No one—repeat, no one—writes historical
romance better." —Mary Jo Putney

978-1-4022-4686-9 • $9.99 U.S./$11.99 CAN

SEIZE THE FIRE

BY LAURA KINSALE

New York Times bestselling author

"Magic and beauty flow from
Laura Kinsale's pen." —*Romantic Times*

AN UNLIKELY PRINCESS SHIPWRECKED
WITH A WAR HERO WHO'S GOT HELL TO PAY

Her Serene Highness Olympia of Oriens—plump, demure,
and idealistic—longs to return to her tiny, embattled land
and lead her people to justice and freedom. Famous hero
Captain Sheridan Drake, destitute and tormented by night-
mares of the carnage he's seen, means only to rob and abandon her. What is Olympia to do with the tortured man
behind the hero's façade? And how will they cope when
their very survival depends on each other?

"One of the best writers in the history of the
romance genre." —*All About Romance*

978-1-4022-4683-8 • $9.99 U.S./$11.99 CAN

WHAT WOULD JANE AUSTEN DO?

BY LAURIE BROWN

Eleanor goes back in time to save a man's life, but could it be she's got the wrong villain?

Lord Shermont, renowned rake, feels an inexplicable bond to the mysterious woman with radical ideas who seems to know so much…but could she be a Napoleonic spy?

Thankfully, Jane Austen's sage advice prevents a fatal mistake…

At a country house party, Eleanor makes the acquaintance of Jane Austen, whose sharp wit can untangle the most complicated problem. With an international intrigue going on before her eyes, Eleanor must figure out which of two dueling gentlemen is the spy, and which is the man of her dreams.

978-1-4022-1831-6 • $6.99 U.S. / $7.99 CAN

HUNDREDS OF YEARS TO REFORM A RAKE

BY LAURIE BROWN

❤❤❤

HIS TOUCH PULLED HER IRRESISTIBLY
ACROSS THE MISTS OF TIME

Deverell Thornton, the ninth Earl of Waite, needs Josie Drummond to come back to his time and foil the plot that would destroy him. Josie is a modern career woman, thrust back in time to the sparkling Regency period, where she must contend with the complex manners and mores of the day, unmask a dangerous charlatan, and in the end, choose between the ghost who captivated her or the man himself. But can she give her heart to a notorious rake?

❤❤❤

"A smart, amusing, and fun time travel/Regency tale." — *All About Romance*

"Extremely well written…A great read from start to finish." —*Revisiting the Moon's Library*

"Blends Regency, contemporary and paranormal romance to a charming and very entertaining effect." —*Book Loons*

978-1-4022-1013-6 • $6.99 U.S./$8.99 CAN